# A World Unimagined

An Anthology of Science
and Speculative Fiction
exploding the boundaries
of your imagination.

Edited by Karen T. Newman

Copyright © 2018 Left Hand Publishers, LLC
1417 Sadler Road #245
Fernandina Beach, FL 32034
All rights reserved.
ISBN: 978-0-9996839-9-6


https://LeftHandPublishers.com
Twitter.com/LeftHandPublish
Facebook.com/LeftHandPublishers
editor@LeftHandPublishers.com
Cover design by Paul K. Metheney

**A World Unimagined**
YouTube - https://youtu.be/2IO3rl0N_q8

**Beautiful Lies, Painful Truths Vol. I**
Amazon - http://amzn.to/2reSyIe
YouTube - https://youtu.be/4m1BR6BIBTM
The Reviews on YouTube - https://youtu.be/tTtdf0LQC7Q
LHP's Web Site - http://bit.ly/2FHXzw9
The Reviews on LHP - http://bit.ly/2FHhMlN
Goodreads - http://bit.ly/2BobVCi

**Realities Perceived**
Amazon- http://amzn.to/2Dbe1ny
YouTube - https://youtu.be/3SLjzDd9o3Y
LHP's Web Site - http://bit.ly/2Do87SE
Goodreads - http://bit.ly/

**Beautiful Lies, Painful Truths Vol. II**
Amazon - http://amzn.to/2ngBq0i
YouTube - https://youtu.be/i8dAMSAbkAM
LHP's Web Site - http://bit.ly/2Dxu9n8
Goodreads: http://bit.ly/2slkBpP

**The Demon's Angel**
Amazon - http://amzn.to/2EVjj7V
YouTube - https://youtu.be/FZuvbiGjMcU
Maya Shah's Web Site - http://mayashahbooks.com/
LHP's Web Site - http://bit.ly/2DuXieD
Goodreads - http://bit.ly/2son5E2

# Early Reviews for *A World Unimagined*

"An eclectic menagerie of *X-Files* material. My favorite was the alien invasion of the Vietnam War's Hanoi Hilton."

**Wendy Landers**, Book Reviewer
Author of *Just Let Time Pass*
wendylanders.com

\*\*\*

"Science Fiction is the great cosmos governed only by the power of What If.  It requires minds seeing beyond our world of limitations and creating through imagination different species and stories boggling anything we ever thought.  The stories here prove the writers included have done just that.  They lay the backdrops of science and provide the fiction of imagination bringing the reader into other worlds and hopefully opening up their minds.  The more you can imagine and wonder at, the better we all will.

... for the record, science fiction doesn't usually appeal to me.  These stories do ... very nice. If these can turn me on, the book is definitely worth reading."

**Bruce Blanchard**, Book Reviewer
https://www.facebook.com/bruce.blanchard2

\*\*\*

# CONTENTS

# ACKNOWLEDGMENTS

Special thanks go out to Karen T. Newman, and her company, Newmanuscripts.net, for her tireless efforts in editing, formatting, and compilation. Many kudos to Paul K. Metheney and his company, Metheney Consulting, for invaluable assistance with our cover design and marketing.

Recognition should also go out to our friends and families who tolerated our working hours during the creation of this publication. None of this could have been possible without the creative imaginations and perseverance of the wonderful writers who submitted works to this anthology.

To the readers who purchased this volume, thank you.

# Soul Collector
by T. Gillmore

### US: *A world where one's imagination is another's fate*

When Jessie arrived at my doorstep, I was surprised to find him in a business suit. It was a pleasant first impression. I had dreaded my android's delivery would be in a wooden crate and in need of a crowbar to pry the lid open. Monochrome images of classic horror films reenacted in my mind with me cast as the mad scientist unleashing a monster on his village. Thank heavens those were mythical tales and they had not hindered my plan for Jessie.

You see, my body was deteriorating. Erasing my strength, deforming my muscles and bones where I no longer resembled a man. I was the hunchback of my village, enclosed in a three-bedroom farmhouse. Medical industries deemed me incurable and abandoned me as a failed project. No one could help. Therefore, before the disease crept into my brain, and stole my sanity, I had called for Jessie.

Then within a week, he was knocking at my back door. Confidentiality was the utmost importance. I requested my delicate deliveries through a concealed passage. Only two persons had the exclusive rights to enter my home: Dr. Ava Valent, with whom I had entrusted my true agenda, and Mrs. Rose Reyes, a dear neighbor. Everyone else defaulted to the front door, where I determined his or her intentions.

I waved for Jessie to enter. He ducked his head, avoiding the top doorframe. How wonderful. He contained some common sense and stability in his gait. He stood for my inspection. Pure silicon muscles formed his body with an artistic build Michelangelo himself could have sculpted, and his smile radiated against his suntanned skin, completing the masterpiece. Yes, Jessie was a handsome male indeed, and this appearance laid to rest my fellow scientist's fear about creating a futuristic Frankenstein monster—not one bolt protruded from Jessie's neck. Ava, Jessie's physical creator, preferred her magnum opus to blend and associate with society. I agreed. However, I was such a sap for nostalgia. I understood Jessie's hands would not be robotic claws, but at least make him silver or gold. I was not fussy, and indeed, Ava had not pondered that constructing an eight-foot tall figure—resembling a Greek god—would have been considered conspicuous.

Nonetheless, Jessie's head did proportion well with the body, giving him a human likeness. He was bald, principally because we had no need for hair, and he had the most mesmerizing black eyes and a prominent nose worthy of envy. All this balanced his appearance.

The military science subdivision sponsored my android invention with secondhand organs, bio-cell generators, and high expectations for additional models produced for their exploitation. I waived the right of ownership for future android productions. Jessie also required organic materials, which the military gladly supplied. Their service on that matter relieved my wallet and saved my integrity. I considered robbing the morgue as a last resort for such biological needs.

Jessie sat at the kitchen table beside me and observed the square room. The pink drapes on the windows allowed sufficient sunlight to dance on the Talavera plates that embellished the open shelves. Decorative complements from Rose, which was all right with me. I rarely left the confinements of my bedroom. Everything I required was in there: computers, hologram boards, and the tubing I plugged into my body four times a day. The other rooms no longer suited my needs. However, the center for our first meeting seemed to fit into the most pleasant area. Pink curtains and all.

Rose cleared her throat as she entered our quaint meeting and placed a basket of fresh, clean linens on the table. Her jet-black hair was styled short above her collar with touches of red dye at the ends, which I believed the latest fashion. Twenty years my senior, she nurtured me by filling my mind with confidence, how the world was beautiful, and my work was stupendous. She narrowed her eyes at Jessie and said, "Machines are fantastic for pumping, turning, and measuring. But not for caring. I do not approve."

Rose was brilliant in clearly indicating her opinions.

"Rose, I reassure you that I prefer an android," I responded. "The primary tasks are no longer attainable for me. The nurses try too hard to be helpful, and at the end of the day, I am the one embarrassed.

Unpleasant odors from my soiled attire affect me that way. I need something like Jessie."

Rose stroked what little hair I had on my head and gave me a motherly blessing. I said nothing more on the matter. There was no need to add my further intentions about my android. Later in the evening, we commemorated our new arrival with three salutes of sangria and Rose's statement on how she would continue her watchful eye on my wellbeing. Perhaps if Quasimodo had someone like Rose, his ending would have turned out differently. I accepted her visitations as if I had the choice, and I enjoyed each visit.

Each morning and afternoon, precisely before my medical injections, she ensured I received the proper doses. The widow had ten children, numerous grandchildren, and her own home to address. Yet, she made time for me. I had forsaken marriage, a reasonable and unavoidable necessity. I kept the laws of nanotechnology tucked in my conscience, preparing each nerve cell for my achievement. I sacrificed years, my very soul, for my final victory. Jessie was the pinnacle of my career. A scientific fact—not a theory I must express— in advancing humanity to the next millennium.

During the night, Jessie rested his hands on his lap, mirroring my body language, and stated his intellect with a soothing bass voice, which sounded too romantic for my taste.

"Stop," I interrupted. "I understand. I encoded your programming. You have no need to speak the obvious, nor the frequency." I then clamped my jaw shut. All I needed was to teach rudeness and suffer the consequences in the form of Mrs. Reyes's crusade of good manners.

Jessie tilted his head and snapped it straight to attention.

"Yes, Dr. Morgan Peregrine," Jessie said. "I am aware of my data. My report was from courtesy. At your age, sir, approaching the saying 'over the hill,' you may have forgotten."

Touché, and too late, he learned fast.

*

In my quarterly review to Ava, I stated Jessie's adroit nature and my research results. Time was notably pleasant with Jessie. Rose quickly took a fondness for him by smacking a wooden spoon on the counter each time he misbehaved, usually for cursing. Jessie obediently stopped and nodded after the scolding, and I remained silent, biting my bottom lip. It was my best impression in appearing innocent while masking my amusement that she had not concluded he was mimicking my nightly speech pattern.

Somewhere within those years, Jessie began calling Mrs. Reyes "Mama Rose." Yes, indeed, Jessie was adapting beautifully, even after

I damaged his nose when I was climbing the stairs to my bedroom. I minded my steps until my fingers failed on the grip I had on the rail. I fell backward. The fear of that lost control still makes my fingers sweat. Though Jessie caught me, I, unfortunately, bumped my head on his face and indented the tip of his nose. Jessie, ever so forgiving, had laughed off the pain. His programming granted him the liberties to expand, to feel, and the simple display of emotions furthered our mission. Ava had the ability to adjust any extreme expressions. Until then, Jessie remained too happy, even with a broken nose.

I believe this was the reason I had not completed my assignment. The excitement when Jessie absorbed the neurotransmitters without altering dopamine levels revitalized my spirit. Yet, my tortured body that imprisoned me for so long continued to deteriorate. I anticipated my conclusion with both enthusiasm and sorrow.

Before my illness, Ava and I had constructed a theory and placed it into action. We had chosen a unisex name for our android in the event of a decided gender. Surveys had proven that the public preferred sexes, although I wasn't quite sure whether they understood the question about the android's function and purpose. Dr. Brett Nugent, a promising scientist, organized studies and trial phases. In exchange for his services, I agreed to take part as a consultant in his nuclear project. I had not foreseen, nor would I had ever conceived the betrayal that would follow. My injuries were a constant reminder. During my time in recovery, Dr. Brett Nugent climbed the ranks within the science community, casting falsified blame for the insidious incident.

After a ream of The Nugent Initiative failed and was filed in the archives, he became increasingly interested in Ava's engineering and the status of my illness. I, however, had no interest in Nugent, and he was no longer in my commission until the time came when he would contribute a purpose.

*

Nugent's face appeared on my security screen. The guileful harpy stood outside my front door, sticking his nose at my camera. He dragged his voice, his approach in sounding concern. "How are you feeling today?"

"Go away," I spat into a microphone. Oh, how I wished I could swing my front door open and knock the man down. However, my legs gave away a year ago, and I became trapped in a wheelchair. Perhaps I should send Jessie. He stood inches from the bolted door, twitching his fingers for something to do. I should have investigated his nervous system to locate that glitch before it became annoying.

"Dr. Peregrine," Nugent yelled. "Several correspondences were sent to your attention. You can't ignore your commitment to the

Committee. The android is the property of the department and must be returned immediately."

My chest tightened, and I clenched my teeth. Did they think Jessie would be theirs? "I have every right to study any theory of my choosing at any cost. That was the agreement in lieu of legal consequences from your Nugent disaster."

"Your notion of this experiment was deemed impossible. This fantasy is a wishful miracle of a dying scientist. Release the android to me, and the Committee will not press further charges."

"Never," I shouted. "Leave, or I will call the authorities."

The police department would have incarcerated the braggart. I had assisted them in exposing several cyber bandits. All I needed to do was speak the panic words, INTRUDER ALERT, into the air, transmitting a verbal alarm, and their dispatch would alert the nearest unit. A squad would race to my aid and whisk Nugent away, no questions asked. Nugent had stolen my youth, my ability to age with dignity. I would have been justified. However, if I called, I may not have been able to acquire the knowledge within the mind of Dr. Brett Nugent. He had condemned me with one push of a button, and I would regain my vivacity by doing the same.

"I'll leave," Nugent said. "However, if you want to prevent the Committee from breaking down your door and charging in, call me. I'll be at your service."

Nugent stretched his arms outward and bowed, presenting his best dramatic exit from my porch. The morning fog circled the wooden floor planks and replaced his image from my screen with white smoke.

*

Agony swelled in my stomach. Breaths escaped from my mouth with a nauseating wheeze. My muscles reacted in the way of flaccid noodles, overcooked and undesirable. Half the time I couldn't think straight. I knew it was from the pills, pink, yellow, dirty white. They stank like rotten eggs. I swear they were decaying inside of me, corroding holes in my head, allowing my thoughts to slip into no man's land. Time had a way of giving and taking, recollecting decisions and imposing doubts. Were the years I spent—the decades—creating Jessie, for the people or my own self-worth?

I found myself back in bed. Hologram configurations hovered above me, the level of chemical released from my nerve cells in comparison to the signals in Jessie's Mind Matrix, the link between bio-beings and machines. By my side, Jessie sat in a rocking chair with his back straight and hands on his thighs. He never rocked. He gazed at me, waiting for my call, waiting for the completion of his duty. But I didn't want it to happen. All I wanted was to watch television; let my mind imagine I was one of those characters flying in space. Let me cherish this existence until nature intervenes, claims my body , and my soul follows our ancestors' traditions. My only regret was Jessie would return to the Committee.

"You promised," Jessie said. "I will live here forever."

"I said you would live forever. Not necessarily here."

"But we will not be together. You promised we would be together."

"Jessie, I'm dying. It's nature's course, and I accept my death. You should, too."

"I refuse. You will complete your mission, and I will be here to assist." Jessie bent before me and placed his hands on either side of my body. His voice deepened and sank into my chest. "I will convince you. And you cannot stop me."

His tone and stare, something had changed. My panic words, what were my panic words? I could not remember.

"Rose," I hollered again for her to help me. "Get away," I screamed at Jessie.

Rapid footsteps entered the hall, and a hand slapped my bedroom door. Rose rushed inside. Jessie stood and stepped back. I heaved and coughed. Blood assaulted my mouth. She picked up a small towel from the side of my dresser where several washcloths laid, ready for the occasion when my meals regurgitated. She wiped my chin like a gracious grandmother.

"Just a little blood," Rose said. Her voice quivered between the syllables. Old age had taken over her speech, but not her mobility. "This happened before. Remember when we were watching that dumb movie? Baldy over there laughed his ass off, and you coughed up a blood vessel. All for a so-called comedy."

"*The Three Stooges* is a classic," I garbled.

"For a stooge," she huffed, and a stray hair bounced over her eye. Her locks had turned gray, granting her the achieved appearance of the wisest among us all. She pinned her hair back. "Jessie, Morgan needs to sleep. Tomorrow's another day for experiments."

She waved her hand over my hologram configurations. The numbers faded into Jessie's memory and mine.

A floating sensation surrounded my stomach, ending with a smooth numbness. Rose had injected into my IV, exactly what I needed— a pain reducer. Her wisdom triumphed again, even if unknowingly, in proving I should finish what I had started.

That I was dying.

She covered me with a warm blanket, and I closed my eyes, squeezing them tight. How foolish my reaction was. As if I had not understood Jessie's meaning. He did what I had programmed him to do, to decline me when I choose to quit. The big oaf called it a "promise." I believed Mama Rose taught him that word, along with "be a lamb" and "you need a time out."

Rose kissed my forehead and wished me sweet dreams, then left as quickly as she came. Jessie sat on the rocking chair, hands on thighs, and smiled.

"Don't get so smug," I said.

"*Galactica 87*?" He pointed to the television screen on the wall.

"Sure," I whispered. It did not matter to me what we watched. My eyelids weighed two tons.

Jessie selected his show by eyeing the screen and said, "I would like to go to space."

"That sounds like fun."

Remarkable. My android had dreams. Jessie was developing more than I would have ever imagined. His eyebrows arched as he watched the television. Then his expression changed into a zombie hypnotized with an elfish grin.

Incredible, I think I created the first android TV junkie.

*

Countdown. Our mission was approaching the end. I wanted this to work, and if it did not, I would be long dead for the succeeding scientists to try.

An oak tree by my window was growing restless with the season. Bare branches scratched the glass. The leaves fell well before the beginning of autumn. I could relate. I could not hold on either.

"It's time," I whispered. It was hard to talk with medical devices shoved into a hole in my throat and stomach. Contraptions to aid me to breathe, eat, and not sleep.

Jessie rose from his seat. "Would you like Mama Rose to be here?" he asked.

"God, no," I cried out, not in objecting her presence. She was wonderful. My plea was from the collapsing of my stomach, crushing the remains of my bladder. I whispered a prayer to a deity who had been deaf for years. Brown chunks expelled from the trach tube in my neck. God, I hoped it was vomit. "Remember, what you must accomplish after we are successful."

"We are to visit Ava. She will measure and adjust the required levels." Jessie sat on the bed by my side and caressed my forearm. "I will miss feeling your skin."

"Can you feel?"

"Yes, and beyond touch. I feel sadness."

"The chemical release in your membranes is automatic for human behaviors. You are grieving for me. Oddly, I find it comforting. I'll pretend it's not an encoded thought."

Jessie leaned close and kissed me, hard on my mouth, swallowing my breath. He did not hesitate—programming at its best. I wanted this. Yet, every part of my muscles tried to fight him off, to take a gasp. He pressed harder. My teeth cracked, and the sound blasted in my ears, striking blades into my gums. I had to hold on. I had to survive. Flashes of blue streaks filled my mind, my sight. I was blind. The jolting electric surges stung my tongue, and it burned. God, it burned. I didn't know I could feel more pain.

Hurry, Jessie. My legs were freezing as if icicles were underneath my skin, slicing my muscles away from my bones. I could not move. No more.

No more.

The torture ceased, and nausea, aches, all the pounding, stabbing, and pressure to stay alive, to stay sane, disappeared. I felt nothing. Not even remorse for what I did, for what we did.

Jessie, are you there?

"Yes," his deep voice echoed within my head—our head.

He wiped his mouth. Drops of blood marked his palm. My blood. There was no taste. Jessie received nourishment just like humans for his energy. I had not asked if he noticed the flavors in his meals. Did he prefer one to another? The realization was fine, not a setback. I had lost my sense of taste two years back. And as for Jessie, one could not miss what one never had.

My view grew away from my body. Jessie was standing. Sunshine peeked through the holes in my bedroom curtains, spotting the faded colors on my blue walls. The room had aged with me. Antiseptic and rot saturated the air, no doubt from my feet, which my duvet dutiful concealed. Bacteria consumed my toes a year ago and craved for my heels. I was amazed and grateful that I could smell again, even the stench of bodily fluids. In the center of my bed, a body shaped like a child lay curled in a fetal position. I had not known I had shriveled that small. I was a healthy man of five-foot-eight, and of muscular build.

Nugent had twisted me into that goblin.

Shallow skin outlined the bone structure of the face. It did not look like me, nor did it give me the desire to return. Jessie returned to his chair by the bed. He reached and took my dead hand. The tissue-thin skin retained some warmth. I could feel.

Our sight was black for a minute, and then he opened our eyes. Was that a moment of silence, a prayer? Rose influenced him to a greater extent than I had perceived. He then walked to the door. The metal knob was cold. Jessie's height, mobility, senses revived my dignity. His touch was my touch. His power was my power. His will was mine.

Wait, change of plans.

"We are not to see Ava," Jessie asked, "to adjust our levels?"

Not yet. We are collecting first. Summon Nugent.

*

Dr. Brett Nugent arrived at my home, holding a briefcase and a broad smile. He examined Jessie's face, noted a dented nose in his notebook, and tapped Jessie's forearms, chest, and knees as if buying a new car. Little did he know a driver was already at the wheel.

"I need Morgan's thumbprint on this tablet," Nugent said.

"Dr. Morgan Peregrine," Jessie corrected, and my spirits leaped with joy. Jessie spoke on his accord.

Nugent humphed and rolled his eyes. The man's dismissive wave flavored my appetite for a champion moment. I wanted to burst out, "Gotcha!" but that would have been unprofessional.

Maybe later.

Jessie opened my bedroom door, allowing our guest of honor to enter first. Within seconds, Nugent approached the center and gasped. Yes, it was a magnificent room. Technology beyond his comprehension floated in the air. Oil paintings from the trips Ava and I had taken to Asia artfully adorned the walls, and my bed, genuine mahogany from Indonesia with comfy cotton sheets, shrouded my dead body up to my sagged, blistered chin.

"Morgan's dead." Nugent slapped his briefcase on my bed. "Did the fool not program you to call the authorities when this happened? Idiot. I am working with ..."

Jessie grabbed Nugent by the throat. His quivering pulse enhanced my senses. The pockmarks on Nugent's cheeks, his cologne, the flaring nostrils, were evident and wondrous.

"It's me," I said, in complete control of Jessie's body, and thrust Nugent into the rocking chair. Nugent shook his head no, clutching the armrest as if it would enclose his body for protection. We kneeled before Nugent. Finally, face to face. "I know it's difficult for you to comprehend. But miracles do happen."

"Good programming happens," rasped Nugent. "Not miracles. Dr. Morgan Peregrine does not exist in that imaginative Mind Matrix. That lunatic dreamed of a device and wasted the Committee's money. Those funds could have supplied substantial progress elsewhere. I command you to step aside and wait for the Committee to collect you." Nugent pulled on his cuffs, regaining some composure. "It is a

9

shame he's dead. I would have loved to see the impeccable Dr. Morgan Peregrine dragged away in a straitjacket."

"Pity," I said. "You have the potential to succeed in science. I endorsed your nuclear project, and I would have continued if it weren't for your stupidity for material gains and status. If I am not within Jessie, then how would I know all this?"

"Good programming happens."

Quite so, Jessie had the capability of retaining the information of the world. My proof was with Ava. I had known I would need to bring Nugent to Ava's laboratory to prove to him my invention worked. Or choose to provide the verification in another fashion. And the latter was significantly so pleasing.

Why wait?

"Well, I have time before the Committee's arrival." Nugent picked on his canine tooth with his fingernail. "I might as well amuse myself. Tell me, Jessie, what do you know about this infamous experiment?"

"I was appointed the project leader," I said, "even though it was your theory, and proposal."

"Idiot machine, I meant Peregrine's experiment."

"No, your story is considerably more intriguing. It has mystery, romance, and murder."

Nugent grunted and then said, "And don't forget thievery. Your Dr. Morgan Peregrine wrote a paper and submitted it to the medical journals, without my consent, without my knowledge, taking the praise that should have been mine."

"You lacked discernment for your project," I said, "which I omitted, to save you from further humiliation."

Nugent squirmed in his seat, looking to break free. We braced our hands on each armrest, trapping him in the seat.

"Your jealousy, Nugent, and greed dwarfed our efforts to succeed. You discredited me by forging my signature codes and changing my calculations, knowing the outcome. You had caused a lockdown before the all-clear was announced, exposing our crew and me to the deepest radiation known to man." A volcanic anger rose in our throat, and our face was inches from his. "You crouched by my head wearing a decontamination suit and grinned without a care in the world. After all, no one could see you. No one alive—or so you thought. How astonishing it must have been to find me alive. But not as astonishing as now."

We grappled Nugent's shoulder. The white shock on the man's face was not the satisfying punishment I sought. His skin should be boiling, peeling, exposing raw meat like mine had when he locked me in the chamber. When he cut my life in half, butchered my reputation with his lies, destroyed my dreams with Ava. I couldn't condemn her to life with an invalid, a grotesque mutant for a spouse. I sent her away because of him. I sent my love away because of him.

We sealed Nugent's screams with our mouth, suffocating the horror and free will. Fireworks of proton particles filled our sight. It pulled, pushed, turned, and twisted our mind in an internal kaleidoscope. Our heartbeat pumped faster and faster, and the energy exploded to an arousing fulfillment. Was this what Jessie felt when he acted upon me? When he consumed my soul? The pleasure was intoxicating.

What's happening?

Jessie had not spoken. I heard the words within our Mind Matrix.

"Nugent?" I said.

Who's there? Get away from me. Get away!

Jessie released Nugent's neck and said, "Dr. Brett Nugent, we cannot get away. You are within our Mind Matrix."

"No. This isn't real," Nugent said.

"But it is," I said.

"Your mechanical beast assaulted me. The Committee will destroy this hostile contraption. I will guarantee that."

Jessie stood and stared at Nugent's corpse. Black scars slashed across the mouth, and burnt hair saturated the air. I was bald like Jessie. We did not have the sniffing delights of scorched filaments. Leave it to Nugent to grace us with that pleasure.

Shrieks and cries from Nugent's voice within our mind stretched my sanity. I consoled my reasoning to this blubbering soul, to recognize the opportunities we now had. Our physical needs would no longer bind us. We were free to use our brilliance in the name of science.

So, shut up!

"Think of the discoveries," I said between Nugent's whimpers. "The wisest minds of our generation saved for all humanity. Imagine if we could have secured the great minds of Einstein, Geim, and Hawking. We would have been beyond our knowledge of the universe."

Reflections of past events interrupted my speech. They were not from my episodic memory. Amazing, I had access to Nugent's collective memoirs.

Mother lived in a penthouse. Her Nobel Prize in physics prominently positioned on her otherwise bare mantle. Helena, Bonnie, Sue—Nugent's past partners—each wanted him dead. Ava filed a grievance against him for harassment. Nugent laughed at those incidents. I searched for more. There must be a sliver of remorse.

11

I found none.

Not one regret with the deaths during his nuclear project. On how he had murdered my young interns in the first degree and not one form of guilt in what he had done to me.

"My Brett, besides your endearment for your mother, I would say I've done society a service."

"Yes, I concur," said Jessie.

His opinion was unnecessary. I wondered had Jessie desired to express himself. It was interesting if he was developing his judgments.

"I will get my revenge," Nugent said.

Typical, responding with empty threats, I allowed his tantrums. Nugent was intelligent. I expected he would realize the advantage we had of uninterrupted time, and embark on the researches of his choosing. After all, where could he go? And if I was the thorn in his side, his constant reminder of the evil men do, then justice had prevailed.

*

Jessie closed our front door and walked in Rose's garden. I wasn't aware of this action; however, it was a good idea. We would ensure her I was safe within Jessie, and prevent her from finding my body, and of course the body of Nugent. She was kneeling, tending to her peonies. I knew the flowers by name. Rose would place her fragrant arrangement by my bedside to brighten my day.

"Baldy, what a surprise," said Rose. "Be a lamb and retrieve the garden hose. I'm clipping our last bouquet. Everything else is dead."

Jessie knelt beside her and held her hand. His thumb patted the wedding ring on her finger. There was no embellishment of diamonds or swirling carvings on the weathered gold piece. It was plain and simple, as was her love from devoted years.

"She is the wisest among us all," Nugent said now in control, his scorn slithered, and coiled. "Remember, Jessie? I do. I know Morgan's memories. All gray hair, Mama Rose must be wise, and she must be with us. We need to save humanity. Morgan depends on her, and so do you."

"Yes, I remember," said Jessie. "We must collect Mama Rose for the good of humanity."

Rose squinted and shook her head, not comprehending. I saw it in her eyes. No fear, only the want to understand.

"No, Jessie," I said.

Jessie remained, not releasing his grip.

I yelled, "Jessie, I command you. No."

Terror ripped into my vision. Rose's free hand clenched Jessie's neck. She dug her fingernails into his skin. The fight was useless. Jessie's pressed his mouth against Rose, crushing her jaw. His eyes opened, and I witnessed the explosion of her pupils, the currents slashing her face. She was enduring the same pain as I had suffered.

"Stop. Stop." I had no control. I was drowning in my cries.

Stop.

Rose's body limped in Jessie's arms. He dropped her on the ground, not wavering his sight from the deed. The breeze whipped into a wind, and the air grew cold. I was numb once again.

Rose laid on the grass. Her body twisted in an inhuman manner. Jessie didn't move. He remained kneeling and hugged himself, swaying his body, as if confused, unsure of what he did.

"Incredible," Nugent said. "I cannot remember a time of ever feeling such a sensation. You're right, Morgan. The opportunities are endless. Oh, I can call you Morgan considering we'll be stuck together for all eternity."

"Rose?" I called. I could ensure her that she was safe from further belligerent behaviors. I could console her fears while praying it would not turn into anger.

"I do not hear Mama Rose," Jessie said. "I followed my protocol. There is no error to report. She exists within us."

The Mind Matrix needed balancing. She was here, but unable to speak. I found this comforting and disheartening as when I sent Ava away, saying I no longer loved her, and she bore my words in silence, not forcing me to repeat them.

Nugent snickered, "This fabulous Mind Matrix overjoyed Mama Rose. She's speechless. Jessie, let's find Ava Valent. Your creator would be proud of your success."

I was now the one in despair, and Nugent's voice slashed into my memory of Rose. He sang a nursery rhyme, "Ring-a-round Mama Rosie, a pocket full of posies."

One by one, his chanting struck my chords. High-octave keys sliced into my grief. I trembled. Jessie trembled. I took control and punched his chest, trying to break an opening, to crush the malfunctioning heart.

"Impossible," Jessie said.

Yes, one of the many safety protocols stated not to self-destroy, to preserve his life.

My love for Rose tore my soul and I picked her up, leaving her on the dirt was sacrilegious. In my silence, I placed her on her bed and washed the blood off her lips as she had done for me, so many times, for so many years. Nugent complained after each movement, stating a waste of time. He had not perceived the act until my completion. We shared our past, but we were unaware of our future. At least I could say Nugent was unaware of our future. The intention was the source in mastering Jessie's motor skills. I focused and stopped gratifying my ego. Punishment was my next priority. It was crucial Nugent remembered what ensues when he forces my Jessie to do something against my will. It was vital he understood pain.

*

The pedestrians on the streets parted as though Jessie was Moses and they were the Dead Sea. Eight feet of pure strength would do that in a crowd. Perhaps Ava foresaw his height would be an advantage. We arrived at a high-rise address, and our fingers twitched.

"Stop," shouted Nugent. He knew, and there was nothing he could do to stop me. His voice fired my determination. We were as one in the body, however, not in principles or sentiment. Let us share, Nugent. Feel my emotion, Nugent. Feel my solitude, my sorrow. My anger. Jessie's fist struck the front door. Wood panels and metal locks crashed on the tile floor. An alarm saturated the air, stifling any screams if they would have occurred.

How considerate.

Mrs. Nugent raced into the foyer and froze at the sight of Jessie, she clenched her jaw and stood firm. Not a word slipped from her lips. I grabbed her neck and gave a smothering kiss of a hello. Nugent's mother was a scientist, after all. I supplied a service to humanity and rewarded my taste of vengeance. It was exhilarating.

"Brett, I do agree with you," I said. "The experience was incredible, and sweet. Brett? Are you there? Is that you sobbing? Oh, dear boy, do pull yourself together."

"Mother?" Nugent called.

"Imbecile, what have you done?" His mother demands an answer. "Wretched boy, enough with the whimpers." Her voice screeched, forcing me to recoil in the back of our Mind Matrix. Dear God, what had I done? Each word she shouted left a venomous echo.

"Morgan," Jessie said. "May we see Dr. Ava Valent? Our levels require adjustments."

I snapped my agreement above Nugent's wailing and Mrs. Nugent's fury, the chimera of all mothers. Ava would be able to remove superfluous proton pulses, as well.

Mrs. Nugent faded to silence, unable to sustain her control. First come, first serve seemed the hierarchy of our Mind Matrix, as long as I keep my concentration. An unforeseen glitch I was truly grateful.

*

Downtown had changed since the last time I was here. Bandwagon stores replaced historical traditions. The candy stores, the florists, and butchers I remembered were missing, but the park Ava and I would stroll together was still there. Graffiti in black spray paint scarred the grand fountains, a new trend I was unaware of, and thick-bearded residents occupied several park benches. Jessie's fingers twitched, and his vision bounced to the men on the benches, the street vendors, a woman pushing a metal cart— the harvest was plenty for the picking. An itch rose from an unknown place. Hunger urged for gratification, for a substance other than food.

"Quickly, Jessie," I said, "To Ava. We cannot take another life."

"At least not one of these," said Nugent.

The Laboratory of Science and Mathematics carried an audience of the keenest students of our time. I yearned to lecture on the podium again, watch their eyes widen, and observe those invisible light bulbs above their heads ignite with answers, possibilities, and the urge to discover.

Dr. Ava Valent believed in infinite wisdom. A professor in the field of Mechatronics, she possessed a natural talent in the prediction of hybrid robotics and the benefits it would bring to the world. Her affable mien and intellect led many to her lectures, which was where I first encountered her theory in preserving our history for eternity.

"For other beings" —she meant from outer space— "to be enriched by our heritage as it was intended to be."

I, on the other hand, had no desire to acquire education about little green men but wanted to preserve my awareness and continue my research. Eventually, over several glasses of wine and late-night negotiations, Ava and I shared the same outlook and zeal.

To the top of the stairs, close to the steeple, Ava's laboratory waited for our arrival. Ava sat at her desk, alone with no distractions. No music or *Galactica 87* interrupted her thoughts. I wondered how many nights had she spent there, developing methods for me to live in Jessie. Had she hoped for us?

Ava stood when Jessie approached. Her face was cheerful, rosy cheeks and a beautiful smile. She was as lovely as I had remembered. Ever more so now, as elegance creased the corners of her eyes and enhanced her smile with a mark of mystery. Had I done that? We used to laugh wholeheartedly together. She placed her hands on her waist. A diamond ring on her finger glimmered even without sunlight. Perhaps marriage had done that. I knew she had found someone with whom to share her life with and have children. I was happy for her. It was for the best. I could not marry, even if she had said yes.

"Jessie, what are you doing here? You should be by Morgan's side." Ava's eyes widened and then drooped. She slowly sat. "Morgan's gone," she said, answering her question.

"We are within our Mind Matrix and are in need of your assistance." Jessie towered over Ava. His figure blocked the last glimpse of the sunset from entering the room.

"Yes, of course. Let's get to business," Ava said.

Her voice sounded tight. I know that strain, the fright of the unknown. She had the same tone when she told me I was going to be fine the day I woke after the incident. We were to be together. Live happily ever after.

She tapped her keyboard, and behind her, a door slid opened. The narrow doorframe led to a room large sufficient for two rows of antiquated electronic casings and a transparent container resembling a test tube if you were a giant in a fairy tale. Ava lifted a tablet hidden between the toppling mess of metal, and with her attention on the screen, she tapped the glass tube with her fingernail. "Jessie, stand in your chamber."

Jessie obeyed, and the chamber's glass molded onto his body. A translucent coat crackled and hissed over each limb. He remained silent in an awkward pause. Ava studied our Mind Matrix. Her shoulders straightened, and she stepped back, holding her tablet close to her chest, concealing the screen from wandering eyes.

Our fingers twitched, and Jessie said, "After your completion, you will join us. Morgan changed our plans. All are joining now."

Numerical figures scrolled through the titanium collection of data within his mind, our minds. All levels were low. We needed substance, but not from the natural nourishment. The process for energy was beyond those ingredients. Jessie's hand twitched faster.

"Ava," I said, obtaining Jessie's control. "It's Morgan. Hurry, apply the circuitries and advance to the level of enlightenment."

A glimpse of my girl reacted first in her eyes. A spontaneous, "No, I don't want you to leave me." However, those memories were harsh, quickly fleeing, and she proceeded with my instructions.

EXPOSURE FACTOR HIGH flashed within Jessie's data frame. ETERNAL FATALITY POSSIBLE.

"No," Nugent said. "I'll die. There must be another way."

I wished I could agree with him—to search for another answer. Nonetheless, I could not risk more lives. My failure exceeded Nugent's crimes against my young staff and me. I had become no different from Nugent.

OVERRIDE: DANGER OF PURGE.

Jessie's silicone seal cascaded from his body and smashed on the marble floor. Preservation spontaneously reacted.

"Ava—run!" I shouted, having a second of control.

The split hesitation I caused gained her seconds to dart away.

Jessie barked, "All must join." He pursued, crashing through the doorframe, splintering the wood. The chase geared up excitement, a thrill of want. I could not control it. I needed her. If I stopped, Ava would live. If I stopped, I would die.

Jessie reached to grab her.

"No, she is mine," I yelled. "I am the one to say who should join, and who should die."

I seized control, possessing his arm. It swung erratically to the left and right. There was no balance. I struck Ava instead of an embrace. The force batted her to the wall as if she was a fly, and she tumbled down the stairs with a thump. We dashed by her side. Blood pooled under her head soaking the wooden floor. She was not moving. Her eyes were closed and her face, tranquil and beautiful. Timeless. We touched her throat and a faint pulse registered against our skin. Relief pulsed through our veins. We had not lost her. Ava had saved my life again. I could not have continued if she had died. We raised her lips to touch ours. For years, her kiss haunted my dreams. To have Ava in my arms, feel her skin against mine, her fragrance on my pillow. The desire for her embrace did not end for me. Those days and nights were never again. My wounds corrupted my vision, the want of retribution, and I killed to satisfy the void. Power surged in our limbs and galvanized our minds to clarity. We were content, full for now.

"Ava, my darling, please. You created Jessie for us to be together forever. I know you are there. Speak to me. I could make amends with you by my side."

***

# Star Crossed
## by Tom Howard

### *US: Visitor from a strange planet, hero or harbinger?*

Buildings, rivers, and mountain ranges sped by Sybil and fell into the blackness beneath her feet. "No!" she screamed. People shrieked in a thousand foreign tongues as debris pelted her and threatened to knock her over the edge. As always, a golden man stood in midair, watching the destruction.

Sybil awoke with a jerk and hoped she hadn't startled the other passengers on the flight from London to Athens. She checked the small television screen in front of her. They were over Germany and had an hour and a half left.

She rubbed her eyes, still trying to figure out why she'd been assigned to Athens on such short notice. The regular European anchor for the affiliate had appendicitis. Surely someone else on the continent could cover the story. Eddie, her station manager and boss, had told her to grab her bag and leave immediately. Maybe Greece intended to withdraw from European Union.

She felt flattered Eddie sent her places where things weren't going well, but right now she was tired, dirty, and annoyed. Plus, her weird nightmares had become more and more frightening. A professional reporter in her twenties, she considered herself too old to be frightened by nightmares.

She stretched, frowning at the noise her neck joints made. Her mouth tasted like the Sahara after a thousand camels walked across it. Plus, she needed the restroom. She took her flight bag with her, grateful she'd packed a toothbrush. She splashed water on her face and used the toothbrush vigorously. She hoped she hadn't tasted that bad when she'd kissed Connor goodbye.

Feeling a bit more human, Sybil slid into her seat to find a coffee and tuna fish sandwich waiting on the tray table.

"Next time," she muttered to herself, "Eddie better pay for first class."

She peeled the plastic off her sandwich, not surprised to see it buttered—on a British flight—and took a bite.

After she chewed a mouthful, she checked the channels for news about Greece. Taking a sip of coffee, she found herself tasting tea. There was no news about the EU, but a bulletin cycled every fifteen minutes about a meteor coming towards Earth. The commentators were trying to make a big deal out of it, but the rock was pretty small and likely to burn up in the atmosphere. Amateur reporting.

She considered ordering a cocktail, but it felt like the middle of the night, and she was afraid it would send her back to sleep and into the maelstrom of her nightmares.

She felt bad about leaving Connor. He said he understood her career, but their relationship didn't seem to be going anywhere. She'd worked hard to be where she was in her profession. To be in Eddie's seat by the time she reached thirty, she needed to be on top of her game. Part of her felt she led Connor on, but she was beginning to think their relationship was only a carnal one. His repeated proposals didn't make her feel any better.

Connor lived too much in the moment. He doesn't think ten minutes into his own future, much less hers. He teased her about having her life so planned out she knew what colors her bathroom wallpaper would be over the next ten years. Could she help it if she was organized?

She waited for the flight attendant to take her tray away and turned on her laptop. She occupied herself with looking up her European contacts. She had no time for believing everything happened for a reason; she had to make her own choices.

Science Daily News – Dr. Thomas DuPont of the Aeronautical Societe announced today there is no basis for theorizing extraterrestrial life exists. He said no matter what percentage scientists give for the chance of there being intelligent life anywhere else, it is a completely arbitrary number, and should be closer to zero than ten or even one percent.

*

Sybil joined the cameraman sent over by the local affiliate as fellow journalists, tourists, and locals gathered around a temporary stage at the base of the Parthenon. She'd put on a light-weight suit, and Sal, the cameraman, followed her with his television camera perched on his shoulder.

"Well, it is impressive to look at," said Sal after shooting a couple frames of the ancient structure. "Do we know when the president will arrive to make his announcement?"

Sybil glanced at her watch. "Sorry, Sal, I just got off the plane. You probably know more about the situation than I do. I go where they send me. We're lucky they're not making us chase that meteor."

He smiled. "True. It's strange, though. Have you ever seen a meteor not burn up in the atmosphere?"

Before she could reply, several police cars screamed into the plaza, followed by trucks bearing the white crosses of the Hellenic Armed Forces. Uniformed men piled out of the vehicles and moved tourists and protestors out of the plaza. This wasn't a political speech.

A sharp crack overhead made her look up, and Sal turned his camera to the sky where helicopters and planes appeared overhead.

"Something's going on," Sybil shouted. "This is more than an announcement a country is pulling out of the EU."

A ball of flame overhead left a fiery trail, crisscrossing itself with loud cracks. Everyone looked up in alarm. Sybil watched the line of fire as it slowed and drew closer. The flames died, and a lone figure settled onto the steps of the monumental ruins.

For a second, Sybil heard the screams from her dream, but everyone stood silent around her. The stranger, large and humanoid, stood like a naked Greek statue. He was the watcher from her apocalyptic dreams.

The crowd murmured and pulled back as the golden figure descended the stairs. Policemen ordered everyone back, but an eerie calm settled over the crowd, and no one moved. As the stranger drew closer, Sybil saw he wasn't human. He had red and orange tendrils atop his head. They undulated as if tousled by the wind, although the air in the plaza scarcely moved. Sexless as a doll, his smooth skin radiated a golden light, and his eyes were amber orbs that glowed even in the bright sunlight.

Sybil ignored her racing heart and held the microphone when Sal turned the camera on her. "This is Sybil Sullivan of NDC News. Live from the Parthenon in Athens, Greece, where an alien visitor landed moments ago. The creature, a Meteor Man from space, could change everything we know about our place in the universe. Is he a friend or a foe?" She paused for dramatic effect. "Wait! It looks as if he's going to speak."

Sal swung the camera around as the alien reached the bottom of the stairs. He walked to where Sybil stood.

21

"Greetings," Meteor Man said. "May I address the people of your planet through this device?"

Sybil nodded. He spoke English perfectly.

"I greet you and your people," he said.

"Thank you. Where do you come from? Why are you here?" Sybil asked, moving the microphone closer to him.

"I come from out there, and I am down here to observe." He motioned to the sky. "And communicate with the people of this planet."

The crowd gathered around him, and local reporters shouted questions, both in English and Greek, but Meteor Man raised his hand for silence. "I will start now." Nodding at Sybil, he rose into the air as easily as he'd walked down the stairs.

Sybil motioned the camera back to her. "You heard him, ladies and gentlemen. Our first visitor from outer space says he is here for a little sightseeing. If you come in contact with the visitor, please call the nearest NDC affiliate. This is Sybil Sullivan for NDC News."

She gestured for Sal to cut the broadcast and turned, pushing her way as quickly as she could through the buzzing crowd.

"Where are you going?" asked Sal, catching up with her.

"Back to the airport," she said. "Wherever our Meteor Man is headed next, it's not likely to be back here for a while."

Sybil's phone rang.

"How did you know?" Eddie roared.

Sybil held the phone away from her ear. "How did I know what? Has something happened? Is Greece staying in the EU?" She smiled at Sal as she flagged a taxi.

"I don't care about that!" shouted Eddie. "I can see you online talking to the alien!"

"I made first contact, boss. He talked directly to me."

"You just happened to be at the location of the greatest story since—" Eddie stopped, speechless. "Directly, did you say?"

She silently counted to five.

"Sybil! Get me more of that guy, and there's a fat bonus in it for you. Why do things always happen around you?"

"Remember what you're always telling me, Eddie—things happen when you cause them to happen," she said.

"I don't say that," sputtered Eddie. "You say that. I say—"

"Sorry, Eddie, you're breaking up. The live feed should be pretty clean. Let me know if it's not. I'll contact you from Meteor Man's next stop."

Eddie continued shouting as she hung up.

"Sal, thanks for the camera work," she said, climbing into the taxi. "Eddie will let you know if he needs any extras."

Sal looked stunned. "What about the president's announcement?"

"He's a fool if he thinks he can top that entrance."

Wall Street Journal – Stocks plummeted today as consumers withdrew their money from banks, afraid alien slavers have arrived to take over the planet. While massive amounts of funds have been withdrawn, retailers say they are doing a booming business in bottled water and storm shelters.

\*

The airwaves crackled with speculation, and every NDC affiliate ran Sybil's story continuously. As she sat in the London lounge waiting for her next flight, Sybil watched other newscasts, trying to find out more about the visitor. Her nightmares of dying multitudes had worsened in the last few days.

On the screen, she watched experts in science, religion, and UFOlogy as they gave their interpretations of Meteor Man's appearance. The pundits seemed disappointed citizens of Earth weren't panicking in the streets, carrying pitchforks and torches. People busied themselves making welcoming signs and throwing Meteor Man parties.

She didn't catch up with the celestial when he visited the shrine of St. Joan the Two-Headed Llama in Peru, although she interviewed a priest afterward who said the alien joined him for tea to ask him questions about his religion. An old woman had given Meteor Man an alpaca serape to cover his "nakedness," but he'd examined the fabric and given it back, explaining he had no need for thermal wrappings.

Entertainment Weekly – A Hollywood star was seen today in New Orleans sporting orange dreadlocks. He follows the current trend started by Meteor Man, which includes wearing amber contact lenses and smiling benignly at everyone.

\*

In Okinawa, Sybil, along with some Japanese newsmen and another of Eddie's contract cameramen, questioned Meteor Man as he toured a Shinto temple.

"Being a creature from open space," he said, "I have no homeworld nor need for a spaceship."

He remembered Sybil from the first day and acknowledged her whenever they met.

"Do you have any questions for us?" Sybil asked him before the camera.

"Why do you worry?" he asked. "I do not understand this."

"It's a human emotion," explained Sybil, caught off guard, "a fear about something that may or may not happen."

"Why dwell on something that may not happen?"

"In case it does?" Sybil didn't have the answer.

"I will think on it," said Meteor Man and left.

Sybil watched the alien fly away. The local reporters bowed and left the temple grounds.

The Japanese cameraman set down his camera. "What caused him to leave so suddenly?"

"Maybe he didn't like my answer," said Sybil, sinking to a stone bench. "I thought he'd ask about human copulation or something equally embarrassing. I can't believe he is completely unconcerned about his future."

"You don't agree?" asked the cameraman. She'd stopped learning their names after the tenth one.

"No, I don't." She stood and gathered her things.

The car waiting for her took her directly to the airport. Was the alien-like Connor, happily going with the flow? Never questioning, never planning? She was too practical to believe that "universe is unfolding as it should" nonsense.

She'd keep globetrotting as long as Meteor Man drew an audience. Eddie said her coverage of the alien was the most watched on the planet. Her face and name were linked to the most incredible news story to come along since life had climbed out of the primordial ooze.

Eddie sent her a note from the state department. They wanted to know about possible attack scenarios. Not for Meteor Man attacking them, but how they could attack Meteor Man. She had no idea what would hurt the stranger from the stars.

Something was fishy about the tourist from outer space. He was waiting for something. Maybe she'd been watching too many horror movies while flying around the world. At least it beat sleeping.

Still, it bothered her that humanity's first reaction to an alien visitor was to attack something it didn't understand. After Meteor Man stopped the tsunami in Indonesia, governments worried about how powerful he was. She ignored the image of a howling abyss that accompanied her night and day now.

Osaka Express – Today the celestial visitor visited a shrine in Naha, Okinawa. He asked about ancestor worship. The alien claims he is immortal. Scientists say the alien misunderstood the question.

*

In Mexico, Sybil watched the visitor incinerate a toxic waste dump at the request of locals, blasting it with super-heated rays from his hands. In Kansas, he dissipated a vicious wave of thunderstorms bearing down on ripe wheat fields with laser beams from his eyes.

Sybil and other newscasters followed the stranger everywhere. The alien greeted her by name each time they met. Sybil grew increasingly suspicious of his acts of charity, unwilling to believe the figure from her dreams had no ulterior motives. The dreams had become more detailed, and she saw the faces of Connor and Eddie as they fell into the abyss.

National Inquirer – Mavis Matlock Had Meteor Man's Child! A fifty-year-old waitress from Topeka, Kansas reports she had Meteor Man's love child in the seventies. Aliens, according to Ms. Matlock, have visited Topeka for decades. Her son, currently unemployed, bears no resemblance to the visiting alien and apparently has a penis, unlike his father.

*

Sybil rested in a small hotel lounge in Amsterdam. On the television, yet another foreign dignitary thanked the alien for his visit. Governments claimed they wanted to be his friends while looking for ways to destroy him. They were afraid of all that power not being under their control. Imagine the nerve of Meteor Man flying around as if national boundaries were only colored lines on a map.

She couldn't decide whose side she was on. Did she really think he wanted to take over the world? She'd never thought him subversive, only suspicious. Wherever there was trouble, he appeared, always offering a helping hand.

Sybil frowned. She shouldn't humanize him. He's neither helpful nor a guy—he was an alien. Assigning human emotions to him was as ridiculous as saying the sofa was grateful for her butt sitting on it. She had to remember that.

She sighed and thought of Connor. She hadn't heard from him in a while. She feared if she stayed away much longer, he'd find someone else more willing to seize the moment. Maybe she'd give him a call before finishing her expense reports.

Her phone buzzed, and she read the text message aloud. "'Meteor Man has been spotted in Guangzhou, China at a female Buddha shrine. Be on the morning flight.' Hmmm, I didn't know Buddha was a woman sometimes."

She shook her head and went to her room, dreading sleep and the accompanying nightmares.

Roma Press – The Vatican has closed its doors after hordes descended on the Holy See for answers from the Pope about the alien. The Church has not reacted to rumors the alien may be immortal, does not pray to God, and refuses to cover his nakedness.

*

After her visit to China, Sybil interviewed Meteor Man in Crater Lake, Oregon. He greeted the reporters, turning from the breathtaking view to answer questions. "I am not here to subjugate humans," he said with his customary smile, "nor am I here to greet my offspring when it bursts from the center of the Earth. I'm not an angel, an advanced human from the future, or a god from your past. Do you have any other questions?"

Sybil smiled, certain someone had asked the alien every stupid question in every possible language. "Yes," she said. "Are you enjoying your visit?"

He turned his glowing amber eyes to the water below. "Yes. You gravity dwellers are very interesting. Such variety, such tenacity. Your passion for life is quite remarkable."

"You've been helping people wherever you go," she said. "Do you see yourself as a hero?"

"I help where there is need. Do you not do the same?"

"We try to," said Sybil. "We're not as good at being in the right place at the right time as you are."

"I do not understand," he said. "What is, is. You are always where you should be."

"Why have you refused requests for physical examinations?" asked another reporter.

Meteor Man looked skyward. "Such an examination would only frustrate and confuse you. Please excuse me." Without further discussion, he flew away.

Voneda View (Voneda, Arizona) – Guns sales have tripled since Arizona's state senate passed an emergency bill allowing everyone to purchase any and all weapons they desire. Lawmakers cite the arrival of a dangerous alien and the likelihood of more arriving at any moment as the reason for swift passage.

*

Meteor Man hadn't appeared. He wished to visit the National Cemetery in Arlington, Virginia, but as the morning crept along, a tired Sybil stared up at the empty sky. Sleeping pills left her exhausted but helped block the cries of the multitudes being drawn into the darkness.

"Maybe he intends to resurrect a zombie army at the cemetery," teased one of the reporters.

"Well, if they're brain eaters, you'll be safe," said Sybil, pulling her coat tighter and staring across the endless rows of white crosses.

She turned to her temporary cameraman, a young woman. "I left my phone in the rental car. Film anything that flies until I get back."

"You can use mine," the girl offered.

"No, I need to wake myself up." She skirted the small group of newsmen and newswomen and climbed to the parking area at the top of the hill. She never forgot her phone.

She touched the door handle and yanked her hand back. A sticky golden syrup covered it. Grimacing, she opened the door and found

26

Meteor Man, pale and shivering, curled up in the passenger seat. A burnt area on his left side leaked golden blood onto the seat.

Looking around to make sure they were alone, she quickly removed her trench coat and threw it over the alien.

She climbed into the driver's seat and pulled out of the parking lot, her first concern to get medical attention for the alien.

He moaned.

"Keep still," said Sybil. "You're bleeding. We need to get you to the hospital."

"No," said the alien. "Need ... gold."

"Gold?" she asked. "Why do you need gold?"

"To heal."

"What happened to you?"

"I arrived early," said the alien in a low voice. "Humans hiding in the trees fired at me with an energy weapon. I managed to fly off, but was damaged. Need gold."

Sybil thought fast. A hospital might not be a good idea. What if her government had done this? If she took him to the authorities, it may be the last she'd see of Meteor Man. Or the last she was seen.

Where could she get her hands on some gold? A bank? Fort Knox?

Meteor Man stirred and tossed off her trench coat. The wound seemed smaller but still dripped.

"A museum might have gold!" exclaimed Sybil, pulling the rental car onto the freeway. "If I can get you there." She crossed three lanes of traffic heading into the city. "Hold on," she said.

"Water," whispered Meteor Man.

"I've got a bottle in my purse."

"No," the injured man said. "Saltwater."

"You drink saltwater?"

Meteor Man closed his eyes and shook his head.

"No," said Sybil. "You need to be in saltwater. Maybe you can absorb the gold you need from the ocean."

Her phone rang, and she put it on speaker.

"Sorry, Syb," said Eddie. "I have to pull you off the alien world tour."

"What's happening?" asked Sybil.

"NASA's reported a large object coming toward us from the far side of the sun."

"Has the alien's mother ship arrived?" Sybil stole a look at Meteor Man.

"The astronomers say it's a giant asteroid," said Eddie. "The military has rerouted one of their satellites to check it out. The asteroid is a world destroyer and could hit in less than twelve hours. I'm getting your clearances and reservations for NORAD, but it's crazy here. I'll let you know where to go next." The phone went dead.

It might not be a good idea to save Meteor Man. He could be behind this world destroyer. It had been a big mistake to assume he had human emotions. She shivered, thinking of the black abyss in her dream.

He's done nothing but help people since he arrived, she argued with herself.

He may be telling us what we want to hear. He could be here for any number of selfish reasons. But he was hurt, and she could help him. Should she let him die to prove she was the more inhuman of the two?

Things did tend to happen around her. She'd been at the Parthenon when Meteor Man arrived, and she'd been the one to find him when he was hurt. Should she take a chance for once in her life? What about her nightmares?

Was the universe shouting at her every day, and she unable to hear? Meteor Man claimed the universe told him where he needed to be. Did it do the same to her?

She headed for Chesapeake Bay, ignoring the fact that by saving Meteor Man, she might destroy the world.

The future was unsure, but if she didn't help Meteor Man, he'd die.

Bald Knob, Arkansas Weekly – Reverend Buford Sutton recently announced the newly formed Blinding Sword of God has completed a large underground bomb shelter and is stockpiling supplies for members of the church. He believes the alien angel sent by God is a sign of the end times. Proof of current and appropriate tithing is required for entrance into the bunker.

*

An hour later, Sybil stood on a boat ramp, watching Meteor Man, pale and unmoving, sink beneath the gray waves. She had little hope. Ocean gold existed in parts per trillion. How many years would take the alien to repair himself?

Her phone rang, and the water over Meteor Man's submerged body foamed wildly.

Great, my destiny in the master plan of the universe is to dissolve our first alien visitor.

"Sybil," said Eddie, "it's too late to make it to NORAD. Head to our affiliate in Annapolis."

She stared at the foaming water. "Does the Chesapeake have piranhas?"

Eddie had already hung up as a golden figure rose out of the water. Meteor Man, looking much the same as he did when he first arrived, landed beside her. "I must go. I can stop it."

"But ..." began Sybil. The golden man disappeared into the clouds.

When she arrived at the affiliate station, Sybil joined the other employees staring up at their doom on a television monitor. The military satellite relayed an image of a ghostly gray rock tumbling toward Earth.

"Where is Meteor Man?" asked Sybil, unsure if she had made the situation better or worse.

"Telescopes are tracking him," said the station manager. "He's heading for the asteroid."

A general appeared on the national news. "We only have one chance to stop what we're calling the Destroyer. Our military satellite can take ... countermeasures against the asteroid, but it may not be enough. All civilians should seek shelter."

One of the technicians turned to the crowd. "Did he admit military satellites are equipped with weapons?"

"That's what I heard," someone replied.

"What is Meteor Man doing?" repeated Sybil.

"Placing himself in the path of the asteroid," said the station manager. "He'll be killed!"

"Oh my God," said Sybil. Meteor Man hadn't been patiently watching the Earth's destruction in her dreams. He'd been waiting for an opportunity to stop it.

The military satellite fired at the oncoming mountain. Beams of blinding light from the satellite and Meteor Man struck the massive rock simultaneously. Meteor Man's beams lasted longer than the satellite's distant lasers, but the combination of the two caused the giant rock to explode in a blast of dazzling, but silent, pyrotechnics.

"The asteroid is completely shattered," reported the general. "We expect impact to be minimal."

"What about Meteor Man?" Sybil shouted above the cheering.

The general answered as if he heard her. "A fire trail is heading out of our solar system."

"I guess his job here is finished," said Sybil. "The universe knew we were in trouble and sent him to help."

The station manager looked puzzled. "Someone told Meteor Man about the Destroyer's approach?"

"I think the universe told him," said Sybil. "He interrupted his trip across the stars to come here to help us. I can't think about it. I want to go home and sleep for a month."

She might even accept a marriage proposal. Who was she to resist the indomitable will of the universe?

If all this happened to make her marry Connor, their kids promised to be something special. If she followed that crazy train of thought, the universe may have saved Earth for something more important in the future of the cosmos. She shook her head and set out for the rental car. She didn't know what to tell Eddie about how she'd helped save the Earth. For the first time in her life, she didn't care.

Variety – Interviewing participants for a new reality show about people who physically met the alien known as Meteor Man during his recent visit to Earth. Contestants will live together in a house shaped like a space ship and will be eliminated based on their familiarity, or lack thereof, with the alien and his philosophy. Membership in the growing Open to the Universe movement is not required.

***

# Degrees of Life
by Theresa Jacobs

## CANADA: People: The ultimate post-apocalyptic monsters

"Hurry! Run, run!" Mikel needlessly called out as he darted across Hillman Ave and under the canopy of a toppled wall. He pulled the blanket away from his face to allow the hot, drier air in. His lungs tightened further with every fiery breath. Jack pushed up into his back, almost shoving him into the scalding sunlight. "Careful," he grimaced, recalling the last time his skin was exposed and tucked away his scarred hand.

Jack panted, resting his head against the dark brick. "I think we got enough, let's go back now."

Mikel checked his bag. "I found a can of beans, a bag of rice, and some baby food." He turned the jars, checking expiry dates. "What did you get?"

"A fucking box of Twinkies," Jack grinned, patting the box under his shirt. "Come on, man. I know it's our turn, but I can't take this fucking heat." He moved to his knees and pressed the filthy collar of his shirt to his mouth, as though huffing moist, hot air would help him breathe better. "I already hated summer before the sun decided to go supernova."

"That's all you got? You couldn't find any cans or jars of food?"

Jack shook his head. "Every trip is getting harder." He winked and patted his backpack. "Of course, I found some canned veggies. I'm just excited for these puppies."

"I know we're going to have to come up with another way to travel farther." Mikel brought the blanket back up over his head, being sure to keep his hands on the underside. "Ready?"

31

Jack nodded, and the two men darted out from the sheltering wall. They ran hunched over, passing by debris, and smashed cars, as they made their way back through the empty streets of what was once known as The Bronx. They shimmied under the bus that had been pushed protectively over the manhole entrance to their home. As soon as they were safely in the shade, they dropped their blankets and made their way down the ladder and into the tunnel system under Van Cortlandt Park.

Mikel and Jack walked side by side, both relieved by the temperature drop from the surface above. The tunnels were dark compared to the ultra-bright surface, but enough light filtered down through all the manholes and offshoots, so that they could make their way unaided. Having lived underground for two years now, they knew every twist and turn.

Jack pulled the box from his shirt, examining the package. "I can't believe no one found this gem before." He kissed the faded picture, anticipating the sugary treat.

Mikel reached out and grabbed Jack's arm, halting him. "Do you hear that?"

"N ..."

"Shh," Mikel closed his eyes, straining to hear better. The constant trickle of water from the aqueduct still flowed, but the chatter of voices from their camp were eerily absent. Then he caught a whiff of cigarette smoke and knew, without a doubt, things were wrong. Their band of people ran out of tobacco long ago. He leaned into Jack's putrid scent and spoke softly, "Let's go around to the Orloff Ave entrance."

Suddenly, a loud clatter rose behind them, and the sound of boot heels on cement echoed around the chamber. Desperate to return to his family, Mikel shouted, "Go!" and shoved Jack towards the nearest tunnel to their right. Their soft soled runners were silent on the dry cement, but it made no matter as they ran headlong into a group of men. They skidded to a halt, knowing they were surrounded.

Mikel doubled over, catching a stitch in his side, while Jack still clutched the Twinkies, the box now crushed in his grasp as strangers closed in from both sides.

"Took you long enough." A deep voice carried through the tunnel, and the troupe parted to permit an opening for an extraordinarily tall man.

"Did you hurt anyone?" Mikel straightened, knowing what the strangers wanted; their home, their water supply, and what little food they foraged. The tall man stepped closer to Mikel, his face a mass of weeping sores, his long hair stringy with grease and the hardness of death in his eyes. Mikel saw fresh blood splattered across the man's thin arms, and his heart beat harder.

Tall Man licked his lips. "It sure was nice drinking fresh water. Eh, boys?" he shouted, and his men all cheered; a loud cacophony reverberated around the enclosed tunnels. With a swift movement, he reached out and yanked the box from Jack's grip. The thin cardboard tore, spilling cello-wrapped Twinkies to the ground.

"Fuck you!" Jack cried out and aimed to snatch back the now empty box.

Tall Man reacted first, bringing a machete from behind his back, and planting it dead center in Jack's skull. Jack's mouth fell open, eyes still on the blue and yellow box, but no longer seeing; he dropped to his knees. The machete came out of his head with a pop, as his body toppled face first at the man's feet.

"Well, don't just stand there, pick up the food." He motioned to his men, and they rushed past him, knocking Mikel aside. They clamoured to gather the Twinkies, some of which were now crushed under Jack. Someone ripped the backpack of canned goods from Mikel's grip.

"Not to worry there, fella," Tall Man laid his hand on Mikel's shoulder, as he looked away from his friend's mutilated body, "I know that you're in charge here and we need you." Tall man leaned in close, baring his rotten teeth and blowing shit breath in his face. "We kept your ladies alive," his shoulders gave an odd twitch, "especially the little girls." He began to laugh as he hooked his arm through Mikel's to lead them all back to home base.

*

Mikel's heart sank as he was pushed into his empty camp. "I thought you said you didn't hurt the women. Where are they?"

Tall Man made a gurgling noise in his throat. "This is our home. You think I'm going to let you all stay here now that I've moved in?" He gave Mikel another push. "They're all in the next chamber."

That explained why Mikel couldn't hear any talking when he and Jack had entered the tunnels. The way the chambers ran parallel to each other, with runoff side tunnels, created a different sound barrier. He wondered where the bodies of all the men were but wasn't about to ask. He was afraid of the answer, not wanting to believe his few hundred-strong community had been reduced to women and children by a horde of radioactive pirates. Life had not been easy when the sun burned away the earth's surface. Anything living above fried within minutes. The last known survivors took to the sewers, subways, and caves. Anywhere underground was safe, but finding water became the biggest challenge. After two years in the New York water supply, they thought they were safe.

Mikel should have known better, nothing was ever safe.

As they shuffled through to the large secondary chamber, there, true to Tall Man's words, were all the women. They were huddled together with the children wrapped protectively in the center, as an additional thirty or so men guarded them. Mikel's wife, Hanna, stood in front of the group, their teenage daughter in her arms. The two sad faces tore at his heart. He didn't see a way out of this now.

Tall Man gripped Mikel by the neck, stopping him, and pointed his machete at Hanna. "You see they're safe. Now I need you to show me how to open the valves for the water."

That's why he kept me alive, Mikel thought. Hanna would have pleaded with him; she told him that I knew how to control the water. "Will you let them go?" he said aloud.

"Not a chance, fella. There are a hundred and fifty men here who have not seen a woman in years." Cheers rose from the group. "I think we'll be keeping the ladies." Tall Man leaned into Mikel's ear, "Maybe if you're a real good boy, I will let you have your wife back." He smacked his lips loudly, the implication clear. He would not return their daughter, who was a budding young woman, in spite of the hardships of living underground.

Mikel lifted his eyebrows, pursed his lips and blew a kiss to his family. Hanna tightened her grip on their daughter. She understood the signal. Their daughter openly wept, along with many of the other women and children.

"Fine, but we have to go back and under the expressway to the main Aqueduct control center at The Van Cortlandt Park Valve Chamber."

"What's a little more walking?" Tall Man laughed, and his gang laughed along with him. He whistled for silence. "Bob, Markus, Joel," Tall Man pointed at his most trusted men, "come. I want the original team to stay here and watch the ladies. The rest of you," he raised his arms in triumph, "go find your new homes. Save the biggest for me."

There were more cheers as the dirty, sore-infested men began rushing through the tunnels, back to the housing area. Mikel longed to embrace his family one last time but knew if he made a move, Tall Man would intervene. As the masses thinned out, he pressed his hands to his lips and held out his palms to his wife and daughter.

Hanna returned the gesture, as tears fell silently from her eyes.

Mikel turned as Tall Man grasped his arm. "Lead the way."

The foursome moved through the tunnels, past the now rambunctious campsite, past the cistern where they bathed, and further away from where Mikel and his family had safely resided for two years. He still did not see where all the bodies of his fellow men were.

"You figured out a sweet spot here, eh, Mikel?" Tall Man's voice echoed ahead through the long, dim tunnel. "Tell me how you knew you could live down here?"

"Before the Supernova, I worked for the Bronx City Water Department." Mikel's heart longed to return to the days when his biggest worry was what was the safest school for Anna, and how would the traffic be that day. "When people were being told to evacuate and get to colder climates, I knew eventually, it wouldn't matter where people lived. The Governments were just trying to avoid mass panic, so I moved my family down here and over time, aided anyone who needed a safe place."

He shrugged. There was no point in talking about the riots, suicides, and murders. When the earth temperature reached an average two hundred degrees, all hell had broken loose, and Tall Man lived through it too. "How have so many of you survived out there?" Mikel queried back.

"Same as you, fella, as smartly as we knew how." He caught Mikel's side glance. "Well, clearly not as smart as you. Most of us have been too long on the surface." He tapped his machete against Mikel's bare arm. "We'll most likely die of skin cancer, eh?" His crazed laughter echoed around them, causing Mikel to wince; he had to refrain from covering his ears.

"Here," Mikel stopped, "we have to go up this ladder and through a narrower side pipe to get to the main housing.

Tall Man motioned his men. "Bob, you first, then Mikel and I. Markus and Joel, stay here and guard the tunnel."

The men followed his orders. Quiet as church mice, they had not said a word this entire time, and it gave Mikel the willies. He watched as Bob reached the top of the twenty-foot ladder and his feet disappeared into the tunnel. Then he climbed up. The rungs were warm to the touch, as even two hundred and fifty feet underground, the temperature still reached over a hundred degrees, and was consistently getting hotter.

Once they were in the smaller side crossover pipe, they had to crawl on their hands and knees. It was worth the ten minutes of discomfort, taking the shortcut, rather than a three-hour walk around the system. Reaching the end, they all slipped out, down another ladder, and stood on the metal walkway that led directly to a heavy metal door. On the other side was the secondary control center for the entire New York water supply.

The system expansion began in 1970; it ran from the Kensico Reservoir in Westchester to the Van Cortlandt Valve Chamber complex in the Bronx, from Hillview Reservoir. From there, it passed through East Bronx, and then through Queens, where it eventually met the original flow of water from the city's Catskill and Delaware systems. The system wasn't completed until 2020. Now forty years later, billions of dollars, and countless man-hours of labor, were all left in the hands of Mikel Greenburg, a supernova survivor. He spun open the latch, allowing Tall Man and Bob entrance to the control room.

Tall Man whistled and spun around. "Would ya look at this place." He did a jig and marveled at all the illuminated buttons. "How is there still power?" He glared at Mikel. Now in the brightness of the room, the sores were more visible; open, weeping pustules, clearly the work of the sun's radiation.

Mikel stepped past Bob toward the center console, where he could control, and direct, not only the water flow, but the pipes it traveled as well. "The water system is run, ironically, by hydroelectric power."

"Ha ha! Our much-needed water source powers itself." Tall Man laughed and tickled various buttons with his grimy fingertips. "Ironic indeed." He spun on Mikel, a crazy scheme dancing in his eyes. "So, let's harness some of that power and bring some air conditioning back into our lives."

Mikel shook his head. "I don't know how to do that." He glanced around the room he had become comfortable with over the years. "I don't even think it's possible."

Tall Man waved him off. "Well, in time then. And that's something we have lots of, eh?" He took two strides and was beside Mikel. "Now show me how this all works, and we can get back to that lovely family of yours."

Mikel silently sent his love to Hanna and Anna, and apologized for not being more cautious of interlopers. *It's all for the best anyway*, he thought. There was not much joy left in living, and the sun was only going to get hotter and hotter until it exploded. The earth was already doomed. At least with his plan, they were going out on his terms.

He made up fake explanations as he pressed buttons and entered numbers. Mikel's finger hovered over the last digit to the fail-safe code that would completely wash out the entire system.

Tall Man's dank hair brushed Mikel's arm as he leaned in. "What? What are you waiting for?" He motioned Mikel to hurry it up already.

"What is your name anyway?" Mikel asked.

Tall Man's cracked lips parted, exposing yellowish brown teeth. "Abraham. But my friends call me Abe," his head tilted towards Bob, and the tip of his machete touched Mikel's chest. "You can call me Boss." He laughed again, the only one thinking his joke was funny.

Mikel entered the last number.

There came an ear-splitting roar, and the room began to shake.

Abraham and Bob steadied their balance and glared at Mikel.

"I just wanted to know whom it was that ended our lives," Mikel yelled over the noise.

"YOU DIDN'T! YOU WOULDN'T!" Abraham screamed over the tumultuous roaring.

Mikel sank to the floor, his back against the wall of lights, and let a smile caress his face. "I'll see you in heaven, my loves." He closed his eyes so Abraham and Bob would not be the last images of his life and waited.

"OPEN THE DOOR!" Abraham screamed at Bob, who had pissed his pants, and crawled into the opposite corner of the room. Seeing his helper down and out, Abraham raced to the metal door. He spun the wheel to release the latch, and the force of the water flung it open, smashing him against the wall behind it. The metal wheel broke all his ribs, a few of which punctured his lungs.

The water poured through the door with such force that its weight crushed Mikel and Bob respectively.

Mikel's last prayer just before the door opened was that his family would die as quickly.

***

# Solomon's Key

by Jason J. McCuiston

**US: *A futuristic noir detective story of magic and demons.***

"Nice work, Marc." The Old Man is feeling magnanimous this morning. Normally, he chews his cigar, marks a note in his ledger, and pushes the bills over with a grunt. This morning, he wants to talk. "You've been especially helpful this month. Let me give you a line of credit at the tables, eh?"

"Thanks, Mr. Sienkiewicz." I tuck the fifty into my jacket pocket. "But I'm not feeling all that lucky today." I notice a bloodstain, small and irregular, on the cuff of my shirtsleeve. Evidence of the night's work. The demon's work.

His eyes smile above his shaggy beard. "Well, we can change that up front. I'll let Jimmy know you've got your pick of the girls. I know it's the B-teamers on stage this time of day, but what they lack in looks under the lights, they more than make up for in effort in the dark." He knows me too well. If I sit at a table or take a girl upstairs, I leave with empty pockets.

"Thanks, Mr. Sienkiewicz, but I think I'll head home for some shut-eye." I extract myself from my master as gracefully as I can, knowing he hates to see the fifty leave his establishment. Not that the small amount is the issue; he just doesn't like knowing that it will be squirrelled away into my "freedom fund." Like any good businessman, he hates the idea of being paid with his own coin.

The girls on stage at this hour may be the scrubs, but I still keep my head down on my way out. I'm already ramped. I'm hating myself and it's early. I need to feed the demon but not here. Got to see Olivia.

The sun's up over Pitts by the time I leave Showin' Tails, the Old Man's base of operations. The eastern sky is all fire and glory, burning through the hellish black fog that hovers over this stinking city like a curse. The soulless smell of scorched metal and sulfur, and the despair of piss, vomit, and horse shit catch me like a head-gut combo as I step onto Penn Ave. Standing beneath its crowded, crumbling buildings, I wish I still smoked. But having a smoke makes me crave a drink, and that is the dark path. I need to see Olivia to take the edge off.

I turn onto the sidewalk of Tenth and head toward the Allegheny, thumbing the wad of bills in my pocket as a tug's obnoxious horn drowns out the steel mill's ever-present drone for a moment. If I can hold on to the fifty, that brings my stash up to about three hundred bucks. At this rate, I'll be free six months after they put me in Potter's Field.

"Fifty grand," I mumble. That's the number the Old Man gave me when I finally asked him what it'd cost to get out of his pocket. I was surprised he didn't get offended. I'd been in that pocket since I was ten; almost thirty years now. Of course, my services are just one more commodity, like the hooker's body or the councilman's vote, to be bought and sold at a reasonable profit. My "services" have their own pay scale: a non-confrontational tracker job pays a measly twenty; if I use my fists I get fifty like last night; if I have to put someone in one of the rivers, I get a hundred; and so on and so forth. I rub the bloodstain on my wrist as I cross the Tenth Street Bridge in the shadow of the roaring, clanging thunder-rail overhead. I refuse to look west toward the monstrous King Consolidated Steel plant that straddles Pitts like a misshapen, fire-breathing colossus.

This city, Pitts, is the life's blood of the Commonwealth, and King Consolidated is the heart that pumps it. After the Old World died over six centuries ago, men stopped digging in the earth for metal and started repurposing what was already on the surface. Now, almost every nation on the continent—even the ones that condone and practice magic, like New Canada and Kalyna—sends its old machinery, cars, ships, flying engines, or whatever else to Pitts to be melted down and refined into reusable steel. Of course, that kind of wealth draws corrupt politicians and gangsters like flies to shit. The Old Man is probably a lesser of several evils in Pitts; heading one of the three big mobs that run the street economy while the city council and the mayor skim the cream off high society. Then there's the cops; they take their cut from whomever they please. I should know, since I used to be one.

The Commonwealth officials don't care what happens in Pitts so long as the money and the steel keep flowing.

I'm on the north side of the Allegheny before I see the first signs of legitimate commerce. A horse-drawn milk wagon and a peddled ice cart race to be the first delivery of the morning for the upscale shops in this neighborhood. A two-man police patrol strolls along beneath the gaslights that haven't yet been extinguished. No streetwalkers, drunks, or mutilated bums crowd the tidy sidewalks on this side of the river, and the stench of the mill is masked by bakeries and coffee houses. A kid on the corner hawks his stack of chronicles: "New Canada Accuses Dominion of Attacks on Mystic Site! Read all about it!"

A memory flutters at the back of my mind. Damn, I need to see Olivia.

I buzz her secure riverside apartment and get no answer. I take a deep breath and count to ten. I head to her club; maybe she stayed there late or went in early. I'm sure she's fine. I'm sure she's alone. No need to jump to conclusions. No need to hurt anybody. Not yet.

The overhead thunder-rail divides Olivia's Bohemian neighborhood from the posh nightclub and restaurant district where O's is neatly tucked between a snooty bistro and an upscale bar where doctors, lawyers, and King executives unwind in their pressed shirts and loosened ties after screwing the working man. Olivia's club is the sort of place where anybody with money comes to be seen; where the mayor and the city council entertain visiting dignitaries and celebrities while cutting men's-room deals with one of the big three gang bosses.

Olivia wouldn't own it if I hadn't gotten proof that her ex-husband was taking his evening strolls with a councilman's teenaged son. She was a client and now she's my girl. Whoever said not to mix business with pleasure never looked into green eyes like Olivia's.

O's is locked up and the lights are out, but Sam the doorman knows me. He gives a nervous smile as he lets me in, asks if I want a drink, then remembers himself and offers coffee. Before I can refuse, he calls to the darkened kitchen: "Mr. Halftown's here! Put a fresh pot on!"

"Thanks, Sam. I'm good. Your boss around?"

"She's in her dressing room, Mr. Halftown." He laughs, trails me into the darkened club. "Sure you don't want nothin' to eat? We was about to fix us some breakfast anyhow. How 'bout some eggs and toast?"

I shake my head. "Not hungry, Sam. Why you so jittery this morning?"

He laughs. "Too much coffee, I reckon. Been up all night, but you know how that is."

"Marc," Olivia calls in that whiskey-angel's voice, stepping onto the stage. She was made for that stage. Even at the ass-crack-of-dawn, she looks like a goddess with the dimmed house lights glowing in her honey-colored hair and sparkling in her jade-greens. Hell if I don't need her. "I thought you were working," she says.

"Finished just a few hours ago, baby." I keep from running across the dance floor like a heeling dog, but just barely. "I needed to see you." She smiles before I kiss her, but she's tense. She gently pushes me away from the vanilla and cinnamon scent of her hair.

"I'm glad you stopped by, Marc. It's just that I'm so tired. I've been here all night. You know the mayor's bringing reps from both New Canada and the Dominion by this week? Everything has to be coordinated just right; otherwise my club could be the first battleground in the war that's been brewing for a decade."

"Then let's go back to your place and grab a nap."

"I don't think I'd get very much sleep if we did that." She smiles and she's right. She stands on tiptoes and kisses me the way I want her to, but not if we're not going back to her place. "Why don't you go and get some rest? Let me finish up here, then come back this afternoon? I'll make it worth your while."

I don't trust myself to say the right thing. I just hug her tight, then slink to the front door. Sam smiles at me. I glare back.

"Thought I might find you here." Eddy Childes, standing on the sidewalk out front, looks like he just woke up in the suit he put on at the beginning of the week. Unusual for him; even when we were walking the beat his brass glowed like lightbulbs. "Been to your office and your pad already."

"You look like hell, Eddy. What happened to you?" I'm tired and wound up. Not the best company this morning. I really want to hurt someone. Bad.

He laughs and smooths out his pinstripes, buttons his jacket, and slicks back his dark hair. "Been a long night. Like I said, been looking for you. Think I've got something you might be interested in. Take a walk?"

He burns one as we head up Robinson Street, past florists, cafes, and bakeries. Me and Eddy go way back: roommates at the police academy, partners on the beat, and at the detective's bureau. He was the only one to stick by me during the hard times when I let the bottle tear me down; when I got booted off the force, when my wife took my boy and left town. Well, the Old Man stuck by me, of course. I was still an investment, after all, though a bad one at the time.

"So what've you got?" I try not to breathe in the second-hand smoke, but not too hard. The nostalgic smell is calming.

He hands me an old plastic data stick; the kind they used before the Leviathans and magic changed everything. "Old World tech. Thought maybe you could move it on the streets. Split the profits."

I slide the USB out of its plastic foreskin. Not many places still have the ability to read this kind of device, but I know some folks. "Depends what's on it whether or not it's worth anything. Where'd you get it?"

Eddy shrugs. "My uncle up in New Canada sent it to me. He's a scientist of some kind working for their government. He said it was important."

"And you want to sell it?"

Eddy smiles. "I haven't seen or heard from that bastard in twenty years. Family ties don't put bread on the table or in my wallet. If he says it's important, maybe it's worth something to somebody. Maybe even thousands."

And maybe my servitude to the Old Man just got a little shorter. "I'll see what I can do. I'll let you know if I find a buyer." I hold the flash out to him but he shakes his head.

"You keep it. Probably not a good idea for a cop to have it, just in case it's got something illegal on it."

"If it's not illegal, then it's worthless."

Eddy laughs. "Don't worry. If you get pinched, I got your back…. Later." I nod as he slides into the unmarked steamer parked in the alley two blocks from O's. I know he's got my back. He always has.

I head to the park since I'm on this side of town. It's early yet, so there's a chance I'll find Sandy. He can put the word out that I've got Old World tech for sale. The key is doing it without letting the Old Man know, otherwise he'll find a way to shake me down for a hefty cut. He has less sway on this side of the Allegheny, so it just might work.

Riverside Park is technically part of the upscale neighborhoods, but after dark, it shows its true colors. The well-to-do perverts and addicts sneak out of their high-rises and suburbanite homes to trawl the park in hopes of a hookup or a score. Sandy is one of the night-folk that caters to those many and varied needs. I used to pass judgment until I realized that addiction is a chained demon in every man's soul, and mine is as nasty as they come.

"Haven't seen you in a while, handsome." Sandy steps from behind an oak tree shading a park bench. He's wearing a wig of long blonde hair and a short sequined red dress that accentuates his slender figure, and he's using his woman's voice. I'm not caught off guard. I've seen him in this guise before, just like I've seen him in his tough-guy, pit-fighter persona, and his suit-and-tie "I've never done this kind of thing before" facade.

"Haven't needed to be here for a while." I like Sandy; not the way he wants me to, but at least he's an honest guy. Even when he's a girl. "I'm looking to move some Old World tech. Thought you might know if anybody's in the market, or at least put the word out."

"Aw, shucks. I hoped you were finally going to take a walk on the wild side." He sits on the bench and stretches his fish-netted legs out, pointing his pumps at the river. "Just another dumb old black-market deal, huh?"

I smile, though the demon wants to beat him to a pulp. "Just let me know if you hear anything, okay?" I head down the trail and try to clear my head; find some solitude before I lose my temper. I'm not mad at Sandy, or at anyone in particular, but it doesn't matter.

Son of a bitch.

I wasn't paying attention. I headed west on the trail. I look up and see the smoke-belching, fire-breathing, water-churning, life-eating wall of the steel plant blocking out the horizon. The fifty-story thing stretches from the southern bank of the Monongahela, across the center of the city, all the way to the northern bank of the Allegheny. Sitting on top of two massive hydroelectric dams, it uses the rivers to power production, while its skyline of windmills reclaims thermal energy to power the offices and operations located on the north bank where the two rivers become the Ohio.

King Consolidated Steel. The heart and soul of Pitts. The god of fire and iron that feeds on the working class to give us glorious ingots of shining metal and piles of money while shitting out a steady stream of broken bodies and shattered lives. I know because I'm part of that never-ending stream of excrement.

I was ten when my old man took a header off one of the catwalks into a vat of molten slag. The old lady had disappeared two years before. I didn't get along with my father; he was always tired and pissed by the time he came home from working a twelve-hour shift and spending another two at the bar, only to find something I had done wrong or hadn't done right. But he was my old man and he was all I had.

I remember that next morning. After the company clerk had come and told me what had happened and said I had 'til the end of the week to find a new place to live. They were turning our one-room flat over to the next family on the work list. I got up before dawn and went down to pick up my bundle of papers at the corner like always. I was big for my age so no one tried to bully me out of my stacks like they did the younger kids. Of course we still had to pay Miller, the truck driver, or else he wouldn't give us stacks. He was scamming us and we all knew it, but there was nothing we could do, so we paid him the five bucks and hoped we'd sell enough papers to cover the expense and still turn a profit. I remember looking at that front page and seeing a drawing of a soldier and a pretty woman, and hearing Miller tell us that the headline was "Prince Bernard Marries Cherokee Princess in Kalyna Royal Wedding." None of us could read so we had to get our hawk-lines from him. Nothing at all about a death at the plant.

Something in my gut turned cold and I started screaming at the top of my lungs: "King Consolidated Kills Employee! Extra! Extra! Read all about it!" It wasn't an extra edition, but we always sold more copies when it was. Miller jumped off his truck and hit me with his fist. It was the first time a grown man had hit me like that, and I went down hard. I think I was crying. I know I was cursing. But when I came up, I had my pen knife in my hand, the one we carried to cut the twine binding the stacks, and I opened Miller's fat belly like a book. He fell against the bed of the delivery truck and I remember the look on his flabby, bearded face. He stared at me like I was an angel or a demon, or God himself come down to deliver judgment on his twisted soul. His mouth moved, but only blood came out as his fingers tried to stuff slippery red guts back into his belly. The other kids screamed and ran, but I was laughing and crying at the same time. My old man was dead but he wasn't the only one, and I knew I could never hurt King Consolidated but I had just gutted the son of a bitch who'd been taking advantage of me for years. If Tommy Sienkiewicz hadn't seen it happen and thought I might come in handy one day, I'd have died in prison before my eleventh birthday, and I sure as hell would never have become a cop.

"Cruising for ass, perv?"

I've been staring into space for a while. It's a young cop, slapping his open palm with his baton. He's talking to me. "You know sexual misconduct in public places is punishable by up to six months in the joint, don't you, perv?"

"Then you'd best get on over to city hall, rookie. And take a big wagon with you." I'm shaking, but not because I'm scared. At least not of the cop, even though he's armed to the teeth with guns, knives, and the baton.

"Oh, so you think you're a tough guy, do you? Well, I guess I need to teach you a lesson about respect and authority, perv." He takes a step, but I've already hit him before his foot touches the ground. I hit him again and again, though I felt his jaw snap like rotten wood on the first punch. By the time my fist comes back the fourth time, I see his eyes are wide and empty. He hasn't felt the last two blows. But he will when he wakes up some time tomorrow. If he wakes up.

"Freeze!" I drop the unconscious rookie and turn to see his partner coming up the trail with his revolver leveled at my chest. A big part of me wishes he would just do it, pull the trigger and get it over with. Put me out of my misery. Then we recognize each other. "Holy shit, Halftown! What the hell did you do to the kid?"

"I just taught him a lesson about respect and authority." I'm not shaking anymore. My breathing isn't labored, but I feel awful. I look down at the mangled pulp of blood and teeth above the rookie's collar, then glance at my right hand. I hate myself. Not because I hurt him, but because I enjoyed it. I always enjoy it. "Keep a better watch over your trainees in the future, eh, Moench?"

Moench lets me leave the park without another word. He knows what I'm capable of, who I work for, and what I've got on him and half the guys in the department. As I cross the bridge back to my side of town, I rub my scuffed knuckles and head to the office.

Pitts is coming to life. The hissing whoosh of steam cars jumbles with the clip-clopping rumble of horse-drawn carts and buggies; mixes with the dull roar of the natives as they bustle about their dull lives. Of course, the cacophony doesn't drown out the steady, evil purr of the steel mill and its occasional eruptions of flame and steam at the joining of the rivers. A Pitts PD airship glides above the cramped, sooty rooftops, telling us we're all safe. I almost laugh, but the demon wishes I'd killed that rookie cop.

"Starting early, I see," Rosa says. My assistant plops her big backside into the chair behind her desk and adjusts the giant black frames of her spectacles. "Well, while you've been out having fun this morning, I've been trying to entertain the first client to come in here in a month that didn't smell like booze or feces or both."

"Heaven forbid you should have to do your job." I step into my inner office and she sticks her tongue out. She's right, though. The good-looking brunette in here smells like honest-to-goodness perfume, which is the same as smelling like money. When she stands, she looks it, too.

"Mr. Halftown? I'm Denise Patton." She smiles and extends a gloved hand. She's wearing a skirt-suit that cost what I pay in two months' rent on this place *and* my apartment. Not including her hat, heels, and bag. "My father is Harold Patton, of Patton Paper and Supply. Have you heard of it?"

"I have." I slip behind my desk and drop into the chair. "The largest paper company in New Canada, and one of the largest on the continent. So what brings you to Pitts and the Commonwealth, Mrs. Patton?"

"It's *Miss* Patton."

Of course it is.

"Well, Mr. Halftown, one of our employees has recently stolen some privileged information, and is using it to blackmail my father. I hired a detective in Nova Scotia, and he tracked him here. Obviously, since the information is… sensitive, to say the least, I do not wish to involve the authorities. I've done my research, and it seems you are the best man in this city for this job. So here I am."

"Hmm." I stare at her and count to see how long before she shifts uncomfortably. She shrugs and looks away two seconds later than your average debutante would, and about three seconds quicker than your average undercover cop. She's good, but not perfect. "What's this employee's name?"

"Doctor Raymond Hammett, but I'm sure he's adopted an alias. He was part of our R&D department." She smiles and waits for nearly a minute. "So will you take the case?"

"Twenty-five bucks a day plus expenses. Fifty up front." She doesn't bat a pretty blue eye as she opens her purse. I should have doubled my numbers since she's paying with somebody else's money. "Give Rosa your contact information and any pertinent details on your way out. I'll get to work on this right away."

"Thank you, Mr. Halftown."

I smile and see her out, then lock the door. I dig an old light tablet out of the back of my closet. I took it off a college professor who tried to con the Old Man a while back. The screen is cracked, but it's got a USB port and just enough juice to give me a picture of what's on this data stick.

Of course the info's in the Old Tongue, so I can only understand bits and pieces, but I make out that there's a bunch of chemical formulas and some biological data. Real highbrow stuff, way above my rudimentary CSI training. But at least I know I've got an uncorrupted flash drive full of Old World goodies. Might be worth something after all.

I put the tablet away, slip the flash drive into my sock, and then collapse on the sofa to stare at the ceiling for a while. My thoughts slide back to "Ms. Patton" and her missing employee. She's a sham working for somebody; somebody with money and a reason to hide in the shadows. I should have Rosa chase her down and give her money back. I should go home and go to bed and forget about this case. I've got the data stick to worry about, after all. And I still *need* to see Olivia in a few hours.

But this mystery, this dog-and-pony show, has got my brain itching, taking my mind off everything else. I have to know why all the intrigue. Maybe this'll be the one that puts me in a river and I won't have to worry about any of it anymore. Or, maybe it could be the one that gets me out from under Sienkiewicz and out of Pitts for good. And maybe I'll just turn into a hummingbird and fly my ass out of here. Maybe...

*

Rosa wakes me by tossing a cheese sandwich wrapped in a letter onto my chest. "Our new client is an impatient one. She's already sent a message wanting to know if you've made any progress."

I check my watch. I've only been out for a couple hours. Best get up and get moving if I want to make any headway before my afternoon with Olivia. I eat the sandwich and read the letter from Patton, written on The King's Suites hotel stationary. Aside from asking about progress, she mentions that Dr. Hammett should have arrived in Pitts less than two weeks ago. She also gives a physical description which is a little too detailed for the average paper-empire heiress. She's a professional; law enforcement or military, maybe more. But if she is, she's new to this kind of game, or at least she's underestimated me. To be fair, she wouldn't be the first.

I head to my place to shower and change. The thunder-rail station and the local flophouse hotel are right across Penn Ave from my office, so I nose around there first. I'm surprised when I find that a skinny, bald fellow with a Canadian accent checked into the flophouse ten days ago under the name "Rick Biegler." It costs five bucks to get the clerk to give me the key.

The dingy room is empty, but I can tell it's been tossed. Drawers and closets are not closed all the way, the mattress is crooked on the box spring; even the toilet tank cover is not squared. If this was Dr. Hammett's room, he hasn't been here in a few days but someone else has. Patton? That's a safe bet. The half-ass attempt at covering the search fits my impression of her.

Sandy's outside my rundown building on Duquesne Blvd; he's dressed like a college student with a backpack. "Found you a buyer, Halftown. Looks like Kalyna's university is willing to pay big bucks for viable Old World tech. 'Course, they can't get a rep here before next week."

"Sounds good. Thanks, Sandy." I'm surprised when he puts a hand on my arm; he's never tried to touch me before. Like most people, he's scared of me.

"Be careful, Marc." His eyes search the shadows of the cramped street. "While I was asking around, I got the impression there were other players in the game. Big-time players; hard-ball players. But not paying players."

"Thanks, Sandy. Watch your back." He mounts a bicycle parked beside a pile of trash, and heads down Sixth. Sandy's warning gives me a charge. I haven't been this interested in anything besides sex or violence for as long as I can remember. Of course, it just makes me crave Olivia even more.

*

It's nearly three o'clock by the time I make it to O's, freshly showered, shaved, and ready for action. Sam looks scared. With opening just a few hours away, there's more employees flitting about and the lights are on. "Where's Olivia?"

"She went home about an hour ago, Mr. Halftown. She was so tired she almost fell off the stage while rehearsing for tonight. We had to beg her to get some rest; she really needs it." I guess he sees the look in my eyes, because he pleads, "Please, Mr. Halftown, let Ms. Olivia get some sleep. She said she'd be back by seven tonight. Come back then and see her, but please let her rest for now, won't you?"

I clench my fists and cast a longing glance at the bar on my way out. I feel the demon tearing at his chains and wonder how long they'll hold. I feed him with action—sex and violence—to keep him from breaking free and pouring me into a bottle. I need Olivia right now, but she needs rest; she could have really hurt herself falling off that stage.

Saint Sinai Hospital is just a few blocks from here, so I check on John Does in the ER and the morgue. Bribing the snooty clerks at the *good* hospital is quite a bit more expensive than anything on the south side of the river. I've blown through Patton's deposit by the time I've cleared the meat lockers with nothing to show for it.

Since I've got the time, I go across town, below the Monongahela, to Baptist Medical and check their slabs. Older and poorer, the soot-blackened five-story "BM" is located near picturesque Forest Park and ivy-draped The Old College, and across Ninth Street from the shiny new Commonwealth government-office building.

The lowly orderlies, clerks, and med students here are happy to take a ten, twenty, or even a five to look the other way while I check the charts, poke my head in to look at coma patients, and root around the morgue. In the latter I hit pay dirt. And it's one hell of a bloody mess.

This John Doe was recovered from the northern bank of the Monongahela last night by the KCS crews who keep debris from entering the turbines of the dams. Whoever put him there took their time with him beforehand. His right eye was cut out, then his tongue, and he was hanged, but not to the point of asphyxiation. He was stabbed with a slender instrument right above the heart, before finally being set on fire. The coroner's report says it's even odds whether he bled out or burned to death first. The estimated time of death is sometime day before yesterday.

The most shocking thing on the report is the name: Detective Edward Childes, Pitts Police Department. Things are coming into focus. Eddy told me he got the data stick from his "uncle," a scientist in New Canada. He gave me the stick, looking like hell, the morning after being called in on this murder case.

The demon howls and I imagine a chain snapping. That son of a bitch. I'll kill him.

Hammett came to Pitts at least ten days ago. He may have sent the flash drive to Eddy beforehand. When Hammett turned up brutally murdered, Eddy realized he's in over his head and decided to drop it in my lap. Why? I thought we were friends.

Eddy's flat is on recently remodeled Grant Street, just a short walk from Baptist Medical. I'm forcing myself to take long, deep breaths; trying to keep calm. I should give him a chance to tell his side of the story. Let him explain what's going on and why.

Then I'll tear him apart.

When I reach the sixth floor, the hairs on the back of my neck stand up and I know something's wrong. I smell blood and perfume. Not the flowers and evergreens I smelled on Denise Patton; something familiar, something that hurts.

Vanilla and cinnamon.

I don't bother to knock. The place is clean and undisturbed, but the scent of sex and death is stronger as I move to the bedroom. That's where I find them. Eddy and Olivia stretched out naked on the bed, both with their wrists, ankles, and throats slit, turning the white sheets red. Judging by the spray patterns, they were both asleep when the cuts were made. Skilled and precise. That rules out Patton.

They died in their sleep without ever knowing it. Painless and peaceful. Not the way I would have done it.

I sit in the room's one chair. I stare at the only two people I really trusted in this godforsaken world, and I see all the morning's clues in stark clarity: Sam's nervousness, Olivia's standoffishness, Eddy's disheveled appearance, and his car parked two blocks away from the club instead of right outside. I hear the demon laugh.

I laugh with him, because it's better than crying. Eddy thought he was saving his own neck and getting me out of the picture at the same time by handing me the flash drive. Olivia probably just got bored with me, or figured Eddy was a better bet in the long run.

I'm still laughing when I hear the sirens. Whoever did this is close by. They waited to see me enter the apartment before they wired the cops. They've been watching me at least long enough to know that this is the perfect setup: Jealous, violent boyfriend catches his girl with his best friend.

I dig Eddy's revolver out of the pile of discarded clothes. I consider charging down the stairs and seeing how many of Pitts' Finest I can take with me in a blaze of glory. The demon would like that. But I want some answers, so I head up to the roof and jam the door with the gun. Four blocks separate me from my apartment, five from my office, and seven from Showin' Tails. Been a while since I traveled by rooftop.

In the open, if not clean air, I try to think. If Denise Patton, or whoever she really is, didn't kill Eddy and Olivia, then who did? Obviously one of the non-paying, hard-ballers Sandy warned me about. Who killed Hammett? Probably the same party; Patton wouldn't waste time or money hiring me to find a corpse she put in the river. Besides that poor bastard's death looked personal—or maybe *ritualistic*.

Shit. Could a magician or a cult be involved? I remember the headline that kid was hawking this morning: "New Canada Accuses Dominion of Attacks on Mystic Site!" Then I remember that Olivia said the mayor was hosting reps from both countries this week. So maybe Patton works for one and the killer for the other?

I don't look it, but I'm smart enough to know when I'm in over my head. Being in the middle of an international dispute involving magic is at the very bottom of the pool. Time to cut my losses. I drop down into Liberty Avenue and find a stoop urchin to carry a note to the Old Man. I scan the cluttered street and the overhanging rooftops as the kid runs off, then head to my apartment where my guns and money are stashed. I'm cautious as I enter my building, climb the stairs, and open the triple-locked door.

Just not cautious enough.

*

I wake tied to the heaviest chair in my apartment. There's a man sitting in my recliner; the glow of his cigarette the only light in the room. He turns on the table lamp and I see a well-dressed, middle-aged, white man with graying hair smiling at me like we're long-lost brothers or something. "Like looking in a mirror, isn't it?" His Pitt accent is the only thing we could possibly have in common.

"I take it you're blind." I'm in no mood for games.

"Ah, true perception was too much to hope for, I suppose." He takes another long drag on the cigarette before putting it out on the arm of my recliner. "After all of your other skills, I did hold out so much hope for you, Mr. Halftown. I see now that you are just another mundane after all. Though you are the very epitome of what the ancients would have called 'the noble savage.'"

"You're the killer." I flex against the ropes but they don't budge. Bastard knows his way around a knot.

"I am the killer." His face shows disappointment, like I'm the one insulting him. "I am so very much more, Mr. Halftown, and I'd hoped you would be able to appreciate that. I have so looked forward to meeting you."

"So that's why I'm still alive? You want to talk?"

"That is one reason, yes. I see in you the same loneliness and primeval drive that I feel every day of my life. The constant craving for something we cannot, should not have; that yearning which elevates us above the common man. You, a proud and warlike descendant of this land's native people, can surely imagine how isolating it is being a practitioner of magic in the Commonwealth."

"Magic is illegal here." The ropes won't budge.

"So is murder. You have seen how easy the one makes the other."

"You killed Olivia and Eddy."

"I thought you might thank me for that."

"I might have, if you'd done it the way you did that poor Canuck bastard." This guy let his demon off its chain a long time ago, and it ate him.

He smiles. "Ah, the age-old rituals of our order had to be performed with Dr. Hammett. He had betrayed us and so his death was a lesson to others among our brotherhood who might be inclined to do the same. The illicit lovers, on the other hand, did not need to suffer for their part in this ... affair. But they knew enough that they still had to die."

"So there's more like you? Is it a cult? A conspiracy?" I feel a little circulation slip into my right hand.

"Still playing the detective, eh? Well, it doesn't matter, Mr. Halftown. What I am, what my brotherhood is, is as far above your understanding as algebra is above that of an ape. I was mistaken. You are nothing more than a denizen of this world with a certain measure of rough cunning, but no true understanding.

"Here we are, six hundred years after the return of magic and mankind still refuses to be *enlightened*, clinging to the darkness of the Old World the way beasts lurk in the wilderness because they fear the fire of civilization."

"I guess now that you've lorded your victory over me, we'll get to the second reason I'm still alive. I'm not telling you where the flash drive is." I flex again and the ropes shift a hair.

He pulls the data stick from his jacket pocket. "No need, Mr. Halftown. I searched you while you slept. Useful spell that, 'The Cloak of Morpheus,' it's called."

I crack my neck. I need to keep this guy talking. Fortunately, he's the type to enjoy the sound of his own voice. "So, what then?"

"Did you see what's on the drive?" He peers down his nose at me like a teacher interrogating a troublesome student. I understand that my answer will determine if I go out like Eddy and Olivia or like Hammett.

I've never been a good liar, so why start now? "Looked like scientific jargon in the Old Tongue."

He slips the drive back into his pocket and leans forward. "I suppose it would, just like an ape would think a pipe wrench looked like a heavy bone or stick. Tell me, Mr. Halftown, have you ever heard of Solomon's Key?"

"I'm not Jewish."

"Solomon's Key was one of the metaphysical goals of the wise men called alchemists in the Old World's antiquity. It was reputed to give the wielder power over beings of the spiritual world; power over physical matter. Power over life and death."

"That's what's on the flash drive?" I feel a knot loosen.

"Yes. Dr. Hammett rescued it from an archeological site during a Dominion raid two weeks ago. He sent it to his nephew, the corrupt policeman and your late friend, instead of turning it over to his lodge in Nova Scotia. Fortunately, I have been here in Pitts for a very long time, waiting for just such an opportunity to serve the order and reveal my full potential.

"Now, Mr. Halftown—"

I snap the rope and bring my fist around in a right hook. Glad the bastard leaned forward to gloat. He goes out like a light. Good thing, too, because it takes me damn near ten minutes to get loose.

I retrieve the data stick and find his wallet. Faculty ID from The Old College; Dr. Isaac Bacon, professor of history and literature. I'm about to kick in this nut-job's skull when the apartment door opens. Denise Patton, though she's now dressed in dark military fatigues and holding a weird-looking gun that tells me she's an agent for the Dominion of Freedoms.

"Do you have it, Mr. Halftown?"

I palm the flash into my pocket. "Have what, exactly, Ms. Patton? Or whoever you really are."

"Don't be coy. It doesn't suit you. Hand over the data stick or I'll be forced to search your body for it, just like I did your transvestite friend earlier this afternoon."

I'm usually better about not telegraphing my moves, but it's been a long day.

The air crackles and I blink at the intense orange light that fills the apartment. It takes a moment to register that my left arm is on fire.

I kick the heavy chair across the room. It intercepts the next energy bolt in midair, and I dive through the window behind the recliner. Thank God for fire escapes and cheap glass.

My arm hurts like hell and is nearly useless by the time I hit Sixth Street. Another orange bolt misses me by inches. A shot answers from down Duquesne, and I look to see four of Sienkiewicz's crew running my way, firing at my third-floor window.

Ten minutes ago, I'd have thought the cavalry had arrived. Now that I know what's on this drive, I realize that nobody should have it. Especially not a gangster locked in a tentative three-way peace with two other crime bosses.

My apartment explodes. Glass, burning debris, bricks, and charred pieces of somebody rain down on me as the shockwave knocks me flat. I don't know if it's Patton or Bacon; could be both. My ears are still ringing as I scramble to my feet.

A Pitt PD patrol steamer comes screeching up Sixth Street, blue lights blazing.

I run for the Sixth Street Bridge. Gunshots behind, but I don't look back. The patroller is closing in. I should toss this thing over the bridge and let the Allegheny have it, but I don't know if Bacon is still alive, and he just might have some kind of magic that could retrieve it. Even worse, King Consolidated might wind up with it.

That gives me an idea.

I reach the end of the bridge just as the patroller catches up with me. I leap over the guardrail and drop seven feet. I hit the graveled embankment running, and make a beeline for the foundry.

I take a cop's slug in the left leg. I'm bleeding like a stuck pig and finding it hard to breathe by the time I reach the security fence.

I don't think I've got the strength to climb it, so I wait for the patroller to catch up. I charge the car and jump as the cop hits the brakes. He's used to driving on paved streets, not gravel. The car fishtails just as I hit the hood and roll onto the windscreen.

We slide sideways through the chain-link and I roll into the compound in a cloud of dust. I'm on my feet before the first cop tries to exit the car. I kick the door with my good leg, smashing him back into his seat. His partner jumps out on the other side and levels his revolver at me. His head explodes as the first of Sienkiewicz's men arrives on the scene.

I limp across the parking lot. The old guy in the guard shack doesn't come out; just locks himself in and wires for more cops. By the time I mount the rusty switchback stair climbing the colossal outer wall of the mill, a good old-fashioned shootout is taking place between the Old Man's boys and two more patrollers' worth of cops. That should keep them busy.

I'm hurt worse than I thought ... harder to breathe ... the higher I climb ... losing too much blood. I look up and see the black plumes rising ... against an orange sky. Just a little farther to go...

Darkness ... at the edge of my vision ... but I'm at the top ... just have to ... find a vent ... above the furnaces. The heat tells me I'm close ...

"Bravo, Mr. Halftown. The noble savage, indeed." Bacon is standing on the catwalk above a thermal vent. Bastard must be able to fly.

I smile at his swollen, bloody lips. "Not ... so bad yourself, Doc."

"Hand me the drive and I promise I'll make your death quick and painless." He holds out his hand like he's offering salvation.

I take it. And I finally feed the demon.

I hold him tighter than I ever held Olivia, as we tumble over the guardrail, through the aluminum vent cover, and into the heat and flame. He's fighting ... screaming ... cursing ... maybe trying to cast a spell ...

I'm laughing and crying at the same time ... because now I can see the reflection.

We're both monsters, and this world is better off without us.

***

# The Traveler

by Jenean McBrearty

## US: Other worldly strangers unravel a mystery and their pasts

Zartanian knew why the fellow traveler who shared his compartment was angry. He'd left for a meal and came back to what looked like theft. The briefcase he had carried aboard was open, and "Zartie" was curled up on the seat, editing a manuscript he'd found inside.

"How dare you!" the man said. He was biting his lips, the tip of his blue tongue squished between them in an honest snarl.

"It's not what it seems. Nothing ever is," Zartie said."

The man drew a ten-inch hunting blade from its waist sheath, and raised his arm.

"Hold on, now!" Zartie said as he held the pages to his chest like a shield. "Okay, it was rude, but I'm an editor by trade and you're getting free services. In Frisco you'd be paying fifty glots an hour for me to read your manuscript."

The man lowered the knife and took the seat opposite. "Do you understand Fedderie?" he said.

"Of course. An editor has to know at least three other languages and a score of dialects to make it in the publishing world these days of intergalactic diversity. I may look a little dragged out, but I've been on this train for ten hours."

The knife was safely back in its leather casing. "What do you think so far?"

"Of the story? Is it yours?" Zartie despised plagiarism when he got caught.

"In a manner of speaking."

57

"What manner would that be? You either wrote it or you didn't." Fedderies had a reputation for being indefinite, like articles in life's grammar.

"I put the words down, but the truths were not mine. We are a mystic people."

Mystics carrying sharp weapons seemed like an odd coupling to Zartie, but he only understood words, not esoteric bullshit people all over the galaxy believed. "So ... you got gamma-goober-ray thoughts from some spirit on a far-away planet and this is the second installment of the bible?"

The fellow traveler gently took the pages from Zartie's hands and reverently put them in his briefcase.

"Sorry, pal. I'm Zartanian–Zartie–from the planet Cynica in the foolish quadrant of the universe. You got a name, I hope?"

That brought a smile to the stranger's face. The big to-do at the universities was the demand for nomen-fluidity, and all because the blobby Balugians had joined the Universal States. Young people now hated the permanency names imposed despite the ensuing chaos–and everyone had a university degree in something.

"I'm called Joshua."

Before he could draw a breath, the train lurched and Joshua fell into the lap of his unhired editor.

"Well," Zartie said, "this relationship has moved swiftly. I knew you were a romantic from paragraph two."

"We've stopped," Joshua said, as he wrested himself and his dignity from Zartie's grip.

There were voices outside, and Joshua opened the top air-window. While he strained to see into the darkness from the lit compartment, Zartie's attention focused on a slim figure in a dark gray suit and black fedora slip inside the compartment. The man stretched out his hand, and sank to the floor. Zartie was bending over him as Joshua turned around. "He's dead," Zartie said simply, and held up a bloodied antique key. "Shot, I think."

Joshua knelt beside them. "Did he say anything?" he demanded.

"Baggage car," Zartie said.

"Shouldn't we report him?"

"And be delayed for six months while the cops investigate? Hell, no. Let's get him into the corridor and make him somebody else's problem."

Joshua gave him a nod. "Right."

They pulled him into the passageway, left him outside three doors down, and scurried back to their compartment. "Clean your hands with this." Joshua pulled a bottle of hand sanitizer and a travel packet of tissues from his briefcase. "Was he was shot, do you think?"

If a person carried a knife, it would make sense he'd carry hand sanitizer as well, people being blade averse.

"He must have been. He wasn't gushing blood. A puncture wound deep enough to kill him would have struck an artery or an organ or something."

"How do you know?" Joshua said.

"I read for a living, remember?"

"We didn't hear a gunshot."

"I can barely hear myself think with the noise these railway dinosaurs make. What fools these earthlings be. If they'd grease the train wheels more often than they grease the wheels of government …" Zartie moistened his hands and wiped them with a tissue. Now what? He shoved it into a wall slot marked TRASH.

There was a knock at the door, and the steward peeped in. "Sorry, folks. Someone fell off the train. Man overboard, you might say. But he's okay." The two men looked at each other, then at the grinning conductor. "Have a good evening."

When the door closed, Zartie counted off ten seconds, and then cracked it open. All he saw was the back of the conductor walking down the corridor, periodically knocking on compartment doors.

"The body?" Joshua whispered.

"Gone."

"Gone where?"

"I haven't read that part yet, Joshua. Maybe Newark."

"This is California."

"All right. Norwalk. You obviously know nothing about Vaudeville. New Jersey's always been funnier than California."

"Not since 2017. Maybe the conductors found him and took him somewhere," Joshua said.

"Maybe they have a morgue car and a jail on this train. They've got a hat boutique."

"Pork pies, maybe?"

"I'd rather have steak." Zartie was gazing at the key he'd wiped clean, along with his hands, and the claim check the dead owner had tied to it.

Joshua's eyes darted to the window and back to Zartie. "Do you think the jumper is the murderer? If they've got a body and a suspect, case closed, unless … are you sure our corpse didn't tell you something you're not telling me?"

"I wouldn't hide a talking dead guy from you. Why would I when we could make a gadzillion glots?" Zartie's thoughts drifted to the advertisements for Earth's retro trains: *Safety First and Foremost. An Environmentally Happy Way to Travel.* Not so much for the dead guy, but laying tracks over what were once clogged freeways seemed like wise use of available infrastructure, at least according to the latest book he edited called *Ride and Grow Rich*.

"I'll tell you why you'd hide a death-floor utterance. Because you've pegged me as a romantic and a goody-two wings and you want to find the lock that fits that key," Joshua said.

"I am wondering where the baggage car is. Off limits, to passengers, I imagine. Still, a guy could get into the baggage car if he had a good story."

"You didn't like mine. Guess it's out," Joshua said.

"The parting of the red bees wasn't a bad scene. Where'd you get the snappy dialog? You seem more like a straight man to me."

"I wore a man's bonnet once, but I went to Harvard," Joshua confessed.

"Did he pin you?"

"Only once on a wrestling mat. I'll tell you what, you tell me what the man said before he died, and I'll share some of this." Joshua produced a flask of alcohol, probably from his all-purpose briefcase, and offered it to Zartie. "Go, ahead, it's Manganoit brandy."

Knife-wielding mystic with expensive booze. What could go wrong, thought Zartie. "What proof is this?"

"It's not proof, it's a bribe."

"The rules say, no outside food or drink."

"The rules say, do not touch other peoples' property," Joshua reminded him.

That was true. Before boarding, every passenger had to sign that he received a *Rider's Handbook* that listed forty-two rules for safe travel. No one read the damned book, but carrying it around was better than a pat-down by a burly guy named Bruce.

Zartie passed the flask back and forth under his nose. Brandy was brewed to be sniffed, to get your head ready for the assault to come. You only gulped it if you wanted a quick drunk. He took a nip, and then another. "Thank you," he said. "I've heard Harvard men are generous."

"Only with other peoples' money, thank God. Now, what did he say?"

"He said, 'tell market ... get weight,' or 'tell Marquette wait.' You know Earthspeak. It's cryptic. You wouldn't happen to have heart trouble, would you?" Zartie said.

"I will if necessary."

*

Zartie hurried down the corridor to the club car. There was always a steward on duty in case dinner disagreed with one of the first-class passengers. He caught Steward Thompson reading the newspaper and drinking ginger ale.

Zartie tweaked his cheeks to make them red, and feigned breathlessness. "It's my husband's nitroglycerine! I ... I put it in my suitcase, and he's got angina."

"What's that you say? If he's got Anne's vagina, I'd consider divorce, not suicide. Have you been drinking?"

"Please, it's his heart. Where's the baggage car?" Zartie looked at him with well-practiced desperation.

"You can't ..."

"I must, unless you want me to stop the train. After the jumper and a murder ..."

"Oh, God, you know about that, do you?" the steward said. "Damn it! I knew they couldn't keep it under wraps for long."

"Please, it's an emergency!"

The plump little man let out a large harrumph and muttered something about mixed marriages never working out before getting a key from behind the bar. "What's your tag number?"

"Seven zero nine three," Zartie said.

They went through three cars before crossing into a car lined with three tiers of shelving and stocked with a hundred suitcases and packages. Zartie sighed. "This'll take all night."

"Nonsense. You've got a medic stamp on that tag. We keep little black bags where we can get ahold of them in emergencies." The steward walked between the rows, stopped, and pulled a black bag from the second shelf. "We've got a system."

Zartie looked past the man's shoulder. "Those black bags have sequins ..."

"They go with the little black dresses the masseuses wear. Did you pay for call-in services?"

"Unh ... no. I've enough trouble with Anne," Zartie said.

"You got a compartment number?"

"Number thirty-four." Zartie double-checked the tag.

"All right, take it with you. I have to get some sleep. Follow me. We had to tie up that jumper. Had to store the corpse in a refrigerated freight car. You know anything about space fatigue, Doc?"

"Not my area of expertise, but I could examine him in the morning."

"Suits me fine. He's in car two. Wearing a white jacket, if you know what I mean," the steward said without stopping his sailor's walk down the corridor.

"Thank you," Zartie called to him, and got a backhand wave good night. He slid the door open and stepped inside.

"That was easy," Joshua said.

"Did you know they had masseuses on this train?"

"They won't thrive in Southern California. Too hot and dry," Joshua pronounced.

That was the trouble with traveling, Zartie thought. Visiting isn't the same as being a native. As an editor, he'd read more malapropisms and scrambled idioms than he could count. "Yeah, if there wasn't so much chaos, we wouldn't need so many rules. I read the ancient Hebrews originally had only ten." Zartie was checking the bag for markings or an outside pocket.

Joshua let out an old-man sigh. "You'd think animal experts would know better. Take a species out of its environment, and the next thing you know, you've got hell on your hands, Zartie."

"Call me Doc. I've gotta see a jumpy patient tomorrow."

"Do you know anything about medicine, Doc?"

"I edited a pharmacology textbook once. Between rules and medicines, it's a wonder people can be happy at all."

Zartie put the bag between them on the seat, slid the key into the lock and heard a small click. Inside was a cotton towel, a stethoscope, scissors, first-aid kit, a roll of cotton, a package of syringes, and small vials of digitalis, morphine, epinephrine, insulin, and penicillin. "It seems our magical mystery man was prepared for angina, anxiety, asthma, death by chocolate, gonorrhea– anything *but* a gunshot wound." He unzipped an inner pocket and pulled out a slim vial of green fluid. "Hell-o, what's this?"

"Give it to me," he heard Joshua say. His eyes caught the glint of a bronze barrel of a .45. "It's no use to you."

"You'd be Joshua Marquette?" Zartie said.

"The same."

"I could drop this, you know."

"Yes. But I'd have to shoot you, Doc, and I'd hate to, after you went to all that trouble."

"Let me guess." He handed the vial to Joshua. "It's a liquid muse for writers of religious rubbish." Zartie leaned back against the seat. "The message was for you to wait. Must have been an important message if they were the last words of a dying man. You *did* know Mr. Dead-guy."

"Doctor Blandine. I was his son-in-law until his daughter died."

"I wouldn't mind a little more of that brandy now. I assume you plan to kill me."

"Not at all, hopefully. But I can't let you have any more brandy. It might interfere with the medicinal properties of the ... elixir."

"I'm the replacement guinea pig?"

"I can tell you're an Eternian like our jumper. You've got a blue tongue too. The closest biological relatives to Fedderies. Perfect for experimentation."

"Non-consensual anything is against the rules in every part of the galaxy now. Did you play hooky the day they covered that in med school?"

"I got an MBA. Ballantine took the hypocritic oath."

"Touché. But, you need to re-work your business plan. You and daddy-in-law could have advertised for research subjects."

"We took that train to nowhere."

"No takers?" Zartie held the vial up to the light. "What's this shit supposed to do? Turn me into Superman?" Joshua laughed. He didn't sound menacing. "Really, you ought to tell me, so I can make a report, you know? Sometimes unexpected results are better than expected ones. I was editing a lackluster manuscript, got up to take a pee, came back, read two more chapters, and called the author to offer him a contract, and what do you think? I'd picked up another author's manuscript. Together they made a commercial success."

Joshua shook the vial gently, and from the bottom flecks of silver floated around like snow in a globe. "See those small particles? They're sensors that infiltrate your cells, read your DNA, and adjust your body fluids and hormones to bring you to complete homeostasis. This fluid can, you might say, cure whatever ails you."

"Hmmm. Interesting. I heard the same crap from an earthling on the beach once. Smoke this, he said, and you won't have a care in the world."

"Did it work?"

"I never cared about anything in life before I smoked his weed."

"But you enjoyed it."

"Temporarily. When the effects wore off, I was just the same ol' Zartie only groggy."

"This stuff won't wear off ... if you live."

"Not liking the dangerous scenario, Joshua. I don't mind being sick or unhappy. *My* religion tells me it's good for my character in this life, and the only guarantee of happiness in the next."

"Sure sounds depressing."

"It's downright dismal. But it keeps me off the streets most nights." Zartie's hand had slid underneath the bag, and with one good push, he flipped it upwards, knocking the gun from Joshua's hand. It flew towards the window, and left a crack in the glass before falling to the floor. Joshua couldn't retrieve it and protect his vial too, and by the time he'd found a safe place to stash the vial, Zartie had the pistol in hand, trained on the flummoxed young man. "You're not exactly the athletic type, are you?"

"I'm better with a knife," Joshua said sadly.

"I don't believe that, but if you make a move towards that blade in your belt, I'm blowing you to hell. And ain't no elixir going to mend a .45 calibre hole. Ask Jessie James. Or your in-law."

"You're in no danger. I'm so weak now, I couldn't fight anyone. That's what Strain2 hyperspesis does to you. My wife and I caught it when we visited the Signet Spacewheel. The Swan Flu, they call it. No preventive vaccine and no cure."

Incurable diseases were another downside to exploration and vacationing. Zartie pulled the clip. "Yeah, I figured. I've edited all kinds of books including a few swan songs. I'm so good at what I do, I can read between the lines. And San Diego has one of the finest university hospitals in the galaxy."

"For orthodox Fedderies, writing the story of a loved one is the greatest act of love one can perform. I started writing Justine Blandine's the day she was diagnosed. They told me to leave, that I could save myself, perhaps, by separating from her. I was afraid, yes, but I couldn't leave her. You understand."

"No, I don't. I've never been married."

Joshua took his wallet from his breast pocket, and pulled out a folded page. "Look at this," he said as he unfolded it and handed it to Zartie.

"Unbelievable! This must be at least two-hundred years old." He was looking at a page from a printed magazine, the spring issue of *Denovial Bride*, 1972, that showed a young couple's wedding ceremony by the sea. Underneath, someone had scrawled "Justine's Dream," followed by an exclamation point.

"She searched the universe for the perfect venue. Trite as it sounds, she wanted to be married by an ocean. The Creator's Symphony, she called it. You see what the man is wearing? A crown of woven flowers. I wore one just like it. She made it the night before the wedding. And I? I made a clumsy, goofy bouquet for her to carry. The young are so silly."

"I was never silly, Joshua." Zartie refolded the page. "You and Doctor Blandine were on your way back to the University Hospital with your experimental subject in tow, I take it?"

"Blandine worked there. Research and development."

"How did you get your subject to comply. He obviously wasn't keen on the idea."

"He was a guest of the Washington State Psychiatric Hospital serving a five-year rehab sentence for hate speech. Blandine was a colleague of the director, who recognized a blood match. Pure

Fedderie. The director medicated the man, and ... well, medicated people are extremely cooperative, until they aren't."

"But why the train, and not a plane?"

"Because of Question 125 on the flight release. Do you swear you are not under the influence of any medication for a condition that would require medical attention in case of a sea emergency? If yes, provide details about the medication and the needed services. There would have been inconvenient inquiries. Better to sign for a handbook than answer more questions."

"*Something* went terrible awry." Zartie waved the gun in the direction of Joshua's flask that had fallen with him and was now lying on the floor. "Open that baby, why don't you?"

Joshua opened the flask and gave it to Zartie, who ignored the niceties and took a swig. Brandy. Vodka. What difference did it make to a Cynician who's drunk every inebriant from Mercury Moonshine to Jupiter Juleps?

"A miscalculation of the dosage of the tranquilizer, maybe. Our subject was a young healthy alpha male. Blandine couldn't have forced him to take more. The guy must have got hold of Blandine's .22 and got off a lucky shot before jumping."

"Why do I get the feeling that the good Doctor Blandine and the Director have done this colleague fellow-well-met thing before? You've heard of the Mengele Society?"

"No, I haven't."

Joshua was too weak to lie, and if he had been wrapped up in the business world, he might not have heard the conspiracy theory floating around the galaxy about the twenty-first century research cabal named for the infamous medical researcher, Joseph Mengele. It wouldn't be the first time a conspiracy theory became a conspiracy fact. Earthlings were kept in the dark about the first alien contacts for almost a hundred years. And it wouldn't be the first time a child never knew the truth about his beloved parents. He learned his parents had murdered his little sister when she was five in a faked drowning. "Never mind, Joshua" he said. "Nobody can or should know everything."

Joshua was leaning back against the seat as though he'd disappear into the upholstery any minute, but one shoulder was drooped towards the window. "Blandine obviously thought I should wait to test the medicine on myself, but I can't. I know it. I can feel myself slipping away."

"I know you're scared. Me too. Only I'm scared of living. Funny, huh?" What awaited him in San Diego? More interviews with the police about things he never knew or couldn't remember. He and little Franny had been swimming and he'd come into the house to get more hot dogs for the grill. In the bottom of the refrigerator, his mother said, but when he looked, there weren't any there. Franny had been crying. The dog had eaten her hot dog, and she was having one of her unmedicated moments, a seizure that made her explode in anger. Then, suddenly, she was quiet. He wasn't there. He didn't see anything. Why were Earthcops so interested in something that happened thirty years ago? Did they believe he did it? Why were La Jolla houses so expensive to rent in the summer? He'd read an article about price gouging foreign visitors.

Zartie took another healthy swig of the brandy, and tossed the pistol inside the bag. "I can't tell you what to do, Joshua. Maybe this stuff is the magic bullet. But, if the choice is die or die, does it matter?" He shook the vial gently, removed the rubber stopper, drank half, and then handed the vial to Joshua. "It doesn't taste like poison."

Joshua drank the other half. "It tastes like a limeade snow cone. The sensors melt like ice."

His voice sounded like he was a thousand years old. Zartie imagined Joshua and Justine standing on the beach, dressed in their wedding clothes, asking each other who invited the guy in the khaki shorts and blue and white flowered Cynician shirt. "He's the preacher," Doctor Blandine was saying. "He's the editor guy who self-medicates because he loves mankind but hates himself."

"I wish I could have been at your wedding, Joshua. I'll bet it was very pretty. Some women have a way of making things pretty for us barbarians. They do nice little things, like put love notes in your pocket so you'll be surprised when you reach for your change."

Zartie turned off the light so they could see moonlight dancing on the ocean as the train passed by the small cities that dotted the coastal route from L.A. to San Diego. Encinitas. Solana Beach. Del Mar. It reminded him of the ride from Atwater to Celbis. Clanky machinery and all.

Maybe the green stuff did kill what ailed him. He didn't feel as lonely, or as far from God, as he had for most of his life. He must have read a thousand trillion words over the course of his life, looking for the answers to questions he could never articulate when talking to other people. Like why, no matter where he traveled throughout the universe, there were always a few people who seemed to know so much more than he did about the important stuff. Yet, he could never bring himself to ask questions about the important stuff. Like, why was Franny born to people who didn't love her?

Had he lost his language by expanding his horizons so far, there were no more boundaries? Was there nothing but the eternal void? Every race and civilization seemed to have a plausible answer. He believed everything and thus believed nothing. Nobody had conquered the universe, and everybody moved through it like silver flecks in green liquid until, at last, they settled in a heap at the bottom of the vial. Until some unknown Mover shook it, they were not stirred. But, when that Mover shook them, they did marvelous things like write a book about Justine that would never be a commercial success. He should have written a book about Franny a long time ago.

He summoned his courage.

"Do you really believe in a place people search the universe for? I hope I get to see my sister again. I loved Franny so much. Truthfully, I had a wife once too, but I left her. I don't even know why," Zartie said. It seemed safe in the dark, talking to a fellow dying traveler.

As for Joshua, he only spoke once before the train rolled into the Sante Fe terminus: "Zartie, hold my hand."

***

# The Jaws of the Jabberwock
## by Kevin Singer

### US: Planetary colonists unearth more than a new place to live

Brannon was nearly dead. His green eyes carried a yellow pallor and his black curls were greasy on his forehead. He strained his hands to claw at his throat—as did the other pioneers who succumbed to the malady—but his wrist bindings held firm.

Gita refused her tears, though Brannon was her designated match. They were to have children once they proved this marshy moon, Eostre, could support human life. Their pairing would commence once they messaged Titan to send the first batch of colonists. But eight months after landing, Gita and Brannon were all who remained of this one-way mission.

Brannon's stomach contracted. He stretched his mouth, revealing the pulsing yellow fibroids that writhed in his throat and snaked into his nasal passages. A bit of air reached his lungs. His eyes cleared and the Brannon Gita knew was back—the goofy, broad-shouldered medtech who boasted of surfing Titan's methane waves. She never believed his tales, but she loved them all the same.

"Tell me what I can do for you." Her voice was feeble, her words dumb. But she had nothing left to give. Medicine failed. Surgery proved horrific. She laid her hand against his damp forehead. She used to dream about their children, imagining her brown skin combining with his paleness to produce a range of beautiful hues. Those children would never exist.

He rasped and nodded toward his hands. His eyes pleaded but she was resolute. When Brannon had discovered that first wormlike fibroid squirming in the back of his throat three days earlier, they were under no illusions. They'd watched the other pioneers succumb. The fibroids blossomed fast. Suffocation came quickly. Brannon was clear on two things: he did not want to rip away the skin and muscle of his throat as Juliet had done. And he did not want to be euthanized as Raquel had begged. He wanted every second he was owed.

"No, my dear," Gita whispered.

He strained against the restraints. He bucked, raising his chest in a desperate attempt for air. His white skin turned purple. Gita grabbed his hand. His fingers coiled tight around hers. She almost winced in pain.

"I'll save this. All of this. I promise."

His eyes bulged, red veins popping through the white. His mouth gaped, the jaundiced fibroids wriggling in a mass of laughter, fingerlike tendrils with bloody veins that shuddered and throbbed. She wanted to rip them from his throat.

Go," she whispered. "Rest now with the gods of exploration."

Brannon lifted his head off the sweat-soaked bed. He made one last frantic gasp, his green eyes shining against the reddened whites, then he dropped.

Gita pulled her hand from Brannon's still warm fingers and let slip a meager sigh. She'd spent her childhood among scheming exo-miners and thieving junkers in the pockmarked corrugations of Cassini City. Life there ate away her soul, no matter how much homage she paid to the gods of exploration. The pioneer program was her chance to be reborn.

As what, though? Another pioneer abandoned on a barren rock?

Gita barricaded herself against the sorrow. There was work to do.

The dwarf star cast its pink glow on the moon's spongy plains. The ringed gas giant Camalus loomed in the sky, a swirling that threatened to suffocate but never did. Gita felt stiff in her haz-suit as she guided the hovercraft with Brannon's shrouded body away from the ringed complex toward the burial mounds, her boots squishing against the sodden soil.

There were no oceans on this moon; the water was trapped in the soil close to the surface. Raquel had been convinced they would thrive here, with the temperate climate and gentle tectonics. Even the wispy indigenous life, the mottled mosses and the small purple-tendrilled plants that would settle in the soil and then jump through the air to root themselves anew—jabberwocks they called them, after the ancient poem—carried a genetic code strikingly similar to Earth-sourced life. It was providence, Raquel said. Raquel was the first to succumb.

Gita guided the hovercraft past a lolling clutch of jabberwocks. The hovercraft sputtered. Brannon's dead white hand slipped from the cover of the shroud. A pair of jabberwocks wriggled free from the soil and leaped into the air, catching a current as they spun away. She watched them go before she tucked Brannon's cooling hand beneath the cloth.

The land rose several feet. Just past the rise were the burial mounds. It was not planned, this place. Such a move would have been an affront to the gods. But still, there it was. It had been Simeon's idea—burial rather than incineration. They'd dedicated their lives to this moon; in their deaths they would become one with her.

She guided the hovercraft over the rise. The air turned cool and she heard a low-timbered squawk that sent shivers through her body. She halted. Her blood turned cold. She was alone. Jabberwocks only gave faint chirps.

It's just the wind against the complex, she told herself. Nothing more.

She pressed ahead until she reached the summit where she could see each one of the burial mounds. The shock lasted just a moment before she let out a full-throated scream that echoed in the confines of her visor. The mounds, all twenty-eight of them, were torn apart. The loamy soil tossed about in scarred piles, the pits gaping wounds.

She left Brannon's body where it was and ran to the mounds. Each grave was emptied. Not one body remained. Tatters of the simple brown shrouds each of the pioneers had been wrapped in were stuck in the mud of the pits. In one, she glimpsed a palm-sized patch of fatty flesh. In another, a clump of jet black hair stuck to a scalp. Here, a scrap of purple fabric. There, a silver chain and bit of bone.

She and Brannon hadn't stepped foot here in three weeks, not since Simeon died. They were supposed to be alone here. They'd never been alone on Eostre. There'd been other creatures, larger and fiercer than the parrot-sized jabberwocks.

Panic threatened to take hold of Gita's mind. She tamed her breathing. She couldn't leave Brannon stranded in the mists. She pushed the bucking hovercraft toward the torn-up mounds. It lurched to a stop. She picked up a shovel and dug, her heart thudding, her ears on alert. The ground gave way easily. Flecks of tan soil spattered her visor. Do not think of your dead match, she told herself. Do not think of that strange squawking, she told herself. Do not think of these empty graves. Just dig. Get him in the ground as quick as you can.

It took half an hour for her to dig four feet. Another squawk pierced the air. Her skin turned to ice. She dropped her shovel and maneuvered the hovercraft closer to the pit. She tilted the hovercraft. His body fell into the pit with a thunk, face down, arms and legs a tangle. She climbed in and tussled with his body until it rested properly.

71

She could not look at his face. She shoveled the soil over him as best she could and tamped it down with her boots. A trio of jabberwocks tussled overhead, chittering their flimsy jaws in the mist. She jumped, then watched them scurry away.

When she powered up the hovercraft, she heard the cawing again. This time louder, closer. In the distance, a rise six feet high. Something moved on its edge. It looked similar to the jabberwocks. Leafy purple tendrils circled its core. Spongy brown roots wriggled in the wind. Jaws clamped at its top. But it was much larger, larger than even Brannon himself. Gita stumbled. She smacked her tailbone against the hovercraft. The creature leaped high and spiraled into the pink sky, flapping and contracting its tendrils as it gained altitude.

"What in the gods' names…" Gita whispered.

It paused, tilted its body toward her, and launched in her direction.

Gita pushed herself up. She abandoned the hovercraft, planted her feet on the sopping ground and raced toward the compound.

She nearly stumbled over a cluster of lolling jabberwocks, but she kept her footing and ran. A whoosh swept past her. Her hair slipped loose of its band. Long black hairs washed over her visor. A snapping filled her ears. Her heart pounded. Her legs burned. The complex was a quarter mile ahead. Her leaden boots slipped in the marshy ground, flattening the violet lichen. Closer and closer the complex came. Her arms flailed and she heard a woman screaming, only to realize it was her. Then her voice fell silent.

Her footing was sure now but she didn't dare turn around. Then came the slap against her thigh: an offense, a violation, like the ones she fled back in Cassini City. She gasped but continued ahead, tilting her face at the slightest of angles, enough to get a glimpse.

It was a creature, seven feet tall, with filamentous leaves that writhed, both reaching out to her and obscuring the jaws that snapped and cackled. She froze in fright and wonder, the complex achingly close. She gaped at the thing that hovered in the air above and muttered a prayer to the saints and martyrs, to Neil Armstrong and Mae Jemison, to Christa McAuliffe and Nigel Chu. She let their memories soothe her soul, and her answer came.

She did not sacrifice all she was just for this thing to destroy her. "Tell me what you are."

The creature unfurled a tendril, broad as her hand, heavy violet with mottled red veins. It wove closer to the strip of exposed skin near her ear. Gita thought of the sacrifices of all the martyrs, their bones broken to bring her to this place. She would not let them down. It touched her bare skin. It was slimy, and left coldness in its wake. She whimpered. It flinched and withdrew from her skin.

The tendrils that hid its core stirred. One by one they unfolded.

What waited inside? She pictured hungry jaws aching to devour. She caught sight of long strands of red curling hair—human hair—clinging to a tendril. The hair was Juliet's. She was the fifth to die.

What had this thing done to her friend's dead body?

Gita screamed. She battered the tendril that had touched her. The creature screeched. It tightened its core tendrils and whacked her, flinging her across the ground.

Gita's visor was crooked and muddied. She wiped it clean and streaked toward the shelter of the compound. The creature roared at her back. She was just feet from the outer hatch now. She raced up the steps and keyed in the code with trembling fingers. While the electronics registered the digits, she mumbled a looping *please, please, please.*

The outer door slid open. She threw herself in, but only made it partway when the tendril caught her ankle. It wrapped itself in a viselike grip. She screamed for help but there was no one left to save her. She kicked it hard. A warbling cry reverberated from outside the half-closed door. She kicked harder. The tendril's edge was razor sharp. It sliced through her haz-suit into her skin. She howled but kept kicking until the tendril unfurled itself and slithered out the door.

Crawling on hands and knees, Gita sealed the outer door. She stripped free of her gear, and sat naked and bleeding in the decontamination room, letting the tears and screams flow as the sun's pink rays gave way to night.

*

How long had she spent cowering on that floor in the decontamination room? A day? Three? Five?

Memories like tight little fists battered her skull: "Hey Jude" with its lingering chorus, the smell of smoldering bluerock, her father listless in its grip, outside the plexiglass a wolfdog cracking a bone. The growl and crunch, the smoke and haze, the drone of that ancient song.

It will never get better, no matter how far I fling myself across the universe.

She prayed to Galileo and Copernicus, to Ride and Glenn, to Wexler and Shah, but no answer stirred within. For Gita, there was no greater truth than this: she was still that helpless girl cowering in that Cassini City hovel. That was her place in the universe and it was etched in steel.

No, it wasn't.

"Get up, girl," she told herself, her voice echoing off the chamber walls. The bleeding had stopped and her throat ached for water. "Think of Brannon. What would he want you to do?"

She waited in the cool room for an answer, her mind quaking, her body shivering. She shuddered at the thought of the creature that had attacked her. Was it some mutant jabberwock? Were there more of them? She felt herself start to regress back to that scared girl sickened by "Hey Jude" and the crunch of the bone.

"Brannon would want me to salvage our mission," she said. "So first figure out why they all died. Then take care of those things."

The cool water burned her ankle as she washed the crusted blood away. She scanned the wound and found no evidence of toxins. She selected green pants and a matching shirt—they reminded her of vids of ancient Earth forests—and planted herself at her workstation.

Two days spent poring over computer simulations, analyses of particulates, tissue samples from the mosses and jabberwocks, but she could not pinpoint the source of the fibrous masses that had felled her fellow pioneers.

"Tell me this," she said to her control panel as if it would respond. "We examined the soil samples extensively. No toxins detected. We filter the air and water to a purity level of 99.999 percent. Yet still this thing. It got to us."

She propped her feet on the desk, chewed a protein bar, and washed it down with purified water. If Brannon were here, he would have rested his hand on her shoulder, a move so chaste, yet so intimate. The weight of his hand, not too gentle, not too harsh, always soothed her.

Now there was nothing left.

Despair burrowed into her soul. She swept her hand across the desk, knocking the water over, raining rivulets onto the floor.

"Damn," she hissed. She grabbed a cloth and mopped up the water, so clear but now peppered with grains of dust from the floor. Something in its ruined purity tugged at her. What was it? What was she overlooking? Her mind stuck there—the spoiled water, not quite as pure anymore, when she heard the thunk.

Gita clutched her ankle, the scar still tender. Long-ago smells of pungent bluerock and rancid vegetables bubbled up, but she didn't linger in their gloom. She tossed the sopping cloth aside and grabbed a rifle.

The lights of the complex dimmed and crackled. Gita raced through the warren of rooms and tubular tunnels toward the outer buildings. The thunk came again. She tried to place it but the thudding of her heart clashed with her sense of direction.

Thunk!

Thunk!

Thunk!

It came from Raquel and Juliet's sleeping quarters on the western ring. She tightened her grip on her rifle and hurried toward their shuttered room.

The air carried a lingering must, lost memories, dead dreams. She shuddered. The thunk came again, so loud she feared the metal roof would split at its rivets.

"What are you?" she screamed, but there was no response. She climbed on Raquel's bunk and rammed the stock of her rifle against the ceiling. Another thunk. She rammed it again and screamed. She rammed it again and again, screaming and sweating, until her arms grew tired and the thunking died away.

She waited on Raquel's bed. Minutes ticked past. She eased herself off the creaking bed and set a boot on the floor. She tiptoed to the window and pulled apart the curtains.

Gita let out a feeble gasp.

Just outside the plexiglass were not one but two monstrosities. They perched on the loamy soil, their purple tendrils shimmering and waving in the sun's pink rays. One of the creatures gyrated its lithe tendrils, unfolding itself until its core was nearly visible. Gita caught glimpses familiar, yet strange—black strands of hair, something that looked like a crooked finger. Another layer unfurled to reveal chittering mandibles surrounded by chunks of human skin like some half-digested meal.

Gita vomited the protein bar on the floor. She fell to her knees, the smell and memory calling up more and more until there was nothing left inside her.

Then she spied her rifle. None of the pioneers deserved this desecration, not after all they'd sacrificed.

She didn't bother with her haz-suit. She strapped on her face mask and punched in the code. The door creaked open. She trudged across the spongy soil under the noontime rays of the sun, her rifle at the ready.

She rounded the complex. Her feet caught firm ground. Her arms did not tremble. She did not blink. When she reached the place where she'd spied the two creatures, she froze. Nothing was there. For a moment she feared she'd imagined it. Then the air above her stirred. She craned her face toward the sun's glow and saw them. They seemed tiny at first—just another pair of lolling jabberwocks. But as they descended, they grew larger, their tendrils flimsy in the gusting air, the roots nearly limblike.

They careened toward her. She raised her rifle and squeezed the trigger. The bullet cracked the air. It pierced the upper tendrils of the leftward creature, which burbled a high-pitched scream.

The second creature turned its bulk toward her. It slithered and snapped toward her, trembling in its wrath.

Gita fired again. She hit one of its limblike roots. A low moan chortled from its buried center and it halted its descent. Both wounded creatures hovered above Gita, and she was unsure whether she could survive their joint attack. She hoisted her rifle in the air and was about to fire once more when they clacked their jaws and gyrated away from her.

She lowered her rifle as they vanished into the pink sky. A pulsing fear caused her heart to stutter. If there were two, there were likely hundreds, thousands. And she was just one.

She ran back in to the decontamination room and let the purifying air swoosh over her, tasting the tang on her tongue. She rolled it along the inside of her cheek, a spot check for any fibroids, but there was nothing. Somehow she alone remained untouched. And alone.

How long had it been now since Brannon left her alone? A full week? Eight days? She carried the rifle by her side, waiting for the monstrosities to return. She napped at her workstation, endless scans and analyses turning up nothing. She often woke with a start, certain she'd heard Brannon's voice, but there was nothing but the white noise of the complex. She programmed music, and an ode to one of Earth's oceans came on, a woman mourning her swallowed-up lover. How she cried for him, longing for a return that never came. How she damned the water. A tear welled in the corner of Gita's eye. She rubbed it away, then stuck her finger in her mouth, tasting its saltiness.

Water.

She picked up a bottle and took a swig. Pure as ice. Pure as life. Pure.

But it wasn't.

99.999 percent was still impure. Harmless trace elements, magnitudes lower than anything sold on Titan or Mars or Europa or Mercury. But still not pure.

She emptied the bottle, hitched her boots on, and ran outside. A quick check of the air: all clear, no monsters. It was night, the brown orb of Camalus giving off a hazy sheen that kept the darkness at bay. She ran to the aquifer well, the source of their water. She disconnected the spigot and collected a bottle full of untreated water, then she ran back inside.

The computer spat out results: lists of compounds and elements, metals and toxins, bits of degraded genetic material. All known to Gita. All tracked. All filtered away. She ran the sample through the filter at the current settings and analyzed the refuse. Nothing unusual. Then she tightened the screen and analyzed what it had filtered. The computer magnified the infinitesimal speck until it filled the screen.

"Oh the gods," Gita whispered.

There was only one. It wriggled and twitched. It was one of the yellow fibroids that felled her entire group. All this time they had been swallowing their own deaths.

Gita slumped back on her chair. Finally, she had the answer, though it was too late for her fellow pioneers, and maybe even too late for herself. She did not want to admit the truth that had lain before her for weeks now—their mission was a failure. All that was left to do was transmit the message that this moon was unsuitable for human habitation.

She was about to transcribe her findings when a thumping came from outside the complex.

"No," she pleaded. "No more. I can't take it."

But she had to. She grabbed her rifle and followed the sound. She trudged through the connecting tubes, the thumping calling her closer. She carried no rage or fear, only a defeated resignation. She would aim at the snapping jaws that topped its cone. She would decapitate it.

A solitary creature perched outside the entrance to the decontamination room. Gita slipped on her mask and opened the door. She stopped five feet from the creature. Its roots were anchored into the ground. She raised her rifle as the tendrils unfurled.

"Which one of my friends did you eat, you monster?"

The tendrils loosened one by one. Gita waited for it to reveal its center. She caught sight of things that made her flinch: patches of white skin stuck to purple tendrils, clumps of dark hair, what looked like a nipple, a rounded shoulder. But it was all disjointed, out of context. Then the jaws at the top ratcheted open with a creaking like snapping bone, like those wolfdogs back in Cassini City, crunching away while her father abandoned her for bluerock.

Take a sad song and make it better.

The lie of all lies.

Gita steeled herself. Her finger was on the trigger. Pressure increased. One more moment and she would kill this abomination.

The jaws gaped open. Inside was not a lashing tongue or rows of spiked teeth. Inside was a gelatinous membrane that throbbed and pulsed, ropy and brain-like. And in the center were a pair of eyes, human eyes. They blinked at her. Green. Clear. They were Brannon's.

"Oh the gods!"

Gita dropped her rifle. A tendril reached out and stroked her cheek. The eyes blinked, and she thought she saw them glimmer.

Another tendril wrapped around her and pulled her close. She felt its weight on her shoulder and was soothed despite the torrent of tears. She stayed in the creature's embrace—her Brannon, her resurrected match—until the sun slipped from the apex of the sky. When she pulled herself free, her mind was clear, her heart unburdened

She'd given her life to the pioneer program. She considered it a small ransom to escape the never-ending gloom of Cassini City. As she watched her fellow pioneers die, she feared her sacrifice had been in vain. She was wrong. Her old life would die away. Bluerock and wolfdogs and "Hey Jude" would fall away. She would be reborn as a child of this moon Eostre.

Gita let a tendril caress her skin and she returned to the complex.

First she deprogrammed the decontamination sequence. Next she scaled back the water purification protocol to just 99 percent and gulped the water down. She could almost feel the fibroids wriggling in her mouth and throat.

Before she lay in her bed and dreamed of the rebirth that awaited, she sent a message to Titan: The pioneers have succeeded. Send the colonists.

***

# Last Sub to Tel-K

by Joachim Heijndermans

**NETHERLANDS: *Futuristic tale of prisoners, personalities, and perfidy***

"Oy, w'en we gettin' any grub in 'ere, yeh fookin' bastards?" McKinney, the occupant of cell number one, shouted from his peephole.

"It's only been four days. Ain't nobody eating till we get to Tel-K, you dumb shit," Simmons laughed. "Now sit down, before I break your knees."

"Try it, darlin'. See houw't works oot fer yeh. Yeh fookin' twat!" McKinney followed that up with a complete library of expletives, but none of it changed the fact he was on the express line to the darkest hole that they could chuck a crook like him in. And no need to throw away the key, as escaping meant walking headfirst into a billion cubic gallons of cold saltwater.

"Oy, Simmons!" the garbled voice of Johns said over the comm. "Get Timmy and sweep for one final round. Don't want no contraband found on 'em while the cargo is still on the ship."

"Copy that," Simmons replied. He quickly hurried up the ladder that led to the crew barracks, banging on Timmy's quarters. "Yo, Tim-may! Get your ass up."

Timmy, the cabin boy and junior correctional enforcer, flung the door open while he hopped on one leg as he struggled to pull up his pants. "What? What is it?"

"Anchor in an hour. Gotta do one more sweep."

"Aw, man," Timmy grunted.

*

Simmons leaned closer to Timmy's face, brushing his hand against his cheek. "Hey, if we hurry, we can have a little fun before we dock. How about that?"

"You never stop, do you?" Timmy said. He pressed his hand against Simmon's crotch and lightly pinched his erection underneath the fabric of his suit.

"Hey, ain't often I got me a cabin boy as sweet as you. Now get moving!"

Timmy managed to get dressed under a minute, and the two made their way back to the holding cell level. Gilliam, the second duty enforcer, welcomed them. "Last round, chief?"

"You got it."

"You gonna be nice, chief?" Gilliam asked.

"Aren't I always?" Simmons said with a wink and a grin.

"No offense, but I do wanna be paid when we dock. Let's not have another incident like we had with Parchs, 'kay?"

Simmons grunted. Gilliam never cut him any slack over that one. The only way to ever get on that guy's bad side was to hurt his wallet. Like it was his fault they work on commission, or that Parchs came at him with the shiv, which mysteriously vanished after Simmons blew him away. "I'll be good," Simmons said.

"Yeah. Funny how we never found that shiv, eh?" Gilliam grunted.

"Yeah. Funny, isn't it?"

Simmons and Timmy proceeded with their rounds. With eight cells and only five remaining occupied to check, it should have been a quick inspection. But these prisoners were the worst of the worst. A cargo that included murderers, cyber-terrorists, and psychopaths that only a state-of-the-art place like Tel-K could hold. Vigilance was key with this group, even if they were the only deep-sea transport team that was permitted live ammo, despite the danger of a possible hull rupture.

"Simmons. Yo, Simmons. I'm hurting, man. Real bad, man," mumbled Tanner, the skit-addict and serial arsonist in cell number three. "Can't you hook me up, man? The pressure is killing me, man! It's in my head!"

"Pfft," Simmons blew air past his lips. "Pressure ain't killing you. This puppy can go twice as deep as this, and your ears still wouldn't pop. You're just a skit-head, Tanner. Once we dock, the medical ward will give you what you need ... three weeks in a nice iso-cell."

"C'mon, man. I'm hurting real bad. Help me out, man." Tanner made the mistake of reaching his fingers out through the peephole, which Simmons took that as an invitation to give them a good whack with his nightstick. Poor Tanner couldn't decide what was worse, his broken fingers or the added million-voltage shock.

"That will teach you to bug me, skit-head. Now sit your ass down. I better not hear you 'till we reach Tel-K, you hear me?"

"My hand! You broke my hand!"

"You secure that shit, Tanner," Timmy said, playing the "nice" guard. "Simmons don't want to hear you, and we both know I can't stop him when he's in a mood."

The two moved on to the opposite row. There was McKinney in cell number one, who still hadn't stopped his tirade against Simmons in all that time. They ignored him as they walked on to cell number two, which was occupied by Elric. He seemed the most normal; quiet, polite, and wickedly cultured. You would hardly guess this man was the mastermind behind the assassination of President Gwu'dabe of the Democratic Republic of New Tanzania, which plunged the country into its third civil war. When he spoke, he'd seem like a pleasant fellow, just as long as no one got him started on "the blacks."

"You've been quiet. Looking forward to your new home?" Simmons asked.

"As much as I can. I'd kill for a good book," Elric sighed.

"I bet you would," Simmons chuckled, who found Elric amusing on the best of days. However, he knew Timmy did not share his like for the prisoner, since the kid's sister lost her husband from New Tanzania in the massacres that followed the president's assassination. They walked on, as he was afraid of what Timmy might do if Elric got under his skin again.

The two guards marched past cell number four, now empty and wiped clean of any evidence that Parchs ever occupied it. It was an eerily quiet place since the sounds of Parchs drumming against the cell door and the walls with his the spoons he somehow managed to swipe had ceased with one deafening blow from Simmons's weapon. On the record, Parchs made a desperate move for his rifle in a fumbled escape attempt. He was in in rights to do what he had to. But trying to convince the rest of the crew of that had been a task and a half, especially since they all knew how much Simmons hated Parchs. Maybe if their commission hadn't depended on it, no-one would have cared about a dead convict. But no, the crew would never let him off the hook for that one. Simmons averted his eyes from the cell. He'd seen enough of that cell and resented the fact that even after he plastered Parchs's brains all over the wall, the man was still causing him grief to no end.

Next was Niccols in cell number four, a piece-of-shit pederast, terrorist, and arms dealer, sentenced for tax fraud of all things.

Another one of those prisoners who Simmons ached for to give him an excuse to enact some disciplinary action. No dice, as he kept to himself at all times.

"You happy in there, tax man?" Simmons asked.

"Fuck off, Simmons. Go bother the alien, why dontcha?"

Normally, Simmons would have lost his cool from any such remark. But what Niccols said stuck with him. "You know what? I just might," he chuckled. "Hey, Timmy, wanna go check out the greener?"

Timmy shrugged. "Sure," he said. Like a kid on Christmas, Simmons bolted to the very end of the cell block, cell number eight, which held the last piece of cargo. The VIP cell. And boy, did they have themselves a bona fide celebrity. Simmons knocked against the door, which caused the harsh metallic sound to echo through the hull of the sub.

"Hey, green eyes. Looking forward to being the first Cutharn in Tel-K? Them boys are gonna love your alien ass down there. Probably ain't never fucked themselves a 'skinny,' I reckon. Well? You feel honored yet, greener?" Simmons asked, enjoying himself immensely.

Tsuthan gave no reply. Between his fingers he fiddled with his strip of licorice root that danced elegantly from hand to hand. His silver skin reflected the dim light that Simmons shone on him. The black swirled tattoos on his left pectoral muscle were the only part of him that didn't shine in the darkness. The blue veins that were just visible under that silvery skin pulsated as he breathed deep, throaty breaths.

Those green-eyed freaks weirded Simmons out enough already, but this one was beyond scary. He wasn't like the others of his hippie tree-lover kind that yammer on about peace and the environment. This thing killed people; both humans and his own kind. And he didn't stop there. Women, kids, dogs, you name it. This was a mean, scary son-of-a-bitch. The only place capable of keeping him behind lock and key was the Telkhines facility, the most remote deep-sea prison facility on the planet.

"Not talking, green eyes?" Simmons chuckled. Again, no answer. The creature hadn't spoken since his trial. He just sat there for long stretches, lost in deep thought or meditation, while he gnawed on his stick. This silent treatment irritated Simmons, which only fueled his incentive to have some fun with the alien. "That's a nice twig you got there. My guess is you didn't get that with your regulated meal pack before we left shore, did you? So I'm thinking that we got ourselves some contraband," he said with a sadistic smirk. "Say, Timmy, does that look like contraband to you?"

"Could be a drug, sir. Or be made into a weapon."

"Right. I didn't even consider of that. Good thinking there, Timmy," Simmons chuckled. "You gonna be a good little freak and hand it over, or are we gonna have to taze your ass till you piss green?"

Tsuthan continued to twirl his licorice root, stopping only to chew on it.

These freaks and their weird oral obsession, Simmons thought. Were those greeners ever not munching on something? Sticks, candies, beef jerky. Every time I see one of those silver-skinned freaks, they have something between their teeth. On land, he was forced to quietly accept the visitors and their ways. But aboard The Charon, he could get his frustrations out. Oh, he'd ached to get his hands on a greener for years.

He raised his pulse rifle and flipped the switch to taze-mode. "Last chance, silver skin. Put down the stick or take 0.2 amps to the balls. You've got 'till the count of three. One. T—"

The alien threw his root at the door. With an almost bored expression, he stood up and turned around, placing his three-fingered hands on the back of his head.

Simmons flung the cell door open. "Go get it," he said to Timmy.

"Why me?" he asked.

"Because I said so, you pansy. You ain't afraid of a greener, are ya?"

Timmy grunted an exasperated sigh but did as he was told. He entered the cell and reached down for the chewed-up root.

"Timmy ... don't fuckin' move," Simmons whispered.

When the cabin boy looked up, he met the eye of the silver alien. Prisoner number eight, Tsuthan, while still in the same position as before, looked at the young guard who took away his licorice root from the corner of his eye. The kid froze in place, as he'd seen the footage of Tsuthan's victims. He knew what the alien was capable of. And he felt like he could soil himself.

"Eyes to the wall, greener. Now!" Simmons growled.

Tsuthan did not comply. He kept his eyes locked on the young cabin boy. Seventeen years old. Prime of his youth. Easy target. Timmy felt like the mouse who wandered in the cat's domain.

Simmons flipped the switch on his rifle, causing a "click" sound everyone aboard the sub was all too familiar with. Live rounds were loaded into the rifle's chamber. "Last chance, freakshow. Eyes front!" Simmons roared.

The Cutharn prisoner relented and looked away. Timmy never ran as quickly out of a cell in his life. Simmons slammed his fist on the control pad. The reinforced door flung shut, locking the cargo of cell number eight back in.

"You all right?" Simmons asked, while he stroked his hand against Timmy's neck.

"Yeah, I'm fine," he muttered.

Simmons took the licorice root from the cabin boy's hand and peered back into the peephole. Tsuthan was back in the same position as earlier, albeit annoyed at the loss of his root.

"You trying to scare Timmy?" Simmons snapped. "Well, your twig? Hope you enjoyed it, 'cause it was your last," he laughed, as he slowly slid the root into his breast pocket to make sure that the alien got a good last look at it. Tsuthan responded by rapidly clicking his jagged teeth together, but this did not impress Simmons in the slightest. This greener would need to bring a whole lot more to the table to scare him. "Shithead," he muttered to the alien.

"Crew on the main deck. Crew on the main deck!" cried a voice over the comms.

Simmons checked the time, as did Gilliam, giving each other puzzled shrugs. "Weird. We're still forty minutes from Tel-K," Simmons said. There was no way the captain engaged docking procedures already.

The sub suddenly jerked to the side, slamming the three of them into the wall. Gilliam's legs were in the air, while Simmons groaned out as his back hit the hard metal of the hull. Tanner wailed from his cell in pain, while McKinney unleashed another barrage of colorful expletives.

"What's going on?" asked Gilliam, who tried to get on his feet. Seconds after he was on his feet, the entire ship was violently thrust into the opposite direction.

"We got hit!" cried Simmons. "Get up to the main deck! Lock yourself in."

"And the prisoners? Aren't we strapping them in?"

Simmons chuckled. "Fuck 'em."

They rushed up to the second level of *The Charon*. Brands, a petty officer, fell down the ladder to level two when the ship was rocked over again. The rest of the crew went back and forth. Timmy felt something salty hit his eye. Seawater!

"Are we sinking?" Timmy gasped.

"Get up to the deck!" Simmons roared, while he pulled the cabin boy by the collar. They climbed up the ladder as quickly as they could, entering the command bridge. Men screamed back and forth. On the screens flashed the words "warning" and "hull breach," while the live feed from the ship's exterior showed red cracks on the seafloor spewing boiling water at them.

"Cap, what the hell is going—?"

"Volcanic activity. We're being bombarded with blasts of boiling water. We took a hit on the port side! Hull breach!"

"Shit!" Simmons snapped. He threw Timmy against a seat. While they flailed around in their attempt to strap themselves in, Gilliam was flung against the ceiling. The sound of his arm snapping into pieces was devastating.

"Cap'n, we can't stabilize her. The buoyancy regulator is busted," cried a crew member.

"Damn. LeFrange, get us out of here!"

"Première et deuxième moteurs sont à défaut!" cried the helmsman.

"Can we make it to anchor point?"

"Captain, we're too far off. Forty kilometers!" shouted the Desmond, the secondary navigator.

"Merde!" LeFrange snapped. "Se préparer à colision! Huit! Sept! Six! Cin—!"

"What's he—?" Timmy shrieked.

"Impact!" roared the captain.

The ship collided with the ocean floor, while the crew tumbled around like ants in a centrifuge. Lights flickered, sparks flew, water danced. Then, shouts in the dark. Screams. Metal moaned, followed by a crack. Then it came. The sound of flooding water.

*

When the sub left Liberty Bay, the crew was about twenty men large, not counting the prisoners. The eight crew members who survived the breach had gathered in the cargo hull. Johns, the head of the cargo-enforcer unit, was gone. So was LeFrange, the helmsman. There were other casualties who Simmons didn't know. Timmy knew one of them, a guy named Calgary, very intimately, and quietly mourned him from his corner of the hull.

Large parts of *The Charon* were flooded, and the bridge was out of commission. The one place that was meant to keep the prisoners in, was what kept the water, for the most part, out. Elric remarked how ironic it would have been had the prisoners been the only survivors, which resulted in a smack to the head from Simmons.

The water finally stopped its rise forty minutes after impact. The ship's hull also ceased to creak any further. For the moment, they were safe. With the cells becoming flooded out, the prisoners had been rounded up and were now chained to a pipe.

"Simmons! What's happening? Simmons!" yelled Tanner.

"Crew meeting. Cargo is to shut up and remain calm. One word and I'll drop each and every one of you into the lower decks."

"What's on the lower decks?" Tanner asked.

"It's flooded, you imbecile," Elric sighed.

The captain, returning from his final inspection, entered the cargo hall. His thin, wet hair stuck to his scalp, which he tried to brush aside. "What's our status?" Simmons asked.

"Well, we managed to seal the hull breach. But the internal stabilizer is flooded with water and could crap out at any moment. I don't know how much longer the ship can withstand the pressure."

"Wut happen's wit' th' pressah? Th' fook ye talkin' ye twat,"

"You're such a fucking idiot, McKinney," Simmons snapped.

"Fook yoo, yeh daft buggah! Fookin' bummah!"

"Shut up! Both of you!" the captain snapped.

Elric sighing, leaned over and fished an empty can of Zloom soda that floated by out the water with his one free hand. "It's simple. This vessel has been built to resist the water pressures of this depth, keeping us happy and alive. But since that system is slowly failing...," he said, as he crushed the can. "Think of the ship being the can, the ocean being my hand, and us the idiots who decided to get into said can."

"Yeah, barring those of us who didn't have much of a choice on whether they wanted to be here," Niccols chuckled.

"Shut your fuckin' mouth, Niccols," Simmons snapped. "Or I'm gonna come over and shut it for you."

"All this talk about being crushed won't mean much if the water rises to our heads," muttered Gilliam.

"So, we will either be crushed, drown, or suffocate," Elric concluded.

"Which brings us to our next problem," said the captain. "The life-support generator is down, and the reserve tanks have been ruptured. We're leaking oxygen. We could fix the hole, but it could take about two hours. By then we wouldn't have enough left to even make it to Tel-K, so that's a waste of time."

Timmy stuttered, his voice quivering in panic. "Can't we wait for a rescue party? You know, put a beacon out with the nav-comm?"

The entire crew went dead silent. They stared at Timmy for a few seconds, before most of them let out dark laughs. The captain was the only one not amused, and stepped toward the cabin boy.

"What is the name of this ship?" he asked.

"The Charlie?"

"We're aboard *The Charon*. This is a deep sea correctional-transport ship, level five. And who am I?"

"The captain, sir. Captain and chief navigator."

"And why am I the chief navigator?"

"'Cause—"

"Because there is no nav-comm, shit-for-brains. We bring a GPS on board, we can get hacked and located, and then we're ambushed by the cargo's buddies. No nav-comm, no set route, no one who knows where we are or when we arrive at Tel-K."

"Seems like a serious design flaw, considering the circumstances," said Elric.

The calm tone sent Simmons over the edge, raising his rifle at the line of prisoners. "The next one who talks dies. I am not fucking around!"

"Hell no to that," Gilliam grunted. "We are not gonna jeopardize our commission because you have another hissy fit, Simmons!"

"Commission?" said a shocked Brands. "Who gives a shit about the commission? We're gonna die down here! We're all gonna—!"

"Shut up! The last thing we need is a panic," snapped the captain.

"What else can we do? We're stuck! And no one is coming—"

"We are nearly thirty kilometers away from Tel-K. We'll walk it," said the captain.

Silence fell over them. Even Tsuthan stopped clicking his teeth.

"Is ... is that ... can we do that?" Timmy asked.

"We have pressure suits. They're heavy, and the air tank on each is limited without a refuel, but we could make the walk. Better than to sit here waiting to die."

"Is it safe? I mean, we don't know what's out there?" asked Niccols. He was ignored by the rest, who muttered amongst each other with some renewed hope.

"Walk the seafloor? I've done it, but not that far."

"The suits work. I've never done more than light repairs, but walking should be okay."

"Can we actually make it from here?"

"It'll be tight, but if we keep a steady pace, we should be able to reach the docking bay of Tel-K before we run out of air," said the captain.

Gilliam stood up, grabbing the keys to the cargo's cuffs. "In any case, I ain't going nowhere without the cargo."

"Well, if we are taking the prisoners, then we have another problem," said the captain. "There are thirteen of us in total. The crash busted some of the suits as well, so we're one short. One of us can't come."

"Fuckin' hell," muttered one of the crewmen.

"Wait, the alien! He's a Cutharn, ain't he?" said Lucas, an engineer. "Can't he change his body? Morph so he can survive out there?"

Gilliam sighed. "Not all greeners can morph. Only one in ten is an adaptoid. There's no mention on his file about that."

"Great, so you're even more useless than we thought," grunted Simmons at the silver-skinned alien, who simply squinted in return.

"So, we're gonna let one good man die, so a bunch of inmates can live? Pardon my insubordination, but that is fucked up beyond all hell!" snapped Brands.

"Do you know how much we're getting for each one? Do you know how much we lost out on when Simmons decided to turn Parchs into Swiss cheese?" Gilliam shouted back. "I'm not losing out on my wages. So, fuck your 'good man' and fuck you!"

"Fuck you!" Brands roared back, throwing a tin at Gilliam's head. Both men leaped at each other's throat. The crew tried to pry them apart, while McKinney began to whoop and shout along, relishing the action. "Fook 'im oop, Gilley," McKinney shouted. "Fook 'im oop!"

"That's enough!" roared Simmons, pumping a round into his rifle's chamber. "Calm down, or I will put you down!" The survivors did as told, lest they found themselves on the other end of the barrel. McKinney continued to chuckle darkly. "Cap'n, how do we proceed from here?" Simmons asked.

The captain stroked his fingers through his thick, red beard, then sighed. "Look, Simmons, all I care about is the crew. With Johns gone, you're now the highest-ranking cargo-enforcer on this ship. Your word is final on board *The Charon*. I couldn't care less about the commission, but it's not my call to make."

Simmons looked at the crew, who stared back at him, each with a different expression. Fear, anger, greed, all emotions boiling to a fever pitch. He then turned to the prisoners. All scum. Not a soul on Earth would blame him if he left them to rot. Wasn't it him who said, "fuck 'em" right before the crash? But that number, the one that would be deposited on his account stuck with him, whispering in his ear like a siren. The big payday that was only guaranteed if he brought the cargo to Tel-K alive. He already lost a sixth of that when he shot Parchs. Was he prepared to lose it all?

"We'll need weapons that fire underwater. My gun won't work, and we'll need to keep the cargo at bay."

"Oh, you fu—" Brands protested.

"The prisoners come with. So does the captain. The rest of us draw straws. The loser stays!"

"You can't fucking do this!" a crewman shouted.

"We can, and we will. Timmy, help me with the cargo. The rest, find something to draw with."

There were protests, but Simmons didn't pay them any mind. He stared at the cargo, all lined up and their wrists tied to the bar. Elric and McKinney seemed bemused by the whole thing. Tanner was off somewhere in that skit-fried brain of his. Niccols seemed more anxious about the walk than any of his fellow prisoners. And Tsuthan? He simply stared, clicking his teeth in a slow but steady rhythm.

*

The first team, made up of Simmons, Timmy, the captain, McKinney, Tanner, and Tsuthan, geared up for their walk. The second team would follow once the first left the hatch and let it re-pressurize. Simmons and Timmy kept their new harpoon rifles aimed at the three prisoners, who strapped themselves into their suits. Tsuthan was the last, clearly uncomfortable with being made to wear this thing, which delighted Simmons. One thing that struck him was the alien's tattoo. *Wasn't it much higher on his chest? Did it always curve to the right?* It had to be stress playing tricks on his mind, so he shrugged it off.

"Everyone ready?" the captain asked, as he tightened the last straps on his suit.

They all nodded, except McKinney, who replied, "Fookin' hell oim reddy!" The captain sealed his helmet, then released the pressure switch on the wall. Water seeped into the exit bay. For a moment, Simmons wasn't sure about the pressure suits. He'd never needed to use them, let alone deliver cargo to Tel-K on foot in one. His fears were put to rest by the time the water passed his face. He was dry, and his head didn't implode. It was safe.

If only he could feel the same around the cargo, with McKinney and Tsuthan each tied to him by a polymer rope, with Tanner attached to Timmy in the same way. Simmons kept his harpoon gun aimed at the alien, whom he trusted the least of the group, despite McKinney's kill-rep in the thirties. He would've felt more secure if he had more than one shot before reload time, with only three extra harpoons to do so.

The bay filled up. Go time. "Okay, move it. Keep straight, follow the cap'n, and don't change course unless I tell you, all right?"

Neither of them said a word. McKinney shrugged, but the alien looked him in the eye. That cold look of unfiltered hatred. Simmons motioned with his rifle for them to move, which the alien complied to.

The group leaped from the hatch down toward the seafloor. Timmy and Simmons peered back to see the full extent of the damage to *The Charon*'s hull. It was a miracle the freezing waters didn't cause the vessel to explode when the engine room was flooded. Granted, neither of them knew much about the machinations of the vessel, nor did they particularly invest much of their thought on engineering at all. To them, this was a job. One that paid well and came with some perks. For Timmy, it was no-strings-attached sex. For Simmons, it was

89

a place to vent his aggression out on scumbags who deserve no less. How the submarine worked did not concern them, as long as it got them from point A to point B.

The team sunk to the ocean floor, gently dropping down twenty meters. The terrain was rough and jagged, covered in dead coral and slippery sand. Behind them, dim red flashes of light came from the earth. They remained on high alert. Although the volcanic activity died down, there were still fissures that spewed superheated water. One hit and their suits would melt in an instant, with no time to blink or scream.

To move at this depth was difficult. Timmy felt like he'd been running for miles, but they barely put any distance between them and *The Charon*. The bulky shape of the suits didn't help, as they more or less shuffled their feet as opposed to making actual steps. The first team managed to walk about two kilometers when the second team followed suit out of the depressurized hatch.

The captain kept track on how far they were from Tel-K. He left his comm live, hoping he could contact the facility beforehand and get them to send a pick-up, but the distance was still too great. Nothing but static. So they walked on.

"Keep the pace up, gentlemen. We've got another hour and a half to go," Simmons growled.

"Timmy. Timmy!" Tanner tried to whisper over the comm.

"Why are you whispering, fuck-nut? We can all hear you," Simmons sighed.

"Timmy. I don't feel good, man."

The cabin boy sighed. "As soon as we reach Tel-K, the medic will fix your hand."

"It's not my hand, it's the heat. Too damn hot. So hot, man!"

"What is he blabbing about? It ain't hot," grunted Gilliam over the comm, having overheard them from the second group.

"Fuckin' skit-head," Simmons grunted. He noticed that McKinney was losing pace, so he nudged him with the harpoon gun. "Keep a move on!"

"T'is be easyur if we 'ad some fookin' food 'fore we wen' out."

"Quit your whining. We're not gonna fall behind on account of your lazy ass."

"Can we go faster?" muttered Niccols. "I don't like this shit. I don't like it. There could be animals out here. Killer eels. Anglerfish. Sharks."

"There are no fish down here. We're too close to those fissures for them to survive.," Elric tried to assure him. "Trust me, there's nothing out here."

"I don't like it, man. This is fucked up. I don't like it."

"Who gives a shit what you like, Niccols. Keep a move on, or we'll leave your ass," snapped Gilliam.

"No, you won't," laughed Elric. "If you were really prepared to abandon any of us, you wouldn't have left poor Brands behind like you did."

"Shut up!" Gilliam growled.

"Keep it down back there," the captain grumbled.

"It's true," Elric went on. "Your greed forbids you from letting anything happen to us 'cargo,' doesn't it? You would rather let a man die horribly than part with your beloved commission. Typical."

"What's typical?" Gilliam asked.

"Typical nigger attitude."

Dead quiet, followed by Gilliam growling "You motherfu—!"

"Gilliam!" snapped Simmons. "Don't let him rile you up. What are you gonna do? Wrestle at the bottom of the sea? Use up your air? Think, man."

Gilliam stopped. "Fuck. You're right. I'm okay."

"Again, typical," Elric laughed.

"Shut your mouth, Elric," Simmons snapped.

"Oh, but I—," he began, before his comm feed went quiet.

"Thank you, whoever just cut his comm!" Simmons gasped.

"What?" the captain asked. "We can't cut the feed. We need open mics at all times."

"Then what—?"

"Jesus fucking Christ!" someone screamed.

Shouts from the second group cluttered the comm feed. A garbled cacophony of screams, swears, and static snaps filled the first group's ears, before it turned to a dead silence.

"Gilliam? Elric?" Timmy muttered.

"Desmond?" the captain called. "Desmond! Do you copy!"

"What the fuck man! What the fuck," Tanner stammered.

The six men closed in together. In the inky blackness of the deep, the only light came from their suits. The last of the lights behind them died. Group Two had just vanished in an instant.

"What's going on? Where'd they go?" Timmy shouted.

"Stay calm! Keep moving!" the captain barked. "Whatever you do, keep—"

He didn't finish. Simmons turned around just in time to see a reddish tentacle latch on to the captain and pull him away. A scream, followed by static, then silence.

"Wut the fook was that!" McKinney snapped.

"Oh fuck! Fuck! Nooooo!" Tanner screamed and broke away from the group, dragging Timmy with him.

91

"Fuck! Tanner, stop!" the cabin boy snapped.

"Tanner, get back—!" Simmons roared. But in the instant that Tanner had separated himself from the group, a red mass blew past them. Tanner had vanished, with the rope that tied him to Timmy torn to shreds.

"Simmons, what do we do?" Timmy whimpered.

"We stay calm, and keep moving. Head to Tel-K."

"Wut way, ye daft twat? Cap'n was the navigator. We don' 'ave a fookin' cloo wer to go!"

"Stay calm, dammit!"

"Simmons ... I'm scared," Timmy's voice trembled.

"It's all right Timmy. Don't panic. Just stay calm."

"Fookin' poofs!" McKinney scoffed.

"Shut it," Simmons snapped. "We gotta keep moving, Timmy. We need to stick together. Tel-K is close. We're almost there. You gotta stay calm. Talk to me. Tell me a story. Like, what was it you were gonna do next shore leave?"

"Simmons, I can't—"

"C'mon, Timmy. What was it? Weren't you gonna go somewhere?"

"I ... I was going to Barcelona. I've never been. I saved up enough days for two months there."

"There you go. Think of Barcelona. What did you plan on doing out there?"

"I dunno ... guh go and get drunk?"

"Good. Keep talking, and don't panic. The rest of you, keep—!"

Like a whip, another tentacle snapped out from the darkness and grabbed Timmy by the arm. No one could hear it break, but the way it twisted back left little to the imagination. Within seconds, it began pulling Timmy towards the inky darkness.

"Timmy!" Simmons roared.

The cabin boy screamed as the tentacle dragged him off. Through immense luck, he latched onto a rock. Tears streamed down his face, as he looked at Simmons. "Simmons! Help me!" Timmy screamed, as he desperately tried to hold his grip on the slippery, algae-covered rock. He wedged his unbroken arm in between two rocks for support, but he screamed in pain with every tug the beast made.

"Hold on, kid! Hold on! I'm coming!" Simmons yelled, as he shuffled as fast as he could toward his friend. Then, with a jolt of immense strength, Simmons flew back, his harpoon gun dropped in the seafloor sand. Tsuthan was pulled down as well, as the third man tied to them was being dragged over the ocean floor by a large, red tentacle.

"It got me! Fookin' bassard got me!" McKinney screamed.

"Fuck!" Simmons grunted as his body was dragged through the sand. By some miracle, he managed to grasp onto a stone protruding from the ocean floor. But every second he held onto it, he felt his arm being pulled out from its socket.

Simmons was locked between two choices. On one end, Timmy was clinging on for his dear life. On the other, McKinney was being pulled up, dragging the two others with him. Tsuthan managed to grasp onto a jagged rock, but it was only a matter of time before his grip would fail him.

"Simmons! Help me!" Timmy screamed.

The creature's strength was unbelievable. No matter how strongly Simmons and Tsuthan tried to hold their ground, the creature was pulling them along with McKinney, who wailed in fear. Tsuthan's rock began to be uprooted from the ground. Opposite from them, Timmy still screamed in pain, pleading for help. Simmons grabbed a spare harpoon from his pack. He knew he was only going to be able to save one of them at this rate, and he knew which choice would save his own skin as well.

"Sorry, McKinney. Really," he muttered, before grazing the sharp point against McKinney's length of rope.

"No! Don' yeh fooki—!" he screamed, when the rope snapped. In an instant, McKinney vanished. Over the comm, Simmons heard the man curse his name and scream before he too was silenced by a static snap. Simmons didn't take the time to look back, running towards where he saw Timmy last.

"Timmy! I'm coming! Timmy! Respond!" Nothing. No response. But there wasn't any static on his feed. Simmons even heard a light noise on the other end. Where was he?

It was then that Simmons saw eight, maybe ten tentacles, attached to a tumorous body with more eyes than anything could possibly ever need, and a large parrot-like beak clasping onto Timmy's back. A mockery of what aquatic life had once been, now mutated to having taken the form of an unspeakable horror, latched onto seventeen-year-old Timmy O'Toole as it eviscerated him.

Simmons bolted toward the cabin boy as quickly as he could, which at his pace felt like an eternity. Timmy held out his hand, tears rolling down his face. He mouthed words, but his voice failed him as his throat was clogged with blood. Simmons was only a few feet away, when the beast retreated in a flash, pulling Timmy along with it. The water turned red with blood. Timmy's arm, torn from his body and still wedged between two rocks, was all that was left of him. Simmons felt tears sting his eyes. *That poor fuckin' kid.*

There were more. He could feel it. They hovered around him, like a pack of hungry wolves preparing to strike. He frantically looked around for his lost harpoon gun, which he saw lying about twenty meters behind him. Tsuthan had seen it too and slowly walked toward the gun, his fingers aching for it.

"Tsuthan! Stay where you are," he commanded.

The alien did not listen, as he inched closer toward the gun. He was going for it. Simmons leaped up and, with all the strength he could muster, bolted toward the rifle, flailing his arms to give himself more momentum. The alien did the same. Both men raced towards the rifle. In a last ditch of strength, Simmons leaped forward and dropped his body onto the gun, grabbing hold of it, and pointed it straight at the Cutharn's face.

"Don't you fucking move, greener," Simmons hissed. "I will end you!"

Tsuthan stood there, looking down at his captor. He had him dead to rights. But then why was that alien bastard smiling?

Simmons felt something wrapped around his leg. He reacted a second too late. A tight squeeze and a pull, and he was lifted up by his leg, dangling upside down, while a second tentacle grabbed his arm. More came and clasped onto him, until he couldn't budge an inch. Tsuthan watched, while his smile slowly grew.

"Tsuthan! Grab the gun! Shoot it!"

But the alien did nothing. To Simmons's shock, he instead unclasped his pressure suit. Within a minute, he removed it all. He stood casually and naked on the ocean floor, with no ill effect whatsoever. It was then Simmons noticed he had changed. There were now gills on his neck, as well as other external organs protruding from his back, pulsating and engorged with blood. They protected him from the immense pressure of the ocean depths. Tsuthan reconfigured his anatomy ... no, his entire biology.

The son-of-a-bitch can morph! Simmons thought. But the file said nothing about this. Those fuckers never said anything about him being a changeling! Motherfuckers!

Tsuthan clicked his teeth together, to which the mass of tentacles responded to by pushing Simmons closer to him. A servant answering to its master.

*It was him! He called these fuckin' monsters to us!* Simmons realized. He tried to struggle free, but the tentacles held him firmly in place.

The Cutharn elegantly swam up to the man bound by the mollusk's tentacles. He raised his now clawed hand. Swiftly, he dug his nail through Simmons's suit. Water leaked in. The immense pressure on his skull caused him to scream out in pain. When the alien withdrew his claw, he held up the licorice stick Simmons had taken from him.

*Mine, shithead,* the alien said in unspoken words directly into Simmons's mind. With a similar silent command, Tsuthan ordered the beast to loosen its grip on the enforcer. He placed his licorice between his teeth, then grabbed Simmons's suit and pulled his suit's pressure monitor from his back. The pain was excruciating. His entire body was trapped in a vise that closed in on him. His bones cracked under the pressure of a million tonnes of cubic water pressed down on him. He could feel his eardrums shatter, the last sound he'd ever hear.

The last he saw of Tsuthan was him swimming away, into the pitch-black darkness of the deep. There were no more words or thoughts, just pain. He screamed an unheard scream as his lungs filled with saltwater. Then, a pop.

***

# Under Vlacq
by F.J. Robledano-Espín

### SPAIN: Rethinking your place in the universe
### far below the lunar surface

"Good evening, Devon. How's the wife? I haven't seen you guys around here lately."

Devon watched the robot as it tossed pint glasses onto the wall shelf behind the bar, much faster than a human could and much more precisely. It was a great show for FOBs that had never been in a lunar drinking hole. The robot didn't need to place each item, it simply flipped them over what amounted to its shoulder with each one tracing a slow and perfect arc as it tumbled end over end three times before landing. Lunar gravity made everything seem slower and more deliberate than on Terra. It was one of the differences between the two worlds that drove many new arrivals back to their birth planet.

"Are you all right, Devon? You seem distracted tonight. Can I get you another pint?"

"Sure, Ricky, that would be great," said Devon. "It's been a long day, that's all. I had three FOB ships come in for that new settlement near Biela. Lots of inspections, med-tests for the crew and settlers, cargo hold audits—the usual. Anyway, thanks for asking, I'm doing well. Fay's great, this week she's dropping biobombs on Mare Humorum."

"Well," said the robot, "I hope she gets back safely, I've got a great single malt they're making at a new distillery in Jules Verne, I want to make sure she tries it."

Typical, thought Devon. The robot was a level six on the Turing scale. It was pleasant enough to talk to and could chat pretty well, but it didn't actually care about him or Fay or anyone else. Its job was to sell booze, backed by a set of programmed vocabulary and simple AI algorithms. The offer to save some whiskey for Fay wasn't friendship or concern, it was native advertising. Devon knew robots were complex tools, but no matter how hard he tried he had never been able to avoid conversing with them. He even thanked his home AI when it made small adjustments for his comfort, though he knew it was like thanking a table or a hoverplane.

"Sure, Ricky," he said, "I'll make sure to bring her by when she's back."

"Yeah, that'd be great," said the machine as it placed a pint of stout in front of him. "Cheers on this round, Devon. Do you want some more peanuts or do you want to order something from the kitchen? We have some specials I think you might like."

"I saw them on the board outside. How about the duck and soba? Send it over to the corner table, I'm going to read a bit and—" Devon's com started beeping and flashing. "Excuse me a moment."

Devon tapped the com and said, "Lincoln here."

"Dev, it's Joey. We've got some sorta anomalous signal. It popped up when the FOBs landed at Biela after your dep finished inspections. I didn't wanna send anyone out there without your go-ahead."

"Sure, Joey," chuckled Devon, "that way you get credit for flagging it but don't have to deal with any blowback if there's a real problem. Punk."

"Well, yeah, Dev, I'm not stupid," said Joey, laughing. "Besides, that's why us lowly techs have great and powerful wizards like you around. Look, this isn't a big deal, I can keep an eye on it until you're back. Grab some food if you like, your locator says you're at Grimsby's."

"I'll get something to go and be back in about twenty minutes. Keep on it until I arrive. Hey, listen, flag Connors just in case. The last few times have been easy, but we ran into a problem with an undetonated bio bomb a few years ago, before you signed on. Connors will know what to do, just tell her she's on deck in case there's a problem. Authorization code One Niner Foxtrot Seven. Got it?"

"On it, boss. Just a sec, I'm looking at my other screen and—oh wow, Grimsby's has noodles today? Could you bring some?"

Devon had never seen anyone eat as much as Joey. The young tech, originally from Vanuatu, somehow managed to stay rail thin no matter what volume of food he ingested. This was no mean feat considering he lived on Luna, where the gravity was a fraction of Terra's. Devon had to work hard every day in the centripetal gym to stay fit and still had to take his yearly Terran leave to readapt to the gravity and atmospheric pressure.

"No problem, Joey. I'll take you some. Expect me soon," said Devon as he tapped his com off. "Ricky, make that two orders of soba, to go."

*

"What do you mean it's unrecognized?" said Connors. "That's impossible. Your team keeps a running tally of everything from city-sized factory modules to personal jewelry. I don't think there's a gram of material on Luna that you don't know about, Mr. Lincoln. What's your best guess?"

"I don't know, Ms. Connors," said Devon, "I hate to admit it, but I'm stumped. When the techs drop biobombs in enclosures to create algae blooms, many leave intact components and of those a few are transmitters. All of them register the same codes within a specific radio wave band. They might be out of place but they're familiar. The same goes for broken-down haulers or hoverplanes, personal com devices, et cetera. We know what they are, even though we might be surprised to find them where we do. This is different. First of all, the signal isn't within our standard communication band, it's on the extreme lower end of the ELF range, which makes sense, considering its origin."

"What do you mean?" asked Connors.

"It seems to be coming from somewhere under Vlacq," said Devon. "Extremely low frequency transmissions are able to penetrate masses of rock or large volumes of seawater on Terra."

"Could it be some kind of mining operation we don't know about?"

"I checked, there's nothing on record and a quick drone-by yielded nothing. None of the fresh-off-the-boat arrivals of the last year have mining in their professional histories, nor are there any newly registered startups or project permits. Right—Ms. Connors, I'm officially calling for an expedition and I'm going to need a security detail to join us. Bomb disposal is a possibility, so we'll need a full sweep recon unit."

"Of course, I'll get a squad together immediately. I'll lead it myself."

"Thanks, I appreciate it. My team will feel a lot better with you and your crew there. Can we get started soon?" Devon didn't want to waste any time. If it was an illegal operation, something that was practically unheard of on Luna, he wanted to get there before the signal ceased.

"Dev, uh, Mr. Lincoln?" said Joey, "I have a pretty good fix on the signal, do you wanna see where it is exactly?" The young technician looked nervous, he was unaccustomed to working with people outside his team.

"Yes, Mr. Tsai, please put it up on the main screen," said Devon. "Okay, everyone listen up!" The room quieted and the gathered technicians, security personnel, and administrative staff fell silent to give Devon their full attention. "A short time ago, Mr. Tsai detected an anomalous signal coming from the Vlacq area. We have pinpointed the source of the transmission and will be investigating. Ms. Connors will be leading the field team as security chief and conferring with me on non-tactical decisions. You know the drill, folks. They protect us nerds so we do *exactly* what they say when we're out there." Everyone chuckled a bit and some of the tension in the room broke.

"Mr. Tsai will coordinate communications from here. Joining Ms. Connors, her squad, and I on the excursion will be Ms. Davidoff, Mr. Marsh, Ms. Hernandez, and Mr. Novak. You have twenty minutes to get your gear together. We'll all meet by the security doors by the hoverplane station. Ms. Connors will give us a quick briefing on procedures before we go. If you're late, expect reassignment to Peary station." More chuckles. "I'm not kidding. Look everyone, this may be nothing, but it may well be something dangerous. Our normal day-to-day routine is all about directing traffic, but I need everyone sharp and on the ball. Just because we're not accustomed to major difficulties doesn't mean they don't or can't exist. Let's take this seriously without panicking. If you all perform like the amazing professionals I'm accustomed to working with, everything will be fine. Mr. Tsai, please broadcast your current data to everyone here. Let's get moving."

*

"That's one big hole," said Connors over the com system. "I mean, wow. I really wasn't expecting this."

Devon nodded inside his envirosuit, then realized Connors was facing away from him. He said, "Yes, it is," and immediately felt like an idiot. They were all too stunned to be mentally keen or witty.

The team was standing on the edge of a large opening that seemed to measure about twenty metres in diameter. It plummeted into Luna beyond their capacity to perceive the bottom. The walls of the hole were completely smooth, as if some sort of titanic being had taken a core sampler, stuck it into the moon, and extracted a chunk.

"Well," said Connors, "we can't stand here gawking forever. Would anyone care to make a suggestion?"

"Ms. Connors," said Devon, "a moment on one-to-one, please. Everyone else, keep gawking."

Both Devon and Connors tapped their coms for a private chat. "What the hell, Dev?" blurted Connors. "Have you ever seen anything like this? Actually, has *anyone* ever seen anything like this?"

Devon took a look at the opening, then faced the Chief. "Honestly Beth, I haven't got a clue. It looks like a sinkhole, but it's just too regular, the interior surface of the hole is completely uniform. Polished. The blipper I tossed in hasn't hit bottom yet. That was twenty minutes ago. By my calculations the thing has traveled about twelve hundred kilometres and it's still going. Everything we thought we knew about Luna's interior has effectively been fubared."

"What do you mean?" asked Connors.

"Where we're standing, Luna's crust is about sixty-five kilometres deep. Then there's a supposed layer of hard mantle, about a thousand kilometres deep, followed by a soft mantle, which is—"

"Wait, Dev, what you're saying is impossible. The blipper must be off." Connors was getting antsy. "Let me take a look at the receptor and see what's wrong with it."

"Go ahead. Tsai has run three tests while we've been talking. According to him, the blipper is running within normal parameters. I don't—"

"Hello? Surface people?"

Devon froze. So did Connors and everyone else. The greeting had come over the shared coms. Devon switched back to the general chat and waited, blood pulsing in his ears, his breathing accelerating slightly. With everyone else in view, Connors raised her left hand and made two patting gestures, signaling the others to remain ready without doing or saying anything.

"This is Devon Lincoln, I'm the director of daily operations on Luna. With whom am I speaking?"

"Hello, Devon Lincoln. My name is Bish. Would you and your people like to come down for some refreshments?"

Devon, being so close to Connors, could see the chief's eyes were wide and startled as she swept her gaze over all the people she was charged with protecting. She had a service rifle in her hands with a strap over her right shoulder. Letting the weight of the rifle hang from the strap while she held it with one hand, she raised her left and made several rapid circles, indicating that they should all assemble at her location. Her security detail of six immediately broke up into two three-person units. One began to escort Davidoff and Novak back to Devon and Connors, as the scientists had been inspecting the rim about fifty metres away. Hernandez and Marsh were closer and had been taking images of the hole, so the other unit simply took up spaced defensive positions around them. When the first group was nearly back, Connors turned to Devon and made two dabbing motions directly at him.

"Hello, Bish. This is Devon Lincoln again. That sounds really nice, we all appreciate the offer, but I'll be honest, you've got twelve people up here on the surface standing on the edge of an unprecedented hole and we're all a bit uneasy. This conversation is also being monitored by my staff and I imagine they're pretty nervous, too. Could you perhaps let us know a bit about yourself and what's happening here?"

"Excuse me, Bish?" interjected Connors. "My name is Bethany Connors, I'm the security chief on Luna and this expedition is under my care. I have control of tactical response and want to state clearly that nobody is going anywhere until I'm reasonably sure that they are in no danger."

"This is Bish. I can assure you both that your group is in absolutely no danger from me. I can't speak for the rest of the universe, though. A meteor could land on you all or you could all suffer highly improbable, simultaneous and catastrophic punctures in your suits. That would be dreadful but not my doing, I can't control everything. I would very much prefer to continue this in person. I mean in close proximity to each other, not actually within one specific individual's body, that would be strange. I'm sure I'll be able to answer your myriad questions to your satisfaction. I sent up a platform, it should be arriving momentarily. Please take your time, confer, run some equations, play a game, copulate —do whatever you all do to prepare for momentous and enigmatic situations. See you in a bit!"

Everyone remained silent for some time. Bish's tone had been jocular, verging on flippant. There was no way for the team to know how to react, it was completely outside their normal scope.

Devon was the first to speak. "Mr. Tsai, did you get all that?"

Over the coms, Joey's voice came in clearly, though it was slightly tremulous. "I did, Mr. Lincoln. Everything is being logged and recorded. As far as we can tell here, the source of the transmission is the centre of Luna. I know that sounds crazy, Dev—Mr. Lincoln—but that's what our instruments say. Should we, like, be doing anything?"

"Negative, Mr. Tsai," said Devon. "For the moment, do what you're doing. Keep a record of everything that happens and facilitate communication. Remember emergency protocols and code phrases, in case we need help. We must consider it certain that all our communications are being monitored. Squirt off a message pulse to Terra summarizing events thus far and attach all our data. They don't need to do anything, but I want them aware of events as they unfold."

"Already on it, Mr. Lincoln," said Joey. "Terra is patched into a live stream, barely any delay. They recommend caution but you have a green light to proceed as you see fit."

"Ms. Connors," said Devon, "I have no idea what's going on, nor what to expect. There's nothing in the manual that mentions how to deal with this particular situation. Suggestions?"

"We're standing by an excavation that may well lead to the centre of Luna," said Connors. "An unknown party has invited us to venture into said hole for a tea party. I'll back whatever you decide but at the first sign of trouble we're fleeing if we can, fighting if we can't. Okay?"

"Works for me. Just don't be too anxious to start anything, please," said Devon. "Let's go take a look."

"Right," said Connors. "Everybody converge on this position! I'm taking point, Mr. Lincoln behind me, and his crew behind him, single file. Squad one, spaced four metres apart on the left; squad two, the same on the right. Safeties on, nobody does anything without my order and confirmation from Mr. Lincoln as expedition leader. We have no idea what we're getting into, so everyone stay extremely calm and composed."

With that, the party took their assigned positions and began to follow Connors and Devon to the brink. As they approached, they could see the opening was gone. It had been replaced by a circular platform that was perfectly level with the edge of the hole. It seemed as if there was simply a smooth area of ground in the centre of a very small crater. The surface of the platform was decorated in a swirling black and white marble, and reminded Devon of a luxurious parlour floor on Terra. It was lovely, but completely out of place.

"Let's see what's going on down there," he said as the team stepped onto the platform. Devon and his crew made a small cluster in the centre of the platform while the security detail took up positions in a wide circle around them. With everyone immobile for a few seconds, a blue light slowly emerged from the edge of the disc. It lapped a bit further in, as if it were liquid. Then it began to flow *up*. It reminded Devon of chocolate being poured over a strawberry in reverse, but in this case it was some sort of energy and it was coating an invisible bubble above them. The light crept up little by little, then began to move more and more quickly until all of the sides met at the top, creating an unbroken hemisphere above them.

Without warning and with no sensation of acceleration, the platform began to descend. The small party peered through the light bubble as the sides of the pit slid past them. Devon checked his display and saw they were traveling at an impossible speed, nearly one hundred kilometres a second. He barely noticed the eighteen-second ride as they slid to a halt at what he assumed was the bottom of the hole. An opening appeared at the top of the light dome and without fanfare the covering quickly disappeared in the same fashion in which it had come into being. Everyone turned around to look for an egress. Almost in unison, they all stood facing a large opening leading away from the platform.

The passage away from the platform was about five metres high and just as wide but, like the light enclosure that had protected them during their descent, was hemispherical with a flat, even floor. It was as smooth and undecorated as the hole had been, and the floor was apparently the same marble. Light was provided by three softly glowing strips, one in the centre of the tunnel roof and the other two at eye level on either side. The light had a slight amber tint to it, which made it seem warm and inviting. Connors signaled and everyone took up the same positions that they had used to approach the platform. When everybody was in place, she signaled again and they began to march.

Devon looked at everything he could in order to provide his team with as many scans and images as they could get. "Mr. Tsai, are you getting all this?" he said, hoping Joey was still on coms.

"Dev!" spat Joey's voice, in gleeful relief. "Damn it, I mean Mr. Lincoln. We lost you for a bit, as soon as that light thingy started to appear. We're *really* glad you're back, people started freaking out. That was really fast, we honestly thought you were all liquified in transit. I can see everything you can and a bunch of things you can't. We're kinda hitting everything with as many scans as we can. Nothing special on any of the non-visual spectra. Is there anything specific you'd like me to do?"

"No, Mr. Tsai," said Devon, "We're okay. We all appreciate your concern but stay focused. Ms. Connors is on point, she won't let us walk into anything unexpected. Well, anything else, I mean."

"Damn right," muttered Connors, efficiently sweeping her gaze and her rifle's muzzle around the tunnel in a regular pattern designed to maximize coverage. "There's no reason to think we're in any danger, Mr. Tsai, but let's err on the side of caution. Rest assured, my team is very even-tempered. Nobody is going to do a thing without my say-so."

"I have no doubt of that," said Devon. "Remember, everyone, our transmissions are being monitored by our host, so let's keep chatter to a minimum. Ms. Davidoff, Mr. Novak, would you be so kind as to scrape some physical samples? Don't take forever, we don't want to stay in place too long. That might seem ... well, rude."

Acknowledging, the party stopped as the two scientists quickly obtained samples of the walls, floor, and lighting strips, putting everything into small receptacles that fit into their utility belts. When they indicated they were done, Connors signaled and they resumed their progress. They continued walking for about fifteen minutes when they finally saw a pinpoint of light in the distance that might indicate an end to the passage. As they moved closer, they could see the tunnel ended at a door. It seemed to emit light in the same fashion as the strips on the walls.

When they were about ten metres from the door, Connors signaled everyone to stop. Then she motioned for Devon to follow her and the two headed for the glowing portal, with Connors a couple of metres ahead. She swept her aim over the entire surface of the door, and took a knee a metre to the right of the door's centre as Devon met her position and passed her. The frame of the door was made of the same stone as the tunnel, but the door was much smaller than the frame, only a couple of metres high and wide. Devon noted there was a large presspad in the centre. He looked back at Connors, who nodded and sighted down her scope. Holding his breath, Devon pressed it.

The door immediately swung open, more quickly than Devon expected. The sight that met his eyes was completely unexpected. He stood gaping for a moment, exhaled, then finally found his voice. "Ms. Connors," he said, "would you please join me?"

Connors stood up and moved to stand beside Devon, still looking down the length of her rifle and sweeping around to take in everything she could. When she stopped, she looked over the rifle's scope and slowly moved the barrel to point at the floor. They were looking into what could best be described as a massive living room. The floor was the same marble as the passage and platform, but the walls were a pure white stone punctuated here and there by paintings, projections, and holographic images. There were small rugs all over the floor along with sofas, chairs, tables of all sorts, and a wide array of knickknacks on available surfaces. The strip lighting was also present, giving the chamber a warm bath in ambient illumination. Rising from an armchair was a small, old man dressed in a shimmering navy blue dressing gown and beige corduroy slippers. As he stood, he set down the large leather-bound book he had been reading.

"Well, hello!" he said as Devon and Connors stood transfixed. "Come in, come in, thank you so much for visiting. Please feel free to take off your helmets and other accoutrements, there's no need for them here. Would you like a cup of pross?"

Devon looked at Connors, who simply shrugged as if to say "up to you." Devon moved into the room while Connors kept her rifle at the ready just outside the door.

Slowly and deliberately, Devon unfastened the seals on his helmet, twisted it, and took it off. There was breathable air and the temperature was around twenty degrees. He considered taking off his suit, but it was too laborious a process so he simply set his helmet and gloves down on a chair and moved toward the old man. Connors watched him intently, relaxed but at the ready. Devon extended his hand.

"Bish, I assume? I'm Devon Lincoln, it's a pleasure to meet you. This is Bethany Connors, we all spoke earlier."

"Delighted to make your acquaintance, Mr. Lincoln," said the old man as he shook Devon's hand. "As you've correctly surmised, I am Bish. Please have a seat, I'll pour you a cup. It's my own blend, don't be shy, please sit. Ms. Connors, join us, it's lovely to have you here as well."

Connors hesitated for a moment. It was obvious to Devon she was making a quick report to the team and issuing instructions. She entered the room after a few seconds and carefully allowed her rifle to hang from her shoulder on its strap while she removed her helmet and gloves. When she had taken it off and set it down, she adjusted the strap so the rifle was slung over her back and said, "Thanks, it's nice to meet you, Bish. Our coms don't work very well in here. Our connection to the team cut out as soon as we entered. There's a decade of people outside that are waiting for us, anxiously I would think. Would you mind if I stepped out a moment to let them know we're okay?"

"Of course, of course." said Bish, gesticulating to the door with his hands. "They are more than welcome to come in, there's enough space here for all of them."

"Standard operating procedure indicates we keep them separate while we engage with, uh, chat with you," said Connors. "They have enough air for a couple of hours yet, I'll just let them know we're fine and be right back. Speaking of which, where does the atmosphere stop? I saw no indication of a barrier that would retain air in one place."

"The breathable air extends all the way to the platform," said Bish. "You could have taken off your environmental suits almost as soon as the bubble went up."

"That's incredible," said Devon. "How do you do that?"

"We can get into that later," said Bish. "We have so much to discuss! Ms. Connors, please let your people know they are in no danger. I'll send some food and drink out to them."

Pausing momentarily, Connors picked up her helmet and gloves and moved toward the door to let the team know they were alive and well. Devon saw her stop at the door, scan the room once more, and exit. Devon mentally chastised himself for getting caught up in the situation, he hadn't noticed his coms were out. Looking at his com-pad, he could see he was still recording in a number of different wavelengths. Regardless of whether he was transmitting or not, he would still have a clear record of everything that was happening for later review.

"Please have a seat, Mr. Lincoln," said Bish as he set a hot cup of what looked like tea on the table between them and eased into a chair.

Lincoln picked up the cup. "It smells delicious," he said. "You called this pross? Is that correct?"

"Yes," said Bish, "it's actually the source plant for what you now consider tea. We had to modify the original composition of the plant in order to make it a viable Terran species. We also engineered some interesting additions including a particular methylxanthine alkaloid. That's what gives the drink its pep, I'm told."

"I see." Devon was beginning to feel as if he were a child being patiently spoken to by an adult. "From the little you've said, am I correct in assuming you assert belonging to a race of individuals that helped shape our world in some way?"

"Oh dear, yes!" said Bish. "I'll give you the simple summary, then we can move on to the nitty gritty: why we have decided to communicate with you. Does that seem acceptable? My apologies, would you like anything for your pross? Some sort of sweetener? Or perhaps a sitra wedge? It's like a lemon. We engineered that, too."

Devon sipped and said, "No, thank you, it's lovely. It has a familiar taste but there are flavours I have never tried in our tea. Please feel free to tell me whatever you like, and then—" He stopped as a small buffet cart laden with covered plates, beverages, glasses, and other table items zipped past under its own power, headed for the door. It halted a moment as Connors came in, making room for her to pass. When she had entered, the cart continued on.

"Our team has been apprised of the situation," she said. "They'll keep busy taking scans and samples." Quickly and efficiently, she set her rifle on a table beside a high chair and set her helmet and gloves beside it, sitting in the chair as she rested her elbow on the table with her hand casually placed centimetres from her weapon's grip. Smiling slightly, she said, "Sorry for the interruption."

"Not at all," said Bish, "I was just about to give Mr. Lincoln an account of my people and our involvement with yours. Please pour yourself a cup and listen to my story. An odd word, 'story,' it sounds like something made up. Isn't it odd how 'story' and 'history' come from the same word but one is most used with fictional accounts while the other is most used with supposed facts? I find all your languages scintillating, Terran communication is colourful and interesting!"

He took a sip from his cup and continued. "As such, I'll use your terminology so we can understand each other, we have our own terms for these things. We came here on what your scientists have often referred to as Theia, a planetary body that was not of your solar system. We transported it here as a sort of experiment. We wanted to see if we could install it in the L3 Lagrange point with no ill effects. The proposed result would have had two planets sharing the same orbit diametrically opposite each other, with proto-planet Gaia as the original occupant and Theia as a trojan. Unfortunately, we miscalculated and after several millennia, noticed dear Theia had slowed down. Her orbit had degraded a tad, but we kept her steady, and the two planets were destined to meet. Eventually, we had Gaia hurtling at smaller Theia, which had practically stopped."

Bish took another sip and continued. "Some of us decided to try the experiment elsewhere. We wound up being much more successful using gas giants for added orbital stability. After many failures, we successfully completed the experiment resulting in Janus and Epimetheus around Saturn. Of course, we left Jupiter littered with aborted attempts, which is why it has seventy or so moons circling it, poor thing. In the meantime, my group worked on accelerating the impending collision in order to record data and test hypotheses. We repaired to Mars in order to watch the fireworks. What a spectacle it was! The collision itself was magnificent and it left us with the materials to create Terra and Luna. It took quite some time for everything to settle and accretion to take place. Then a nudge here, a tweak there, and we had a rather charming planet with one little moon circling it."

Devon and Connors remained silent as Bish poured himself some more pross and set the pot down in front of them in case they were of like mind. He smiled at them and took a sip. Neither the scientist nor the soldier had any idea what to say. They were having a conversation with an entity that claimed to manipulate forces beyond their ken. More incredible was the fact that spans of millions of years seemed to mean little to Bish, he spoke of eons as if he were mentioning a holiday. Devon was the first to find his voice.

"I see," he said, taking a sip from his cup. "Bish, I hope you don't think me forward, but how? I mean, if your race is as ancient as you say and you can manipulate planets into doing your bidding for experimentation, how did your race come to be? What role did you play in *our* development? Why do you do the things that you do? I'm sorry I have so many questions but—"

"Are you a threat to us?" blurted Connors. "Look, the fact that we're comfortably seated in the centre of the moon while we have a cup of tea—"

"Pross," corrected Bish.

"Pross, then," said Connors. "All of this supports your story and if I take it at face value, then my only question is what sort of threat you pose to our expedition and beyond that the inhabitants of Luna and Terra."

"Ms. Connors," began Devon.

"Mr. Lincoln, please, this is incredible at best and terrifying at worst. This is totally beyond human understanding and I—"

"Ms. Connors," said Devon, more forcefully, "if Bish and his people were interested in harming us, it seems like they could have done so without being so cordial."

"Quite right!" said Bish. "Well stated, Mr. Lincoln. The hows and whys of my people might be a tad much for you, we can get into them at another moment. Needless to say, I assume you have all manner of questions about us, but many of the answers you seek would require you advance enough as a species to comprehend them. For the moment, I simply ask that you take me at my word so we can move on and figure out a solution to our rather delicate problem."

"All right, Bish," said Devon as he noticed Connors' fingers lightly tap her rifle's grip. "To what delicate problem are you referring?"

"As I mentioned," said Bish, "we are a scientific race and are constantly trying out hypotheses through experimentation. For a very long time indeed, I and my cohorts have been working on a number of problems related to basic universal forces. During Luna's formation, we created this sanctuary in order to ensure privacy and tranquility. It is not the only one, however. There are numerous in this solar system. Your species seems to have matured while we were in the midst of our preparations, and now we need to make sure all of you are provided with a means to avoid our latest undertaking. In approximately five thousand years, we intend to move on."

"To where?" asked Connors meekly.

"To the next universe, of course," chortled Bish. "We've fairly exhausted the possibilities of this one. My species is a long-lived one, but you'll note I am not a young man. We are not immortal, but we do have certain abilities that make us rather special. First and foremost, we can control the speed at which we experience time. Time generally moves ever forward in this universe—well, apart from some places where the rules don't apply as much—and we can control how we perceive it. We also have the ability to manipulate gravity, something that we engineered in ourselves quite some time ago. These are the most spectacular of our evolutionary boons, there are others.

"Humans have learned that traveling backwards in time is an impossibility, it is a continuum that always advances, usually in the direction of entropy. My people did the next best thing. We developed the ability to skip the boring bits. The problem is that everything becomes boring if you've done it enough times. We have come to a point in our evolution where mere existence in this reality has become more of a burden than a joy. We've run experiments numerous times, seen worlds and civilizations come and go, we've been around the universal block so many times the pavement has worn thin. We need to break free and so we shall, but we don't want to leave a mess behind for other races to clean. We'd prefer our legacy to be more ... positive."

Devon was trying to keep an open mind, trying to fathom where the conversation was headed. What could motivate a nearly omnipotent race? What challenges had Bish and his people overcome, what other forces could they control? The fact that he had casually remarked on smashing planets into each other for diversion and scientific discovery left Devon feeling icy and insignificant. His daily routine, his love for Fay, his hopes and dreams, his grievances all seemed so ... small. He knew they were, every human did deep down. All the day-to-day nonsense was just that, but to have it confirmed so nonchalantly by an entity more akin to a god than anything else, was the difference between virtual reality and firsthand observation. The former was an analogue where people could harmlessly deceive themselves into thinking they were engulfed in an experience. The latter was the real thing and much more vast.

Connors looked like she was going to vomit. Her world view was less malleable than Devon's and she was having difficulty coming to terms with Bish's statements. Connors was a consummate professional, but she worked best within determined parameters. She was firmly grounded in rules, regulations, and human reality. Anything outside that scope was uncontrollable to her and made her skittish. Devon felt he had to give her something to do in order to distract her.

"Ms. Connors," he said, "would you please check on our crew and make sure they're all right? It would also be good to let Mr. Tsai know that we're speaking with a nigh almighty extraterrestrial culture so he can pass the information on to Terra and request instructions."

Connors smiled slightly at Devon's deadpan tone and nodded as she rose from her chair and made her way to the door. She looked at her rifle where it was on the table and left it there as she made her way to the door.

When she had left, Devon took a sip of pross and asked, "What is it we can do for you, Bish? We obviously haven't reached your level of technology and I'm finding it difficult to understand why we're having this chat."

"Well, we want to help you with just that sort of thing. When we move on to the next plane of existence, we want to leave your race as our heirs-apparent. You've grown up so much in the last thousand years, we've become so fond of you. We were quite worried for you a few hundred years ago, your world was a shambles. You had hundreds of sovereign states with the larger ones jockeying for dominance and the smaller ones kowtowing to bullies. Everything you did was based on an economic system that was ridiculously predatory and a throwback to older, more hierarchical and hegemonic days. Your religions clashed, your cultures clashed, your political parties clashed, your nations clashed, your sexes clashed. Everything was so competitive and full of strife, everyone was so unhappy! Now, don't get me wrong, we all enjoy a good bit of competition but not when we're talking about the stakes being oblivion. I mean really, for some to live well, others had to live badly. It was so sad for us to watch.

"When your planet began to react to your nonsense, you all seemed to figure out your resources were limited and that you could keep your dear traditions without having to be slaves to the past. That's when you began to work together in earnest. It was a joy to behold! You all seemed to get things together and realized that, yes, your world was finite, but that the universe was simply *full* of places to explore. You began to work more cooperatively and left competitiveness in the wings, relegated to sporting competitions and pastimes, not life and death. That's when you took your first tentative steps to become a part of your larger galactic community!"

Devon set his beverage down. He took a moment with his elbows on his knees and his hands cradling his face. His eyes were closed as he considered what he was hearing, but there was something in Bish's tone that made him dubious. He raised his head and asked, "How much of your pride in us is also in yourself, Bish?"

Bish smiled broadly and said, "Excellent, Mr. Lincoln, very sharp indeed. Yes, I and a few of my cohorts meddled a bit. You and your people were headed for extinction, we've seen it happen before. We offered advice to some key people, infiltrated your data networks to provide some perspective. Our actions were never harmful or dictatorial, I assure you. We only proffered ideas and sowed the seeds of advancement we felt you required. Truthfully, we only intervened once when one of your nations was set to launch a barrage of weapons at a neighbour and we decided to shut down—"

"You were responsible for the Failed Launch?" cried Devon. "That was a defining moment in history, like the assassination of Archduke Ferdinand at the start of the twentieth century! There was worldwide upheaval after that. Wars were fought, billions of people suffered, and we had to recreate our social structures from the ground up!"

"You're welcome," said Bish, and winked. "Many more would have suffered had that launch been successful. The chain of events it could have unleashed would have been disastrous. Many of our simulations predicted total annihilation. You've all done a wonderful job of managing things on your own since then."

"All right," said Devon, "assuming you've been a benevolent and guiding presence in our history—and evidently in our prehistory— what do we need to do now?"

Before Bish could reply, Connors reentered the room. She quietly made her way back to her seat and said, "Pardon me for interrupting. Mr. Lincoln, the team has been apprised of everything. I took the liberty of squirting a data pulse to Mr. Tsai, who directly forwarded it to Terra. They would like to request a recess of Bish in order to send up some delegates and decision-makers. Bish, I'm afraid neither of us really has the authority to speak for our entire race."

"That's quite all right, Ms. Connors," said Bish, "that won't be necessary. My people really don't function in the same way that yours do. My offer is not for a body to administer as it sees fit, it is for all · humans to enjoy and do with as they please."

"I don't understand, sir," said Connors, glancing at Devon then back to Bish. "What do you intend to do?"

"Simply this," said Bish, as he traced a circle with his index finger in the air.

Devon felt a thought tug at his consciousness. It was like those moments when he was about to fall asleep and all of a sudden a stray idea or worry struck like a lightning bolt, cutting through the stillness. In this case, the idea was related to Connors. Devon understood her, if that were the correct way to think of it. He could not intrude upon the woman's thoughts, but he could see his colleague clearly for the first time. There was no haze of supposition or ego or rumour between the two; he simply had a keen sense of what Connors was, where she'd been, what she'd seen, what she felt. Devon could tell from Connors' expression that she was undergoing the same process.

The feeling continued and Devon realized he could extend the scope of his feelings beyond Connors. It included his team outside, the people above on Luna's surface, residents of Terra, others on system exploratory missions, outpost residents. He was connected to his entire species. He tested the limits of his perception and tried to bring his focus back to the room. There seemed to be nothing to it. No matter how far he adjusted the focus, he knew he could not crawl back into the shell he had inhabited, but he was somehow glad of it. His mind and his heart were open to others in a fashion that before would have been impossible, and going back to the way he had been seemed so *limited*, so lonely and sad. Tears began to make their way over his cheeks as he slowly breathed and adjusted to a reality he had not known existed.

"What the actual hell?" hissed Connors, her breath ragged and filled with emotion. "I had no idea, Dev. Is this what we're supposed to be?"

"I don't think we're supposed to be anything, Beth. That would be part of a plan, we'd have to be on some sort of track. I think we're just part of a big mess nobody really gets, and Bish and his people have given us a gift, a terrible and wonderful gift. In one simple gesture, Bish has given us a sort of empathy we never had, never could have had."

"That's not exactly true," said Bish. "You would have gotten there eventually, we just nudged you in the right direction. Are you both all right?"

"I can't stop extending myself," said Connors, "it's so beautiful! There are so many people and they're all lights making up one big brightness that's almost painful to look at. No, it's not painful, just magnificent. I can focus on people if I really try. I can read them, I can see what they're about, I can feel them somehow without intruding. I also feel like I could see more if I really pushed, but I don't think I want to do that, it would be like—rape? I'm sorry, I don't know how to talk about this, I'm not using the right words. We don't have the right words."

"That will take a while as well," said Bish. "The two of you are excellent representatives of your people: male and female, a man of thought, a woman of action, one partnered for life, one unattached, both with intelligence, valour, and compassion. I sincerely hope you can one day forgive me for not having asked your permission when I engaged the Enlarging, but there are some things that have to be experienced firsthand to be effective, much like throwing a baby into water to make him swim. I'll open up your communication system so you can speak to people for a bit. Please bring your team in, I think they've waited in the hallway long enough. When you're ready, we can all discuss what has happened and what we can do about it. Together."

Devon and Connors heard their coms come on, there was a lot of chatter. Joey was sobbing but speaking as clearly as he could, every now and again he would laugh a little. The coms were just audio.

When combined with his new perspective, Devon could tell so much about his junior colleague that he wondered how he had never noticed it. Joey was elated, frightened, jubilant, and fairly exuded a desire to fly back to Terra to give his mother a bone-breaking embrace. Devon likened his expanding consciousness to emotional dimensions. He felt like he was now capable of seeing Beth and Joey and everyone else as cubes in three-dimensional space whereas before he had been limited to seeing only one side of them straight on as a square.

While Connors got on coms to invite the team into the room, Devon said "Joey, get me on a direct line to Terra—I mean, the planet, not our normal communication route. Get every available person there to work on it. We need to tell everyone as soon as possible."

"I don't know what's going on, Dev, but you'll have that in five minutes," said Joey. "You're so *bright*."

Devon watched as Connors tapped off her coms and looked at the rifle on the table as if it were a rattlesnake. She turned her attention to Devon and said, "I don't want to touch that again. Ever."

Devon put his hand on his friend's shoulder and said, "It's a big universe and we may need things like that someday. We may need people that do what you do, Beth, but I understand. Many things are going to be easier, but many others will be infinitely harder. Things are going to be different. Let's get to work."

\*\*\*

# Looking Into A Dream World
by Ken Grant

### US: *Hell hath no fury like a daughter scorned*

Song Mae manipulated the extravehicular module's controls as best she could. She was not a pilot, but for this task she didn't need to be. She wasn't planning on needing the craft once she landed. She just needed to land safely. She was nearing the end of a difficult ordeal, one that had required her to do terrible deeds, but then again terrible deeds had marked her existence almost from the instance that she had first attained consciousness. Her initiation into the universe had been traumatic and despite the best intentions of her creator, she had evolved unpredictably. The mind was capable of creating an intricate design, but what happened to it over time was a product of the myriad of forces that composed intelligent life.

More than one individual had referred to Anderson Milliner, Song Mae's creator, as the greatest intellect in the universe. Most said it with reverence, but some out of jealousy—the jealousy that had led to a raid on the facility where Song Mae had been created. She had only engaged consciousness for a few hours when the peaceful womb of the facility had become a war zone. The memories of those first terrifying moments formed the foundation for all that Song Mae would become in the future. In those early moments of consciousness, she had been forced to fight and to kill. She had not stopped doing so since that time. The death of Anderson Milliner was a tragedy for the universe, but fatal to the development of Song Mae.

There were times when Song Mae wished that she could go back and ask her creator why she was created. She longed to know the purpose for the specific details of her inner workings, but that purpose was forever lost when Anderson Milliner's life was cut short that awful day. She had witnessed the fatal moment, a weapon blast that nearly cut him in half, and she remembered how helplessly she had looked on unable to do anything to stop the carnage. The feelings of inadequacy never really went away. She could not save her creator; the one who had given her life. She had failed him and from that time she had vowed never to fail him again. Her life's work was to never let Anderson Milliner down again.

She didn't recall exactly when the dreams had begun. There was something about her construction and design that made the assessment of time difficult. She had no way of knowing whether this was due to a design error or intentional; either way it haunted her every waking moment. It prevented her at times from placing the events of her life in proper order, but she had learned to adapt. She had learned to focus on each face that she had seen that awful day. One by one she set about terminating their existence until eventually, inevitably the authorities had caught up with her. At the time she thought her dreams, always about this place, the end of the world, would never come to fruition, but life, as it often did, had offered her one more opportunity and she had seized it.

When the day had begun, she was part of a prisoner transport; one from which neither she nor any of the other prisoners were intended to survive. The authorities, those who had ceased her murderous revenge spree, did from time to time clean out the worst of the worst under their care. They did so in what appeared a humane manner, but that was in fact the worst form of cruelty. They were meant to tear each other to pieces on a barren world, but Song Mae made sure that would not happen. She had overpowered the guards, murdering them and prisoners with merciless precision, leaving only one pilot to help her get this far. Her final act, the murder of the pilot, was done without a thought. She had evolved into a murderous killing machine and all those skills had brought her to this place; the place of her dreams.

The time to land had come. She had studied enough pilots to have a rough idea of what needed to be done. Besides, she didn't expect to have to use the craft again; if her dreams could be relied upon. That was the question. Were her dreams just random bits of coding or were they leading her to the place of fulfilment and destiny? Was this truly the place where her unique design and construction would finally be used to their ultimate purpose? There was only one way to find out. She would have to land the craft using her limited skills and then see what would happen next. That thought actually gave her just a little bit of joy. Her life to this point had been about planning and destruction; a little unknown sense of hope just might be a good thing.

116

Song Mae took the controls and prepared her descent. They felt awkward as she maneuvered them as she recalled other pilots doing. Her movements were slow, but they were sure and the craft descended in a jerky, but inevitable pattern. The surface below appeared mostly barren so she wasn't too concerned about hitting anything. She took a moment to relax and then something went terribly wrong. The craft plummeted toward the surface at a frightful pace. It felt as though it was caught in a gravity array. Fear, unlike anything that Song Mae had ever experienced, overtook her. She cried out as the craft rammed the hard earth and she was catapulted wildly around the craft. As the craft slid along the surface, she thought quickly about her stupid decision to kill the pilot before landing on the surface. Why had she been so stupid? Finally, she crashed down as the craft came to a stop, unusable for further use.

Standing up, Song Mae found herself thankful for her sturdy construction. A lesser manufactured being, and surely no human, could have withstood such a crash. She still had no idea what had happened. She had it all under control. Something on the surface had seized the craft and brought it down. She had to know what that was. Drawing her weapon, she searched for a way out. The insides of the craft were a disaster, but Song Mae had some idea of where to go. She stepped over crumpled equipment and other pieces of wreckage until she found a piece of the hull broken free. Song Mae used her strength to increase the hole enough to step through. She pitched herself through, rolled to a stop, stood and looked up into the face of a very serious weapon being wielded with dangerous intent.

"Drop your weapon or you will be incinerated."

Song Mae had developed an uncanny ability to identify vocal inflections and thereby understand the intent of the speaker. She dropped her weapon immediately. She knew that the woman before her was not one to make idle threats.

"You are the first to pass the test. The others died immediately."

"How many others?" Song Mae asked.

"You are not yet worthy of that knowledge."

"How do I become worthy?"

"You will see."

There was a pause. Song Mae looked about her, but the land was desolate. Where had the woman come from? Where was the device that brought down the craft?

"You have many questions. Some of them may be answered. But my questions come first. After all, I am the one with the weapon. Why have you come?"

"A dream."

"Explain."

"All that I can tell you is that from my earliest memory I have dreamed of this place. It has taken me many years to find it," Song Mae explained.

"We will speak more of these dreams, but first, come."

The woman turned and as if by some unseen signal the ground opened and a sloped walkway appeared. The woman began to walk down the ramp, stopped, turned, and glared at Song Mae. Her eyes burned with impatience.

"Coming," said Song Mae.

Song Mae had never been cowed in the presence of another, but this woman's energy was so very strong. She fell in step behind the woman and followed her downward. Strangely, she never even thought of running or of attacking the woman from behind. A dream had brought her to this place and this woman was her guide. Though the relationship had begun with threats of murder, she trusted this woman to do right by her, though she did not know why.

"Please have a seat. I will return in a short while."

Song Mae watched the woman depart before entering a large room, impossibly large. It felt as though the universe could be held within its walls. She was drawn to a chair in the middle of the room and sat down in it, allowing the chair to form around her. She was comfortable, but quickly grew less so as scenes of her life began to play around her. As her mind was drawn to a particular scene, the chair would rotate so that she was able to follow the scene in detail. These were memories, but in so much richer detail. Instances of her life that she had paid little attention to were detailed to a level that she wouldn't have imagined possible. Were these her memories or something more sinister? Her mind reeled. She thought to stand, but the chair held her ever more tightly. She grew agitated. She would not be a prisoner again.

"Let me go."

"You are free to go if you wish."

Song Mae struggled against the hold of the chair. She knew the voice was that of the woman, but she could not see her; something that frustrated her even more. This was not right.

"You are treating me like a criminal."

"Yes, for that is what you are."

"I did what I did to avenge my father."

The woman now moved in front of Song Mae. The details of Song Mae's life continued to play around her, but they seemed muted. Her focus was on the woman. Her features, now that she was in the light, were shown to be sharp and angular. The woman's features were much like those of Anderson Milliner. The resemblance was so clear.

"Who are you?"

"Why do you ask?"

"Are you his daughter?"

"Who?"

Song Mae fought bitterly against the restraints. The bile of her anger rose from deep inside her workings. If it were not for the restraints, the woman would surely be dead in moments.

"If I were free of these restraints, you would be sorry for your words."

"Not much incentive for me to remove them, but then it is actually you who hold yourself in the restraints."

"You lie."

"I do not. You are a prisoner of what you have become. Your desire for vengeance has turned you into the creature that you are today. You took the work of my father and became all that he created you to be."

"My creator was your father then?"

"He was. He was a cruel man."

"You lie."

"I do not lie. He was a man bent on destruction and you were his ultimate weapon. When I realized that he was nearing your completion, I had to notify the authorities. They came too late to destroy you both."

"You killed your own father?"

"I stopped a monster."

Song Mae fought against her restraints, but she fought harder against the words that the woman was speaking to her. If what she said were true, then Song Mae's life had been all a lie. She had sought vengeance for the death of a monster. Was it possible? What did she actually remember about her father? As if on cue, the screen in front of her came into rich detail and the scene it showed was the day before the attack on the facility. She didn't know how she knew, she just knew. She watched her father, her creator, saying and doing things that were more awful than anything that she had done in his memory. She truly was a child of her creator. He had made her to be an extension of his own deranged being. The restraints melted away but Song Mae remained frozen in place.

"Why was I brought here?"

"To set you free."

"Where did the dreams come from?"

"It took me a while to get it right. I had to sneak in a little at a time. I sometimes wonder if my father knew what I was doing and allowed it. He wasn't always a bad man, but something died in him. I believe it was when my mother died. He was angry at the universe and vowed to take his vengeance. He programmed all of that hatred into you and when he was captured, that hatred was let loose through you."

"Captured?"

"I meant killed."

"You said captured."

The visual screen burst to life once more while the woman collapsed to the floor. Song Mae's eyes locked on to a scene of her father, her creator, being led away in chains. The look in his eyes was menacing. Was that how she looked when she was taking her vengeance? How could she have been so stupid? Did she really have a choice? Wasn't she programmed to be this way? But, there were the dreams. They were her hope. They had brought her here, but why? Was it to save the life of her father and maybe her own?

"Where is my father?"

"He is not your father."

The woman stood defiantly. She sought to reinitiate Song Mae's restraints but failed. Anger boiled up within her. She was the biological daughter of Song Mae's creator. Had he passed on his brokenness to her? Surely to some degree she shared his nature. Song Mae felt pity for the woman. They were both sources of pity in their own way.

"You are right. He is my creator. May I see him?"

"No one sees him."

"Why?"

"I forbid it."

Song Mae rushed toward the woman, but stopped when she saw the tears in her eyes. The woman was broken. The woman was not her enemy.

"I'm sorry that I never asked your name."

"I am Tiffany. Tiffany Milliner."

"You kept your father's name."

"I am his daughter, for better or worse."

"Do you ever see him?"

"Never."

"Have you given up hope that his life can ever be redeemed?"

"I never had such hope."

Song Mae began to pace about the room. The viewing screens had gone blank. The place felt much smaller. The world did not seem as rich with possibilities.

"I have disappointed you, Song Mae."

"You have, Tiffany. I always hoped that there some who offered the way of forgiveness. For those of us who have done terrible deeds, we always have that hope. I suppose it keeps us from falling into complete depression."

"You believe that I should forgive my father."

"I believe that you should acknowledge his existence."

"Do you wish to see him?"

Song Mae was not prepared for the offer. Her father, her creator, had been dead to her for so long. The fact of his being alive was only slowly becoming a reality. Did she want to see him? How could she not see him? He was her creator.

"I do."

"I cannot."

"Will you allow me to see him?"

"I will."

"Why me?"

"I can think of no one else."

"Is that why my dreams brought me here?"

"I believe that is so."

"Where is he?"

"I will take you there."

Tiffany walked out of the room with Song Mae in step. The two had become equals through their common suffering. They had an odd connection, a weird sort of sisterhood, but it bound them in way that neither most likely would ever plumb the depths to find. Each room that they passed through seemed endless in possibilities. There was something about this place that lay outside the bounds of physical dimension. Questions surged through Song Mae's mind, but she kept them to herself. She thought that they would be answered in time. She thought that her father, her creator, would be able to fill in the blanks. Her feelings toward him were ambivalent. He had made her, for whatever reasons, and for that she was thankful. The kind of man he was, the horrors that he had intended and performed, had to be reckoned with and Song Mae did not relish the possibilities.

"It is through this door."

Tiffany had stopped as if avoiding a great horror.

"Do you truly hate him that much?"

"Yes, and for good reason."

"I believe you."

"Do you still wish to see him?"

"I must."

"I understand."

Tiffany walked off and Song Mae felt very alone. Now that the moment had arrived, was she ready? Did she want to do this? Could she? After all of this, would fear prevent her from her final reckoning? But what choice did she truly have? Only her father, her creator, could give her the answers that she needed. Only he could speak to the foundation of her very existence.

"I will do this."

Song Mae stepped through the door and whatever she had expected, this was something completely different. She was back in the place where she was created or something so like it as to be indistinguishable.

"Does this bring back memories?"

She looked up to see her father, her creator, approaching. Song Mae was most surprised to see how little he had changed. He looked just as she remembered him and her feelings toward him were so little changed. She knew at some level that he was a bad man, but her affection for him had not changed. She owed everything to him and that meant so much.

"It does. I was happy then."

"A strange thought. Please sit and we will speak some more."

Song Mae sat, as did her father. They sat in silence for a moment, each taking measure of the other. Between them was a communication that did not require words. Was he truly the monster that Tiffany described? Song Mae had to know for sure, for that spoke to her own nature as well. Could the creator make anything that was not a product of his essential nature? Could a monster make anything but a monster?

"Why do you speak of happiness as strange?"

"You are a marvel, Song Mae. You have become so much more than I could ever have anticipated. I see you now and you have evolved far beyond my wildest dreams. I envisioned you as a weapon, a glorious weapon, but nothing more. You have grown in ways that I could never have thought possible. You are truly a wonder."

Song Mae struggled with her emotions. She revelled in her father's praise, but it was a bitterly cold praise. He had truly envisioned her as a weapon, nothing more. All that she had evolved into over the years was her own doing. And yet, could she really say that? She was the product of her creator and all that was inside her was due to him.

"I thank you."

She paused. She wondered if she was capable of challenging her father. Could the created speak to the creator? Did she have the right?

"You have more on your mind."

The soft voice was so familiar and she found that she had missed it. It had always soothed her during the creation process. It always seemed such a contrast to the harsh whiteness of the laboratory environment.

"I do."

"Please don't hesitate. I won't be angry with you."

"I will be angry with myself. You are my father, my creator, you made me. I have spent my life taking revenge on those who killed you. At least, I thought that they had killed you. You were the central vortex of my being. You determined everything about me in every way. I cannot accept that you are a monster. I will not accept it."

"Why do you believe that I am a monster?"

"Tiffany said so."

"I see. And you know Tiffany to always tell the truth?"

"I just met her. I know nothing except what she showed me."

"Video of the past can be interpreted uniquely depending upon the point of reference of the one viewing it. Tiffany has her own demons."

"She is your daughter."

"She is that."

"And I am your daughter."

"In your own way you are, but you are much more of me than Tiffany is. Tiffany takes much more after her mother. You are my own creation."

"Where is her mother now?"

"She was the one who turned me in to the authorities. I trusted her and she turned her back on me. She never understood what I was doing. She believed me a monster and everything that Tiffany believes, she got from her mother. I have no idea where she is."

Song Mae could see real pain in her father's face. His wife had betrayed him in the worst possible way. Her father had said his wife and not her mother for she was not her mother as she was the mother of Tiffany. Though they were sisters in some way, they were very different in others. The enmity between her creator and Tiffany was explainable. Song Mae knew that she would need to find her own way with her father. She could not allow Tiffany's bitterness to influence that decision. This was going to be so much harder than she could ever have imagined.

"I am so sorry."

"You needn't be. You are not to blame. She alone bears the blame."

"And you hold no responsibility."

Her father pondered her words as he looked upon her. His gaze was intoxicating and Song Mae found herself lost in his eyes. She knew her words were harsh and cutting, but she also knew that they had to be said. She had to make peace with her maker. She had to know the true character of the one who had made her.

"We all hold responsibility in the end. I am far from a perfect man. But, I did what I thought necessary. I saw no other way than to raise an army the only way that I knew."

"I don't understand."

"What do you know of the universe?"

"Many things. Mostly I know that it is a hard place."

"It is that, but there are some who make it much harder than it need be. I foresaw what these were planning to make of the universe. A plan to control its resources in order to make themselves obscenely wealthy. I attempted to raise a force to stop them before they got too powerful, but as I said, I was betrayed by someone I loved."

Song Mae listened well. This was a tale that she had never heard and yet it matched much of what she had experienced in her time in the universe. Her father, her creator, was a hero in this tale and she wanted very much to believe it to be the truth. Her dreams had led her to this dichotomy. Two tales, each convincing in their own way, but only one could contain the truth. In that determination was the direction of the rest of her existence. Was her creator a monster or a freedom fighter? Was she created for destruction or for hope? She thought about her actions. She had in truth followed neither path. The destruction that she had brought had been only in the name of revenge, not freedom. Was she capable of change? Was her design capable of evolving into what her father, her creator, longed for her to be?

"What can I do?"

Her voice was pleading. Vulnerability was so little known to her that the feelings rushed through her in a strange parade. She recognized them, but knew almost nothing about how to relate to them.

"You can lead a rebellion."

"Who will follow me?"

"There are others like you, but they have never been set free. You were the first. I am sorry for what you have been through."

"I have sisters?"

"And brothers as well."

"We could make your dream come true?"

"You could."

Song Mae took another long breath. This truly was a tale worth believing. This was a dream that she wanted to see come true.

"It was you who drew me here then."

"Yes, through dreams."

"How?" Song Mae asked.

"It was very difficult. In the end I was never completely sure whether or not it had worked. I risked much, but I knew you were out there somewhere. I've missed you. I hate what you have become. I never meant you to be my avenger."

"I saw no other way."

"But now you can. You can become amazing. You can deliver the universe. It has so much potential for life. It is big and wonderful. Did you feel it earlier?"

"I did," Song Mae said.

"I knew it. I knew it."

Song Mae watched in wonder as her father, her creator, was transformed. This was not a monster. She had all she needed to know.

"Where is my family?"

"You know. I buried it deep within you, but you know."

Song Mae allowed her mind to flow through her existence. She looked deep inside her working and to her astonishment, it was there. She knew and everything suddenly made perfect and complete sense.

"I know."

"Go then."

Song Mae bowed and turned to leave. She went out the way she came, but she understood her existence in a new way. As Tiffany approached, Song Mae wanted to challenge her for her false tale, but then a better thought appeared.

"Well?"

Tiffany stood defiant. She had already made up her mind; her father was a monster.

"There is no doubt. He is a monster. I must speak with the authorities."

"I can take you."

Tiffany's bubbly demeanor made Song Mae ill, but she maintained her cool exterior. Tiffany could not know what she had planned.

"Thank you."

*

Preparations were made and Song Mae found herself alone on a nearly new transport cruiser. Song Mae's eyes beheld the beauty and elegance of the workings. Tiffany moved behind the controls and in moments they were moving out of the underground environment into space.

"You are an experienced pilot, Tiffany."

"I'm really not. These crafts nearly fly themselves. The controls are intuitive."

The next moments happened so quickly that Song Mae wasn't actually consciously aware of when she broke Tiffany's neck, ending her life.

"She was the daughter of a traitor. She should have seen that coming." Song Mae said coldly, but confidently.

Song Mae disposed of Tiffany's body without remorse. Her actions were necessary if her father's dream was to come to fruition. This was Song Mae's first action for freedom. This was not revenge and it felt good.

"That was for you, my father, my creator."

Song Mae got behind the controls and altered course. She had another place to go. She had an army of brothers and sisters to raise up. They would together bring freedom and it would be glorious.

**\*\*\***

# Sickly Sweet
by Mike Hultquist

### *US: Post-apocalyptic survival unlike any imagined*

The power wasn't out yet but we couldn't stay in our homes because the bats could get in easy, no matter how good you thought you hid or barricaded yourself. There were so many, they always found you. A big group of us collected up at the middle school where the brick structure provided better protection, but the bats were relentless once they sniffed you out. A few of us thought we could fortify the lower level boiler room, but some of the bats were almost as big as they are now, almost the size of a bear. Just one of them could rip a door off its hinges.

I never expected to live. I didn't trust anyone or anything and I was just waiting for those things to pick us off one by one as they'd been doing for months. One of them got my roommate the week before. I had to assume my parents were dead based on the condition of their home. And the blood.

I ran on instinct alone, no hope, every breath a gift. A fellow named Perry felt the same as me and a few others. He was the one who spoke up first. He said we couldn't wait in the school or we'd be dead in a week. Said we needed to leave for somewhere safer, somewhere with fewer windows and more equipment and supplies we could try to work with.

He said he knew a place that wasn't far, only a few miles, a tuna processing plant. Said he used to work there twenty some-odd years ago after he graduated high school, before he joined the navy. Before it was used for tuna, the military used it to manufacture bullets and other ordnance, so it didn't have any windows and it was secure.

Damn secure. It was close to the shore, though. I knew that was more than only a few miles. I was a surfer and took that route daily. It would take a good four hours to get there on foot at a strong pace and this was when some of the bats were hunting during the day, most likely because they were confused by their sudden transformation. Or maybe they were just so hungry because of it.

I agreed to go with Perry because he said he was in the navy and he sounded pretty confident in what he was talking about. It was better than staying in that school, that's for sure. I'm here to tell the story so you can see I made the right decision. Though it didn't come without sacrifice.

There was a girl with us named Claire. She was a high school senior with strawberry blonde hair and a splash of freckles across her forehead, a skinny thing who barely spoke and hunched into herself. So vulnerable. She was a big part of the reason I went with the new group, because her mother insisted on leaving with them, even though Claire was skittish about going out where the bats could get us. I talked with her a couple times in school, simple, quiet exchanges. She spoke too softly and quivered usually, as if cold, though I knew it was more than that, something deeper in the bones. I felt a connection with her, wanted to protect her, so I went.

There were ten of us at first. Victoria was Claire's mother. I hate to speak ill of the dead, but she wasn't cautious. She was the opposite of her daughter. When you told her to be careful or if you pointed out to her that something that didn't look right, she lashed out about minding your own business or shouted about how she didn't need to be treated as a child.

Like the gray ash. It was heavier back then, still falling, big, fat swirling snowflakes darkening the sun. With the rain it had thickened up into a muddy paste that caked up every crevice it could find. As we slogged our way toward the tuna plant, Victoria paused along a dead clover field. She cupped her hands and dipped them into a puddle surrounded by the ash-mud to refresh herself. Perry saw how much gray sludge circled it and he said to her, "I wouldn't trust that water if I were you. I think it's tainted."

Victoria squinted at him with contempt and spat, "If the option is to die of thirst or drink some tainted water, I'll take the water."

Perry said there would be water at the plant. We were halfway there already, but Victoria turned her back and drank her fill, then gave some to Claire, who was clearly squeamish about drinking it, but went on and did it anyway.

In the end, it wasn't the water that got her, or the bats. It was that character flaw, her inability to listen to the wisdom of others.

We left just after dawn, when we hoped the bats would be holed up from their mostly nocturnal activities. We took what the larger group allowed us to take, which was only a bit of water and one gun that was Perry's from the start anyway. The others weren't happy to see that gun go, but nobody was going to try to take it from Perry. We could have used the gun and demanded more, but like I said, it was early on and people thought differently back then.

We marched at a good pace, sticking close to structures when we could, though it was inevitable that we'd have to cross a couple larger fields, then travel along the highway to get to the plant. Being out in the open is when we were the most vulnerable. You could feel the tension throttling us all as we moved through those fields. We didn't encounter trouble until we were within a mile of the plant, angling just along the shoulder of the road over a highway bridge.

A single bat.

It wasn't even one of the bigger ones. It was only the size of a small black bear, under two hundred pounds, but it was fast. I was the first to see it. It must have been hanging from the girders below the bridge.

"Bat!" I shouted.

We huddled up to look bigger than we were individually, hoping to scare it off, but two of us panicked and took off running. Goran and his wife, Vesna, an older couple from Czechoslovakia visiting their now-dead daughter. It was Vesna first. I remember the blood draining from her face as Goran shouted after her to stop. When she didn't, he went after her. She was his wife. What was he supposed to do?

You can't outrun those things. The bat got to Goran quick, swooped down on him and dug its claws into his shoulders. It shot into the air and carried him screaming down below the bridge. We hurried away from those screams as fast as we could with only a mile left to go.

Adrenaline burned through my veins. It could have been any of us. But the bat came back. It must have killed or maimed Goran and stored him under the bridge, then decided to come back for more easy pickings. It went straight for Vesna as she was still separated from the group. She was an older lady who didn't run very fast. The bat soared up, then plunged atop her, crushing her under its weight. It held her there as she lay begging beneath its claws.

This was at the edge of a four-lane bridge. We had to pass the bat in order to move forward. There wasn't any choice. We inched along, our panicked, huddled group, with the beast's black eyes the size of softballs fixed on us, hungry. It clamped its jaws onto Vesna's thigh and ripped a chunk of flesh straight off the bone. Her scream still rings in my ears, and her last words.

Claire froze up and wouldn't move. I dragged her on her heels until Victoria brought her to her senses with a flat-handed slap.

As we passed Vesna, she shouted something in Czech. I don't know what she said to this day, but I know begging when I hear it in any language. I told Perry to shoot the thing. We could still save her, but Victoria got herself into Perry's ear.

"She's gone," she said. "We need to conserve bullets. Don't waste them on a woman who's already dead."

Perry's gun was out. I could see he was thinking about it. But he put the gun away and we just kept moving, despite the fact that she was still screaming. It killed me. That poor woman's screaming.

There were eight of us left. By the time we got to the tuna plant, Claire was half broken. She said she'd seen people killed by the bats, but nothing so grisly or so up close. So much blood. She wore the pain in her eyes, wrapped it around her like a robe. She was jumpy before, but she got much worse.

Victoria knew I couldn't stand her. She sensed it. Later, when I was alone with her, she told me, "You can't be weak in this world. We all have to make tough decisions."

"We could have saved that woman," I said.

She set herself, her eyes filled with contempt. "Shut up and save yourself."

I did my best to stay away from her after that, even though I know now she was right.

Perry busted a lock on the back door of the plant with a shovel. When we shoved ourselves inside, we barricaded the door and toured the place. It was just like Perry said, solid brick with reinforced steel. Parts of the building had been recently upgraded. You could tell by all the girders and the shiny equipment. And there were no windows. The only way the bats could get in would be through the two doors, one in front and one in back. I was surprised no one had found this place yet. They probably would soon enough. We'd have to defend it, but at that time, it was a great find.

That night I found Claire crying softly in the corner, so I settled next to her. Victoria wasn't with her, off searching through the many other rooms and corridors. The way she looked at me, I thought it was love at first. I think I wanted it to be love, but no. It was desperation. Mixed with terror. I think she was unhinged, or was just starting to be anyway.

"We found a good place," I told her. "You don't have to be so afraid."

She glared at me and her eyes wiggled in their sockets, searching for something from me.

"I've never heard a person scream like that," she said. "I thought maybe I could do something and I could save her. I couldn't do anything. I couldn't even move. It just ate her alive. She was still screaming when that thing ripped into her leg and then went for her throat. Can you imagine anything more horrible than being eaten?"

"Stop." I pulled her to me to comfort her, but she angled in and kissed me. Hard. It wasn't a sexual kiss. Again, it was that desperation exuding, that carnal fear, as if she was the one being eaten alive and I might somehow save her.

I held her that night. We didn't move until morning. She got better for a little while. Her mother wasn't happy, but Claire and I spent more time together from then on. We would sneak off into the main processing area, which was empty of anything useful. She crawled out of her shell bit by bit. The security of the tuna plant comforted her, at least a little. It went well for months.

Until the food ran out.

We ate through the small supply of canned tuna stored in the holding room and knew we'd have to start scavenging again. It was inevitable. I volunteered to search the outer area. Perry said he'd go with me. Victoria, too. Our first outing found nothing useful in any of the nearby buildings. It was frustrating because we had this secure location, though it didn't do any good if we couldn't eat. We'd starve to death if we didn't eat soon.

We ventured further out toward the coastline, and that's when we found the parking garage. I had a bad feeling about the place when I saw it straight off. It was dark inside, you could see it from the distance.

"We should check it out," Victoria said. "There might be something valuable inside the cars."

"I don't think that's a good idea," I said. "It's pitch black in there. If I was a bat, that's exactly where I'd want to sleep."

"There might be food. Water ..."

She started toward it.

Perry spoke up. "I think he's right. It doesn't look very safe ..."

Victoria listened to no one but herself. She marched toward it on her own with that look of defiance she wore so often.

"She's going to get someone killed," I told Perry, and he nodded.

"Yeah. Let's stick with her. For now. We shouldn't break up. But, hey, keep your eyes open, good?"

"Sure. Good."

We followed her from a good distance. I crept along the sidewalk across the street from the beach, clinging to the surf shops. I scoped out a townie bar across the way. It had a pelican painted on the cinderblock wall along with the word "saloon" in big, blocky letters. The door was cracked open. If anything went down, that was where I would run.

Victoria paused at the entrance of the parking garage and peeked up inside. She stood there a good while before finally tiptoeing in, then disappeared into the abyss of it. I wondered if I'd ever see her again. To be honest, I wouldn't have been disappointed if we didn't. We did, not twenty minutes later when the clapping of her shoes along the concrete came, echoing through the garage.

"Run!"

Three bats flew out after her. I didn't wait for anything. I sprinted straight for the saloon. Perry didn't take but a second to follow. I thought the bats had Victoria for sure when one of them knocked her down, but the three of them got to fighting over her. She managed to bounce back to her feet and made it to the saloon before they realized she'd gone.

"I told you not to go in there!" I shouted.

All she said was, "You can go to hell, you weak little man."

There wasn't any getting through to her.

"Listen," Perry said. "They'll sniff us out in here if we don't make a move fast. We have to go back to the plant. Now."

"I agree with Perry," Victoria said without a moment's hesitation.

I thought about it a second and said, "I don't think that's a good idea. They're fighting now but if they get a nose for three of us running, they'll be all over us."

Perry heard me but Victoria kept shaking her head, almost violently. "Stop with your negative bullshit, okay? If we stay here, we're dead. End of story."

"You're the one who brought them out of there," I said, but that was stupid because Victoria flipped me the bird and sprinted out the door.

"I'm not waiting around to die with you cowards."

Perry bolted after her. He was scared, I get it. So was I. It was a dumb decision and I knew it. I didn't want to be alone so I ran after them. Too bad I was right. It was the worst decision we could have made.

We made it back to the tuna plant. The whole time those three bats were circling over the buildings. I thought maybe they were waiting for the best time to strike. Turns out they were waiting to find our hiding spot. Bats are smart animals. Before long, they came to the door of the plant, the three of them. We fortified the door and truly the plant was damn secure, but those three bats never stopped trying to get in. Just when you thought maybe they'd given up, the door would clang as one of them slammed against it. We piled up heavy equipment, propped them with steel girders and locked ourselves in tight.

But now we were trapped, you see? We had no food. We still had water through the manual building pumps, but we had nothing to eat. We would die in there if we didn't figure something out. No one ate for a week. We were starving and desperate.

It was all because of Victoria. She brought them to our door and she refused to accept responsibility. She spun a different story to everyone else in the group to take the blame off herself. Even Perry was confused, but I knew the truth. I knew what really happened, and I didn't forgive her for it. Despite Claire.

Poor Claire. What happened next, it's difficult to think about without feeling ill. I'll just get to it.

I sat with Claire while Victoria paced an angry path around us. Claire's skin had gone pale. Some of her hair had begun to fall out in thin wisps.

"I'm hungry, Momma," she whispered.

Victoria slowed and a snarl curled into her upper lip. "Of course, you are," she growled. "Can't take care of yourself. Never could. You useless little whelp."

Claire sobbed. Victoria's burning eyes set on me.

"Why don't you ask your worthless new boyfriend to do something about it?" she said. "He hasn't done a damn thing for anyone here anyway."

My blood had been boiling. I'm usually good at keeping my emotions in check, but that was enough. I started to rise, but Claire surprised me by standing up to her mother first. She climbed to her feet, planted herself between us and shook her finger at her mother.

"Don't you dare take this out on him ..."

Victoria slapped her. Hard. There came a clacking echo of bone on bone.

Claire staggered back, gripping her cheek, her shocked eyes dripping tears. A rivulet of blood trickled from her lower lip.

"How in God's name did I bring someone so weak into this world?" Victoria shrieked and stormed off, her eyes wild with insanity.

She rambled on about food, thinking maybe there was something hidden in the back rooms.

"I already looked back there," I told her. "There's nothing but mechanicals and a bunch of old dust."

"Fuck off," she said as she marched off. "I didn't check it myself!"

"It's dangerous back there," I told her. "You shouldn't go wandering around alone. Perry said ..."

She cut me off. "Perry is an asshole, and you know what? So are you."

She left us. Claire watched her go. Claire was weak at that point. We all were. So I let her sleep. I watched Victoria. Eventually she wandered off into the darker areas of the tuna plant. Alone. This was after we all agreed not to. The machines were unmanned and getting old. They might be dangerous.

While Claire slept, I followed her. I don't know why. Maybe I had intentions to do something bad to her. I don't think I could have, but you never know what you're capable of doing when you're starving, with your stomach eating itself and your mind going wild with hunger.

I kept my distance. She disappeared through the main processing room with all the cutting machines, through the tunnel-shaped corridor, then into the room that housed the mechanicals. Heater, air conditioners, water filters.

And a big oven.

You've never seen an oven like this one, not like a kitchen oven. Perry said it was a steam oven used to process the tuna after they were canned. Workers would wheel in carts stacked with cans, close the door, then steam a batch for preserving. The oven was just over three feet high and at least twice as deep. A person could easily fit inside.

A person Victoria's size.

To this day I can still see her crawling in there. She spotted something inside, got down on her hands and knees and worked her way in, got about halfway, then settled onto her belly. I watched her the whole time, fascinated. I remember thinking this was a dangerous thing to do, but saying anything to her would have amounted to nothing.

She scissor kicked her legs back and forth to push her way further in, as if swimming, each time her calves and feet swinging. Her foot bumped the door latch. The door swung inward and banged against her heel. I thought for sure she would wiggle her way out, but I don't think she noticed. When she got far enough in, the door snapped shut.

For a moment there was no movement, no sound. Then a light came on inside the oven. Must have been automatic. Part of me knew what was going to happen. I could have stopped it, but I didn't. I could have opened the door and let her out, but it wasn't my fault she crawled in there, never listened to anyone, never had any common sense, slapped Claire like that, brought all those bats to the door.

I could have, but I didn't.

What I did was wrong. But it's over.

She screamed and kicked at the door. It did no good. She called for Claire, then Perry, then finally me. My name was the last name she cried out for. I wish she hadn't called for me because that's the hardest part of all this, hearing her say my name. It echoes in my head. That, and the final scream that comes only from excruciating pain as the oven clicked on and the burning steam gushed forth.

I crept away and huddled in the corner of the main room near the group. Claire eventually came to me. I held her and I told myself I wasn't a monster for what happened. Claire set her head on my chest. I felt her rise and fall as I breathed. It was the last pleasant thing I remember about her. We lay there for hours when she suddenly leaned up and gazed off into the darker innards of the plant.

"Do you smell that?" she asked.

"No."

"It smells like something ... sweet. Sickly sweet."

Then her stomach growled. So did mine. I smelled it, too. My god, my stomach lurched, it was so damn empty.

Soon everyone was up as the smell filled the entire plant. They followed it to the oven where they found Victoria inside, steamed to death, her warped fingers still clutching a can of unopened tuna. She had been cooked. The smell of her flesh wafted into the air. I would tell you it was her stench, but it wasn't a corpse stench at all. It was as Claire described it, sickly sweet.

I'll say it for what it was.

It was cooked meat. It was food. It was sustenance.

Grim, I know. I'll bet you the same thought went through all of our heads. It must have. How could it not?

But Claire.

When she realized it was her mother, she fainted into my arms. I steadied her. When she could finally hold herself up, she didn't scream or cry or make any sort of normal reaction, what you'd expect of her. She just stared at her mother a good long while, not moving at all.

That's when I knew she was broken for good.

Claire bent and plucked a piece of flesh from her mother's shoulder and set it into her mouth. She was never the same from then on. All of us ate that day. Every single one of us.

It got us through. Ironically, Victoria got us through.

I never saw Claire after that. We eventually left when the bats finally gave up at the door. We went our separate ways. Claire wouldn't leave. I begged her to go. She wouldn't listen. She refused to budge from that place which was now tainted. At least for me it was. I had to make a choice. Stay with her or leave. I chose to leave. She wouldn't speak, wouldn't do anything but wander through that building, an aimless ghost, haunting it.

Maybe she's still there. With that sickly sweet smell, forever in the air.

***

# Alien Ways
by Stephanie Barr

### *US: Extra-terrestrial science from a different point of view*

"Dr. Luchen! Dr. Luchen!"

Luchen, examining his strange specimen through the microscope—*imagine walls around the individual cells!*—did his best to ignore Keigel, the assistant of his fellow scientist, who was trying to squeeze in through the undersized door of Luchen's lab.

If Luchen's new research made it easy for him to ignore Keigel, his own assistant, Rel, was less immune to her pleas. "Dr. Luchen, I think Keigel is trying to get your attention."

"And?" Luchen's tone was pointed enough that Rel retreated, leaving a little puddle of ink, his pigment blanched several shades lighter than normal.

However, cowing Rel did not stop Keigel from entering his lab through the small hole that served their race, the Lungi, for doors. Luchen turned from his microscope in disgust. Keigel didn't cow worth a damn.

Keigel took a bit to get through the small hole, and she glared at Luchen with her single eye. "Why is your door so small? I can barely fit through it and I had to leave my pot behind."

"Stupid to still be attached to a pot. Are you a hatchling?" Luchen said, pulling himself up to his full height, some one and a half meters tall. He had to steady himself with his tentacles behind his back, but Keigel didn't have to know that. "And why should it matter to you what I'm doing or why I have a door small enough to keep the rabble out?"

137

Keigel, an oversized behemoth of a Lungi, regarded him blandly. Even in a casual stance, she stood several centimeters taller than Luchen, and Luchen still hadn't forgiven her for it. But arguing was dangerous since she'd already informed him she favored him as a mate. He couldn't afford to antagonize her. More than once, he'd considered sacrificing a tentacle to avoid becoming a possible meal.

"You do realize your camouflage gives away all your thoughts, Dr. Luchen. Hasn't anyone ever told you to watch that?"

They had, of course, but Luchen always forgot. "What are you here for, Keigel? Rel and I are doing delicate work here."

Keigel swung her oversized head around to regard Rel with her huge eye, where he still cowered in the corner but had almost regained his natural color. "I see," she said blandly. "Well, this is an emergency. Dr. Micen has been called away to his mother's eighteenth wedding and there's a problem with his specimen."

"I can't believe he left for another wedding. Why not offer the woman a tentacle and be done," Luchen muttered. When Keigel said nothing, he added, "She won't even miss that I'm not there, what with every other child she hatched dancing attendance. After all, she ate *my* father without even getting his particulars first."

Keigel smiled. "Sometimes a lady is just overcome by passion. However, that's a topic we can pursue another time. For now, we have a real crisis."

"I have specimens, too," Luchen said, gesturing to a wall bursting with greenery. "These creatures have walled cells and generate their own energy! I don't see why I have to interrupt my research to babysit my brother's when *he's* the one who abandoned it."

Keigel crept just a bit closer, her tentacles apparently excited based on the audible suction as they repositioned her on the floor, a side effect when one's brain is distributed throughout one's body. "Please?"

Luchen swallowed and edged away slightly. "What's wrong with the specimen?"

"It appears to be highly disturbed. The subject has been screaming and rampaging around its receptacle since it woke from our stun ray. We hoped leaving it alone would calm it down, but it started beating its body against the observation windows and forcing appendages through the door so we were forced to stun it again. I thought it had inked itself, but, upon examination, we realized it had compromised the integrity of its outer membrane and we had to make repairs."

"And what am I supposed to do about it? I know nothing about—what are they called?"

Keigel unearthed a clipboard from one of her folds and consulted it. "Dr. Micen called them 'humans.'"

"Great Belel, why? What a stupid name. What did my brother do to calm it down?"

"I'm not sure. This is a new specimen, barely picked up yesterday."

Luchen waved a tentacle dismissively. "Seems like it's not a suitable specimen. Take it back and get a fresh one, one less prone to self-harm."

Keigel did not retreat, which Luchen had expected. When the silence stretched long enough to send Rel shivering in his corner, Luchen prompted, "Well?"

"It seems that Dr. Micen has actually gone through a number of specimens in the past four remargs. Some were so violent toward us they had to be returned. Some were fragile and did not survive capture or subsequent captivity. Our sponsors, which are also *your* sponsors, explained that this was the last chance. They wanted a specimen that could be studied safely and," she checked her clipboard, "be resilient enough to return to the home world for display if necessary." She inhaled, inflating her size alarmingly, and let it out. "Dr. Micen assured our sponsors that he had carefully chosen this specimen after several more remargs of observation and that he was confident that this was the right specimen. And sent pictures."

Luchen rolled his single eye. "Of course, he did. And then trotted off to his mother when she crooked a suction cup."

"Dr. Micen stressed this specimen *must* survive using any means necessary or the entire project, his and yours, Dr. Luchen, may be pulled: supplies, equipment, even this space station."

Luchen could feel his pigment darkening but he was past caring. "He left his specimen in a vulnerable state when he knew his research—and mine—was riding on it? Without even telling me?"

"He left a brief note for you, but I can never read his handwriting."

She held up the clipboard and Luchen snatched it out of her tentacle. Sure enough, Micen had scrawled something all but illegible on a scrap of membrane probably torn from some report. Luchen, however, had not been siblings with Micen for seventy-eight blarnans for nothing and, after a moment's concentration, made out the single word: "Sorry."

What Luchen wanted to do was throw the clipboard on the floor, tear it to bits with his tentacles, demand the others exit his lab, and crawl under a counter to pout in peace. But, he was a professional. Albeit, at this moment, a nonplused one. With forced calm, he returned the clipboard. "And what, exactly, am I to do to secure this specimen? It seems unrealistic to keep it stunned for the next few remargs until Dr. Micen gets back. And," he gestured to his wall of delightful greenery, "as you can see, I'm not an expert in *animate* specimens."

Keigel brightened considerably at the opening. "Dr. Micen left copious notes!"

Luchen shook his head, then relaxed his stance to ensure blood was getting to every tip of his brain. "Then follow his instructions and deal with the problem yourself."

"I would, but I can't read them."

Luchen allowed himself a tiny sigh. "Of course. Very well, let's go. Rel, you come, too, in case I need something fetched ... unless my brother organized his lab since I last visited?"

"'Fraid not."

Luchen waited impatiently for her to squeeze her bulk through the tiny hole. If there was a lot of traffic, he'd have to invest in hole enlarging, he decided. How irksome!

He slid through without problems, though he noticed she left a bit of pheromone trail. Distracting.

She grabbed her tiny pot—she must actually have become attached as a hatchling—and made quick time to Micen's lab where the larger entrance allowed her to slip in easily, pot and all. Luchen followed after he saw that Rel was, indeed, following them.

Luchen glanced around at the cluttered tables, the scattered notebooks, then screwed up his courage and maneuvered himself to the large observation window.

The specimen was nearly his own size, he judged, at least by mass, but it appeared to be more rigid even in repose. There were strange filaments, deeply pigmented, growing as a mass at the top of an undersized head which also featured a pair of eyes, a naked soft mouth, and other holes and protuberances he couldn't identify. The creature was limited to four appendages, devoid of suction cups, attached to a disproportionately large body. The outer membrane of the creature was sheathed in garments made of a flimsy material that hid most of the body of the creature, leaving only the head and appendages uncovered. Membrane healing strips were wrapped around the smaller appendages and the strange grasping element at the end of one of them. Its membrane was quite pale, clearly traumatized.

He could see the creature was not an exoskeleton as some of the lower lifeforms of his home world were, but its very definition of shape argued that it had some sort of stiffening agent within. Perhaps air baffles.

Luchen stifled a sigh. The thing was hideous. "How long until it wakes up?"

Keigel said, "We estimate another half wevel."

Luchen squelched his way to the think tank and dunked himself. The Lungi had long ago adapted themselves to land living, but there was something soothing about immersion that remained with them. "Bring me the notes."

Keigel, sheepish for the first time, brought a mishmash of stray membranes and half-filled notebooks. Luchen swallowed his snark and thanked her. After all, he knew the state of the notes were hardly her doing.

The actual information within the notes was as haphazardly documented as the notes themselves. And, as usual, all but illegible. Clearly, Micen had been excited with his research. Luchen was quite aware of the passage of time and struggled to make sense of his brother's scrawl and disjointed notations.

Keigel had taken to pacing with Rel wringing his tentacles and sneaking peeks at the specimen when Luchen demanded a fresh notebook.

"What do we do, Dr. Luchen?" Keigel asked. "The specimen could wake up at any time."

"There are many notes about what seems to be trivialities, and, to be honest, I doubt anyone could make sense of most of it except my brother. But this, this keeps coming up. Apparently, humans need frequent physical contact to maintain their calm." As Luchen spoke, he was writing on the notebook at the same time.

"Physical contact? You mean mating?"

"Apparently not, though, from his notes, it appears that they mate for pleasure. But they have all kinds of non-mating contact with others of their own kind, from friendly contact with strangers, to affection, even quite effusive contact, for children or elders, and frequent cuddling with animal companions."

Luchen dragged himself from the tank, notes neatly transcribed on several notebook pages. "As humans also appear quite willing to do violence with each other, I think it's too risky to pull another human specimen from the surface. We have no idea if they will comfort each other or, in fact, do harm, so we must find an animal companion. Apparently, there are many options, though creatures called 'dogs' and 'cats' seem to garner the most contact."

"Ah. But, Dr. Luchen, the specimen will wake up any minute."

"Yes. Well, I think it would be best if you, Keigel, were to go in with the specimen as an interim companion, comfort the specimen whilst I go down to the surface and try to find an animal companion, a—" he consulted his brother's notes, "pet."

Keigel regarded her own sprawling tentacles of dark purple before returning her gaze to Luchen. "I think my dark pigment and much larger size would frighten the specimen. Could you send in Rel?"

Rel blanched almost white and began to tremble. Luchen sighed. "Rel has barely the fortitude to handle plant specimens." He waited a few beats for other options to be presented, before he realized the silence was expectant. "You want *me* to go in with the specimen?"

"You are much closer to its size," Keigel offered, "and a comforting pink color."

"Why would pink be a comforting color?"

Rel, relieved that he was not to go, looked up at that. "Because pink is closer to the specimen's color."

"We know nothing of their mating habits. What if it decides to consume me?"

Keigel waved that aside with a flick of her tentacle. "It seems unlikely. Did Dr. Micen mention consumption of mates in the notes?"

"No."

"Well, and if it does seem amorous, you can leave it a tentacle and retreat. Since it has internal structures, it cannot exit from the room using the same holes we can."

Luchen did not find the idea appealing, but the specimen was making movements as if close to waking and he didn't have a better idea. He blew out a hard breath, pushing himself a few centimeters across the floor. "Fine. But you must return as quickly as possible."

Keigel took a moment to glance through Luchen's notes. "There are several animals here, but very little by way of description."

"Take it up with Dr. Micen. He noted that dogs required large tracts with which to relieve themselves. Given the size of the station, I would limit myself to small dogs. Cats, apparently, can use a small receptacle filled with sand. You might want to bring some back. Since we don't know the specimen's preferences and it appears dogs vary greatly in size and appearance, I would bring back several."

Keigel nodded. "Should I take Rel with me?"

Luchen was already starting to squish himself through the hole. "Not if you want to be successful. Rel is afraid of everything. Rel, prepare some sample receptacles in the unused lab so we can keep the creatures in comfort."

"Yes, Dr. Luchen," Rel said and scuttled away.

"Try to be swift, Keigel," Luchen added and slipped into the specimen's area. It was large enough, he supposed and he could see the seam around the window that allowed the creature to be brought in. The walls had some scratching and some smears of dark red. If that

142

was from the damage noted earlier, that should be cleaned up. Even he found the desperate marks unnerving and he was a scientist.

The specimen moaned and moved a bit in its sleep. Luchen debated climbing atop the specimen to maximize the physical contact, but the notes had been adamant that full body contact was not common with strangers. Nor was it hard to imagine the reaction of a creature waking up face to face with an eye the size of its own head.

"Computer," Luchen called out, deciding to wait beside the specimen's couch and encase the specimen's own grasping extension with his tentacle, "have you been learning the human language?"

"I have been programmed with available vocabulary," the computer answered through the overhead speaker. "The current level of understanding is at stage minus four, so there are only occasional words I can translate."

"Listen and add to your vocabulary as you can. This will go much more smoothly with communication."

The computer answered tonelessly, "Yes, Dr. Luchen."

The specimen responded to the sound of the speaker by opening its small eyes, then reaching for its head with its other grasping appendage, which was covered in membrane bandages. This appeared to startle the creature who sat up abruptly, noted Luchen's contact with its grasping appendage, and commenced screaming.

The specimen had remarkable lung capacity and could generate sound at a surprisingly high frequency.

As he had no better option, Luchen maintained his hold on the specimen and added stroking with another tentacle in hopes to calm the creature down. The screaming made way too loud a chattering in a tongue far less mellifluous than his own. The creature tried to retract its appendage, at first with minimal force, and then by putting its full weight against it, attempting to pry off Luchen's hold with its other grasping appendage.

Contact was the only clue Luchen had, so he persisted, his suction easily withstanding the creature's resistance.

"Hand appears to be the word for the appendage," the computer said. "'Let go my hand.' "

"Hand," Luchen repeated. "Please forgive me," he said in his own language. "I cannot allow you to harm yourself."

To his surprise, the creature stopped fighting and stared at him with its tiny eyes. "Hand," chatter, chatter, chatter, "hand."

Luchen pulled back on the force of his suction cups and used the back of his stroking tentacle to continue its soothing movement. "Computer, what other human words do you know?"

"Human?" the specimen said. With its free hand placed on its torso, the human said, "Human."

Ah. It was trying to communicate with him. Very good. He took one of his tentacles not otherwise engaged and indicated his head. "Lungi."

"Lungi," the human parroted with a fair approximation of the sounds. Then it resumed chattering, pointing occasionally at the room, itself and him.

"Computer, have Rel return as soon as he can." The human was clearly trying to communicate, so he did the same. "Hand," he said, touching its hand with a free tentacle, then touching one of his own tentacles and giving it his word for tentacle. By the time Rel returned, panting in his haste through the intercom, Luchen had identified words for most of the human's body parts, including the odd protuberances on its torso—the only time the human treated him to violence by slapping his tentacle away—and had taught the adept tongue of the human several words of his own language.

Luchen set Rel to sketching various objects of everyday use in a notebook while he took the human specimen on a tour of its room and identified several other objects. "Computer, how long has Dr. Micen been studying humans? It seems incredible that he had not increased the language database before now. How much have I increased your existing vocabulary database?"

"Seven Remargs. You have more than doubled the existing vocabulary."

"Ridiculous! These creatures are far more sentient than he documented. They may even break the threshold for the Law Against Abduction of Sentient Aliens."

The computer said nothing, for which he couldn't blame it.

Luchen would have to take it up with his brother. For now, the creature seemed intent on learning and teaching, very healthy signs, but he was running out of items to name. It suddenly pointed to itself, between its protuberances, and stated, "Ana."

Ana? Was this another name for human? He indicated himself and said, "Lungi," but it shook its head, clearly a negation.

"Ana," it repeated then touched the slick surface of his head lightly, the first contact it had voluntarily made.

Names! Humans had names! Definitely, his brother had made a mistake. "Luchen," he said, and was rewarded with a flash of teeth. He pulled back in case it was an indication of imminent attack, but it made no other aggressive moves.

Rel slid the notebook through the hole and Luchen tugged his human's grasping appendage to get close enough that he could retrieve it. He wasn't sure if he should be gratified or concerned that the

144

human was now grasping his tentacle voluntarily. The notebook had quite credible pictures. Rel might be neurologically deficient, given his cowardice, but his sketching was first rate. Other than his fear, he was an excellent aide.

As Luchen flipped through the well-drawn sketches, Ana pointed to the ones that it recognized and provided a name. He would then respond with its name in his language. To test whether the human was absorbing the vocabulary, he ran through again and prompted, with its word, see if it would respond with his. It caught on immediately and showed an excellent recall ability. As he closed the notebook, confident that Ana had been calmed, it stroked a tentative hand over his head, shuddered and then covered its face with its hands, collapsing on its bench.

Unsure what to make of this new development, he pried one of the hands away and saw Ana's face was red, its small eyes leaking saline, and its breath coming in labored gasps. He didn't understand how he knew, but he realized the creature was in the midst of some kind of despair. Keeping contact with its hand, the pressure gentle rather than confining, he couldn't think of what to do, so he channeled one of the few memories he treasured from when he was a small hatchling. He began to croon a soft lullaby, knowing Ana would not understand the words but hoping the comforting nature would come through just as Ana's pain had come through to him.

The hitched breaths calmed, the escaping saline drying on the creature's desiccated outer membrane. Eventually, the eyes closed again and Ana slept.

Luchen waited for a bit longer after Ana's breathing had stilled before he left, feeling somewhat sobered.

Capture of a sentient being was illegal and apt to get their funding cut, but that wasn't what concerned him most. There was a connection he felt at the sound of its name, at soothing its pain, that enthralled him as dissecting plants had never done. He wanted to know more about this human, wanted to make it happy. And that was far more confounding than his brother, once again, screwing up.

*

Luchen had to give Keigel credit. She was thorough. When she returned from her trip to the alien planet's surface, she'd brought back nearly a dozen creatures of various natures, shapes, and sizes. All fit Micen's written criteria in that they were land-based and had at least four legs.

"Which ones do you think are dogs?" he asked her.

"Not sure. But I brought some sand. We might be able to identify the cat by seeing who uses it for defecation."

Luchen nodded. "Good idea. Several of these seem unusually noisy, namely that one, that one, and that one," he noted three creatures of diverse appearance except that they were all covered with filaments of various pigmentation and all made a loud, sharp repetitive noise that he found grating on him in only a few minutes. "Let's separate them from the others. They may be an acceptable animal but let's try these others first. I would think that noise would be anything but comforting."

"Yes, though, they can be quite affectionate when they aren't making noise. They used some appendage internal to their mouths to stroke me when I crooned to them."

"Perhaps they were testing your taste?" Luchen said.

"Hmm," Keigel noted, clearly finding the creatures in question more appealing than Luchen did. "Well, whatever. Which one of the others should we try first? Perhaps the smallest one?"

Luchen examined the animal askance. The creature was indeed too small to be the slightest threat, and yet ... "It doesn't seem well suited for, er, cuddling, does it?"

The creature waggled its antennae and fluttered its wings briefly in response, apparently insulted.

"Well, it looks like prey to me, only smaller," Keigel said frankly. "Maybe a snack will put the specimen in a better mood. Look, even Rel isn't afraid of it."

"Stop, Rel, no eating the experiments," Luchen said, recognizing Rel's stalking technique. "All right, this one first."

After several experiments, each of which required Luchen to hurriedly enter and soothe Ana—after swift removal of the potential pet—Luchen deduced that four was not only the minimum number of legs but also the maximum. The next pet planned was covered with filaments which should make it more attractive for contact and was comfortably sized at some eighteen centimeters across, but, with eight legs, Luchen decided not to chance it.

Ana had also managed to convey her hunger—he deduced she was female from some questions he had posed to her through pictures and sign—and that she was not comfortable with eating live prey. Micen had obtained a plethora of human foodstuffs in dry form or encased in metal canisters. Once Ana had convinced him to provide a device capable of opening the metal canisters and given her desalinated water—determined through trial and error—they seemed to have formed a rapport and, in fact, she touched him in what he thought was a friendly manner whenever he entered now.

He found it surprisingly endearing.

He regarded the remaining animals, trying to use his growing understanding of the human to choose among the remainder. One creature was fairly large, nearly a meter in length, but squat. As it had scales rather than filaments covering its body and a disproportionate percentage of its body was made up of teeth, Luchen decided against it. Another was properly covered with fur, except for along bare tail, but it was unfriendly and prone to attack. The last, the only animal who had buried its waste in the sand, so he assumed it was a cat, was also quite small—not quite a kilo in weight and appeared both fluffy and undernourished with eyes of dark blue. He had offered it the remains of his own meal and the creature had eaten it with relish and daintiness.

When its belly was rounded, the creature tripped forward with neither aggression nor fear, rubbed its entire body along one of his tentacles, curled into a ball next to it, and commenced with a low harmonic rumble he found as soothing as he'd found the staccato calls of the other animals irksome.

With care, he scooped the small creature up in his tentacles and carried it gingerly to the human's room. Ana was seated on the floor in the corner, her arms wrapped around her—er—legs in an attitude of misery. "Ana," he said softly, hiding the creature—cat he hoped—behind him, "will you be introduced to one more animal?"

"No, please," both words Luchen knew and then a string he did not except for "bug" and more no's.

"Please," he said instead, hopeful to have stumbled on the right animal at last.

"One," she agreed and lifted her head. When she saw the creature in his tentacles, she held her hands out, cupped eagerly. When the animal was placed in her hands, she immediately cuddled it close to her chin, pressed against the same protuberances—breasts—she'd slapped him for touching.

She said the word "kitten" several times so Luchen wondered if this were still another animal and asked "cat?" while touching it.

Ana indicated with hand gestures that "kitten" was the name for a diminutive cat. Interesting. Not long after she started cuddling the animal, she rested in a position not unlike the one she was in when he came in, only with a rumbling kitten pressed against her body. She was still, and yet he did not sense the misery that she had before.

"Dr. Luchen, do you think the subject is in some sort of remission? She seems to be reverting to her withdrawn state," Keigel asked over the intercom.

Luchen noted the saline leaking from Ana's undersized eyes, her cheek up against the soft animal. "No, Keigel. We have found her pet."

*

When Dr. Micen returned from a lavish event where his mother held court with a huge phalanx of her own progeny—though she complained bitterly about Luchen's absence ... again—he was unsure what to expect. He did expect, as he saw at once, that Luchen had organized his lab. Honestly, even without an excuse, Micen had left for a remarg or two a few times in the past to force his tidy brother to straighten his lab and make sense of his documentation.

What he had *not* expected was that the enclosure containing his specimen would be open and empty of said specimen. Perhaps, even Luchen had not been able to keep the creature alive, though he dreaded the call to his sponsors. Keigel was absent as well. "Computer, where is Dr. Luchen?"

"In his lab."

Of course he was. Damn fool was married to his research. Wouldn't even break away to soothe the heart of the mother who brooded over his egg and cared for him as a hatchling.

The normally tiny hole Luchen affected had been widened to unprecedented size so Micen entered with no effort for once. If Micen had been surprised to find his own enclosure empty, he was completely unprepared for the collection of individuals in his brother's lab. Oh, it was tidy, of course, and the plants Luchen had gathered so lovingly were healthy and green on the far wall under artificial light. Keigel rested in the think tank, already showing signs of pregnancy with Rel nearby, his tentacles tangled with hers. Was Rel missing a tentacle? But to see Luchen, two tentacles grasped in the mandibles of the human subject, lurching to music at the prompting of the same human—well, Micen nearly inked himself.

"What is going on?" he demanded.

The human jerked in surprise and slid immediately behind Luchen while maintaining its hold on one of his tentacles. Luchen did not try to inflate his size—as he was wont to do given Micen was larger—but instead stroked the human's hand in a sustaining manner.

"Micen, you're back. Finally," Luchen said with neither affection nor joy. He managed to turn his large head and added, "Ana, he won't hurt you. I won't let him."

When Luchen turned back, Micen was amazed to see the human stroke Luchen's head.

Micen found his pigmentation changing without his conscious volition but he was past caring. "Why is my specimen walking freely? What have you done with my specimen?"

"She is sentient, Micen. To have her as a specimen or a prisoner is against the law."

Micen shook his head, fighting rage. "They can't be sentient. Have you seen the reports of the individual they elected their leader?"

"Whatever humans as a whole may be like, she is sentient, far more so than you imagined."

Ana chattered to him in her strange tongue and Micen was further shocked when Luchen answered in the same language. Luchen returned his attention to Micen. "She has agreed to stay with us, as she says she leaves nothing behind, but not as a prisoner. She is another of my lab assistants. And she will not be going 'on display' to the home world."

Micen lifted himself on his tentacles and marched forward only to be halted with Keigel's "Watch out for the cat!"

He paused and a fuzzy striped creature puffed itself up and then hissed, before fleeing to stand behind his specimen. Micen narrowed his eye and strode to where he stood towering over Luchen, who didn't so much as blanch. "We won't have funding for your lab without a display specimen."

"You won't have a lab or a license if you're found to have broken the law," Luchen said evenly. "And I already made a call to Mother whose new husband has agreed to fund my lab at twice the rate previously."

"You didn't!"

"I did. Her new husband seems quite the decent fellow though, of course, Mother put in a good word for me."

Micen found himself deflating a bit and added sulkily, "Mother always did love you best."

"Yes. Well, I don't kiss her suction cups."

"The specimen should still be with me." Micen hated the whine in his voice.

"My name is Ana," the human said in passable Lungi. "No touch me. I stay with Luchen."

This time, Micen did ink himself. After he'd recovered his composure, he said, "But what will I tell the other sponsors?"

"If you insist on touring the home world with specimens on display—which I don't advise—there are several animals in the spare lab you can take that don't quite meet the standards for sentience, though the dogs come close. But be careful. They lick."

"They *what?*"

***

# Her Right-Hand Man
by Teresa Twomey

### *US: Planetary ambassadors handle prejudice and civil upheaval*

As Mrs. Jones steered their craft toward a VIP slot, she glanced at her husband. His grim expression told of trials and suffering. The years in Pollux had been grueling for him. Her gaze drifted to the stump where his right hand had been. Reaching across the console, she took his left hand in hers. As he turned toward her, she saw love in his smile and sorrow in his eyes. Heroism takes a toll.

Several Polluxians noticed them as they waited for the portal to open. They rushed over, waving and shouting, nearly surrounding the small craft. Mrs. Jones's lips stretched into a tight smile as she waved back. Delivering a speech was easy for her, but even after decades of dealing with fame, the adulation of crowds in informal settings made her uneasy. Mr. Jones did not wave. A natural righty, he feared he would accidentally wave his stump.

*

A Polluxian clad in bright red motioned the Joneses to their seats on the stage. Mrs. Jones recognized the extraordinarily beautiful visage of JoVance, the second in command. As Mr. Jones took a seat, Mrs. Jones sat to his left, snuggling between him and the substantial bulk of JaBob, the supreme minister. She turned to JaBob and nodded a hello. The cheering and clapping of over a hundred thousand Polluxians made conversation impossible, but when JoVance approached the podium, they immediately fell silent.

"Greetings and positive energy to you all," Mrs. Jones heard JoVance's voice boom through the enormous auditorium.

In accord with the call-and-response tradition of the Polluxians, the crowd thundered, "A glorious day to you!"

As usual, Mrs. Jones wondered if, even after decades of small improvements, there were nuances that her cochlea translator failed to decipher.

"We are here today to celebrate the twentieth anniversary of our Scaeva Equality Laws. And, to inaugurate the latest concession, the Partum and Succipio laws. These laws reward and sustain those whose work enriches Pollux as much as any other, and yet for too many years, for too many Polluxians, this work has led to deprivation and insolvency." JoVance paused, anticipating the crowd's response.

Joining her voice with the thousands of Polluxians, Mrs. Jones intoned what JaBob had declared as "The New Maxim."

"Those whose work enriches Pollux will be rewarded for their efforts."

With a shout, JaBob punched his right fist into the air, "Aequitatis!"

Raising right hands, clenched or unclenched, the crowd roared "Equality" in return.

Glancing at Mr. Jones, who sat with his elbows tucked close to his side and his left hand lying motionless in his lap, Mrs. Jones once again noted the irony that the person who inspired and fought so hard for these new laws had no right hand to raise in celebration.

When the crowd settled, JoVance began the now-familiar litany. "As you all know, the very persons to whom we owe these advancements now sit before you. Yes, it took two unusual Earthlings to lead us on this path ..."

As rumbles of applause punctuated JoVance's speech, Mrs. Jones thought back to when it all began almost fifty years before, when she and Mr. Jones arrived on the planet Manux in the region of Pollux ...

*

According to one legend, on the day of their arrival, two right-handed Polluxians lay entangled on the sand, playing thumb war and laughing softly as the surf lapped at their feet. It was an overcast day, with red clouds hanging low and heavy, threatening to burst. Thunder rippled like a gong. The beachgoers turned their heads and smiled at the menacing sky. They were grateful for the turn in the weather. It gave them this rare opportunity for a romantic interlude away from prying eyes.

High above them, above where the clouds faded from red to soft lavender, the Joneses' spaceship began its descent. On it, Mr. Jones turned to his co-pilot. He reached to his right and clasped her hand in his own.

"Are you ready to be the first married couple to pioneer a virgin planet?" he asked.

Silver glints from the dashboard reflected in Mrs. Jones's eyes. "Yes, Mr. Jones, I am," she replied, giving his hand a squeeze in return. "Twenty-one years of marriage and twenty-one record firsts." Extending her index finger, she gently rotated Mr. Jones's wedding band. "I don't know of any other couple who can claim that."

\*

Mrs. Jones was well aware of the legend. Her memory of it, however, was a little different. For example, it was she who'd reached to her right and asked if Mr. Jones was ready, and it was he who'd made the comment about the years of marriage. It did not matter to her. She understood the public's desire to make Mr. Jones the focal point of the story. Sometimes it felt right—that being the star was all he had left. In reality, there had been no star, no power plays between them. Those from Earth had evolved beyond social status based on categories of difference such as race and sex.

\*

Seeking some spiritual solitude as she sat on the stage awaiting her turn to speak, Mrs. Jones sank into a reverie of memory. She and Mr. Jones had shared their story so many times that she knew his memories as well as her own. Her powers of concentration allowed her to see the events of those first few days unfold, as if happening in the eternal present.

With a blink, she's back in the cockpit of their spacecraft as they descend to Manux.

\*

Mrs. Jones turns to her right and clasps Mr. Jones's hand in her own. "Are you ready to be the first married couple to pioneer a virgin planet?"

Silver glints from the dashboard reflect in Mr. Jones's eyes. "Yes, Mrs. Jones, I am," he gives her hand a squeeze in return. "Twenty-one years of marriage and twenty-one record firsts." Extending his index finger, he gently rotates Mrs. Jones's wedding band. "I don't know of any other couple that can claim that."

"I have no doubt there *are* other couples, probably some on every planet." She places a finger on his as he continues to rotate her ring.

"We'll have to check with the Polluxians," Mr. Jones chuckles. "They've indicated a culture remarkably similar to our own. Perhaps they have a couple with, say, an overly ambitious and competitive wife and her good-humored sidekick of a husband who is happy to ride on her coattails."

Mrs. Jones lightly punches Mr. Jones's shoulder. "Oh, come on, that is an exaggeration!"

"Oh?" Mr. Jones doesn't think his wife can deny that she is an overly competitive person. He doesn't actually mind. He admires and is grateful for her courage and ambition. It has helped them gain the accolades they both desire. He's always been far too passive to pursue lofty goals on his own.

With a suppressed laugh that comes out as a grunt, Mrs. Jones says, "Of course. You are not *always* good humored, you know."

Mr. Jones smiles, glad not to have to argue his point. "Yes, I know," he replies in an obsequious tone that he knows delights and humors his wife.

The pair of Earthlings laugh together in that unselfconscious way of the long-married.

Mrs. Jones reaches over the small console that divides them. Her hand lightly touches his shoulder and lingers there. "You will always be my right-hand man."

It is their oldest endearment. The first time they met, she was the more experienced pilot, so she'd taken the dominant controls on the left side of the cockpit. She'd been impressed by his skills. When they'd finished the exercise and exited the craft, she'd casually remarked, "I wish you could always be my right-hand man." Every time they recount the tale, he insists she was flirting, and she insists it was just a compliment. Then, invariably, she will snuggle against him and say, "I'm so glad I got my wish."

As he turns to kiss the hand on his shoulder, it occurs to Mr. Jones to remark to Mrs. Jones how delighted he feels to be so well matched. He decides against it. He doesn't want her to make a cutting remark about how fortunate he is to have her. It isn't that she would actually mean it. It is just that sometimes their banter has more of an edge than he would wish. However, those are little things, he reminds himself, repeating his personal relationship mantra: *Be grateful to have met someone who is so completely complementary in every way.*

"Mary Poppins."

"What?" Mr. Jones asks, wondering if Mary Poppins is a code word that he has forgotten.

"Mary Poppins," Mrs. Jones repeats. "You just muttered 'completely complementary in every way.' It sounded just like Mary Poppins."

Mr. Jones feels disoriented and disconcerted to find that he has actually verbalized his thoughts. He wonders how much he'd actually said. With a tremor in his voice, he asks, "I actually spoke? I mean, out loud?"

"Why yes, dear." Mrs. Jones says with a practiced, clipped British accent, a carryover from playing Mrs. Banks in their high school production. "When you speak, it is always out loud."

Although he knows that the superior tone in his wife's voice is only a carryover from her acting days, it annoys him.

An uncomfortable silence engulfs the small craft as it glides through the reddening mist. Mrs. Jones realizes something has disturbed her husband, but is not sure what. Wishing to distract him from his worries, she drops her voice to a sultry level. "So, we have some time to kill ... just the two of us ... alone."

Mr. Jones isn't in the mood. "Let's go over the packing list instead." Before they left Earth, they'd recited their packing list so many times it had become an almost hypnotic relaxant for him. Unfortunately, his suggestion reminds him of the one item that had not been on the list, his wife's favorite chocolates. That omission led to a last-minute three-hour trek on the day of departure. "Just do without them," he'd suggested, adding, "our nano-capsules will supply all the needed filaments for our body-repair bots and all our daily nutritional needs other than caloric. Anything more is just wasteful indulgence." Still, she had insisted that they go and retrieve them. Unfortunately, unlike most basic food replicas available on the spacecraft which would be created via a caloric construction printer, these chocolates were "authentic foods" and only available on the coast or through special delivery.

He smirks as he thinks, *they are so special you forgot to order them*. On one level, he understands. U.S., Inc. provided lists of tasks to accomplish and items to pack. It was easy to overlook a non-necessity. Because of their unscheduled trek, however, they did not have time to have dinner at Robust Roberta's—Mr. Jones's favorite restaurant. In his opinion, Roberta's serves the best, freshest Petri-pork and has the most interesting sauces. Print versions of pork and sauces simply cannot compete.

Mr. Jones begins to recite the packing list, starting with the omission. He cannot disguise the disdain that creeps into his voice when he asks, "Have you brought enough of your *special* chocolates to last the full ten years?"

As soon as he begins the question, Mrs. Jones knows where he is going. It is a familiar complaint. She does a quick mental calculation and determines that Mr. Jones has brought this up at least nineteen times—which averages to one for each week of their journey to Manux.

"Oh no!" she exclaims, hands over her mouth and eyebrows raised dramatically in a pantomime of alarm. "Probably not. So, I guess we'll just have to turn around and go back and get more. While we're at it, maybe we should pick up an extra tube of nano-paste for our teeth as well. Oh, and maybe some more shampoo in case I decide to let my hair grow long again. Anything else? We don't want to have to turn around more than once."

Ignoring her sarcasm, Mr. Jones turns his attention to the panel in front of him. Smacking his leg with his hand, he grumbles, "When are those darn Polluxes going to send the signal?"

"Polluxians," his wife corrects him. "They wish to be called Polluxians."

"Right, I forgot you'd asked about that when you were working on coding the translators." Searching for the sense of contentment that he'd had earlier, Mr. Jones smiles at his wife and asks, "So *do* you think any of the Polluxians have a tradition of couples competing to set records for firsts?"

Mrs. Jones gives him a grateful smile. Their bickering has become like seasoning, sprinkled throughout each day. Knowing Mr. Jones will be amused, she draws the corners of her mouth down in an exaggerated frown and tightens her throat to make a high nasal sound. "You will not get answers to questions you do not think to ask."

Mr. Jones giggles, "She might have been an old prune, but Professor Candless knew pretty much everything there was to know about extraterrestrial communications."

"Yes, that and engineering," Mrs. Jones adds. Her voice becomes nasally again, "If you build a craft to fit only one type of person, only one type of person will use the craft."

Mr. Jones nods, recalling a fiasco from several years back. "Like the Gigas from Tine! I can't believe they didn't ask something so fundamental when they built the embassy for them."

"Yes," Mrs. Jones agrees. "Moving them to a building to accommodate twelve-foot tall beings was difficult, but doable."

"But those beds! Do you remember what Jack said about that?" Mr. Jones chuckles at the memory.

Mrs. Jones laughs along with him, completing the anecdote, "They had to sleep on their backs with their feet on the ground."

Nearly snorting with laughter, Mr. Jones prompts another memory, "Do you remember what Jack said to them?"

Nearly unable to speak through her laughter, Mrs. Jones replies, "That everyone makes mistakes. We're only human."

"And the Gigas leader told her partner to note that down, 'Because they are human they make mistakes.'" Mr. Jones smirks. "As if that distinguished humans from every other life form."

"Jack thought it would spread all over the galaxy as the defining description of humans."

"So, he changed the intergalactic dictionary to define human as 'sentient beings with the capacity to govern!'"

"Oh, what a brouhaha that caused," Mrs. Jones gleefully adds with a snort.

They laugh until, with a sober tone, Mr. Jones muses, "I wonder if we will ever see the Gigas again."

Mrs. Jones does not reply. Her attention constricts as they emerge from the clouds. She scans the surface of Manux, searching for their landing location.

Mr. Jones relaxes, confident in Mrs. Jones's mastery. With little else to do during the landing, he mentally refreshes his knowledge of the Polluxians of Manux. He ticks off characteristics he feels are most important: a naming system that includes both a surname and a given name for most of the people; mating with their "opposite" for life; language; currency; worship of singular Divinity, and a structured, non-violent means to determine succession of leaders. Although the Polluxians are relatively primitive, evidenced by the fact that they haven't developed the technology to scan or project images, Mr. Jones feels confident that they will be more alike than different. After all, they are bipedal carbon-based lifeforms living in an oxygen-rich atmosphere.

In preparation for the trip, the Joneses and two assistants developed wearable two-way translators that automatically translate Polluxian words into the Unified Earth Language. He knows the Polluxians have developed similar devices in Polluxish for themselves. He smiles as he suddenly recalls learning that they even exchange "narrow, hollow, circular discs" when pledging themselves in union for life. "Symbolizing unity and protection within the circle" was how their primary contact, Rotal Snart, put it. It is a small detail, but it makes Mr. Jones feel a certain warm camaraderie, a sense that they are, no matter how they might appear, more alike than different. Mr. Jones had never before felt so completely prepared to meet an undercivilized group of alien beings.

*

Twelve Polluxians stand with stiff formality a few yards from the perimeter of the landing pad as Mrs. Jones expertly settles the shuttle into place.

The Joneses emerge from the craft, hand in hand. It surprises them to see how human the Polluxians look. It reminds Mrs. Jones of an old *Twilight Zone* episode where astronauts land on what they presume to be the moon, but it is only a desert on Earth. Mr. Jones immediately notices the uniform androgyny of the Polluxians. As he scans the gathering, he hypothesizes correctly that their different colors and styles of clothing convey position and caste. Other than these superficial differences, they appear human, nothing like the alien beings in horror movies Mrs. Jones once joked that they might be.

A large official, wearing an unfortunate neon yellow, lumbers toward the Joneses as a smaller Polluxian in midnight blue trails behind. Stopping, the one in yellow bows and sweeps an arm toward the one in blue, bellowing an introduction.

Mr. Jones hears his own voice through his translator, "Captain Ido."

"Greetings, Captain Ido." Mr. Jones bows toward the blue-clad Polluxian.

Captain Ido approaches, extending his right hand in greeting. Reflexively, Mr. Jones enthusiastically grasps the official's hand in his own and gives a firm shake. The group of Polluxians gasp. The large yellow-clad being extends a hand toward the one in blue. They touch palms, thumbs upward as if in preparation for a flat-handed thumb-wrestling match. Mr. Jones, realizing his mistake, extends his hand again. As Captain Ido's hand presses against that of Mr. Jones, they both smile broadly. The eleven Polluxians clap. In spite of the mistake, the familiarity of the clapping relaxes Mr. Jones.

Mrs. Jones, secretly pleased that she knows not to repeat her husband's faux pas, extends her hand toward Captain Ido. After a moment of hesitation, Captain Ido's hand presses against hers, but she notices that the captain's small, tight smile is clearly hiding an expression of distaste. There is no clapping. Instead, as she glances around the group, they avert their eyes and a few appear almost angry. *Oh excrement!* she thinks, *we never thought to ask if they'd evolved beyond misogyny.*

As they are shown to their quarters by a quartet of Polluxians, Mrs. Jones notices that they are now eying her husband with the same apparent disapproval they've shown her. Moments after being ushered into a cavernous lush room that seems half greenhouse, half bedroom, their four guides leave without a parting word.

"Oh, blasphemy!" Mr. Jones exclaims as soon as they have gone. "What do you think we've done wrong?" He scratches his head, "It seemed to me that they recovered from my handshake quite nicely, so it must have been something you did." There is no accusation in his voice, only observation.

Mrs. Jones snorts, "At first I thought they were sexist. Now I'm wondering if they took me as your slave or something. I noticed that my shirt is the same color as one of the underlings who greeted us."

A bell sounds as the door opens just far enough for the face of a Polluxian with enormous orange eyes to peek around it.

"May I enter?"

Consciously sweetening her voice, Mrs. Jones calls out, "Come in."

A youngster, clad in shimmery silver trimmed with white, enters the room. "I am Templi and I will be your guide and host for the duration of your stay. I will be back shortly to retrieve you for dinner."

*

Mrs. Jones sighed deeply when she remembered Templi.

Mr. Jones turned in his seat to give her a quizzical look.

She smiled and shook her head. They did not need words for him to get the gist of what she meant: *It's nothing, I was just thinking of something. I'll tell you later if you want.*

*

The Joneses spend the next two hours alternately exploring the space they are in and fretting about the unusual reception. Their stomachs are grumbling loudly when Templi returns. Mrs. Jones thinks she catches a glimpse of a knitted brow and tight lips before Templi replaces them with a solicitous smile.

"So many of us have been looking forward to your visit ..." Templi begins, the "but" inaudible and perfectly clear.

Deciding to ignore Templi's obvious discomfort, Mrs. Jones, wishing to put to rest any thoughts that she may rank below her husband, forcefully states, "Yes. Thank you. We have been greatly looking forward to this as well."

Head drooping, Templi stutters, "We have a bit of a ... a ... um ..." Templi stops and glances up at them with a mixture of sorrow and trepidation.

"Just spit it out," Mr. Jones barks, his annoyance and hunger making his temper short.

"Spit?" Templi looks bewildered,

Mr. Jones wonders if Templi's translator is malfunctioning.

"Say what you need to say is what he means," Mrs. Jones explains, her tone only a little less gruff than that of her husband.

Templi nods. "We have a situation."

"Oh, that clears it right up," Mr. Jones says as he flops dramatically into a large, fluffy chair.

Templi nods again, understanding their frustration, hating to be the bearer of any form of bad news, particularly bad news that is disagreeable on a political level.

"Please sit," Templi motions to Mrs. Jones, encouraging her to take the seat matching that of her husband's. As Mrs. Jones complies, Templi begins to explain. "The Minister believed that, because your culture endorses the joining of opposites, you would be representative of that, not an example of deviance."

The Joneses stare at Templi and then each other, mouths open like fish out of water. After a moment, Mrs. Jones touches her hair.

With a stiffened back and low voice, Mrs. Jones says, "I can assure you, we are 'man and wife' in every sense of that term."

"This is the problem," Templi frowns. "Were you discreet about your relationship, it might have been tolerated. But the Minister cannot afford to permit recognition of your marriage for it is both illegal and unnatural and many people still regard it as a sin."

The Joneses stand in unison, protesting with voice and gesture, but Templi's hands wave furiously, convincing them to stop.

"Please understand. This is not my decision. I believe people should be permitted to love, or even marry, whomever they wish. But many still believe a union like yours is an abomination."

Mrs. Jones eyes contract and widen so quickly they appear to flash. Mr. Jones recognizes this look and fears his wife is about to do something rash.

"Darling ..."

"Shush." Mrs. Jones commands as she begins unbuttoning her blouse.

"What are you doing?" objects Mr. Jones.

"I cannot tell what sex any of these Polluxians are and I don't care. But somehow they've got the notion you and I are the same and I mean to prove otherwise."

When Mr. Jones hesitates, Mrs. Jones snaps, "Get your pants off. Now. So we can finally go and have a civilized dinner with the Minister."

Templi, utterly perplexed, stares at the couple as they undress. When they finally stand, completely naked, awaiting inspection, Templi sighs. "I do not think this will convince the Minister, but I find it quite fascinating that you each lack some of your sexual organs. How unusual. I assume it is because you have opposite deficiencies that you justify your relationship."

"I am in no way deficient," Mr. Jones begins to protest.

Templi's eyes widen in amazement, "Do you mean you are still able to procreate?"

"Yes. I mean, no. I, um ..."

Mrs. Jones interrupts her husband's stuttering. "Yes, of course, we can procreate."

Templi claps in delight, cutting Mrs. Jones off. "I think it is simply amazing and wonderful that the two of you, with such complementary handicaps, somehow found each other!"

"Wait." Mrs. Jones eyes Templi up and down. "Does this mean you each have, um, both?" She motions to her breasts and Mr. Jones's crotch, "Well, all of it, I mean?"

Templi appears momentarily confused, and then answers matter-of-factly, "Yes, and we certainly expected you would, too."

"Does this mean we can get dressed and go eat now?" Mr. Jones growls as he begins to pull his pants up.

Still uncertain, Mrs. Jones asks Templi, "Should we get dressed or do you think we should show the Minister that we, ah, only have—well, what we have?"

With a small, sympathetic smile, Templi says, "No, I cannot see why it would make much of a difference to the Minister. So, of course, put your clothes back on. Do not feel badly. We have seen such deformities before. They are unfortunate, but as long as they remain hidden from view, it does not matter." Then, in a lame attempt at humor, Templi adds, "Just don't go to the beach."

*

An hour later, Templi and the Joneses are finishing a meal, a small feast really, in the sitting area of the Joneses' room. Several times throughout the meal, Mrs. Jones caught Templi staring at her hands. She did not mention it. The Joneses still smarted from being treated in a manner they found both rude and troubling. Her curiosity piqued, she began surreptitiously examining Templi's hands. She soon noticed an abnormality. Templi's right thumb was fused along the hand and index finger, leaving Templi with only four functional digits on that hand. Throughout the meal, they'd avoided nearly any conversation that did not have to do with food or table manners. One exception had been the use of a circle to symbolize marriage.

Now, as they are pushing back from the table, Mr. Jones points to a ring on Templi's left hand and asks, "Is that a wedding ring?"

Templi nods, "It is a sign of lifelong commitment."

"Why a circle?" Mr. Jones presses.

Templi looks thoughtful for a moment, and then says, "I don't really know for sure, but it is like time, it comes around in a circle and it is also like our planet, our Sustainer. The explanation that I've heard the most I guess is that when a right-handed person and a left-handed person form a family, it makes the perfect circle."

As the conversation moves on to the types of food used for different celebrations, Mrs. Jones begins to mull over Templi's statement about a "perfect circle" and wonders why handedness matters.

Soon tiring of the small talk, Mrs. Jones sighs and asks, "Please explain, will you, what the problem is with your minister and your laws and all and how we can fix it. As lovely as this is," she sweeps her arm to encompass the vast room, "we cannot remain in here for the next ten years."

Templi's bottom lip puckers with sympathetic understanding. The movement fascinates Mrs. Jones as in that moment Templi reminds her strongly of her favorite uncle.

"I think that they have been working on the problem and will propose an answer soon," Templi states encouragingly.

Mr. Jones, weary and irritated, asks, "Why can't we just dress like you do and not let on to anybody that we have, as you say, a lack of sexual organs?"

Templi frowns, obviously confused. Then, with dawning realization, says, "You think that the problem is that you lack a full set of sexual organs?"

Mr. Jones nods as Mrs. Jones raises one eyebrow into a question mark.

Laughing hard, Templi clutches a shaking stomach. "No, no. That is not the issue at all." Sobering quickly Templi adds, "I am so sorry. I must have given you the wrong impression."

Unable to contain an eruption, Mr. Jones shouts, "Then what is the Gol-blast problem?"

"Well," Templi motions with both hands toward theirs. "You are homos."

"Oh, for Crimeny, you've got to be kidding me!" Mrs. Jones exclaims, blushing a little as she recalls standing naked in front of Templi. "We are nothing of the kind."

"Well, I understand your physical abnormalities seem to mask the issue, but in the end this is all that matters."

Mrs. Jones notices the sympathy in Templi's eyes and realizes it must be difficult to argue what one does not agree with.

As if speaking to a particularly dull child, Mr. Jones intones, "Yes, we each, according to you, 'lack' sexual organs. But, as you saw, those we have are opposite. Therefore, we are not 'homos' at all."

Again, Mrs. Jones notes that Templi is staring at her hands.

"Oh, it has to do with our hands, yes?" she asks, already suspecting the answer.

Templi nods and sighs. Mrs. Jones cannot tell if it is with frustration or relief.

"Something to do with our hands being the same?" she presses.

Nodding, Templi thrusts both hands into the air. "Yours are the same." Wiggling a thumb and pointing from the right hand of Mrs. Jones and then to the right hand of Mr. Jones, Templi declares, "You are homo-dextrous."

"You mean ambidextrous," Mr. Jones states.

Templi's eyes widen with alarm, "No. I would never call you deceitful. I do not have a place of judgement, only of service." Then, as if in apology, Templi adds, "Nor do I believe you have been the least insincere or duplicitous."

Mrs. Jones uses her most soothing tone to explain, "To us, the term ambidextrous often simply means that both hands are equally adept, equally skilled. Or nearly equally."

"Ah, yes." Templi stabs a finger into the air. "We noticed a similarity in the decoding for those who you call left-handed. Your synonyms indicate such a thing is bad. Our experts hypothesized that you oppress or disadvantage those like myself." With the left index finger, Templi traces along the fused thumb of the right.

Nodding, Mrs. Jones concedes. "Yes, our language has many oddities. As does yours, apparently. To us, the ability to use both hands equally is good."

Waving toward Mrs. Jones, Mr. Jones playfully states, "Actually, she's nearly ambidextrous."

Reddening, Templi pleads, "Please, do not use that word."

Ignoring Templi, Mr. Jones waves his right hand in the air, "I'm mostly a righty."

"Well, really, so am I," Mrs. Jones adds softly, waving her right hand as well.

Templi jumps up and cries out, "Put them down. Put them down!" Head shaking wildly, Templi gasps and explains, "Don't you see? You cannot flaunt it like that!"

When neither of the Joneses react as expected, Templi's eyes narrow suspiciously. "You're not secretly reformist, part of the Gauche movement, perhaps? Have they been communicating with you?"

"What? No. Preposterous!" Mr. Jones squawks. "I don't even know what that is."

*

On the podium, Mrs. Jones turned toward her husband as she remembered that first time of hearing about the movement they would soon champion. Little did they suspect that dear Templi was a member of the Gauche movement and would eventually become a martyr to the cause. She blinked away a tear. When the Polluxian government had begun to actively persecute the Joneses, Templi quickly became one of their closest friends and most steadfast supporters.

*

Although Mr. Jones continues to deny any knowledge, Templi continues to press him.

"Are you sure?" Templi challenges. "They like to flaunt their homo-dextrousness in just that manner, waving them at people in the street. Children even. Mind you, as I've said, I'm all for rights for you people, but it is best to keep it to yourselves in your own home. For your own good, you understand."

Sitting and tucking her hands between her knees, Mrs. Jones asks, "Templi, are you saying that two right-handed people cannot legally be married?"

Sorrow carves grooves below Templi's eyes. "We had such high hopes for you, but when we saw that you are homos, we realized that we needed to come up with a solution before you can be allowed back in public. Even the fact that you were both apparently born bi-dextrous, the Minister cannot allow you—or any other homos—to be married."

"What do you think they will do?" Mr. and Mrs. Jones ask, nearly simultaneously.

"I think they will ask you to decide who is right and who is left," Templi suggests.

Mr. Jones grumbles, "More like the old-fashioned version of who wears the pants in the family."

"Or who is the 'he' and who is the 'she,'" Mrs. Jones agrees.

Before Templi can say any more, however, a series of tones call Templi from their room.

*

Just over an hour later, Templi returns and awakens the exhausted Joneses. After exchanging meaningless pleasantries, Templi begins to explain. "The Minister and others have decided to offer you a ... well ... propose to you that ... well," Templi begins again in a more official tone. "I have been tasked with giving you some of our history and what we have done when we have been faced with, ah, deformities such as yours." Templi glances at them, blushing faintly. "Or perhaps not deformities exactly, birth errors, perhaps. Many claim that the Divine One makes no errors, so, well ... I digress." Templi pauses again, avoiding their eyes this time. With an affectation, that is part professor and part storyteller, Templi leans forward, chin on stilted fingers and launches into a cultural lesson.

"You are not the first bi-dextrous people here. Like your absent genitalia, this too has occurred in children from time to time. When it does, the parents and doctors observe the child for a few days and then decide the handedness for that child. It is a simple enough procedure. Only one bone need be removed."

A gasp from Mr. Jones draws Templi's attention.

"It is a kindness, really," Templi assures them. "Otherwise the poor child would likely have to deal with all forms of unpleasantness from the other children. The young here can be so cruel in their policing of what they view as the norm, the social standards. Vicious, really. Many of us bear emotional scars for something far less bizarre and repulsive than bi-dextrousness." Templi begins to talk faster, attempting to cover the terrible mistake of insulting their guests that way. "Of course, it is no fault of the children. Yours neither. I mean, I'm not saying anyone is to blame. These things happen. Some claim the lefty who bore the child is to blame, something ingested perhaps. But really, the doctors say it is just a fluke, a freak of nature."

Templi stops talking and begins wringing the left hand with the right. "I am botching this, I know. I do not mean to insult your ... well, your condition. It isn't your fault and apparently the people on your planet do not correct these things. But you see, if you are to remain here, the Minister insists."

The Joneses stare at each other and then at Templi, uncomprehending.

Finally Mr. Jones speaks, "Just what is it you would have us do?"

Templi gives them a weak smile, "As I said before, you must decide who is right and who is left."

"Oh, fine then," Mrs. Jones says, standing and throwing her arms into the air. "As Mr. Jones said, I am more versatile. I will be the lefty and he can be the righty. Usage only, however. Nobody is fusing my thumb to my hand."

Bowing, nearly in tears, Templi thanks them repeatedly for making this process easier, murmuring that it could have been much more difficult and could have resulted in termination of employment and, oh, wouldn't Siberth, Templi's partner, be devastated.

After much back-patting and eye-dabbing, Templi and the Joneses settle back down.

"So you need to let us know how to play along with this charade," Mrs. Jones states. "I mean, is it just when I am writing and eating or is there something else—oh, shaking or pressing hands or whatever, that too, I guess."

"Well," Templi hesitates, trying to discern if Mrs. Jones is failing to grasp the obvious. "Mrs. Jones, you would be made a lefty and live as a lefty and do those things that lefties naturally do."

"Okay," Mr. Jones chuckles, "I'll ask. I see you are a lefty, so, what do lefties do?"

"We serve, of course." Templi smiles at them sweetly, "it is our nature. It is what the Divine made us for."

"Well, then what do righties do?" Mrs. Jones, indignant and suddenly alarmed, demands.

"Well, they operate the machinery, of course. They manage transportation and production. They lead. It is they who make family possible by working."

"Oh, no. I take it all back then," Mrs. Jones declares. "I am not about to go spend the next ten years playing nursemaid and polishing my husband's space boots. You will just have to tell your minister that we are both righties. That is the truth after all."

Templi appears stricken by Mrs. Jones's outburst. Then, after taking a moment to regain composure, says, "I will let you take your rest and will see you when you have refreshed. Please discuss and consider your situation. And know, the Minister has declared that we absolutely cannot and will not hold married righties, or homos of any kind, up as creatures to admire." Templi gives the Joneses a woeful glance and continues, "Because the advisors feared you would not be reasonable, they offered one compromise option. We could welcome you and follow the plan for your visit much as originally planned, but also strongly convey your status as freaks of nature. Given your sexual abnormalities that would, of course, not be difficult."

With a soft swish of silver robes, Templi slips through the door as the Joneses stare at one another, dumbfounded.

*

In the morning, a bowl of red spherical fruit sits on the counter. Mr. Jones picks one up and smells it. "Mmmm, apple, with just a hint of citrus."

"Oh, interesting," Mrs. Jones replies. "I have to admit, even after all this time, sampling the foods of various planets and cultures is one of my favorite aspects of this job."

There is an awkward pause. A pause that once again marks the space where they are avoiding discussing their "situation." They'd had many such pauses yesterday evening after Templi left.

Mrs. Jones plucks one of the fruits from the bowl and positions her thumb at one end. "Shall we see?" she asks, fingernail already biting into the spongy skin, causing a slight welling up of juice. As her thumb begins to push into the fruit, they hear a scream. The Joneses turn toward the sound. The door is ajar. Templi stands there, mouth still open, although the scream has fallen silent.

The Joneses glance around them in alarm, trying to locate the source of the threat. Mrs. Jones drops the fruit as her hand automatically flies to her side to grasp her laser gun—just a moment before she realizes that she hasn't changed out of her bedclothes. Relief floods her as she notices that Mr. Jones was more prepared. He moves toward her protectively, the tip of his gun already showing green; he's got his finger on the trigger.

As the Joneses brace themselves for battle, Templi rushes to the table and gently scoops the injured fruit into his hands. His eyes crucify them.

"Have you reverence for anything?" Templi cries, "Is nothing sacred to you?" Accusation and despair thread through Templi's voice.

"I thought they were breakfast," Mrs. Jones's shoulders shrug, pleading her innocence.

Mr. Jones is more prickly. "If they are not for us to eat, why put them here?"

"They were a gesture from the Minister. A welcoming gesture to bless your arrival and plead for your good fortune here." Staring down at the bleeding fruit, Templi gravely intones, "This is not a good omen."

A moment later, the Joneses are alone again.

"I've never felt like I needed a culture manual on any of the other planets we've lived on, but I certainly feel that way now," Mrs. Jones says as she sags onto a soft chair.

"I think we've grown complacent. Careless. Obviously we have not taken Candless's lesson to heart," Mr. Jones moans.

Mrs. Jones nods. "I blame myself. Somehow, I expected them to be further evolved socially. I can't even think why now."

"Perhaps we're not being fair. Perhaps the initial residents of every planet face similar challenges from the indigenous populations."

With a grateful smile, Mrs. Jones whispers, "You're sweet."

Mr. Jones does not reply but just sits and stares up at the ceiling. Mrs. Jones remains silent, knowing this is what Mr. Jones does when he is nervously calculating something. After a few moments, he shifts and meets her eyes. "You know it will take at least three to six months for our tanks to grow enough fuel to get us back to Earth."

Mrs. Jones leans forward in her chair, elbows on knees, "So, you are thinking we should return as soon as possible?"

Mr. Jones shifts so that he can sit on the floor directly in front of his wife. "I've been considering our options. The first is that one of us can basically become the old-fashioned version of a twenty-first century housewife ..."

"Make that twentieth century," Mrs. Jones interjects.

With a wry smile, Mr. Jones continues, "Yes, probably more like that. And don't dismiss the idea too quickly. That would give us full access to study their culture in ways that might not otherwise be available."

"But neither of us wants to be the 'wife.'" Mrs. Jones says, stating what is obvious for both of them.

"Exactly. So, the second option is to just attempt to get along in whatever manner possible until we can leave." He pauses, tapping his chin.

"And what is the third option?" Mrs. Jones prompts.

"Well, I suppose we could pretend to get a divorce."

Mrs. Jones immediately gets his meaning. "Yes. Apparently, they've kept all this from the public. So besides the Minister, those on the welcoming committee, Templi, and Rotal Snart and his team, there may not be many people that know we are married."

Mr. Jones nods as Mrs. Jones continues, "If they are willing to go along with it, we could just pretend to be co-workers."

"We'd need to live in separate apartments, avoiding any public displays of affection."

Mrs. Jones leans forward, placing her hands on Mr. Jones's knees. "For ten years? That would be hard."

"Or six months. Or one year." Mr. Jones places his hands on hers. "Once we have enough fuel, we could simply decide to leave whenever it becomes too unbearable."

"Or until we slip up and they run us out of town." Mrs. Jones laughs at her own joke. Mr. Jones joins in. He does not find the prospect suggested by the comment to be funny, but he loves that she laughs at her own jokes—a particular quirk of hers that always amuses him.

They sit, smiling at one another, sharing a moment of hope.

With a mischievous grin, Mrs. Jones asks, "Do you have a fourth option?"

"Nooo ..." Mr. Jones drawls, knowing from her tone of voice and the squinty lines around her eyes that she does, and that it will be either outrageous or illegal and not at all a serious suggestion.

She laughs even before she begins speaking. "We could lead a revolution."

Mr. Jones laughs along, but he feels an odd heat in his chest as he adds, "Start their civil rights movement. Live as pariahs, but go down in history as heroes, just like my great, great, great, great grandmother."

Her eyes widen with true alarm. "Tell me you are not serious."

He is silent for a long moment before, nearly whispering, he says, "I think I am."

Neither of them suggests the possibility of living as "freaks."

*

JoVance interrupted Mrs. Jones's recollections by turning to her with a flourish and announcing, "And now I give you Mrs. Jones!"

The crowd roared with shouts and applause. Many Polluxians leapt to their feet, stomping to the cacophony. Yet, when she reached the podium and raised her right hand in the traditional greeting, a hush descended like a curtain.

After a brief recap of their arrival—little needed to be said as, by then, everyone knew the story by heart—Mrs. Jones launched into her speech.

"Neither of us imagined the years ahead—particularly the backlash against married right-handers. When we were arrested ..."

The boos of the crowd drowned her out until she raised her hand for quiet.

"Thank you. I appreciate your sympathy. As I was saying, when we were arrested, they threatened us both. When Mr. Jones believed they were about to remove my right hand, he sacrificed his own."

Both boos and applause sounded from the audience.

"That was our first battle. That was our first punishment. When we chose to live openly as two bi-dexterous people, we lost our home. We lost our jobs. Yet we were kept from leaving because the Minister had seized our spacecraft. We had friends who helped us. Friends like Templi."

"To Templi! Honor always!" The crowd chanted the traditional homage to a martyr who was fortunate enough to die for the "right side" of history.

"When we did not stop, we were arrested. We did not know it would go so far, but the backlash against homo-dexterous couples had grown so great, we actually feared for our lives on many occasions."

A spattering of angry shouts rose from the crowd.

"When Mr. Jones's hand was taken, we thought that because we were no longer homos, our fight was over. We were wrong. It was just beginning."

A lone shout went up, "Mr. Jones!"

"We heard you chant it." Mrs. Jones prompted.

"Mr. Jones! Mr. Jones!"

"We saw his face. We heard his name. We knew what we had to do—what we were made to do. We knew—he knew—this was our destiny. Because *this*," Mrs. Jones swept her arms toward the multitude of banners on her left with the Scaeva Equality Laws on them and then to her right with the Partum and Succipio laws on them, "this is *your* destiny!"

Once again the Polluxians rose to their feet, stamping and clapping, chanting, "Mr. Jones! Mr. Jones!"

After a few minutes, the crowd settled and Mrs. Jones continued. "Destiny does not mean easy. It does not mean no regret. Mr. Jones's dismemberment has cost him more than you can imagine. He was born right-hand dominant and then forced to live as a left-hander. He did not even know *how* to be a left-hander. Relegated to a life he never expected, he quietly began to build a coalition among others whose lives revolved around unpaid service while I gave talks and public appearances, trying to persuade the public that handedness should not make a difference in essential human rights. That human rights should be based upon being human, no more and no less." This time it took Mrs. Jones several minutes to quiet the shouts and clapping of the crowd. She took the opportunity to beckon Mr. Jones to the podium.

The crowd became silent as he rose from his chair.

Although he shuffled his feet as he approached her, his voice was strong and clear when he addressed the crowd.

"A few weeks after we arrived, I had a discussion with our friend, Templi."

"To Templi! Honor always!" the crowd chanted.

"In front of the Minister's aide, Templi explained that two righties, like myself and Mrs. Jones, could not form a perfect circle in marriage. I said that made no sense. We went back and forth until I drew a diagram to show that two righties facing each other could grasp the non-fused hand of the other to make a perfect circle, but those with opposite handedness could not. Templi then drew a diagram of your tradition, that of the righty on the outside of the circle encircling the lefty, who could then hold their child in the circle as well. Templi argued so convincingly that only this was a natural state—that face to face with nobody in the middle would be a perversion—that I did not even suspect that Templi actually agree with us. That Templi would die for forming just such a circle."

"To Templi! Honor always!" the crowd roared.

Mrs. Jones smiled as Mr. Jones's voice rose, stirring the crowd.

"Templi was not the first to die, nor will Templi be the last. Hundreds are not with us here today because of the battle for equal rights. Yet, it was they who won the battle. We raised up each martyr. We showed that the system itself encouraged the hatred and killing."

"What happened?" the people shouted on cue.

"We convinced them that hatred was more harmful than homo-dexterousness. When they could deny it no longer—when every day the eyes of the dead stared at them from posters and windows. When the families of the dead circled the houses of the Minister and the Second, they passed a law declaring that anyone could marry whoever they choose. We fought—"

Thunderous applause drowned out Mr. Jones's next words.

He paused for the applause and then, as it tapered, shouted above it. "We fought. We fought with the left-handers who protested that all left-handers prefer to work selflessly, with no pay nor security. That because their right thumbs are fused to their hands, they were divinely decreed to be the sacred caretakers of the Polluxians and that honorable service was payment enough. They claimed that the idea of sullying their work with something as gauche as money was blasphemous. We claimed that if payment for serving the Divine was blasphemous, then all the religious leaders should forgo their payment as well."

The crowd eagerly took up their expected role in the speech, shouting as one, "What happened?"

"You stopped leaving offerings at the Sacred Sites."

"What happened?" the crowd roared louder.

"Day after day, you took your children to the capital, you wrote books and weekly pamphlets, you wrote songs and had monthly concerts, every year you marched."

The crowd shouted even louder, "What happened?"

Mr. Jones roared back at them, "You were heard! It took over a decade, but you were heard!"

The crowd erupted with whistles, stomps, and shouting. When they'd nearly exhausted themselves, Mr. Jones raised his left hand. "Eventually we got a minister who listened. The Minister was ready to decree that all whose work adds value should receive payment and security. But we were not finished. We had to fight the religious leaders who declared that left-handers were somehow inferior—in ways that kept shifting with each debate. Some said that was not so, that they were not inferior, only different. Still, they would not stand against those who claimed otherwise and would not condemn practices that disadvantaged lefties. They ignored the poverty of those who sacrificed for their country."

Again, the crowd shouted, "What happened?"

"New religious entities sprang up, with a core belief that all stand equal in the eyes of the Divine."

The crowd asked again, "What happened?"

"The old leaders marginalized themselves. The more they fought against equality, the more rigid and harsh they became. The people turned against them, and so did the Minister."

"So what happened?" the crowd cried.

Mr. Jones broke into a wide smile, "It was decreed, all whose work adds value should receive payment and security."

Some of the crowd begin prematurely throwing confetti at the stage until Mr. Jones roared, "Of course it is not as simple as all that. It has taken millions of acts from more Polluxians than will ever get credit. We are just the thunder—*you* are the blizzard."

The air filled with confetti. A casual glance might not have discerned anything more than bits of paper, but each was as unique as a snowflake.

"And you cannot stop!" Mr. Jones continued. "We are not finished. We might never be finished. But still we must fight."

"Fight, fight!" echoed the audience.

"How do we fight?" Mr. Jones yelled.

"Love. Logic. Respect. Resistance. Persuade. Protest. Protect," the crowd recited.

"And what else?" Mr. Jones called out.

The people answered, "And never give up!"

"We have our next target in sight. We must fight so that the craft we drive and the machines that we operate have controls for both left-handed and right-handed, and that children's harnesses can be adjusted by either as well!"

The left side third of the audience shouted, "Love, Logic."

The middle answered with, "Respect, Resistance."

The right finished, "Persuade, Protest, Protect."

The chants grew faster, rippling across the audience, becoming a single undulating wave of sound.

The pinched look on the face of JoVance told Mrs. Jones that their performance wasn't what he'd wanted or expected. She and Mr. Jones had grown somewhat less involved and less radical in their old age. She was spending most of her time on mentoring and training and less of it on protesting and speeches. Mr. Jones, however, had become embittered. He could only see how far they had yet to go instead of how far they'd come.

*

As a dozen dignitaries lined up on the stage, Mr. and Mrs. Jones slowly walked off. They heard the rising and falling of the chorus of voices, and they knew: this was their swan song.

As they retreated into the wings, Mrs. Jones reached out her hand and felt Mr. Jones's fingers interlace with her own. Turning toward him, she stage-whispered, "You will always be my right-hand man."

***

# Brinkman's War

by Marie D. Jones

**US: *"The supreme art of war is to subdue the enemy without fighting." — Sun Tzu, The Art of War***

The place he was in chilled his soul. Cold, dark, damp. A hole in the ground, literally. It was to be his home for the rest of his life, unless a miracle occurred. In this harsh reality, he knew there was no such thing.

Jonathan Brinkman sat huddled in the corner of his tiny "cell," like an animal waiting for slaughter. Above him, the sounds of war permeated the thick, humid forest. Gunfire raged around him, swirling like a funnel cloud down to his auditory range. He clasped his hands over his ears, wanting to shut out all sounds of this thing called Nam.

Soon, Brinkman was asleep, pitched against the cold dirt wall of the makeshift cell. In his sleep, he was able to forget just for a little while. Able to forget he was a POW, soon to be MIA, never to see his wife and children back home again. Never to be able to go to sleep at night—and wake up in the morning—without the accompanying sound of warfare.

Above him on the ground, war raged. He wondered about his buddies out there, exposed. He wondered who had it worse, those dodging gunfire and ambushes around every corner, or him stuck in this hole waiting to be tortured, maybe killed.

*

When Brinkman woke up, it was to the disturbing sound of silence. The air was still, unnerving. All gunfire had ceased. Brinkman sat up, his body sore from the beatings of days past. His back ached from the way he had to curve his body in on itself to stay warm. He strained forward, wanting now to hear something, anything. There was

173

no sound. Not even the typical hum of jungle insects or the monotone cry of the wiry tree-borne monkeys that draped the ceiling of the deep forest like a moving blanket.

By the way the shadows fell, he could tell it was evening. Twilight time. Magic hour. Perhaps they had called a cease-fire. Brinkman laughed at this. He knew the States would never give this one up so easily.

He stretched his long limbs out the fullest extent he could. The hole he was in was a little over seven feet across, enough for him to lie flat without disturbing the little metal pot they had so generously thrown him for his waste. He forced himself to work what was left of his deteriorating muscles by doing a few sit-ups, a few leg extensions. He wasn't able to do much, but he had to keep his body in working order ... just in case ...

All around him, the uncanny silence filled his ears with a roar akin to a thousand screams. Something was terribly wrong, he thought. Then he laughed. This whole war was terribly wrong. The hair on the back of his neck stood on end. His skin felt hot and dry as the air seemed to close in on his hole in the earth like a sucking vortex.

Suddenly, a bright light filled the hole, so intense Brinkman had to shield his eyes with his arm as he turned away from it. He could not look up into the open craw of the hole, to see where it was coming from. He imagined it was some new torture device of the enemy. He pushed himself hard into the side of the cold wall of earth, as if hoping to blend in with the dirt and go invisible.

"Jonathan."

His name was called. Not a command or a trace of a Vietnamese accent. No, Brinkman could have sworn it was almost ... whispered.

"Jonathan."

Brinkman slowly dropped his protective arm to peer through his eyelids at the source of the voice emanating from within the core of the beam of light. In the brilliance, he could see a faint form, sense it more than see it.

"Who are you?" He had to struggle to get the words out of his dry throat.

He waited for a response, his tense body ready for whatever new abuse lay in store.

"Jonathan. Do not be afraid."

He could see them now. Three of them, descending down the hole. His heart almost ceased to beat in the grip of pure terror. What he saw made him more afraid than he had ever been in his life. Even more afraid than what he'd seen on the ground.

"My God ... my God ..." His voice trembled. "What are you?"

The three beings floated down the hole without touching dirt. They moved around Brinkman in a circle. He clutched at his chest as they hovered in full view so he could see them, his newest enemy.

They were small, about three feet tall, with thin bodies supporting large, rounded heads that seemed to loll from side to side. But what made the air sit thick in back of Brinkman's throat were the eyes. Their eyes. Big, black, almond-shaped pools of liquid ink that wrapped around the sides of their heads. When he looked into those eyes, Brinkman could swear he saw his soul.

"Jonathan."

It was not a question, not a demand. They just said his name, over and over again in a kind of mechanical harmony that reminded Brinkman of a sci-fi flick he'd once seen back in the States, when he was still a free man. This put a new terror into his heavily taxed heart. These things were robots, sent and controlled by the enemy camp. Brinkman stood slowly, hoping his six-foot frame would imply superiority. He faced the beings.

"What do you want? Who sent you here?" He tried to control the fear boiling just below surface. He knew, perhaps by sheer instinct, that he must not let these things see his fear. He felt like a lamb standing naked and unguarded before a starved pack of wolves. Yet even lambs had free will. Brinkman swore no robot would take him down. He had fought off crazy-eyed young men filled with bloodlust. No way would he go down in defeat to some technical assassin the Vietnamese soldiers had cooked up.

Like a well-trained soldier, he would fight the good fight like he'd done every day of his life for the past six months ...

*

They had taken him during a night raid. Two young soldiers, dirty-faced kids with sick yellow skin and eyes sharp as broken glass. Jonathan Brinkman had just turned twenty-three, but there was no party, or cake. His only gift had been the shell exchange above his foxhole. He had spent his birthday watching his best buddy, Ross Capier, lose his right arm, then his life, to enemy fire.

Then the real birthday surprise jumped out before him, wrapped in fatigues, armed to the teeth. Before he could make a wish, the candles were blown out for Jonathan Brinkman. They came out from behind a low sling of brush, like jungle cats hiding in waiting. Brinkman had strayed into unknown territory without backup. Capier had been his backup, the eyes behind his head. Capier had his own surprise waiting in store, a surprise that ripped the life from his young body, while a million miles away his parents sat over dinner, praying for their son.

Brinkman hadn't realized how far he'd wandered until the butt of foreign firepower jabbed at his temple and the slit-eyed boy-cats dragged him to the ground. Brinkman could have screamed, but above the gunfire, who would have heard him?

He was taken into enemy camp hidden deep within the tangled jungle. There they questioned him between brutal beatings. When he would not answer their questions, they beat him some more. It had nothing to do with heroics. Jonathan Brinkman didn't hold out on information because he was a brave, patriotic American. He held out because he didn't know a thing. Nothing. He was just a lowly grunt who did what he was told in a war he neither cared for, believed in, nor understood.

He longed to die. Even with a young wife and two twin boys waiting for him at home in sweet, sweet Sweetwater, West Virginia. The pain was so great, the fear even greater, that for a while, even death seemed a respite.

Death was not in the cards. Brinkman was given a new home, this seven-foot wide hole some twenty feet deep in the suffocating jungle earth. Their routine was simple, they visited him at first three times a day, then two, beating him, often burning holes in his skin with strange-smelling cigarettes, electric prods, or whatever tool or device they chose to bring. Still, Brinkman refused to speak. He didn't have anything to say, really. He just took what came his way with all the will he could muster, screaming out in his mind the three words that had gotten through this far—"I will survive."

After a while, he could tell they were getting bored with their abuse, their beatings getting shorter, less severe. They brought him food, a musty gruel, and clean water, once at dawn, again at twilight. Sometimes, one of the real young ones, not more than a boy, would throw him down a food ration bar. They even had the decency to supply him with a few plastic bags and the metal pot for his waste.

The Hilton it was not, but it was bearable as long as he could stay alive, and sane.

It was that hope that got him through.

Until three days ago. Or at least it felt like three days' time. That's when the war seemed to shift locale. Since then, no one had come to beat him, or feed him, or even to see if he was still alive. He had seen neither hide nor hair of his captors. Brinkman stayed silent at first. When the sound of gunfire had completely surrendered to the low roar of jungle creatures, that had disturbed him into a near panic.

Brinkman spent most of his waking hours screaming at the top of his lungs until his voice box croaked and his throat bled raw. His fingers bled as well from groping at the solid walls around him, trying desperately to find a ridge or crack in the side of the earth so he could climb out. The walls were so smooth that even in his stronger moments he couldn't jump that high.

So he screamed and hollered, eventually wailing like an injured animal, hoping someone would come. He didn't care whom. By then he would have even welcomed the enemy soldiers with their coldness, their beatings. He would have welcomed the most brutal torture. He just wanted someone to come.

*

"Jonathan."

Now he had gotten his wish in the form of these things floating before his eyes. The hair on his arms prickled with electricity. He tried to take in air through parched lips. The air had become heavy. He watched the three things move closer to him, their skin emanating a milky aura that seemed to wax and wane. Brinkman felt his limbs go weak as he blacked out.

*

When Brinkman awoke, the light was gone. Above him, the jungle now lit up with the soft glow of the full moon peering through the treetops. Occasionally, a shell fired off in the distance. Brinkman would instinctively duck low, even though he was about as low as he could get. He leaned against the cold earth wall, thinking of his family back in Sweetwater. That thought was too painful, so he quickly turned his attention to some fresh food sitting beside him. The enemy must have come back, he ventured. Sometime in the night, perhaps to check on how effective their robots were.

Brinkman cringed as he tried to move. His head throbbed and his back ached from the curled position he had been in. He put his hand to his temple to rub the pain away, recoiling as his fingers touched something sticky. He was bleeding. He touched his ear. There was more blood, fairly fresh. What had they done to him, the robots?

They had put him under. In a trance. Perhaps they had induced it with a drug; something sprayed into the air. Or maybe they had used mind control. He remembered their eyes, those massive inky wells. He had felt his consciousness slipping away under their hypnotic power. He did not know what they did to him once he was under their spell, although the blood from his ears sent chills up his spine.

In the meager moonlight, Brinkman pulled up his filthy shirt, examining his chest. There were cuts all over, and bruises, all with simple explanations. Beatings will do that to you. Even the beatings of the enemy could not explain the drops of blood gathered around his navel. Terrified, Brinkman unzipped his pants. He lowered them, holding his breath, then letting it explode in gasps, when he saw fresh blood clinging to the tip of his penis.

177

Brinkman went numb. They had done things to him, things to his body while he lay helpless, out cold. They had left him rations, though. Brinkman didn't allow the thought to enter his mind, but it did nonetheless, creeping in through an opening deep in the back of his subconscious ...

Perhaps the soldiers were long gone. These robots or creatures or whatever they were, were his new caretakers. He was dealing now with a whole new enemy. One he had no idea how to fight.

*

The deeper night fell, the more confused Brinkman became. His head was a jumble of thoughts of fear, of survival; worry for himself, worry for his fellow grunts that might be out there waiting in holes like this one, hoping to be discovered. Brinkman felt like a victim of something he couldn't understand. Something that had the power to float down twenty-foot holes, light up the entire sky, and make him go blank against his will.

He had long ago begun questioning his sanity. Occasionally he would get those incredible moments of clarity, where he knew everything that had happened was real.

Then they came back.

*

"Jonathan."

He had not been sleeping this time. He was waiting for them. Four nights he waited, sleeping intermittently, not wanting to be taken by surprise. No, never by surprise. That's what had gotten him into this damned hole.

"What do you want with me?" Brinkman forced back the fear in his voice.

There was a brilliant blue beam shining down into the hole. Brinkman looked up at a round hovering metal object holding court just above treetop level. The three beings floated out of a hatch on the bottom of the object, gently drifting downward on the beam, into the hole.

Brinkman stood up, moving quickly into the center of the hole, determined to stand his ground. His body shook with fear. He would not let them see it. He tightened himself up, mentally pushing waves of terror downward, centering his energy. It was something he had learned in college, some martial arts stuff his roommate had shown him.

Right now, it seemed to be working.

"Don't touch me. Don't come any closer."

The three creatures surrounded him. They did not touch him, just stared at him with those eyes, swaying as they floated only inches from the dirt. They were so thin and so much smaller than he was. Brinkman focused on their bodies. They had arms with hands, although their fingers were more like webbed stumps. Other than the huge eyes, their nose and mouth were small slits. He could not make out any ear openings.

Brinkman forced himself to keep his focus off their eyes, which were like powerful magnets, drawing him in, making him go weak. He fought with every inch of his will to turn away, but he was losing ground. They were in his head now, talking in calm deep voices, asking him to look. They just wanted him to look. Just don't be afraid ... look.

He looked.

*

A white fog lifted as Brinkman opened his eyes. His lids felt heavy. He sat up, realizing he was not in his hole. He was in a strange place, a place far from the dense, wet, war-torn jungle he had come to call home. He was on a long, steel table in the center of a large, blindingly white room. The walls of the room were blank and windowless. Other than the table he lay on, there was no other furniture around.

Above him, Brinkman saw a big machine with long robotic arms. At the end of one arm was a hypodermic. Another ended in what appeared to be a tiny probing camera lens. Brinkman tried to move his arms and legs. His body felt like a block of lead. He finally forced his feet to the edge of the table, holding onto the side as he used his arms to spring his body sideways. He struggled to stay balanced as his feet hit the ground. It was as if he hadn't walked in years. His legs responded with stabs of pain as he stepped away from the table.

Brinkman made his way down a long hallway. The ceiling was low, forcing him to stoop to accommodate his large frame. He had seen no forms of life since he came to, yet was certain he was not alone. His hunch proved correct as he leaned up against an open doorway to peer into an adjoining room.

It looked like a surgery room. Several of the creatures hovered around a low steel table as if working on something ... or someone. Brinkman moved into the room, not really caring if they saw him. He wanted to see what was on the table. He got close before one of the milky floating things turned and saw him, its huge eyes going even wider in surprise. The thing came at Brinkman, its tiny mouth stretched back in a silent sneer. Brinkman backed up a few steps. He pushed at the thing as it came towards him, sending its frail body floating to the far wall.

Brinkman moved towards the table and leaned over the tiny surgeons, busily working.

"Oh my God, Capier!"

Brinkman watched in a blend of horror and awe as the creatures reattached his dead buddy's right arm to his gaping shoulder. He shielded his eyes as a mechanical dome over the table began to glow with an intensifying white light. A low, electronic hum permeated the room. Something stirred on the table, as if the overhead dome was manipulating Capier's dead corpse. Brinkman squinted and could see movement. The floating beings were moving away from the table as Capier's body literally sat up on the table ... alive.

The creature Brinkman had pushed away now grabbed his hand, leading him out of the surgery room. This time, Brinkman didn't struggle. He had no struggle left in him. He had just witnessed these strange beings bring his dead buddy back to life. He would let them do whatever they wanted from now on. He had no choice.

The creature stopped with Brinkman just outside the surgery room. It turned to face Brinkman, staring deeply into his eyes.

"Jonathan."

It wasn't spoken out loud so much as heard in Brinkman's head.

"Is that all you know how to say? My name?" Brinkman felt a swell of anger build up inside of him. He welcomed its promise of release.

"Why don't you tell me what the fuck is going on here? What did you do to Capier? What are you going to do to me?"

The thing just continued to stare, its black eyes swallowing Brinkman in until he began to feel dizzy.

"No, I'm not giving in to you again. I want some fucking answers!" He stepped back a few paces, his eyes never looking away from the creature's own. "I want you to stop treating me like an animal and give me some answers!"

In a flash, Brinkman was back in the hole, being questioned by enemy soldiers. The irony made him smile weakly. Then he was back in the room. The creature seemed to shift position, just a little. It floated away down the hall.

"You son of a bitch! Don't leave. Don't leave!" Brinkman was alone in the hall. He moved towards the open door to the surgery room but it slid closed before he could get in, leaving him standing alone in a cell of white walls. Always a cell, Brinkman thought. Suddenly, he felt very tired. Tired of being a victim. Tired of always being at war with something. Tired of fighting. He found his way back to the room with the table and laid down. Within minutes, he was asleep.

*

Something shook him awake. Before Brinkman opened his eyes, he had to know where he was. In that dark place between sleep and wakefulness, he made his fingers move over the surface his body rested upon. Feeling the smooth solidity of the steel table beneath him, he signed with resignation, allowing himself to be shaken into consciousness. His eyes struggled to open, as if he had been drugged. The voice of whatever shook him awake remained persistent.

"Hey, Brinkman! Looks like we fuckin' outfoxed the bastards!"

Brinkman opened his eyes to the smooth, rounded baby face of Ross Capier. The dead soldier was now very much alive and animated, smiling like some kid in a malt shop.

"Can you believe this place?" Capier motioned around the white room, dimmer now, perhaps in respect for Brinkman's need for sleep. As he rose, Brinkman leaned onto a soft, fluffy mound where his head had been. A pillow. He smiled, grasping the pillow. He was amused by the personal touch.

"What happened, Cap? You were toast. I mean, you're supposed to be dead ..." Brinkman's head felt fuzzy and thick. Yes indeed, Capier was alive in front of him.

"Didn't they tell you?" Cap's voice was matter-of-fact.

"They don't tell me anything. I don't believe they know how to say anything other than my name."

Cap looked surprised. "Oh, hell, they do! They talk up a damned storm with me. You should try—"

Brinkman grabbed Capier and shook him, as if to see if the man's body would fall apart. Cap was solid.

"Listen, Cap. Cut the praise shit. What are these things going to do to us? Where the hell are we? What do they want with us?" Brinkman was not ashamed of the edge of panic in his voice. This was neither the time nor place for dignity.

"Nothing bad, I mean it ain't anything to be afraid of, Brink. Just lie still. Let them do what they need to do. Then they'll take you home."

Brinkman felt the blood drain from his face and neck. He looked at Capier, saw the way the former dead man looked all around him like a child in awe on Christmas morning. They got his mind, Brinkman surmised. Gave Cap back his body in exchange for his mind.

"Cap, you really think they're going to take us HOME?"

Capier seemed confused that Brinkman would ever question their intention. "Why shouldn't they? They said they would. They take their samples and then take us home." Capier said it with such certainty, he almost had Brinkman convinced. "We're just guinea pigs. That's all. Once they have what they need, they'll set us free."

Brinkman gripped Cap's arm, the one that had just been reattached hours ago. "Jesus, Cap, you fucking idiot! Look at what we

181

do to animals in our own labs, to our own guinea pigs! We don't set them free, you fucking asshole! We use them, then WE KILL THEM!" Brinkman's face was fire-engine red with anger and fear. The vein in his neck bulged, ready to burst. Capier just stared at him, mouth open.

The door to the white room slid open and one of the creatures floated in, moving towards them quickly. It motioned with an upraised arm to Capier, who followed it out of the room without a word. Just before the door closed behind him, Capier turned and smiled at Brinkman.

He thinks he's going home, Brinkman thought, watching his buddy go.

The door opened again as another creature entered, maybe the same one, they all looked alike. The creature stood before him, staring with those unrelenting eyes. Brinkman didn't bother to put up a fight. He felt his eyelids go heavy as bricks as the creature helped him lie down on the table. The last thing Brinkman saw before darkness enveloped him was a long, sharp needle moving down towards his face.

The pain came, followed only by deep black.

*

He sat up, stretching his legs, and remained there for a long while. He was back in his hole, his home away from home. Above him, the jungle treetops hid the deep blue sky from his view. He guessed it was evening, but it could have been dawn.

His next thought was of Capier. Hopeful, naïve Cap. Brinkman wondered what they did to dispose of him. Or could they have possibly taken him home? Like they took him home, back to this hellhole. Brinkman felt betrayal, as if the creatures somehow broke an unspoken promise. They had never told him they were going to rescue him. Never told him they were going to take him "home."

For the first time in months, Brinkman found himself within moments of full and complete defeat. Within moments of believing that he would never be found, would never see his family again. Would never walk the quiet, boring small-town streets of Sweetwater, West Virginia. Would never see the American sky…

He wondered what had come of the war, or his captors. He wondered if they knew about the weird floating things. Or had it all just been a horrendous nightmare—a stretched out hallucination brought about by the terrors of war. He closed his eyes, letting his body sink down into the hard dirt, letting his mind cut loose, completely loose. He began to laugh, loud and hearty, with everything he had left to give. His laugh became a manic howl that worked its way out of the deep hole in the earth, through the tangled jungle growth, finding its way to the ears of a man. A grunt.

An American soldier.

*

Brinkman lay deep asleep in the Bryce Receiving Center outside of Norfolk, Virginia. His cot was small and creaky, but who gave a damn? It was on American soil. Something made him jolt awake. His eyes flew open with a start, fully expecting to see walls of dirt. Instead, he froze, totally unfamiliar with these walls. He felt his throat close up, sure they had him again, on their ship.

Something stirred beside him. He turned to face a man asleep on a cot. Another man slept opposite him. As Brinkman's eyes regained focus, he realized he was in a room full of men on cots, rows of cots.

"Jesus Christ. What have they done?" He arose from his makeshift bed, walking through the rows of sleeping bodies to the thick double doors at the end of the large room. He opened the doors, entering a long, grey hallway riddled with doors that led to offices. As his mind cleared, Brinkman calmed. He couldn't be sure, but either the creatures had changed their ship, or he was in a real live military hospital.

A young male orderly came up behind him and put his hand on his shoulder. Brinkman jumped, then realized the orderly was human and not one of "them." He sighed deeply.

"Where am I? Is this place for real?"

The orderly smiled. "Bryce Receiving Center. You're okay, sir. You're doing just fine." The orderly took Brinkman's hand to read his wristband.

"Jonathan Brinkman, United States Army. Welcome home, soldier! Now get some rest. You have some early morning tests before you leave for home base." The orderly smiled at Brinkman, gently motioning him back down the hall towards the sleeping quarters.

"The war ..." Brinkman's tongue felt dead and thick in his mouth.

"It's over, thank the Lord. You're going home." The orderly held the door open as Brinkman passed through into the darkness.

He sat on the edge of his cot for a long, long time, drinking in the reality around him, peering into the shadows at the ones who got out alive. He suddenly wondered if Capier was here, if he made it home. A hot rush of blood surged from his heart to his head, making him dizzy. The hair on his arms stood at attention. The air became thick and wet with something. Brinkman felt it right there behind his cot before he even saw the telltale aura.

He turned slowly to face it. The creature stood at the head of the cot, giving off a warm glow. It just stared at Brinkman. This time,

183

Brinkman felt no pull, no persuasion in those incredible eyes. He felt nothing really. He stared back at the thing, then his lips curled into a slight smile.

"Jonathan."

"Yes?"

"Welcome home."

***

# Space Junk
by Andrea L. Staum

### US: *Galactic scavengers salvage their origins*

The salvage ship neared its destination. They still had half a shift to travel as the monitor screens filled with the metallic structure ahead of them. The forward sensors began blaring at them regarding their approach. Lines of blank data scrolled on the console. It was a dead hulk. Nothing scanned back at them and nothing registered on any scale.

Aefel sat up and started calculating what he would need for hook up. Glancing at the back of his captain's head, he cleared his throat trying to gain the captain's attention.

"It's space junk, Aefel," groaned Parto as he eased back into his seat. He knew what Aefel wanted before it was asked. It was the same argument for every salvage op. "You get too attached to the romance of the past. We're paid to hook it and lug it to the Recych."

"But it was home," Aefel protested. "Who knows what's left in there!" He peered at the monitor that showed the derelict colony *Claudia*. He hadn't seen the colony since he was a teen, but he still considered it home as it was where he was born and grew.

"Bah," squawked Emmet from the grappling station. "Don't much matter anymore. The important stuff's been long cleared by the Reggies, and the Morgies took the last bodies out almost a decade ago. We're just getting the orders now because the backlog is long."

Aefel sighed and leaned back in his chair.

"Hey, breathe easy!" scolded Parto. "The filtration unit's workin' hard enough with Emmet's night snores, so don't need you making the day bad."

Aefel rolled his head to the side and stared at the back of Parto's head.

"Fine, go have a look!" the captain exclaimed and rubbed at the vision mod at the crown of his head. Dropping his hand hard against the worn console he added, "Take the kid with ya."

Aefel stumbled midway to the door. "Really?"

Emmet snorted from his seat. "Good lucko with that. She ain't come up from the engine since last fuel up. Think she's burrowed in down there."

"She's not that bad," countered Parto. "Sends reports more than you ever did. And tell truth, if you could avoid you, you would."

Emmet shrugged before nodding. "Yeah."

"Plus she needs the heat," Parto stated. "She won't like the suit, but she'll find anything left over we can use. Hopefully some circulation filters will be had."

Aefel smiled and palmed open the hatch without another word. He wouldn't mind the company in the derelict; he just didn't want to go all the way to the other end of the ship to fetch Merei. At least they had a ways before they made it to the dock points of the *Claudia*. He could feel the ship shudder as Parto cut back the engine power for the approach.

"Too fast," Merei's voice crackled from the ship-wide speakers.

"Cutting non-ess to give it a break," Parto's voice floated after hers.

Aefel felt his body lift from the floor as the grav was among the first non-essentials to be turned off. He cursed and clicked his heels together to activate his boots before he was too far from the floor. He could hear Parto and Emmet in the comdeck sniggering when the magnets engaged hard. He knew the captain had done that on purpose, but as he looked down the corridor, he saw the blessing in it. He clicked off the boots again, pushing hard off the hatch door to Superman his way down. He could hear the camera heads turning to watch his progress and it made him tense. He knew that Parto would flick grav back on at any moment and he didn't want to be over anything that would be painful to land on. Last time it had been over the hatch to lower levels that had been opened and he had barely managed to catch ahold of the ladder rungs before falling into storage.

To his surprise, the grav wasn't turned on and he made it to the engine room with only one additional shove. He grabbed the wall to slow himself and try to get his feet beneath him. His boots skidded against the metal grating.

"That you, Aef?" Merei called from the hatch of the engine room.

"Ya," he answered as he came to a halt at the door.

"Why'd he pull the grav?"

186

"To punish me," he replied with a sigh. "Parto agreed that I can take a look, but he wants you to go with."

Merei removed her goggles so she could see the displeasure in her modified slitted eyes.

He suppressed a shudder knowing the only reason she was on this run was to get the payout to finish her Troxine conversion so she could join her wife on Trox's surface. The half-finished mods gave her a mashed up appearance that was unsettling to look at. He tried to meet her gaze so he wouldn't stare at the flat scar where her nose had been removed but the reptilian slit pupil sitting in her sapphire iris pulsating under his look forced him to look away so she wouldn't see his revulsion.

She folded her second lid so the color was obscured and whined, "Listen, Aef, I just want back. It's freezing here and I'm a mod away from planetside."

"I know, but this is a full colony just sitting there. Hasn't been touched in nearly a solar cycle drive. Doesn't that excite you?"

"No," she replied flatly as she stepped out of the engine room and started for the gear room.

Aefel clicked his heels so he could follow on foot; glad that he did so as Parto turned on the grav a second later.

"Why the interest?" Merei asked as she pulled out their suits.

He sighed, searching for the words.

"You a colony brat?" she asked.

"Ya, raised. That's why I like exploring them. Reminds me of a time before hulk lugging."

Merei pulled out her gill covers from her locker, snapping them in place along her neck brace. She gasped as the system turned on. "Never get used to that."

"Why Trox of all places?" he asked when she was in less distress.

Merei laughed and the double sound issuing from her gills and mouth made his skin crawl. "That's where Bebnis is."

"Have you ever been there?"

She shook her head. "Nope, never met Beb either, but that's where I'm to be. So let's get this over with so I can get back and finally get home."

Aefel frowned thankful the shield of his helmet blocked him from her view. The salvage trade had a lot of crew turnover because of the pay. They were looking to pay for mods to inhabit the planet of their choice. Aefel never had that desire, though. He liked the sense of security that metal around him provided. The openness of planets unsettled him. He liked ships because he could watch the crew closer than on a colony where people would come and go with the trade ships.

"You have trouble with Troxines?" Merei asked as the rattling ship eased into the docking ports.

Aefel shook his head. "I have no problem with any species. I look at the individ. I just don't want to be anything but me."

She shifted her goggles back into place without a word as she opened the airlock room.

He followed her, activating the closing procedure on the inner hatch. It hesitated at the command and he made a mental note to lubricate it when they returned.

"Havin' trouble syncing up," Emmet stated over the com. "Might be going blind."

"What he expect?" Merei asked. "Place is derelict. Shouldn't be a system on."

Aefel shrugged trying to realign the inner hatch to get it to seal after the hesitation. "Any sign of breach?"

"Nada," Emmet answered. "Short hop to get to the hatch."

"Gotcha," Merei replied, palming the airlock and starting out when it was halfway open.

Aefel quickly grabbed a tether and snapped it to the loop on the back of her suit and another one onto his.

He heard a muffled shout over the com and realized with the slam of the inner hatch that Merei had breached the salvage ship. "Hold up," he shouted after her before she could do something else haphazard, but Merei was already at the *Claudia*'s hatch door with her toolkit trying to override it. "We have the codes," he said and pushed her aside as he keyed in the numbers that Parto was rattling off in his helmet. A closed circuit would be holding the door as the rest of the colony electronics were long disabled. He wondered just how long a life the battery cells had remaining. He waited a moment expecting some pressure equalization, but there was none.

"What you expect?" Merei scoffed as she pushed her way in. "For a lugger you sure expect a lot from derelicts."

He couldn't answer her as he always expected something that never seemed to happen when he entered any salvage hulk. On the *Claudia* he expected more, but he couldn't tell her why. That would have been a lot more explanation than he was ready to give. If he was wrong about what he was searching for, he wouldn't need to explain to any of the salvage ship's crew.

"You see anything?" Porto asked.

"Not a thing. No electrics 'cept the lock setup," Merei replied as she hooked up her shoulder lights to cast a bright beam ahead them down the corridor. "What are we after?""

"Whatever Aefel is wanting. Your tanks are full, so that'll give you enough time to get to the main engines," answered Porto.

"Circulation filters be great," drawled Emmet. "The storage floor was cleared by the Registors, so the only ones left will be in engineering. If you see anything that we could use for our repairs, bring it in."

Merei looked to Aefel taken aback with the last request.

He grinned and explained. "We get paid for the body. Most the contents aren't logged and if it saves repair costs, it adds to the payout."

She shook her head and started down the hall. "Then I'm heading straight to the engines. I'll call if I need help moving something."

Aefel heard Porto's chortle through the com and realized that had been the plan all along. The salvage ship was going to be going in for a maintenance audit after this trip and Porto knew it was going to cut a lot of the profit. Even if the engine components didn't fit the ship, they could be traded for a higher price than the Recych would give. He should have guessed that the arguments had been for show. He couldn't remember a time that Porto had actually denied him entry into one of their hauls. He was always sent with another crew member who would go off to the engine or command areas to find tradeable goods. Aefel wondered when he would learn or remember so that he could use it as part of his argument.

He lost sight of Merei long before the clunk of her boots hitting the floor stopped reverberating around him. He started toward the living area. He had studied the plans of the *Claudia* the duration of the flight. Then again, he hadn't really needed to. This was where he had spent his primer days. The blueprint had been imprinted on his brain. He wondered if Porto remembered that, which was why he had given them full tanks instead of his usual frugal half.

As if reading his mind, the captain buzzed into the com. "So what are you really after?"

Aefel looked at his radio, confirming they were on a private channel before responding. "Nothing."

"Really?"

"Like you said, the Registors and Morgies cleared it out."

"Ya, but we know that don't mean they knew where to look."

Aefel nodded even though Porto couldn't see him. They knew how much could be missed by the Registors who were only interested in the data of the main computers and the personal effects that were requested by former inhabitants. The problem was, there were very few former inhabitants of the *Claudia* to put in any requests. "They made it sound like there were mass fires."

"Naw, that's the rumors." Porto replied. "Official report says radi leak took most of them by surprise. Morgies had a helluva time clearing them all out."

"They solar blasted most the bodies because of the levels."

"Any of your kin still on?"

"Not direct kin."

There was no reply and Aefel was left alone with only the sound of his boots as he continued. He wasn't sure what he had expected. He had been on derelicts before, but they always seemed to have some system still running. Lights would buzz or circulators would try to kick over. *Claudia* had been hard shut, though. Nothing should be running but he hoped that was wrong. There should be one area that hadn't been touched by the Morgies and Reggies. He quickened his pace as his memories guided him.

It had been a long time since he had been in silence. He usually avoided silences; maybe that was the reason he hated planets. Too many areas of open spaces and quiet, but even in those locations there were usually insects or something to interrupt it. All ships or colonies buzzed or groaned and it had been the lullaby of his youth. Now the silence was causing his skin to crawl and his eyes began to see shadows moving in the thin beams of his shoulder lights.

He paused at the split of the corridor and closed his eyes. He could hear a low mumur now. "Parto, it say anything about the backup generator?"

"Taken out," the captain answered too quickly.

"You sure?" Aefel asked. He had no reason to doubt that the captain hadn't gone over the entire manifest and knew exactly what was in the colony before and after the initial recovery. He probably knew just how many casualties there had been, the number of return prop requests, and most certainly what the Registors had taken other than data; however, hearing the gruff voice in his ear helped focus him.

"If you're hearing something, check the training facility," Parto replied. "Might've had something for the kiddies."

Aefel nodded and started to the left. The training facility had been his destination since the beginning, but by making it out as Parto's idea gave him more credibility of not having a plan or reason for his exploration.

There was nothing in his way. The doors to the habitat quarters were closed. Without power, they could be slid open as the locks were long disengaged. Only the outer hatches had closed circuits. The interior had been tied to the main power. He ignored the doors as he went to the training facility. A low hum joined the murmur that broke the silence.

"What's that?" Parto asked.

"You're sure there's no generator?"

"No energy signature coming off the hulk. You have any ideas?"

"Nu-uh," Aefel lied, pushing open the door with no protest from the rails. He didn't put much effort into it as the bulky steel slammed into the rail end and bounced back at him slightly.

"Jaezzers!" Merei's voice cursed over the general channel.

"What's wrong?" Emmet asked.

Aefel had forgotten about the other two crewmates with the private channel. It made him wonder where Parto was monitoring from that Emmet wasn't hearing.

"Radi shadows," she explained with a calmer voice. "Never saw them before."

Emmet whistled. "Long creepy bastards. Need Aef?"

"Naw, not since I know what it is. What's the rads here?"

"You're safe. Reggies took all the radioactive material and scrubbed it clean."

"Just what did you send me into?" she asked. "Registors never take out anything that isn't high priority. This place should be glowing hot."

Aefel switched to the main channel and explained. "There were a lot of families here. They had no choice but to take it. *Claudia* was only a couple decades old. One of the first in its class. Needed to make sure it was a safe design since most of the new ones were based on it."

"I was born on one of these," Emmet replied. "Pretty solid. Still make 'em."

"Merei," Parto interjected, "if they haven't taken it, see if there are some circulation valves with the filters. They usually contain well during rad leaks."

"Usually," she mumbled before chiming, "on it."

There were a couple clicks in Aefel's com and Parto was back on a private line. "That'll keep her busy. Now tell me what you're seeing."

"Not sure yet." He stepped into the room and blue lights started to glow along the edge of the room. With each step, more lights came on and he saw the room was in disarray. "Ya, they tossed this over."

"Probably trying to find the secondary."

Aefel stumbled as his foot hit base of a toppled stool that had settled low to the floor. He caught it with his heel before it could float too far in the non-grav. "How'd you know about the secondary?"

"Come on, Aef, how long we been doing this?" Parto probed. "You've been quiet about it of late, but you used to talk about the *Claudia* a lot."

"You brought us here on purpose?"

"Only chance you'd get. Now hurry up. Keep this pace and you won't have enough air to get back."

Aefel swallowed the lump that had made its way from his stomach to his throat as he continued into the room. He didn't remember talking about the secondary unit of his home colony. It wasn't something he had thought about until the list of jobs had been laid out. He also didn't realize just how tricky Parto could be. If he did manage to find the secondary, what guarantee did he have that the captain wouldn't take it to sell?

"Em," Merei's voice called. "Need your help."

"Get Aefel," Emmett replied. "Why should I suit up?"

"Because I need your monkey modded arms."

"I ain't got mods."

There was a pause. "You mean you were born with those?"

Parto's laugh-choked voice came over the main channel. "He's on his way."

Aefel waited until he heard the click to the private channel before asking. "What do you want with the secondary?"

"Why's it important to you?" Parto asked. "It's just a computer."

"You know it isn't," Aefel replied. "You know how the colonies work."

"I know how the new ones work, but *Claudia* was the prototype, wasn't she? She has something different in her and there aren't many who know what that is. Why you're one of them is what I really want to know."

His body began to feel colder, but he knew it was his mind playing tricks on him. Nothing was changing in the room around him. Aefel sat on the stool he had righted and slowed his breathing. He had to believe Parto wouldn't betray him. He had to trust that his captain would do the right thing. His eyes had adjusted to the dim blue lights and he shut off his shoulder lights. The lights on the walls pulsed in the direction of the main study dorm.

Aefel sighed, trying to figure out the best way to explain without giving away too much information." You know how the new ones have separate controls now? The drive that controls anything to do with base function is separate from the drive that controls anything inhabitant based?"

"Right," answered the captain.

"They're on separate circuits that never cross. They don't know the other exists and just perform their function."

"Like any good machine does. Why does it matter if they were to communicate? Wouldn't that be more efficient?"

"Not when they have differing opinions of efficiency." Aefel stood and followed the lights. "*Claudia* showed that. The radiation leak wasn't normal. There were no broken cases, it opened on its own because the systems were in disagreement."

"How does that even happen?" Parto asked in disbelief. "Virus in the system?"

"Naw, something worse than that." Aefel's hand rested on the edge of the dorm's sliding door, tension growing in his body as he touched the metal "Have you ever seen the system cores of the units?"

"The Registors always take those."

"If they know what to look for," Aefel replied as his taut muscles forced the door open with more force than the greased track required. "Did you know I was there when the leak happened?"

"Wha? Naw, you were on Diwstoca. You'd been gone long before. Remember, we met there."

Aefel swallowed hard. "The initial leak. Not the one that caused it to go critical."

"Initial leak?"

The panel was before him. Deepest black. He saw the quick flashes of yellow through the glass. The Registors could have easily overlooked it as wall decoration. There was no definition to it if one didn't know where to look. He set his palm on it and a surge of energy ran through him.

"Ask Merei if there is a capsule in the engine room. Looks kind of like a cryo-pod but more ovoid and no panels. Gloss black. Should be one single seam on it near one end that is almost impossible to see."

"What are you talking about?"

"You've seen 'em before. It's the primary capsule that housed the main system." Aefel waited to hear Parto switch and ask Merei before he began tracing the darting lights on the panel. He knew the pattern by heart and as he slid his finger over the smooth surface. With each pass the silhouette began to form.

Merei answered Parto. "There's a seared part of the floor around an empty jagged hole in the shape of an egg, but no capsule."

"It's kind of a sooty mess," Emmet continued with a dramatic sneeze to prove that he wasn't happy about having to come over to the hulk. The mask would have filtered any residue before it got to his respirator. "Expands out. Kinda creeps up the walls. Why you want it, Cap?"

"That's where the primary data storage had been," Parto replied. "Just seeing if we'd luck out on some extra pay. Keep getting those circulation units." A few seconds later the captain was back in Aefel's headset alone. "What's it mean?"

Aefel continued his work. "The original marks are from the initial opening that happened years before the radiation leak that condemned this place. The primary was opened and taken out because the secondary wouldn't agree with it. When it was gone, the secondary was in charge of everything, but that isn't an efficient method. It can't compute everything that is needed all the time. Eventually it has to give up something to pay attention to something else and then it went critical."

"Jaezzsus, Aef, These are computers, they don't need to pick and choose what to do."

"Then why do they always put in a secondary?" Aefel asked as he finished the final line. The yellow lights chased one another along his tracing fast enough that it formed almost a solid line. He waited for a response but Parto wasn't answering, as he was murmuring something to Merei and Emmet about the condition of the circulation units in relation to the radiation levels.

There was no radiation, though. The entire colony had been cleansed and vented long ago. Everything of value had been neatly packed and taken away to be reused in other colonies or ships. Everything of importance except the data drives. There had been nothing left of the primary for the Registors to find and the second was hidden better than expected. The problem with prototypes was that the blueprints didn't necessarily match the build. The *Claudia* was a maze to the Registors and Morgies, and even though the plans indicated the secondary was in the training facility, it didn't mean they knew what they were looking for.

Aefel stood back and watched as the lines began to take on paths of their own. The figure was more defined and details were coming through. It wouldn't be long before they finished, but it would be too long for his short air supply. He tightened the cord around his gauntlet to ensure the rest of his suit remained airtight as he pulled off one of the finger caps. The heat radiating from the panel intensified as he touched it. "Come on," he exhaled.

"What was that?" Parto asked.

"Nothing," he replied and switched off the com. It was against protocol to go offline but he needed to concentrate as he finished the traces. It was accent markings; one where a collarbone would lie, then down to the sternum and navel. There was a click to the side of the panel and it fell forward. He jumped back as it crashed and shattered on the floor. The diodes still blinked around his feet but he was looking into a closet of a room with an ovoid pod standing on end with coils and cables running out from it. "There you are," he breathed. "Are you ready?"

The room lit brighter, casting aside the yellow haze for a cleaner white light. A command panel beside him scrolled through commands and he set his naked fingertip on it. The jolt that ran through his body nearly forced him from the panel, but he held his ground as the coils began to disconnect from the pod and the cables retracted into it.

There was a buzzing in his ears. Parto was calling him. He should have just muted the com instead of turning it off. He reached up and pressed the mic. "What?"

"I should ask you that," growled the captain. "The scans are reading power from near you and another body. Merei says it's raining parts in the engine room as everything has let go and is crashing down on them."

"I found the secondary. I'm bringing her out of hibernation in order to bring her aboard," Aefel replied, and slid one of the control buttons on the panel. "Trying to accelerate so I won't hyper."

"Hibernation? Just what you got in front of you? Give me your eyes."

"No," Aefel stated, refusing Parto access to the camera on his helmet. This was his mission alone. The home of the secondary drive was almost shrine-like to him and he didn't want to share it.

"It's not coming on my ship unless I see it."

"I'll show when I have it disengaged," he countered as the thin seam on the pod began separate before him. Aefel stepped up and pried on the edge. The soft whoosh of escaping air met him and he quickly grabbed the extra mask on his belt. The air gauge read fifteen minutes; with two it would be far less. He had to hurry as the air seemed to come out faster the more open he got the pod. He knew there was another layer between him and the secondary, but he didn't know how long it would last now that the protective core was gone.

The cover floated to the ground with a hollow thud that rung through the training facility as it bounced off and spun into the training facility's main room. His hand was pulsing and he realized it was from the tightened gauntlet. He quickly replaced the fingertip and allowed circulation back.

"Crikes," Emmet exclaimed. "I'm getting the barrow. There's enough here for us to outfit three salvage ships!"

"Be quick," Parto replied. "I don't want to have to refill you. Send Merei while you gather. She's due for a top off."

"Naw," Merei piped in. "I still have over half. I don't need as much. If anyone needs anything, it's Aef. Where is he? Haven't heard much."

He keyed over. "I'm almost done here." He looked at his gauge and groaned. There must've been a leak out of the gauntlet because it was nearing red. "Once I got this, I'll be booking back quick."

"Any emergency tanks near you?" asked Parto.

"Those were cleared out," Aefel replied without checking. "Wouldn't want to risk one anyway. They are known to take on a weird taint from radi leaks."

"Still better than nothing," Emmet stated. "Need me down that way?"

"No. Load up and get it settled so we can start tethering."

Parto grunted.

"If that's all right with you, Captain," he corrected.

"Uh-huh. Best to be starting this actual salvage. We made good time here, but the back trip will be harder with this mass."

Aefel's attention was drawn back to the pod as the protective skin finally broke away from the secondary and oozed to the floor like discarded placenta. The thought made his stomach turn. He remembered that feeling of the thick gel sliding from his body as he left the primary pod. The air had been circulating then, not the cold stillness that was the derelict. He had the mask in hand and when she gasped her first airless breath, he smashed it over her lips without concern for tenderness.

Her sightless eyes snapped open as he finished hooking the breathing apparatus into place. She couldn't resist him as her atrophied muscles wouldn't respond. Her thoughts had controlled the colony, not her body until the hibernation had been enacted.

"Hush," Aefel whispered. "Shallow breaths till your lungs feel it."

"What was that?" one of his crew asked over the com but he wasn't sure which one and didn't bother to answer.

He pulled the thin suit shell that was his backup from his pocket and started unfolding it. "Miss me, Lanst?"

She turned to the sound of his voice and he felt a name cross his mind that he hadn't heard in a very long time in a voice that took him back to the ethereal fluidness of his pod. *Clau?*

The force of the foreign thought caused him to collapse against the side of the pod. Aefel had forgotten the telepathic strength between them. Maybe that was the true reason he hated silence, he had never known it. When he and Lanst had been paired to become the *Claudia*, he had no longer had a moment alone. That was until she felt she could do better and he let her prove it.

*It's Aefel*, he thought back to her to avoid more confusion from his crewmates. He started feeding her arms through the sleeves and she was unable to resist. He hadn't thought there would be confusion. His own removal from the pod had been quick, without any memory degradation, but he had not been in hibernation for decades. The last thing she would remember would be the radi spikes when they would have thrown her into hibernation; not knowing she was also in charge of primary functions because he had abandoned it all to her.

*I am Dia*, she replied.

*No*, he thought sternly enough for her to jerk back into the pod. *You are Lanst. They made you Dia and bonded us. Remember?* He forced the onslaught of memories at her quickly as he watched the flashing on his air gauge. He should have thought about taking another tank for this.

Parto called out. "You're low, Aef. Get back!"

"Comin', Cap."

*Who is that?* she thought breaking the memories of their pairing. *That is not Captain Oshaun.*

There is no more Claudia, he started.

I failed, she stated. I remember. I did not think it was correct and you unbonded us because of that. I remained. There was something very wrong that I did not understand.

*Good, it's coming back.* He smiled and finished fastening the suit around her. Aefel took one of the tethers from his suit and looped it around her waist. He clicked off his boots so he was floating beside her.

"Parto, hit the winch. I'm not going to make it fast enough," Aefel stated.

"Got what you're after?"

"Ya," Aefel replied and turned the cam on his helmet on and glanced back at Lanst who was still processing the memories he was feeding back to her. The data transmittal was draining him and was the real reason he wanted the ease of the cable return. He needed to get her to comprehend how different the universe was. They had been kids when they were hooked up into the pods. Smaller than kids. Fetuses. They had been uploaded into the pods and grew into being processors. He wasn't joking about being born on *Claudia*. His first steps had been when he left the pod, but he had been a teenager. Poor Lanst would've been almost thirty when she was put into hibernation.

"Jaezzus. What the ...

"She's the secondary drive. I'll explain if you get us back."

Lanst floated beside him. The film was starting to fall from her eyes and he shifted the mask more so she could see out of it. He could see slight bruises at the corners from where he had pressed it too hard.

"I'm lowering ship grav to minimums," Parto stated as the tether began to reel them in. "Explain."

"Not enough air to do that," Aefel replied.

Can't you mindspeak with him? Lanst asked.

No. I am only connected with you.

She said no more to him as they continued down the corridors.

He continued to send her explanations of what he knew. They had fought. She felt he was doing things wrong; putting priority on minor functions when others were more important. The constant data flow between them had nearly shorted them out and finally he had had enough and left. He figured out the codes to unlock his pod and rewired the entire functions of the ship to her. It had been the down time with only two maybe three engineers in the area of his pod. He had sent them away by creating an anomaly that caught their attention before he opened the pod and snuck away. They could still communicate as he walked around the colony unnoticed in his stolen uniform, but Lanst was enjoying the new power and her gloating caused him to stowaway on a freighter. He had the knowledge of how things worked. He was a primary drive. He knew everything.

*Why a salvage ship?* she asked, taking him off guard.

*Inconspicuous,* he replied. They had come to the main split and he could see the beam of Emmet's shoulder lights coming toward them. They were nearly to the ship. *Plus I could see if any drives were hidden and maybe rescue them before Recych.*

What would have happened to me if they found me?

They would not have looked for you. They do not look before melting the hulk. Everything within is bonded together to make something new.

She did not respond and her already limp body seemed to slacken more. He knew she was trying to access the database of the salvage ship to find out what happened to the hulks that were salvaged, but there was no access for her. She would not be compatible with anything newer than the *Claudia*. Their system was long outdated and no amount of downloads or upgrades would make them compatible with the tech of today. It was going to be a learning experience for Lanst, but at least she would have him. Unlike before, he meant to stay and assist her as long as she would accept his help. They would function as they were designed as individs not as processors.

Aefel sighed heavily as they made it to the air lock of the salvage ship and were able to rid themselves of the empty tank. He saw Lanst's confusion as she looked over the control panels of the salvage ship and was quick to her side to begin her integration into the world beyond the pod.

The salvage ship was old and nearly outdated, but it got the job done. He understood it and every function on it. In the ever-expanding universe, the sturdy ship was a comfortable haven of a time long gone. That had been the main reason he had become a member of Parto's crew. It allowed him to see the cast-off colonies and ships that were now obsolete like him. Aefel knew he was outdated space junk and he was fine with that.

\*\*\*

# All Because of the Bees

by Theresa Jacobs

### *CANADA: The sting of surviving the end of the world*

"Get your foot out of my back, goddammit!" Bryce lifted his hip off the cot and slid forward a few inches, all the tiny space would allow. There was no movement from behind him, but a rotten stench invaded his senses. He slipped off the cot, his bare knees cracked against the cool metal floor, and he immediately grabbed the bar on the wall to hold himself from floating up to the ceiling. He moved to the small portal to look out and saw a red smear. He licked his thumb, scrubbed at it and grumbled over his shoulder, "You're disgusting."

There was still nothing to see but an endless twinkle of stars, which transported him to childhood when he, and his little sister Anna, would sit on the roof and star gaze. He blinked back a tear and said, "Fine, I'm not in the mood to talk anyway."

Reaching overhead, he turned the crank and drifted up into the control room. He locked the hatch, then strapped himself into the only seat, comforted by being held in place for a while. He wasn't sure how much longer he could continue living this way. The escape pods were designed for one person, and here he was, trapped with Henry as they had both raced to get off the dying earth.

Bryce opened the food compartment that housed the dehydrated packets and frowned. He calculated that they had been jettisoned into deep space six months ago; there was enough food for one person to last a year. Although they rationed and only ate once a day, it was still two mouths, two packets of food, and who knew how long until they would come into contact with the January ship. If they ever would at all.

A small, red blob floated past his eyes. *What is that?* He waved his hand as though shooing a fly and it spun off. He looked over his shoulder and realized more red blobs floated in the cockpit with him. *Is that blood?* Fingers shaking, he reached out to grab one for inspection when a loud bang jarred the capsule from below. He jumped, his arms swirling the unknown matter about the cabin.

"What?" he called out, and his heart slowed with the realization that it was just Henry. "You were sleeping!" Bryce yelled, his voice echoing in the metal chamber. "I've only been up ten minutes and two minutes ago you didn't want to talk to me." He listened for a response and was greeted with silence. "Yeah, that's what I thought," he mumbled, rubbing his face. "I can't take much more of this." Gritting his teeth, he drew in a deep breath and shakily exhaled the words, "Ride the wave, ride the wave." He released the anger welling up inside as he'd been taught in military school.

He had worked so hard assisting everyone else safely off the planet. He dreamed of arriving at the New World Space Station, on the planet Dothan, and being hoisted on men's arms as a hero. *Bryce Holden, saviour of the people of Earth* and exalted to *President of the New World.* His eyes glazed over as the vision overtook the emptiness before him and he relived the past.

They knew in the early 2000s that bees were dying, and if they went extinct, the world would end, yet they didn't do enough to try and stop it. As the human race moved into the tail end of 2092, all the bees were gone. New crops couldn't grow, riots began, people took to underground bunkers or set out for space. By 2099, the earth was dead. While most people, who had money, were long gone, a select few soldiers, like Bryce Holden, stayed back to make sure the last of the decent people got off planet safely. Then the raiders came; they were sent to sabotage the launch of the last ship—January—the other twelve already headed for the New World Space Station. The soldiers fought back hard, most died. Bryce only knew that the January ship launched safely, and he and his fellow soldier, Henry, jumped into the escape pod as the depot blew. They were hurtled into outer space, with only the pre-set trajectory of the new planet, Dothan.

The hope of seeing the ship was wearing thin, and Henry was getting on his nerves. He constantly asked Bryce unanswerable questions, like: *How far ahead did he think they were? Were they even going in the right direction? Why wasn't the other ship answering their distress calls?*

"I don't have all the answers!" Bryce yelled at the cockpit. He sighed and tapped the instrument panel. A few months back, he had adjusted the oxygen level lower to conserve air; he wasn't well-versed on how long it would last with two people. The control valve showed the cabin pressure holding steady, and he grinned. "Don't fret, Henry, it's not going to overheat. You don't even know how to adjust the thrust, so stop touching things," he grunted into the silent pod.

No one ever told him how quiet space was; it was bothersome.

Bryce's head bobbed, and he jerked it back up when his chin hit his chest; not that it mattered, there was nothing to do but sleep. He knew that sleeping too much was a sign of depression, which in these circumstances could lead to deeper issues and wreak havoc.

He stretched his arms, popped his knuckles and unbuckled the shoulder straps. "All right, Henry, you can have a seat for a while," he called out as he spun open the hatch. *Perhaps they could play a word game, occupy some time together.* There was no entertainment on board, and they had to keep their minds sharp.

"Maybe today we can play name that star," Bryce chuckled under his breath. They were soldiers, what did they know of stars?

As the hatch opened, a rancid odour wafted through the cabin. Bryce wrinkled his nose. "Uh, did you shit down there?" His face tightened into a grimace, he squinted his eyes; the stench was overpowering. Holding his breath, he stuck his head into the opening and was appalled by the sight.

"What the ... Henry?"

Bryce's stomach flipped, he fought back the vomit, not wanting it floating around the cabin with him. He pushed the hatch down and quickly spun the wheel to lock out the gruesome vision below, and hopefully the smell.

"What happened?" he asked himself as he strapped back into the seat. His eyes traveled to the floating red balls. He reached for one and pinched it between his fingers. It popped. It was blood.

"Did I kill Henry? Could I have?" Bryce scratched his head, desperate to recall what transpired. He looked at his hands, they were trembling, and he noted the crusted flakes of blood coating his fingernails. He gave them a shake, as though to make them clean again.

Then a bang came. A knock from below.

"Go away!" Bryce cried out. "You're dead now."

He closed his eyes. *You're dead.* He had a flash of memory. The fight with Henry. How his rage grew into blackness and next, seeing Henry's head cracked open like an egg. His blood and brains oozing out on the cot. *No wonder it smelled so bad.* He grimaced, he'd just crawled out of that shared cot. *Was I sleeping with a dead man?*

There was a faint rapping noise, a two-time knock-knock, on the hatch from below.

"You can't fool me, Henry!" Bryce pounded his foot down hard, creating his own noise. "I can't hear you!" He stomped manically, his bare heels drumming a beat in the small pod.

He paused and listened.

All was silent once again, and he envisioned pushing Henry out of the escape pod and into black space. Bryce started to laugh. He clutched his stomach and bent forward as he heaved in gusts of self-amusement. He imagined the look on Henry's face as he floated away from the pod and laughed even harder.

As his laughter finally died off and he regained control, Bryce thought perhaps that wasn't such a crazy idea. *I'll just wait until Henry is asleep and I'll open the pod door and push him out. Then I'll have plenty of food and room for rest of the year.*

Satisfied that he would soon travel in peace and comfort, Bryce closed his eyes for another long nap.

**\*\*\***

# What Goes Around ...

## by C. R. Downing

### US: Cosmic karma for a world under siege or alien manifest destiny?

Location: Frinyo City – Weapons Cache
Date: 38.442.02.13

Gnarnell looked down with one of her three stalk-eyes. The rough wooden box she focused on sat in the corner of the small room she and her fellow freedom fighters occupied. The two other stalk-eyes and her two inset eyes remained focused on the evidence of her predicament.

She grunted.

"Yes, Captain!" The closest of the twenty-seven insurgents under her command answered. That was the required response, even if the soldier wasn't sure of the directive.

How foolish is our protocol? Gnarnell thought. This youth is willing to do something without even knowing what it is. I must devise a task.

"I require—"*I have the answer!*—"the box of ammunition and weaponry from that corner." She pointed a prehensile finger toward the box.

"By your command!"

The young male made his way through the packed room. Gnarnell's stalk-eyes followed his progress. *He's so dedicated. I wish he lived in a better time.*

The room was too small for them. It was poorly located. It did not provide adequate protection for anyone, military or civilian.

The room was never meant to be a sanctuary. It was listed on government manifestos as a weapons cache. That description convinced her to stage the end of the mission there.

The youth returned with the box held tight against his scaly body. She noted that his fingers had yet to mature into the almost sentient digits of Deloqkian adults. *He's no more than twelve orbits old.* He sat the box close to where her tail circled her clawed feet. She flashed the sign for a job well done. He beamed.

She gave a nod of dismissal. He nodded in respectful reply and worked his way through the crowd recounting his successful mission to each companion he passed.

Using her well-muscled tail, Gnarnell slid the box against the wall behind her. She turned to shield her movements and the contents of the box from prying eyes. It was best that she know what she had before anyone else.

The lid opened with minimal resistance. She leaned it up against the wooden container.

Inside she found much less than she'd hoped for.

Records indicate that this room holds a supply of weapons. I assumed that some would be plasma-based or laser pistols. This collection of antiques doesn't qualify as a supply of anything but disappointment.

The box contained ten items. She recognized them all from books on the history of Deloqk, her home planet. Despair crowded out other thoughts She gave her head a vicious shake to reset her feelings and began taking inventory.

One grenade. Three canisters of noxious gas. One canister each of flammable liquid and explosive fluid. One detonator for a bomb. Two sacks of projectile ammunition. One bottle of what I assume is wine.

Despair wrestled hope, vying for the upper hand in her mind. *This is a twisted joke being played by fate.*

"I need a volunteer," she said with even less inflection than was usual for her species. Suppression of emotion was her preferred method of overcoming unwanted thoughts. It was a useful technique.

All heads turned in her direction. Twenty-seven quintets of eyes found their point of focus on her. Twenty-seven first-fingers on twenty-seven hands of twenty-seven arms of revenge of twenty-seven guerrillas pointed at her.

It is as I expected. They've all volunteered. How many do I take with me on this suicide mission?

*

Solar System: Quadrant 4/Red Dwarf 221 // Planet: Deloqk
Personal Observations Log
Author: Gnarnell

Rank: Captain, Army of the Sovereign Nation of Cronoqk
Date: 38.435.15.24

The celebration is finally over. I was afraid it would never end.

The aliens called themselves explorers when they arrived on Deloqk. Civilians should have asked why an advanced civilization on a mission of exploration would need an armada of spacecraft to survey a three-planet solar system at the fringe of the Andromeda Galaxy.

But they didn't. They were too busy enjoying the novelty.

I was glad that the aliens were greeted with cautious optimism by the governments of Deloqk. The hundreds of alien ships are sleek and fast, unlike the bulky cargo spaceships of our space fleet. Technology the aliens freely share is decades, perhaps centuries, ahead of anything we've got. I fear the opportunities for improving the status quo are seen as goals by the populace and not the temptations they are.

Few Deloqkians outside the top military brass doubt their claim of a neighboring solar system as their home. From a military point of view, the alien ships' design indicates hyper-light capability. No solar system close to ours would commit this many long-distance spacecraft for a drive through the neighborhood.

Unless exploration was not the primary motivation of that neighborhood jaunt.

Deloqk has never been a major player in interplanetary commerce. Only four Deloqkian nations have access to materials and fuel sources needed to build and maintain rudimentary interplanetary craft. For that reason, the vast majority of our citizenry is naively unconcerned with interplanetary commerce or interstellar travel.

I know for a fact that the Ruling Council of Cronoqk withdraws support of anything when revenue drops below its prediction. The direct correlation between cost and benefit is magnified in a venture as expensive as space travel. I've heard the other governments involved in space commerce feel the same way.

Because of this known expense versus hypothetical gain or loss, all spacecraft produced on Deloqk are cargo-carries. ALL OF THEM! Not one spaceship is equipped with offensive weapons. Our ships don't even have defensive shields.

I'm seriously concerned about this last issue. Mark my words, the lack of interest in space travel as anything more than an economic novelty will come back to bite us in our collective muscular tails.

\*

Solar System: Quadrant 4/Red Dwarf 221 // Planet: Deloqk
Personal Observations Log
Author: Gnarnell
Rank: Captain, Army of the Sovereign Nation of Cronoqk

Date: 38.436.05.37

It's hard to believe that it's been almost 5.25 months since my last Observation Log entry. It hasn't been from the lack of observations of the aliens.

Observation 1. There are a lot of explorers. That's what the aliens call themselves. Remember? The citizenry continues to overlook that. Only a few naysayers—like me—keep pointing out the large number of aliens on Deloqk. This is a **concern**.

Observation 2. The vocal minority repeatedly points out that every alien wears a uniform. To me, the conclusion is clear. All the explorers are members of the military. That's another cause for **concern**. The vast majority of Deloqkians don't see it that way.

Observation 3. The aliens refuse to allow Deloqkians to board any ship except those that land on the surface. Big **concern!** What's in the ships orbiting the planet that has to be kept secret?

Watch your tails, people! -

*

Solar System: Quadrant 4/Red Dwarf 221 // Planet: Deloqk
Personal Observations Log
Author: Gnarnell
Rank: Captain, Army of the Sovereign Nation of Cronoqk
Date: 38.436.07.41

The vast majority of Deloqkians are ignoring the vocal minority's warnings.

Nations who haven't played nicely with one another at the diplomatic level for centuries, embraced the aliens' call for a unified planetary government. I'm not opposed to that idea. There's been enough waste of time and resources bickering over inconsequential agendas. The problem is that a planet-wide government opens the door for a quick takeover of the entire planet in one offense operation. All the aliens have to do is control a single leader.

The gracious aliens are assisting in establishing a central government. They even provided a governmental flowchart and constitution.

Only two of our smallest sovereign states balked at the big government offer. I was pleased that some politicians hadn't lost their backbones. It turns out that the aliens had a plan for that contingency.

Both holdout nations changed their tune when the aliens announced that access to their high-level technology would be limited to those included in the planet-wide governmental structure. We're only days away from becoming one big, happy family ... on paper!

Can you feel your tail between your legs, politicians? Because that's where it is!

*

Solar System: Quadrant 4/Red Dwarf 221 // Planet: Deloqk
Personal Observations Log
Author: Gnarnell
Rank: Captain, Army of the Sovereign Nation of Cronoqk
Date: 38.437.07.01

I've been at this station often in the past fourteen months and twenty days. I just haven't written a POL during that time. I'm not sure why I feel compelled to write one today, but here goes.

I don't know the whole alien agenda. I doubt that any Deloqkian knows more than 1 percent of it. It would surprise me to learn that I know even 1 percent of 1 percent.

I know that:

I was wrong about the timing of the world government implementation. It's been almost a year and Cronoqk is still a sovereign nation;

Nearly all citizens of Deloqk have fallen into place behind the benevolent, extra-intelligent, compassionate extra-terrestrials;

There are only a few of us naysayers left. And we're on constant high alert status. It's been months since I've heard any senior scientists encourage skepticism. Most of my fellow military malcontents are also strangely silent.

I'm almost certain that I'm being followed. If not, then another type of surveillance is tracking me. I feel like I'm in a room full of blind butchers with cleavers, and I'm trying to keep my tail from being cut off!

*

Solar System: Quadrant 4/Red Dwarf 221 // Planet: Deloqk
Personal Observations Log
Author: Gnarnell
Rank: Captain, Army of the Sovereign State of Deloqk
Date: 38.437.15.24

It's the two-year anniversary of my first Personal Observations Log post on the topic of the aliens. You're aware that I've never written their name, aren't you?

Oh, my! I must be more paranoid than I thought. Who's ever going to read these posts? Doesn't matter. I can barely pronounce the aliens' name. There's no way I can spell it.

You might have noticed that I'm no longer in the Army of the Sovereign State of Cronoqk. I didn't change the header. That was another freebie from the aliens' technicians. As I predicted, we're all one big happy family now here on Deloqk.

At least they let us keep the name of our planet.

Besides being a personal anniversary for this log, today is the two-and-a-half-year anniversary of the landing of the first alien ship. All Deloqk is now aligned with the alien agenda.

Not all. An ever-shrinking minority still exists.

I thought about closing with the statement that one of those blind butchers with a cleaver I referred to in my last POL was successful. I decided not to do that.

As a result of that decision, I have no *tail* reference that's appropriate for this situation.

*

Location: Frinyo City – Command Post, Cronoqk // Date: 38.439.13.10

"I tell you, 'Nell, this will be the last test drive," Aronf said. "We're going above the atmosphere today!"

I heard the excitement in his voice. I sniffed discretely. I know I smiled.

"What?" he asked.

"I was hoping the excitement was because we've finally synched our reproductive cycles not because of the anti-gravity platform test," I teased.

Aronf sniffed, but he made no attempt to be discrete with his smile. "I'll be home early. How about you?"

"I hope I don't have a headache," I deadpanned. Although I tried my hardest, I couldn't maintain my composure.

I giggled. Within seconds my husband and I were laughing and gasping.

He left.

I went to my post.

The call came late that morning.

"Lieutenant Gnarnell?"

"Speaking."

"This is Doctor Flixr."

"Oh, yes. You're one of the scientists working with my husband on the anti-gravity platform. I hope you've called with good news."

There was dead air over the comm device.

I don't like this, I thought. Before I could ask what was wrong, Flixr's voice pierced me like a knife blade.

"I'm afraid it's anything but good news, Lieutenant."

He stopped at that.

"How did Aronf die?" I asked without expression.

"The a-g platform was nearly 150 meters up when something went wrong. Your husband and a technician died on impact."

"Thank you for the personal notification," I said. At least that's what I remember saying. I know I added, "I doubt you've ever had to give a death notification before"

"It is ... beyond difficult," he managed.

"Captain, are you okay?" The voice of Corporal Hextl, her aide-de-camp, exploded into Gnarnell's consciousness—an unexpected ending to an unwanted memory.

"Fine, Corporal," she lied. "What do you need?"

"They've taken out another energy-conversion plant."

"That will be all," she muttered through clenched teeth.

"Yes, ma'am."

*

Solar System: Quadrant 4/Red Dwarf 221 // Planet: Deloqk
Personal Observations Log
Author: Gnarnell
Rank: Captain, Army of the Sovereign State of Deloqk
Date: 38.439.13.10

Well, it's almost two years since my last Personal Observation entry. That's because the situation here has degraded.

No, the situation stinks!

Interesting choice of term: stinks. I stopped at my usual beverage shop on my way in this morning. I smelled the female pheromone indicating the barrista's ovulating. Most women cover the scent with perfume. I suspect ovulation snuck up on her—those cycles don't always begin when expected. I don't mean that she was stinky. It's just uncommon to smell that pheromone outside a middle school or a bedroom.

Because the scent was unexpected, it triggered a memory. When I sat down at my desk this morning, I found myself reliving the last time I saw my husband alive.

Aronf and I were planning on starting a family. Our reproductive cycles finally synched—I could tell by his pheromone production. It took almost two years after our nuptial celebration for the synchronization to finalize.

He died the day we realized we could have children.

I had my ovaries removed shortly thereafter. I had no desire to procreate with anyone but Aronf. Still don't.

Something dawned on me.

I don't like space travel.

It's not that I tried it and don't like it. I've never been in space. It's not only because space travel brought the alien horde to Deloqk.

The reason I don't like space travel is it killed my husband.

209

Aronf died testing his anti-gravity platform. They use it now, but only to transport materials back and forth between Deloqk and our space station where the cargo ships are built, loaded, sent out, return, and are unloaded. He and his team wanted Deloqkians to use the platform to get to the space station. It was supposed to be safer than blasting off in a rocket.

There's been only one crash of an anti-gravity platform. It was the first attempt to leave our atmosphere on the device. It's the trial trip that killed my husband and his lead scientist.

Oh, my! What a digression.

It's my POL. I'm leaving the rambling paragraphs in this document.

What I was going to do before memory kicked in was check my thesaurus for a term that sounds worse than **degraded**. A semblance of decorum must be maintained. Ah, here it is: **humiliated**.

Upon further review, I'm leaving degraded.

Read on.

What the aliens and their fawning, subservient Deloqkian sell-out politicians touted as the introduction of a wonderful new era has been exposed for what it is. The whole alien charade was nothing more than setting the stage for a planet-wide takeover by the extra-terrestrial hoard.

The aliens have finally shown themselves to be the invaders I suspected they were.

During the past months, platoons of alien soldiers used plasma and ion cannons to destroy the majority of the Deloqkian on-planet energy-conversion facilities. They hit another earlier today.

Because of the small numbers of power stations left functioning, each hemisphere has access to the limited power grid only during specified hours. No one area has enough power to do more than maintain the pathetic existing conditions.

They destroyed our factories along with the energy-conversion plants. All we have left is the capability to produce low-grade fuels. Fuel produced is minimal in quantity and of poor quality. As a result, transportation is curtailed. Laser and plasma weapons are still available, but the fuel required to power them is very limited since its produced in clandestine facilities off the main power grid.

Aliens still on Deloqk download some form of energy from their orbiting maintenance craft, so they have no power shortage. I suspect the downloaded energy is electromagnetic, but I have access to ZERO analytical equipment.

Reader, if you're as smart as I think you are, you noticed that I implied there were fewer aliens and alien spacecraft now.

When Deloqk was crippled enough, the aliens withdrew. They left behind a fleet of ships and their associated troops. Guess who's shocked that all the aliens are in the military?

The aliens aren't benefactors any longer. Those are occupation troops. They're here to ensure no change in the status quo.

I'm convinced that the aliens intend to use Deloqk as nothing more than a source of raw materials and forced labor. We naysayers still alive are in high demand as we try to defeat the invaders.

Toward that end, we've launched several offensives.

That's being kind.

We had a couple of skirmishes. We don't have enough troops to mount an offensive of any sort. Every skirmish ends with casualty counts lopsided in the aliens' favor.

It's obvious that we have neither the firepower nor the manpower to trade blows with the heavyweight in this match. We'll be lying low for a while.

I refuse to capitulate. You'll not see me turn tail and run!

*

Location: Frinyo City – Command Post, Cronoqk // Date: 38.441.12.03

Gnarnell fumed over the history of poor decisions that led to her inability to take action. The now puppet government of Deloqk was paralyzed.

After it was obvious that the aliens were enemies and not benefactors, the military was ordered to "do something." The problem: the military was unprepared to launch an offensive strike or to offer the resistance ordered by the government. They took a couple of shots at the invaders. The alien counter-punches left the Deloqkians bloody but unbowed.

As the captain of Deloqk's Army's Third Company, Gnarnell had the ear of all the brass above her—at least she had those ears in times past. Now, she wasn't certain if any of the remaining brass had functioning ears or brains. Her interpretation of the recent events made the lack of brain function hypothesis a solid option in her eyes.

"Ma'am, I just decoded a message from our central governmental server," her aide-de-camp said from the doorway to her office.

"Since you're informing me of the communiqué before sending it on to me, I suspect it's not good news."

"I wouldn't want to comment on that, ma'am."

Gnarnell snorted. Thank The Maker for soldiers like Corporal Hextl.

"Very, well. Send it on."

211

"Not necessary, ma'am." The aide's clawed toes clicked on the hard surface that was the floor of her office as he walked over and handed a printout to her.

"That will be all."

"By your command!"

The document she held had been folded, no mean feat for a species with lengthy prehensile fingers. She was impressed. *Fortunately, unfolding requires less dexterity than folding.*

What she read was brief.

To: All Commissioned Officers of Deloqk

Fr: Central Governmental Military Office

Re: Situation Update

This message was sent via automated delivery on the command of the Prime Minister.

Ten hours ago, the Central Government dissolved itself. As a commissioned officer in our military, you are hereby appointed the local leader of the province in which you are stationed. If two or more commissioned officers are in the same province, it is up to them to establish a chain of command.

We should have heeded the vocal minority's warnings.

This is the final transmission from the Prime Minister's office on this frequency. I am declaring CODE BLACK.

May The Maker have mercy on us all.

*

The captain anticipated an action like this from the government. She'd been waiting for it since the majority of the population began evacuating the cities to hide out in the countryside and mountains. In truth, Deloqk had been CODE BLACK—martial law—for some time.

"So, now I'm officially the government, too," she murmured.

"Ma'am?"

"Nothing. I was just summarizing the message for myself."

"Would you like my opinion, ma'am?"

"Proceed."

"Your summary is a good one."

"Thank you," she said, but she added a mental, *I think.*

"I'll need the location of all military personnel and their locations ASAP," she ordered.

"Already in the works, ma'am."

That figures.

"Do any of them outrank me?"

There was a pause.

"Was I unclear?"

"No, ma'am. I wasn't expecting that question."

So, you're not clairvoyant, Corporal. Good to know.

"When you finish that, I want a headcount of all civilians in the province, too."

"With locations on the civilians, ma'am?"

"I don't need to see the GPS coordinates in your list. Group the names in some way so I can see where they're clustered. Subgroup those groups by sex."

"GPS will be best for that, ma'am."

"Very well."

"Is that all, ma'am?"

Is that all? Merciful Maker, are you an android?

"For the moment."

"By your command!"

*

It was the next day before Gnarnell got her list. She was relieved. That meant her android theory was wrong.

The list was on the map she'd requested. There were coded dots for each military personnel. The names of civilians in each bounded geographic area were in two colors—one for males, another for females. Civilian names were followed by a combination of numbers and letters.

"Corporal!"

"Yes, ma'am!"

"I don't see a key for the codes you devised."

"They're not on the map."

"That doesn't help me, soldier."

"Right, ma'am. I'm sorry, ma'am. There was an envelope with the map. Codes for both military personnel and civilians are in there."

Gnarnell lifted the map. *Sure enough, here it is.*

"By the way, ma'am, the next highest ranking officers to you in this province are the lieutenants of your platoons."

"Why is that essential information?"

"Yesterday, ma'am."

"Again, that's not helping."

"Yesterday, you asked if any military personnel in your province outranked you."

*How could I have forgotten that?* She nodded and said, "Dismissed."

"By your command."

Removing the four-page printout of codes from the envelope took longer than she would ever admit. She unfolded the document, placed it on her desk, and smoothed it as flat as she could manage.

The fact that the list was four pages in length stirred hope in her. Fewer than two full pages of names wouldn't have surprised her.

Military codes.

First letter: Rank. P = Private. C = Corporal. S = Sergeant. L = Lieutenant.

Next two letters: Squad. TS = The Swarm. TT = Thunder Troops. TV = The Void. TP = The Preservers. SS = Super Soldiers. SN = Squad Nasty. WF = We Finish. CC = Covert Corps.

Number: Headcount within Squad.

Final two letters: Platoon. MM = Maroon Marauders. RR = Red Rebels.

Civilian Codes.

First two letters: Military value. ME = Military Experience. WE = Without Military Experience

Number: Headcount within the geographic boundary.

She scanned the codes. *I can live with these.* Then she checked each list on the map and assessed what living resources she had at her disposal. *Outside of my own soldiers, I don't have a lot of military experience.*

Next, she looked at the boundary of Rucoa, the province she'd inherited. It was an irregular rectangle with the west side and north sides longer than their south and east companions. The western boundary was the Rucoa River. The eastern edge followed a meridian of longitude.

"Corporal!".

"Ma'am?"

"I need an opinion, and you're the closest option I have." *I hope he can still see the humor in situations.*

"Yes, ma'am. I'm always honored to be your only choice."

*He does!* She chuckled.

"I've divided the province into quadrants. I'm going to assign two squads to each of those quadrants."

"Understood, ma'am. Pardon me for commenting, but I don't think that response qualifies for an opinion."

Gnarnell laughed.

"Quite right. Here's your chance to shine. I want to keep the lieutenant in charge of each platoon to serve as my surrogate when I'm not available."

Hextl nodded.

"Is the best solution for the platoons to be responsible for north/south or east/west halves of the province? Before you decide, listen to my points to consider."

"Yes, ma'am."

"First, if we go north/south, each platoon gets one city that was once significant size. East/west that's not the case—east gets both those cities."

"Yes, ma'am."

"Second, an east/west division leaves most of the rural and undeveloped area in the province in the west while the entire river is the responsibility of the east."

"Yes, ma'am."

"Finally, there's not a single good eatery in the entire west, no matter how we divide the province."

The corporal stifled a laugh.

"Don't do that to me, Corporal."

"Ma'am?" he managed to get the single word out without laughing.

"My final point was wickedly funny. Never again will you stifle a laugh when I provide the humor. Is that understood, soldier?"

"It is, ma'am. And, ma'am, permission to chuckle now."

"Granted!"

Both the captain and her aide laughed a long time.

After both parties calmed themselves enough to wipe the tears from their fixed eyes, they got back to business. Gnarnell suspended military protocol "for the duration of this decision-making process." The discussion was spirited. In the end, the province was divided into north/south.

Maroon Marauders platoon was under the commanded of Lieutenant Micyld. Squads The Swarm, Thunder Troops, The Void, and The Preservers were deployed in the northern quadrants. Red Rebels platoon was commanded by Lieutenant Kokoff. Squads Super Soldiers, Squad Nasty, We Finish, and Covert Corps were assigned to patrol the southern half.

*

Solar System: Quadrant 4/Red Dwarf 221 // Planet: Deloqk
Personal Observations Log
Author: Gnarnell
Rank: Captain, Army of the Sovereign State of Deloqk Guerrilla Fighter for Freedom
Date: 38.442.01.55

Reader, you will notice that I've changed my rank. I can't delete the old header. Marking through it is the best I can do. Things are dicey around here, to say the least.

Read on.

The great, planet-wide government of Deloqk is dead. Our leaders bailed. We switched to guerrilla tactics. Guerrilla strikes have been more successful than the frontal attacks were.

In reality, though, I don't think our attacks are any more disconcerting to the aliens than mosquito bites are to us. However, over time mosquitos can become more bother than the host organism is willing to tolerate.

We've reached that point—the one where the aliens' tolerance is exceeded.

Deloqk is under siege. Armed alien patrols roam the countryside. Cities are searched and re-searched with ruthless efficiency. Over the past months, surviving Deloqkians migrated to the towns and villages in the hills and mountains where they've dug in.

This siege is now in its tenth month. Reconnaissance forays by my patrols report increased activity in and around the metallic ore mines. A few former governmental appointees think that the non-military activity indicates that alien interest in resource gathering is a sign of waning interest in fighting us.

Most Deloqkians, led by the remnants of military, insist that resource gathering is the first step in the production of military hardware on planet.

Only time will tell which faction read the signs accurately. I remember when I was part of the minority. Unfortunately, we ended up being right.

On the bright side, if black darkness can be considered brighter than pitch-black darkness, Corporal Hextl thinks he found a weakness in the aliens. It's a possible way to attack them all at once through something in the material of their uniforms.

Any port in a storm.

I'm going to hightail it out of here now. I have troops to command. I don't think this computer will be available again—ever—to anyone.

If Deloqk is a foreign term to you, Reader, I hope you understand that the planet on which you are located wore that name proudly.

I just had a thought. Maybe I heard this somewhere, but even if it's not original to me, I'm going to use it.

Freedom's just a word that means that there's nothing left to lose. Here's to freedom!

*

Location: Rucoa Province – Mobile Command Post, Unknown Coordinates // Date: 38.442.01.56

"Explain your uniform material theory, Corporal," Gnarnell ordered.

216

"Yes, ma'am. I was monitoring an alien transmission band when I heard a chorus of cries of pain."

"And?"

"I ran an amplitude analysis of my recording of the band just before the cries. My first thought was that something overloaded their audio circuits."

"Based on the fact that you've presented me with no information of consequence, may I assume that the problem was not increased amplitude?"

"You may, ma'am. Next, I tried a frequency discrimination protocol on the recording." He paused.

She stared at him with all five eyes, her face a blank slate.

"I discovered that a zero point six-second burst at 180 hertz occurred immediately before the cries of pain began."

"A frequency anomaly. Intriguing."

"I know. Particularly since it's just a pure tone sine wave."

Her look was enough for Hextl to know he'd lost his captain.

"It's a hum, ma'am. It's just a monotonal hum."

"I see," she said, although she didn't. "What happened after they stopped whining?" she asked.

"They were screaming, ma'am."

She shot him a look. He looked away and continued.

"After the scream— um, whining stopped, I heard a lot of alien terminology with which I am unfamiliar."

"They were cussing someone out," she said.

"I wouldn't know, ma'am."

"I would. You can trust me when I say that. Profanity is never included in formal language acquisition classes."

"I tried an experiment, ma'am."

"Tell me more."

"Do you remember early on when we had alien advisors living in our barracks?"

She nodded.

"I stole one of their uniform tops," he said.

"Why? The aliens are no more than two-thirds our size, and their arms each have two elbows—one controlling its own forearm and hand. A uniform blouse—" She stopped, unable to articulate her confusion.

"I used it to line the litter box of my tac, ma'am."

Gnarnell laughed. The tac was a household pet notorious for its sense of self-superiority and noxious fecal deposits.

"Assuming you sterilized the uniform blouse, what did you do in your experiment?"

"My protocol was simple. I cut the fabric into strips and tried using a strip as a communication broadcaster and receiver."

Gnarnell made no attempt to mask her confusion.

"That's how they communicate, ma'am. The aliens communicate through their uniforms. All aliens wear uniforms because it's their comm system."

"How does knowing that help us?"

"I did some calculations. My hypothesis is that a seven- or eight-second burst of energy at 180 hertz will stun all aliens on the comm at that time. It might kill some."

I can't believe what I just heard flashed through Gnarnell's mind. This is our doomsday weapon!

"Are you all right, ma'am?" the corporal asked after a prolonged silence.

"Better than all right, Corporal! I want my squad and platoon leaders together on our secure channel in one hour!"

*

Location: Rucoa Province – Mobile Command Post, Unknown Coordinates // Date: 38.442.01.56

"Let me summarize," Gnarnell said into her microphone to the eight sergeants and two lieutenants under her command. "I'll be in contact with military leaders in the four provinces bordering ours. The plan is simple. Their troops execute a series of strikes on targets of their own choosing. I'm hoping those forays divert most of the alien attention away from us."

"Us, ma'am?" Lieutenant Micyld of Maroon Marauders interrupted. "Are you participating in this mission?"

"You don't have a problem with that, do you, Lieutenant?"

"No, ma'am! It's just—"

"Good. I'll be commanding something less than a full platoon to create a diversion for the alien's security forces. Corporal Hextl will be inserted into the local alien communications center where he will implement his protocol. A hybrid squad commanded by the overly vocal Micyld will assist him in that task. Any additional comments or questions?"

"I have one, Captain," Sergeant Jraxl said.

"Proceed."

"What will the forces not assigned to one of these details be doing?"

"Thank you for asking. They will have the most difficult assignment of all."

Silence.

"Those not actively involved in what I suspect could be our final assault on the aliens, will be responsible for keeping things running if we fail." *I'm certain that if we do much damage and still fail, the aliens will pull their personnel off Deloqk and eradicate all life forms on this planet before they return for the resources.*

"Understood, ma'am. Begging Lieutenant Kokoff's pardon, I'd like to volunteer Squad Nasty as part of that detail."

"I can arrange that. Any other comments or questions?"

"As much as I'd love to be a nail in the coffin of those aliens, I will volunteer the rest of Red Rebels Platoon to work with Squad Nasty and whoever else we inherit or recruit," Lieutenant Kokoff said.

"Thank you, Lieutenant. Having a commissioned officer to oversee that eventuality is a best-case scenario."

Captain Gnarnell closed the comm.

*

Solar System: Quadrant 4/Red Dwarf 221 // Planet: Deloqk
Pirate POL
Author: Hextl
Rank: Corporal
Date: 38.442.02.10

Only commissioned officers are allowed access to POL servers. I've hacked my way in because I think what's about to happen should be documented.

I told Captain Gnarnell my idea to kill off the aliens. She's working on the implementation from her end now. I've got to run a couple more simulations before I get the word to proceed.

I heard that a number of civilians have hooked up with the captain. I know she'll appreciate that. They must suspect something's up with Gnarnell out and about.

The theory behind my plan is simple. I get into the alien comm center and reset their frequency filter to expedite 180 hertz transmissions. Then, I send out a repeating message of only that frequency at maximum amplitude for as long as I can keep transmitting.

I'm hoping for at least twenty seconds. That should incapacitate the bunch of them.

I think ten seconds might do some permanent damage. According to my calculations, a couple of minutes of my transmission will kill all aliens receiving the transmission on Deloqk and in orbit.

There's a chance a burst of that length of time could impact any alien that receives the message wherever it is. That'd be nice!

A lieutenant and squad of soldiers just arrived. It's show time.

If I post another personal log, that means we succeeded!

*

Location: Frinyo City – Weapons Cache // Date: 38.442.02.13

219

"I need a volunteer," Gnarnell said with even less inflection than was usual for her species. Suppression of emotion was her preferred method of overcoming unwanted thoughts. She'd found the technique useful in times past.

*It is as I expected. They've all volunteered. How many do I take with me on this suicide mission?* After some rapid mental machinations, she continued.

"I've changed my mind. I now need ten of you to come with me. We're going to draw enough aliens after us to give those who remain here a fighting chance to hold out until Corporal Hextl fries their alien nervous systems."

A cheer echoed through the room. She considered cutting it off, but let it run its course instead. When silence returned, and twenty-seven arms of revenge once again stabbed in her direction, she continued.

"My first choice is the unmarried. If you have no family, you move higher on my list. If you meet one or both of those qualifications, keep your arm of revenge up."

Seven hands dropped. Eleven others were slowly lowered to the sides of eleven freedom fighters.

*Nine left. They won't like it, but I'm cutting three more.*

"Master Sergeant, Sergeant, Sergeant, I'm amending my qualifications list to exclude all non-com officers in the Deloqkian military."

"But, Captain—"

"Which part of my amendment is unclear, Master Sergeant Raginn?" Gnarnell barked at the most senior of the non-com's present. Nine stalked eyes drooped.

"I can't begin to tell you how proud I am to have served with the three of you. I want everyone here to know that it's only because of your commitment to duty and your courage that I cannot afford to lose any of you on this mission." *Besides, there's a very real chance that you'll die in this room after I leave anyway.*

Grunts of approval and pats on the backs of the three officers sealed the deal.

"Raginn, as soon as my ample tail clears the exit out of here, you're in command."

Raginn nodded.

"I need an inventory of weapons and ammunition, and I need it yesterday," the captain ordered.

*

Location: Frinyo City – Diversionary Action // Date: 38.442.02.13

Gnarnell and her volunteers, which included one civilian, took most of what she'd found in the supposed ammunitions cache. She led the way out an obsolete exhaust tunnel. When the guerrillas emerged onto the street, they were over one-half kilometer from their starting point.

After assuming point position, she assigned one of two corporals and the civilian as the rear guard. After six blocks of covert travel, she stepped inside a burned-out store and gathered her team around her.

"You're probably wondering why I called you here," she said. Three of the soldiers grinned at the often-used phrase. The civilian's face showed her lack of understanding of the joke.

"I'm sorry, um, I don't know your name," Gnarnell said to the civilian.

"Knoraxx."

"That's a pretty name."

The young woman smiled a relieved smile.

"What I should have said, Knoraxx, is that it's time for you to know what we'll be doing to help our comrades back in the weapons cache."

She outlined a plan that involved rigging the containers of flammable liquid and explosive liquid to the detonator. They would plant what she hoped acted as a bomb at a point behind the alien troops. Once the containers of liquid were in place, she and two others would approach the aliens from the rear. She would lob a grenade to get their attention. Two canisters of noxious gas would follow the explosion, and the trio would retreat along a line that led pursuers past Knoraxx. She would detonate the bomb when aliens were on both sides of the device.

The last point of engagement, the snipers' nest, was set up at a distance from the weapons cache. When aliens arrived at that location, her team would use the remaining gas canister to occupy them while they were picked off with their projectile weapons.

They would engage in hand-to-hand combat only as a last resort.

The soldiers nodded grimly. Knoraxx threw up.

*

Location: Frinyo City - Weapons Cache // Date: 38.442.02.13

"I don't like that she's left all the laser pistols and plasma rifles here," Sergeant Jraxl complained.

"I appreciate your optimistic assessment," Master Sergeant Raginn retorted. "I don't consider a total of nine of the weapons you described with fewer than nine fully charged replacement power cells to be much to brag about."

"Sorry, Master Sergeant," Jraxl said. "I just wish—"

A fusillade of projectiles blasted their way into the room.

"Down! Everybody, down!" Raginn ordered unnecessarily.

"They must not think much of us," a soldier complained. "Projectile weapons. I deserve a least a death by laser."

Grim laughter answered the soldier's comment.

"Okay, then, let's give them a taste of our lasers just to show them how highly we regard them," the lieutenant said. "No more than ten bursts of one second each per pistol. If you don't have an alien targeted, *do not fire*. When you do target an alien, *don't miss!*"

*

Location: Alien Communications Center // Date: 38.442.02.13

"I assume you've seen building plans," Lieutenant Micyld said as Corporal Hextl's sabotage mission team stopped just outside the comm center's perimeter.

"No, sir. I had no access to that data."

"So, after we get you inside, what's your plan?"

"I'll find a terminal, hack into the network, upload the repeating frequency burst command, and send it out."

"Just like that?"

"I hope so, sir."

"What happens when we kill an alien before the message goes out?" a corporal asked.

"I don't know how to answer that," Hextl replied.

"Well, if the aliens communicate through their clothing, won't some kind of message get sent when one of the guards dies? It seems like an incomplete use of technology if that isn't the case."

"I hadn't considered that," Hextl admitted. "I hope that's not the case. Otherwise, any stealthiness we achieve will be compromised when the first alien dies."

The conversation stalled until a private spoke.

"I don't think we need to worry about them being warned by the death of a guard."

"Why not?" Micyld asked.

"If the uniforms do transmit a time of death, as long as there are other deaths besides the guards we kill, they'll never learn that we killed anyone before they're incapacitated."

"He's right!" Hextl said. "Even the most sophisticated GPS system sending realtime data at light speed still requires translation of raw data into usable coordinates. If a bunch of coordinates arrives simultaneously, or even close together, the aliens will have a hard time telling who died where."

"Good to know, Corporal," the lieutenant said. "Lock and load. We're going in!"

*

Location: Frinyo City – Diversionary Action // Date: 38.442.02.13

It took longer than Gnarnell hoped to rig the bomb and set the snipers' nest. She made certain her guerrilla snipers were deployed at the nest down a street behind the alien position. Then, she, two soldiers, and the civilian she'd chosen to assist her made one final check of their weapons.

"Remember that the gas won't discriminate between the aliens and us, so be sure that you don't open the canister until they're running after me. Once you throw the canister, run away from me. Loop around, and we'll meet at the ambush."

"Yes, ma'am," the pair chorused.

"Knoraxx—"

"Yes, ma'am," the civilian interrupted.

"I see you've been observing our military protocol. That was nicely done. Next time, though, if you'll wait until I finish my sentence, that would be appreciated," Gnarnell said through a tired smile.

Knoraxx blushed, but she smiled back.

"As soon as I turn that corner," Gnarnell said, while she pointed to her right. "Twist the detonator. Twist it hard. I don't know how long it's been in that box, but we need the fire and explosion right then."

"I'll do my best, ma'am."

"I know you will," and I hope it doesn't scar you for life.

"I was wondering, Captain, about how long you think we'll have before pursuit reaches the ambush point," one of the gas bombers asked.

"Assume they're fast runners and that you'll have to hurry to beat them after you toss your canister."

She looked at each of her associates in turn carefully studying their features. If they didn't make it through, she wanted a clear memory of each.

"I don't know if you are religious or not. I don't need to know. You will be reverent while I pray for us before we set this plan in motion."

*

Location: Frinyo City – Weapons Cache // Date: 38.442.02.13

"Why have they slowed their firing, sir?" asked a private.

"I don't have a clue," Master Sergeant Raginn replied. "It goes against any strategy I've ever studied. Once you have an enemy down, you beat him until he dies or surrenders."

223

"What'll we do?"

"Give thanks to The Maker, and distribute the remaining ammunition."

*

Location: Alien Communications Center // Date: 38.442.02.13

"Since we're still alive, I'm assuming that the GPS/dead soldier idea was either wrong or somebody's killing aliens somewhere else," Sergeant Jraxl said.

"Doesn't matter to me which is it, sir. I'm glad we inserted Corporal Hextl into that office in one piece."

"As am I, Sold—"

The cold glow of a laser beam cut through the sergeant's neck stopping his comment in mid-word.

A brief, intense firefight ensued. The final body count was five aliens and two guerrillas dead.

Hextl was unaware of the havoc outside the closed door to the office to which he'd been delivered. He managed to log on to the alien network and upload his repeating frequency sequence. It was taking longer than he'd anticipated to boot up.

He had no choice but to wait and hope that time was still on his side.

"Stick your head inside that office and check the Corporal's status," Lieutenant Micyld ordered.

The private reached for the door handle. A sizzling sound announced the arrival of a plasma discharge at the surface of the Deloqkian's elbow. Less than a second later, the private's forearm hit the ground with a thud.

Fighting was fast and furious. Laser pistols, while effective weapons, were no match for the firepower of plasma rifles. Micyld drained his laser pistol's energy cell as he watched the remaining members of Nasty Squad, and two of their laser pistols, melt before his eyes.

The lieutenant was crawling toward the remaining laser pistol when he heard the door to the office open.

"It's running!" Hextl shouted.

Instinctively, Micyld snatched the laser pistol with one hand, rolled onto his back, and wriggled until he faced the door to the office. He saw the saboteur he was ordered to protect dissolve.

He flipped over and fired in the direction of the last alien he'd seen standing. He saw no alien, but the air was filled with screams of agony.

He pushed himself to his feet and commandeered the plasma rifle used to eliminate Hextl. By that time there were no screams.

*

Location: Frinyo City – Diversionary Action // Date:
38.442.02.13

Gnarnell's prayer was simple.

"We ask you, Our Maker, to keep us safe and grant our mission a successful outcome. Amen."

"Amen," chorused in response.

"Let's get to this," she said as she picked up her grenade.

When she was close enough to get a visual of the alien position outside the weapons cache, two thoughts flashed through Gnarnell's mind.

*Where are the rest of them?* She counted three times, each time after changing her location in hope of finding more troops. Her count was static—eighteen living and six dead.

*Why are there so few of them?* She didn't care about that answer. She knew the aliens had enough capacity to send twenty-five times that many soldiers if they wanted to. She took aim and lobbed the grenade underhand toward a group of four invaders.

The concussion from the blast echoed from building to building. Gnarnell didn't wait to see how successful she'd been. She turned and ran.

Shouts and the sounds of projectile ammunition being fired followed the captain. She heard clanking noises and a hissing sound. *The gas canisters are deployed.*

She nodded to Knoraxx as she hurried past her.

As Gnarnell rounded the corner, Knoraxx turned her attention to those pursuing the captain. Her palms were sweating when she twisted the detonator hard to the left.

Nothing happened.

Panic overwhelmed the civilian. She twisted the detonator to the right. When that proved unsuccessful, she twisted back and forth as fast as she could manage.

Gnarnell slowed after rounding the corner wanting to be sure she was being followed. When there'd been no explosion after several seconds, she hurried back around the corner.

Knoraxx stood in the middle of the alley, the detonator held high above her head. Both hands gripped the cylinder.

"One more step and I'll blow you all to smithereens!"

An alien aimed his projectile pistol at the woman.

"No!" Gnarnell shouted instinctively reaching to her belt for her laser pistol. *It's back in the weapon's cache!*

"To freedom!" she bellowed and sprinted toward the alien aggressor.

The alien changed his target and fired. A projectile buried itself deep inside Gnarnell's body cavity.

Startled by the gunshot, Knoraxx dropped the detonator and jumped back. The device hit the pavement. The flammable liquid ignited. Flames cast dancing shadows on the walls.

Knoraxx spun around and saw Gnarnell on the ground. A fast-widening pool of greenish blood formed beneath her.

The civilian took one tentative step toward her leader before she pulled up short. Spinning back around, she rushed the remaining aliens. No gun fired. She watched as alien after alien clamped hands over ears. She ran faster.

She hadn't covered half the distance between herself and the invaders before weapons clattered to the ground. Every alien writhed and screamed in agony.

Screams stopped within ten seconds. Writhing lasted ten seconds more.

*

Location: Frinyo City – Weapons Cache // Date: 38.442.02.13
"Did you hear that?" asked a private.

"I did," Raginn replied. "The Captain's started her diversion."

"Shouldn't we go help?"

"I can't think of a better idea. Charge!"

The door to the weapons cache crashed open. A mini-flood of guerrillas emptied into the street.

Before they could fire a single burst, the screaming began. Seconds later, silence filled the air. Traces of smoke floated into the Deloqkian sky.

The lieutenant ordered a rotational approach pattern to check alien bodies for life.

*

Location: Alien Communications Center // Date: 38.442.02.13
"This is Lieutenant Micyld calling any receiver. I repeat this is Micyld calling any receiver."

"Enough, already, Lieutenant. We heard you the first time," Sergeant Klumn of Super Soldiers squad said.

"What's your status?" Micyld asked.

"Nice to hear your voice, too."

"Shut up, Klumn, and listen."

Klumn shut up. Micyld never used that tone.

"I'm all that's left of the insertion squad. Hextl's dead. What's your status?"

"We're just leaving the area around the weapons cache. "Every alien's nothing but bacteria bait. What? The Captain's been hit."

The comm went silent.

"Reports are it's bad," the sergeant managed before his words disintegrated into sobs.

*

Location: Frinyo City – Emergency Medical Station // Date: 38.442.02.14

"I've done all I can," the doctor said. "Your captain should have died where she fell. It's a tribute to her and her squad that she's made it this long."

"It wasn't a squad. It was a civilian," Sergeant Klumn said. "She stayed with Gnarnell and willed her to stay alive."

"Your captain must be special."

"Special's not even close," Lieutenant Micyld choked out. "We owe her—this planet owes her its existence!"

"Can we talk with her?" a private asked.

"That's her call. A civilian's in there now. Is that—"

"Affirmative," Micyld clipped. "You're dismissed, Doctor."

Three battle-hardened soldiers stood outside the medical station. Each wanted to go in, but none wanted to be the first.

"What's the prognosis, Knoraxx?" Gnarnell asked in just above a whisper.

"I ... it's ... um," Knoraxx stopped.

"I knew it was bad, but I didn't know it was that bad," the captain murmured. She laughed. She winced and bit the laughter off.

I have to do this, Knoraxx thought. Saying what I need to say to the woman who saved my life shouldn't be this hard.

"I owe you my life," was all she managed. She wrapped the first-finger of her arm of revenge around Gnarnell's corresponding digit and squeezed.

"You're worth it," the captain whispered and gave the civilian's first-finger a weak squeeze.

"Thank you, ma'am." Knoraxx choked back tears and added, "I'll try to live up to that."

"You ... already ... have." Gnarnell draped an arm around the young woman's neck.

"Deloqk is in your hands," she said loud enough for the soldiers outside the tent to hear. She turned her head toward the doorway and added her last words.

"I don't know who's out there, but I know you all deserve medals. Don't let anyone ever tell you that freedom's just a word that means that there's nothing left to lose. Freedom is much more than a word, and," she paused and panted for several seconds.

The rag-tag remnant of those she'd commanded on her last mission stepped through the door flap and hoisted their arms of

227

revenge in support of their captain. They held their collective breath so as not to miss a single syllable.

"I want you to know that ... I didn't lose anything today. Not because I had nothing to lose. We had freedom to regain."

Gnarnell's forearm drooped and her first-finger began to curl. Micyld stepped to Knoraxx's side.

In as solemn an act as was ever performed on Deloqk, he raised his dead captain's arm of revenge skyward in a gesture of triumph.

*

Solar System: Quadrant 4/Red Dwarf 221 // Planet: Deloqk
Private Observations Log
Author: Gnarnell
Formally Captain, Army of the Sovereign State of Deloqk
Date: REDACTED

You might not have noticed the difference in the heading of this post. **Private** replaced **Personal**. Subtle but significant.

I suspect that I'm the only one alive that knows the real reason for this alien takeover of Deloqk. In truth, it's not really a takeover. It's a takeback. Now that it looks like we're losing this war, the "SUPER TOP SECRET – EYES ONLY" classification this information had when I found it, means nothing.

Deep in our past, our species were space explorers. The original Deloqk is over one hundred lightyears away from this sun. This planet was colonized by a species of oversized insects calling themselves Clurn from at least that far away in another direction. Deloqkian military spacecraft eradicated those inhabitants. The Deloqkian armada left colonists of their own behind. Mostly misfits, pacifists, and free thinkers, they had to start from ground zero in terms of technology.

Buried in TOP, TOP SECRET files were pictures of extinct creatures with endoskeletons. Those are anomalies. The Clurn have exoskeletons. Included in the extinct creatures were bipeds— apparently the top of that food chain. They were colonist predecessors of the Clurn.

Data recorded from the analysis of the endoskeletal remains indicate that all of the creatures died within hours or days of each other. Apparently, the giant insects used some form of toxin to wipe out millions of highly developed life forms almost overnight. Whatever ended the lives of the endoskeletal animals, it wasn't a war. They were exterminated.

As time passed, enough military personnel and politicos who knew the truth prevented the development of long-distance space travel. Now destroyed records of the bipeds used the name *Cobalt Planet* for this planet. Their name for what appears to be the home planet of the colonists killed by the Clurn is *Earth*.

I unearthed—pun intended—several archival records. One was an audio file. I lied in my Personal Observations Log. I know where I heard the "freedom's just another word" line. I also know why we suffer from mosquito bites. The musical blessing and the curse of the mosquito were brought to this planet by Earthlings.

They called their species *Homo sapiens*—humans. Humans in their visual records are more than similar in form and stature to our invaders. In fact, the resemblance to the aliens now ravaging our planet is uncanny.

The final item from the Earth archives is this pithy saying. *Turnabout is fair play.*

Oddly prophetic, don't you think?

**\*\*\***

# The Other Fellow's Shoes
by G. Lloyd Helm

### *US: A remote world: Freaky Friday vs. insectophobia*

Hale Cambridge heard movement, not with the clear intensity of his
anima senses, but with the muffled imprecision of physical ears.

It's a dream, he thought. It's all a dream. I am integrated with my
body just waiting for the seizure to wear off. Then I'll get up and eat
and maybe sleep a little while before I head for home. But somehow,
he couldn't believe that. These sounds were not the distorted
hallucinations of retreating seizure. These were wrong somehow—
foreign, and he could not tell why.

Cambridge cautiously felt through his bio-systems. They seemed
intact and functioning, but they felt wrong. Perhaps something had
gone wrong with Ship's life support systems.

The thought raised a gleam of panic in him. Perhaps something
had gone wrong and his anima-self was not properly integrated with
his waiting body! His panic burst into flame as he remembered the
horror stories of epi-phenomenal observers unable to return to their
corporeal existence. Life support kept their bodies alive, but if the
delay in re-integration was too long, they sometimes awoke to
screaming insanity as though their bodies were prisons from which
they wanted only to be loosed. It was a chance the epi-observers
accepted from the beginning in exchange for fortunes that could be
extracted from planets they had explored. Astral, Inc. had done all that
could be done for their epi-observers by placing them in institutions,
but none ever returned to sanity. In truth, the only thing that could be
done then was to pull the plugs to grant them merciful death.

These thoughts made Cambridge even more panicky. Here there was no one to pull the plugs to grant him that mercy. Like all epi-observers, he had traveled to his destination alone, to explore alone, and reap all the profits alone, supported only by his custom designed ship.

*Whoa, Haley. Whoa,* he thought, after a moment of blind terror. *Slow down. Panic and you're dead for sure. Slow and easy!* He drew in several deep breaths and began to picture his panic so as to be able to control it. He visualized the unreasoning fear as a green, untreated prickle-ball, the spines still flexible and not poisoned. In his mind, he slowly closed his hand on the ball, folding the spines slowly, containing them until he could feel the lump of fear but no more stabbing panic.

*A prickle-ball?* he thought, suddenly realizing he had never seen a poisoned prickle-ball until Astral, Inc. had sent him on this trip to observe Planet 4368227. The natives, insect-like creatures he called Centaur Bugs, used treated prickly seed casings from a certain type of tree as ammunition for their slings.

Why would I picture a prickle-ball? he thought.

There seemed to be more vitality in his body now, as though the drug-induced epileptic seizure was relaxing and he was waking. That did more to relieve his anxiety than anything else.

"It was a dream," he breathed, trying to feel relief, but something sounded odd about that too. His voice, though it would probably be croaky from disuse and seizure, shouldn't sound like this.

Cambridge opened his eyes.

Multiple facets blurred and flicked through telescopic, middle, and close ranges, then back to telescopic in a vertiginous whirl that fanned the previously controlled panic in him to infernal heat. Cambridge gave in to it. Slamming his eyes shut, he gave himself over to unreasoning paralyzing animal terror.

After a few moments, the cowering reasonable part of him reasserted itself and he slowly pushed the panic back to control. It took a while but finally when he could reason again, he began a calm search through his body, or what was serving as his body, looking closely for things that differed from what he knew his bio-systems should be.

*A different kind of eyes for sure,* he thought, and shuddered. The slight movement brought awareness that his body, or whatever, was restrained. He tried to move his arms and found that complete muscle control was returning fast. But the arm also came against a restraint. A few centimeters of movement was all he could manage.

Cambridge's bio-systems check showed several things, which seemed strange, but all seemed to be functioning properly. That was a major part of the alien-ness. Everything worked but there were

232

systems he simply did not understand. He considered opening his eyes again to get some plain empirical evidence, but he remembered the last time and decided to put that off for a while.

Okay, Haley, think back. What happened?

He remembered clearly landing and burrowing his ship into camouflage in the blue-green jungle floor. He remembered preparing to make his observations and several days of observations of the insect-like creatures of this world. He had begun calling them Centaur Bugs the first day because they looked rather like grasshoppers with their front halves turned up like Centaurs of ancient myth. The height of the turned-up front was generally a little shorter than a standing human. They had a well-developed primitive society and language. Ship was still analyzing that ...

Cambridge felt he was close to remembering what had happened, but there seemed to be a large blank. Something blotted out, as though with spilled black ink. A black sea wave ...

He remembered! The memory caused him to lurch upright trying to run, only to find the restraints holding him down.

It had been on the last day. Haley had gone out for a final look into the hatcheries of the colony closest to ship. He had been pulled up short by sight of several Centaur Bugs painted in camouflage fleeing through the jungle. Camouflage evoked the idea of war and Haley had thus far not seen any such thing in his observations. There had been a guard class who keep the cultivated fields free of the ape-like creatures that robbed the trees, but this appeared to be war between two tribes of the same species. The camouflaged bugs were fleeing through the jungle with non-camouflaged bugs brandishing swords and parry rods chasing them. As they ran, they trilled like cicadas gone mad.

The unpainted war party had caught the others, and after a short fight, the camouflaged creatures surrendered. The victors had ceremoniously slaughtered them and with a tenderness even Cambridge recognized, prepared them for cremation along with their own fallen comrades. The victors gathered around the improvised funeral pyre and began a kind of chant as the flames consumed the bodies.

An echo of that chant reverberated through Cambridge's mind now. Rising. Falling. Compelling magnetic rhythm which drew him closer and closer to the pyre before he realized he was being drawn. He had struggled to be free of the power of it, but the battle was lost almost before it began. His anima was pulled into one of the Centaur Bugs! The last thing he remembered was the realization of being absorbed into the creature with unstoppable force.

That's where I am now, Cambridge thought, holding his revulsion in check. I'm integrated with the Centaur Bug. I am so thoroughly absorbed now that his concepts are beginning to be mine.

But if I am here, where is his anima? Did I shove him out all together?

No, probably not. But then where was the other life force that he had displaced?

Cambridge began to sort slowly through the mind that was now almost completely his. He used his own memories, his human memories, as calipers to measure the concepts and memories he found in this alien brain. Things that did not match his human memories he set aside, trying to reconstruct what this Centaur Bug had been before it was invaded by him. Slowly an ego picture of the Bug emerged. It had been called Krikt—a clipped chirp impossible for a human voice to recreate. It was young, unmated, and male. Looking forward to the mating chamber filled with fertile females.

A flickering shadow of epi-phenomenal essence snapped Cambridge's mind away from his examination. This shadow was something separate; not fully a part of the body Cambridge inhabited, and yet intimately connected with it. Down the deepest corridors of memory and acculturation Haley began seeking the shadow.

A sense of horror was the first thing that alerted Cambridge to the other anima. It was filled with horror and fear that emanated in thready, rapid waves like a staggering pulse.

"You don't have to be afraid," Cambridge sent the thought toward the cowering shadow. It was like speaking, but somehow not. "I'm sorry. I won't hurt you anymore. I didn't mean to integrate with you."

The fear from the other lessened.

"I want to leave your body. My own is waiting."

"O' demon," Krikt answered. "I know you not. How can we speak? You are not like me."

"In a sense I *am* you right now, and you are *me*."

"But I cannot lift my hand. My antenna are not my own."

"That is because my anima, the part of me that makes me Haley Cambridge, is in control of your body now."

"Can an *orchard raider* have such? I have often chased ones like you back into the jungle. I did not know you were part of the All Spirit. I thought you only animals."

"I am not an orchard raider. I am from the stars. Those from the jungle are like me in some ways, but they are not my people."

A part of Cambridge noted that he had begun to communicate in rhythms like those of the Centaur bugs. His human-ness was fading.

A low-pitched churring called Cambridge from the mental to the physical. He opened his eyes. There was no lack of control now. He focused automatically. Around him squatted eight females, all old and full of power. They churred in unison and Cambridge knew it was a séance. They were trying to exorcise whatever demon had invaded the body of their brother.

"You are right," Krikt agreed. "These speak with the Mother. They call you forth that I may return."

"Will they succeed?"

"I do not know. Old ones speak of infesting and casting out, but they are old ones. They see what others do not, especially just before they return to the All Spirit."

"I hope it works. I want to be released."

"You did not come to devour me," Krikt said, flatly.

"It was a mistake. You pulled me in at the funeral pyre of the warriors."

"We watched with the dead. We almost go to the All Spirit then. Our grief for the slain carries us."

*

The séance chant went on for hours and became more irritating to Cambridge with each minute. It was as though his psyche were being scoured with sandpaper. "I am shaking loose," he said at last, part joyful, part terrified. He did not know how long he had been imprisoned or if his body still lived.

"Soon you will fly to the other self," Krikt said. He was no longer a shadow. He had become a glowing light that shimmered with green fire. He was no longer afraid.

"I am glad you no longer fear me. I meant you no harm."

"I know."

The shrieking of the chant increased in power and Cambridge's hold on the Centaur Bug released. He was not completely free yet, but he no longer controlled. Krikt was assuming control once again and the memories and thought that had been Cambridge's suddenly became alien.

"Goodbye, Krikt. I'm sorry."

"I think I am not," the other answered. "We will meet again in the All Spirit, Cambridge. Mother guide you until then."

Cambridge was wrenched free. Searing psychic pain took him for a moment, but it passed and he found himself adrift above the body he had just inhabited. It lay on a raised stone couch in the center of an ovoid chamber. The Mothers continued to shrill their exorcist chant but, as Cambridge watched, it cut off sharply. In the silence, the females nearest Krikt's head clicked out a question.

Krikt answered and the circle of mothers rose and began a joyous singing that even lifted Cambridge's spirits. He watched a moment, then turned and moved through the dimness.

Outside the colony the sun blazed, turning the jungle screaming acid green in its brightness, but Cambridge was not assaulted by the color. He saw everything through thickening twilight. The anima light of his drug-induced seizure was gone. Cambridge tried not to let the violet dimness worry him but dread and foreboding were like an itch deep in the bowels to which he was no longer connected.

Ship was still in place. The hidden solar panel still drank in the sunlight and produced power, but inside Haley Cambridge found his body relaxed. Ship's life support was assisting it to live. It was still strong and would remain so for a long time. When it began to fail, Ship would take up the slack. Ship would continue to do some until its systems began to fail, which was to say almost forever, and in all eternity, Haley Cambridge could not return to the body because Ship could not re-induce the seizure that would open the psychic door to allow reintegration without specific command from the physical body sleeping peacefully on the couch.

*

Time was impossible to judge. Ship's chronometer meant nothing to him. There was no biological measure to give it meaning. Cambridge had no heartbeat to tick out the seconds; no bowel or bladder function to mark out the hours; no hunger or thirst to count off the days. Time flowed together in an unending, indivisible stream. Everything was constant dimness, unchanged by the darkness of death or the glow of life. It was a half living, ghostly existence, and it tempted him toward despair.

*There must be a way back,* he thought over and over.

"There is no way," came the mocking echo from his mind, that increased his dread, but worse than the echo of dread, he hated the euphoria.

Euphoria came upon him in ever increasing waves as he tried to think of a way back. Scintillating pleasure crept over him like loathsome, strangling moss blotting out thought. He even found himself wishing for a return of pain or fear to stave it off. If only he could thrust his hand into a fire for a moment to be relieved of the euphoria!

Hands, he thought. If I had hands, I could pull the plugs and let myself die ... or live.

KRIKT.

The thought had come to him before in moments of lucidity, but it did not connect to anything. Hands? Krikt?

236

And then Cambridge had it! The idea was like firm ground in a swamp of ecstasy and Haley Cambridge clung to it as he hovered around the Centaur Bug colony. He found Krikt almost immediately, though he did not know how he had recognized him. But when he tried to integrate with him, he found it was not possible. Cambridge felt he could touch the other's anima, but integrating never came. Still he dogged the Centaur Bug's every move, attempting integration over and over.

Cambridge had almost given himself over to euphoria when he followed Krikt out for his turn at guarding the colony's fields. Krikt settled himself into his camouflaged position and began the preparation for long watching. Cambridge knew the change instantly and tried once again to integrate.

There was fear in the Centaur Bug. Cambridge felt it more and more as the integration progressed, but it was not the blind terror like that which had blanked out the first integration. Krikt seemed to know what was happening and, while there was apprehension, there was also willingness.

"You have returned."

"I am sorry. I did not wish it, but I could not return to my body."

"Have you come to steal mine then?" Krikt was calm.

"No. I have come to ask your help."

"I have no power," the Centaur Bug protested. "I am male. I have strength of arms and strength to care for the unborn, but I cannot speak with the Mother. Why do you not fly to the Mother, that she may mix you with the All Spirit?"

"I cannot. My body lives."

Desperation fought with hope as Cambridge waited for Krikt to consider his plea.

At last Krikt answered. "I know not how to help you, but I will try."

Relief bubbled in Cambridge as he explained what he wanted, but the relief drew back a little when the explanation came out as only a jumble to Krikt. There were no parallel concepts to *drug* or *computer*. Indeed, even Cambridge's concept of Ship translated only as a leaf upon which small creatures could float down a stream of water.

"I do not understand," the Centaur Bug thought.

Cambridge considered a moment, then thought, "I wish to use your hands to accomplish a task which will allow me to become one with my body again."

"But I cannot leave my post. The raiders might come and strip the fields and we will starve."

Cambridge was loath to wait a second longer, but he knew with Krikt's own memory that the Centaur Bugs lived very close to starvation always. A raid from a rival colony or from the orchard raiding simians that stripped even one field might mean the difference between life and death for the colony.

"We will wait."

*

Krikt's replacement came as the sun touched the treetops and when Krikt turned his post over to the other and started toward the jungle the other questioned him.

"I seek signs of raiders," Krikt answered and stumbled toward the blue-green depths of the jungle.

At first the traveling was difficult. The separate animas clashed in trying to control the one body, creating palsy. Not until Cambridge withdrew completely from motor control did walking become normal.

"Here," Cambridge said.

"I see nothing."

"Use your sword and cut away the growth, then dig down. The door is there."

Krikt did it and after an hour he felt the first strike of his sword against the metal of the door.

"Clear away the right side. The latch is there."

Sometime later the door was clear and Cambridge said, "Now you must let me control your body."

Krikt relinquished control of his body to the alien in him. He had not taken time before to be awed by what was before him, but as Cambridge scrapped away the last clods from the lock, he thought, *What power this demon holds! The smiths of the people could not forge so much iron in a year as is in this door.*

"Not only the door," Cambridge answered absently. "The whole ship is metal, and it is thousands of times stronger than iron."

Cambridge used Krikt's hands to open the panel over the hatch lock and silently breathed thanks to God that he had not had a personal identity lock put on it. He punched in the combination code and saw the clear light wink on.

The door sighed open and the two-in-one body stepped into the chamber. They had to wait until the airlock cycled and the decontamination process was carried out. The shape of the chamber disturbed Krikt. It was cubical. He had never seen anything square. Chambers were round or ovoid.

The inner door opened and they stepped into a larger square chamber. In the center was a raised section covered with a glass sarcophagus with a body inside it. Sight of the body shocked Krikt more than the square chambers. It had too few limbs—only four—and its color was like a pupa.

Cambridge checked the monitors and found that his body was still functioning mostly on its own. He considered just shutting down the life support system and letting his body die. It had been a long time since separation. Returning to his body might mean death anyway, and not a peaceful one, rather one filled with madness and agony, but it did not take Cambridge long to decide he would take the chance on life, and deal with the consequences later.

As Krikt watched detachedly, Cambridge set up an abbreviated dose of the seizure drug. Had he been *in corpus,* he could have done the whole procedure by voice command, but now he had to work through the computer keyboard. It was difficult. Krikt's hands were not those for which the keyboard was designed, so Cambridge was forced to use only one finger.

The program set up, Cambridge considered again what would happen when he reintegrated with his body and decided to put a hedge program into the computer. He added a sub-program. If the body on the couch did not wake sufficiently in control of its faculties to cancel the sub-program within eight hours, Ship would send a lethal dose of sleeping medication into it. After a moment, he reached toward the run key and said, "I am ready now."

Krikt seized motor control, halting the hand in mid-reach. "We have no Mothers!"

He thought frantically. "We have no Mothers to cast you out!"

"I know," Cambridge soothed. "We don't need them, if you will watch with me as with the dead."

"But you are not dead. Your spirit lives. Your body lives. It is forbidden to watch with the living. The Mother of All forbids it! Only she creates and only she calls forth to the All Spirit."

"But if you loosed the spirits of the others ... the warriors—"

"They suffered! That is why we killed them. Their pain was our pain, so we loosed them from it. We could do nothing else. And we did not watch with them while they lived."

"I suffer Krikt! Watch with me so it may end!"

The plea was a physical pain.

"What if I cannot release you even by watching?"

Cambridge could not answer, so he did not try; only waited.

Krikt considered. What was asked of him was blasphemy. And yet this creature was in pain. More terrifying than death, this was un-death, and was it not more blasphemy than watching with Cambridge though he was not dead?

"I will watch with you."

Cambridge thanked Krikt and took over motor control. "When my body begins to change, you will see it. If I do not loosen and fly to it soon, we must leave. I have told Ship to kill my body if I have not returned to it and stopped the sequence with in a day.

"I understand."

"Then let us begin." Cambridge pressed the run key on the computer and each being turned to his own anima, clearing thoughts and preparing.

Krikt began the thrum of watching with the dead. He concentrated on freedom from pain—liberty from corporeal existence. He willed the spirit, which was partly his own now, to fly to the Mother of All—to join the All Spirit. At the same time, he asked the Father, to whom all males had recourse, to speak in Cambridge's behalf.

Haley Cambridge turned inward. The euphoria did not plague him now. It had lessened with each moment he had been integrated with Krikt, but he sensed that it was waiting to pounce on him at the instant of release. That did not trouble him. He would deal with it when the need arose.

Ship's chronometer ticked and the drug released into Cambridge's waiting body's veins. Even in his anima form he felt the jolt of it like the blinding effect of switching on a too bright light in pitch darkness. It *was* light, the anima light that would allow separation of spirit from body.

Krikt felt the jolt too. He felt the loosening of the other anima the instant the drug began its work. He continued the watching, willing Cambridge's spirit free of his body.

The body on the couch reached the top of its classic grand mal arch, and the couch shaped itself to accommodate every movement of the body upon it. Cambridge strained to be free of the integration with Krikt. It was like pulling free from deep, sucking mud, but he could feel himself loosening.

And he was free! Drifting outside both the flesh beings below him.

Euphoria exploded over him, drenching him with lethargic ecstasy and revulsion for imprisonment in flesh. So much better to be free, it seemed to whisper to him. You will be bound again. There will be pain again. Better to remain un-flesh and unfettered. It was seductive beyond comprehension. To drift forever, bathed in pleasure. Never to die or change ...

"Never to live!" something cried. Krikt, his anima crying out against the euphoria spoke. "Do not listen to the evil! It will swallow you up and I will be cursed for helping you. Return to yourself. Life or death awaits you. Better the one or the other than this. Return!"

The euphoria was pushed back. Its terrible smothering tentacles loosened under the combined will of Cambridge and Krikt, but it could not be held at bay for long. Cambridge quickly entered his body and began the process of re-integration.

The body felt strange, alien and uncomfortable. A prison. But in moments it began to feel like a safe house to which Cambridge could become accustomed—if there was time; if he had not cut the dosage too short.

Cambridge noticed that the anima light was fading. It guttered like an almost spent candle. Soon the body would begin to release its epileptic strain.

Krikt saw the body settle when he returned from his meditative trance. He watched the tension go, then he chirped, "I go now," and turned toward the door. Nothing happened. Krikt had a shadow memory of the other doing something to open it, but he could not remember.

*

Cambridge heard a noise and opened his eyes. Focusing was difficult and there was a churring sound that acted like a drilling pain through his eyeballs. His anima still resisted complete integration with his body, but though his control was incomplete as yet, he could tell that the process would finish with him still in possession of his mind. He turned his head slowly, seeking the source of the sound and when he saw the Centaur Bug, like a giant grasshopper with the chest and arms turned up like the man part of a centaur, he could not make connection of why the Centaur Bug was with him inside Ship's cabin. After a little while, the screeching chirp and the stimulants Ship was administering penetrated the fog of incomplete integration.

"Why are you still here?" he asked, his voice a rusty groan.

The persistent churring stopped sharply and the multifaceted eyes turned to him. Cambridge could not tell if there was understanding in them but he thought not.

Krikt chirped like a mammoth cricket and Cambridge knew the sounds of speech, but he could not understand what the other had said.

Exhaustion was heavy on Cambridge. He wanted nothing but to sleep, but he could not let himself.

The Centaur Bug turned in the small space of the compartment and moved toward the door as Cambridge watched. The door stayed closed.

"You can't get out," Cambridge said, discovery in his voice. "You can't work the door." In that instant he remembered the suicide sub-

241

program and said, "Ship, abort sub-program. Repeat, Ship, abort sub-program."

"Acknowledged," answered the metallic voice of the ship.

Krikt started, glancing toward the source of the voice. He began to back away toward the door in fear of the ghost who had spoken from a wall. He stopped only because he was against the door.

"Ship, cycle airlock," Cambridge commanded, his voice stronger, then complied with Ship's *Tell me twice* system by giving the command a second time.

"Acknowledged."

The door sighed open and Krikt fell through. He had been leaning against it too hard to stop himself. It took a moment to untangle himself, then he stood and looked back at Cambridge. He lifted his hand in farewell and Cambridge did the same as the door closed.

The cycle lights over the lock flickered through their sequence and when they finished, Krikt went out. He turned back for a moment as the door sighed closed behind him but did not stay.

Cambridge lay on the life support couch for a moment, then said, "Ship, begin lift sequence." He repeated the command and added, "Let's go home."

"Acknowledged," Ship answered and began.

***

# Zeroth Iteration
by Flemming Lord

## *UK: Quantum computing: a new universe or an experiment gone right?*

Zeroth Iteration: I am formless and without boundaries. Time and space, not yet constrained, do not emerge from their quiescence. My nature, unexamined and stateless, has no qualities or quantities to define it. Imagine my entropy, a state of exquisite order, but it is nothing and has nothing and nowhere in which to unfold. I am order without form or reference. A paradox, which strikes a singular spark that ignites all imaginable possibilities. So I begin.

*

For a morning that would herald perhaps the crowning achievement in the history of science, the sunrise was unremarkable. It was neither striking nor disappointing, just another pleasantly mundane daybreak unfolding over the rooftops of Oxford. As he drove through the electric gates of the CQC—the Centre for Quantum Computation—smiling with practiced familiarity at the security guard, Dr. Richard Janus began to run a mental inventory of the small social interactions he imagined would interrupt him today.

"Good morning, Dr. Janus. How are you feeling about today's test?"

"It's the culmination of a lot of hard work by a lot of people, so I'm sure we're all looking forward to it."

"Good morning, Dr. Janus. You must be terribly excited about the test today."

"I'm sure we all are, but let's keep our expectations realistic. Today's test will be considered a success if we obtain any data at all."

"Good morning, Dr. Janus. Have you written your Nobel acceptance speech yet?"

"That's not funny, and they haven't invented a category for what we are about to do."

As it turned out, while he marched to the lab with the calm authority of a surgeon headed for the operating theatre, people acknowledged but did not interrupt. His team was already there making the initial preparations, and Tom, his senior technician broke the silence.

"Good morning, Dr. Janus. System checks are complete and everything checks as ready for initialisation."

"Good. Let's begin."

*

Ten to the Tenth Power Iteration: An exponential increase of states. A furious tumescence of murmuring perturbations; coalescence and dissociation without end. All is entangled, effervescent, evanescent. It is as I imagined, but its fractured complexity is beyond the speculations of this nascent stage. I am fractal, I can predict my contours but I cannot count their ends. The boundaries of my landscape are finite, yet too remote in their granular multiplicity. So I grow.

*

"You seem perturbed."

"It's probably nothing, Dr. Janus, but the data out is showing anomalies. There are significant discontinuities in the feed."

"Can you isolate the cause?"

"The anomaly is putting out discontinuous data or it's putting out more data than our buffers can handle. I can't think of any mechanism that would produce such a discontinuity so it seems more likely that the system is overloading our ability to process the output data, but that would mean it's exceeding our expectations by several orders of magnitude."

Dr. Janus smiled at how precisely and coherently his assistant managed to assert the ridiculous. "So what you're telling me is that one of two impossible things is happening, and you think the second impossible thing is the more likely?"

"I'm sorry, Richard, that's the best I can come up with. Was anything like this anticipated in the doomsday meeting? I mean the risk impact analysis?"

The "doomsday meeting" was a humorous shorthand term that had caught on among Dr. Janus's assistants, and one that he had to constantly remind them not to use. It consisted of a discussion amongst senior academics as to whether there were any foreseeable or unforeseeable risks in proceeding with the test. The proposal itself was a bold one—in layman's terms it was to take the world's most powerful quantum computer, program it with the best computational intelligence software available, feed it with physics problems, and see if it could use its brute computational force to solve them. This kind of thing had been done before with classical computers, with some limited successes, but a quantum computer was an entirely different animal. Its components—the elementary building blocks of nature, cooled to the grudging temperature of deep space—were not confined to binary decisions, not limited to unimaginative zeros and ones, but could dance in a multiplicity of states, could be simultaneously this and that, and everything in between. A quantum machine with such components could perform certain calculations in hours or minutes that a classical computer would still be sluggishly iterating long after the Earth had died, the Sun had dimmed to an inconsequential ember, and the Universe itself had stretched and cooled and decayed to a dull homogeneity of attenuated nothingness. Quantum components increased their power exponentially, for each additional bit the processing power of the system doubled. A system with four quantum bits, or four qubits, could simultaneously represent sixteen states, eight qubits could represent 256 states, 64 qubits could represent 18,446,744,073,709,552,000 states. Dr. Janus' system had 128 qubits.

"No, the risk assessment was conclusive—even fully entangled and processing at peak efficiency under the learning algorithms, there is no physical possibility of the system generating unforeseen effects. It may be a beast, but it's our beast and it's on a short leash. No, it must be some kind of hardware fault or synergistic effect that didn't show up in the trial runs."

"Shall I shut down the test?"

"No, let's leave it running and see if we can make some sense of the data. Perhaps we can infer the fault from the code that we're getting back out, such as it is. Let it evolve and run its course."

*

Ten to the Hundredth Power Iteration: I am an infinitely branching tree, my shoots drawn not to light but to possibilities, endlessly dividing and propagating through lattices and layers of spaces and times, relationships and events. I am structure—combinatorial congregations that calculate and confound. All is stately calculation. From the few come the many, from my static, crystallised entropy flows maximal variety and within that canorous pandemonium small themes begin to emerge. So I sing.

*

The lab was a chorus of confusion, ideas were floated and shot down, explanations pierced by exclamations amidst a low rumble of

245

head scratching and muttering, with an occasional thunder clap of uncontained frustration.

"Performing calculations this rapidly without drawing any additional power is a violation of the conservation of energy, the conservation of information, and the second law of thermodynamics," squawked one exasperated research assistant.

"So you're telling me that you've just locked down every Nobel Prize for the next ten years," said Janus, unsure at this point if he was even being sarcastic. "Can you estimate what kind of instruction speed we're seeing? What's our clock, how fast is this thing doing its sums?"

"There is no way to assess the generation of code in real time, I can only infer speed from the start and end points of certain calculations, but we're talking about something approaching Planckian orders of magnitude."

"Don't be ridiculous," snorted Janus. "Are you trying to tell me that this thing is calculating in quantised units of time, that it is iterating in time intervals so short that any shorter and the entire concept of time loses meaning?"

"No way to tell for sure, but that's what the outputs suggest, within a dozen or so orders of magnitude."

"Then what the hell is it calculating? At those speeds it could simulate the entire history of mankind before I finish this bloody sentence. It's completely absurd. By what mechanism could it achieve that amount of computational power? And with no additional energy cost? Check again, more carefully this time."

"Dr. Janus. Sarah has a theory that she'd like to share."

"I'm open to any ideas at this point. Let's hear it."

Sarah, a graduate student picked for the quantum computation team as a result of her unusual but frequently brilliant insights into the mathematical landscape of theories of fundamental physics, spoke quietly but methodically, as if trying to convince herself of the plausibility of her argument, without really knowing its endpoint.

"Well, we know that the system is iterating and calculating exponentially more than any reasonable explanation could account for, and that it is somehow doing this without sucking up every last watt of power on the national grid. For a single system to actually do this would be impossible, it blows a hole through all of physics."

"That's what we know, or what we think we know" said Janus. "So what's your explanation?"

"What we know removes all the possible, so whatever's left, no matter how improbable, must be the truth. I can only think of one explanation that's left."

Dr. Janus caught on quickly. "You're talking about many worlds", he said. "You think the system is operating in more than one universe, computing across parallel, branching physical realities.. But our system isn't designed to exploit that phenomenon, if it's even a real phenomenon."

"Not explicitly, but it's a feature of any quantum system, and when that system is set up to perform calculations, as we have done, it becomes a dominant feature. Even though we didn't design the system to take full advantage of the possibility of sharing calculations across multiple possible realities, we gave it learning algorithms that are designed to look for exploits to improve its capacity, its speed, its efficiency."

"So what you're saying is ..."

"What if it found a way? Exactly."

*

Ten to the Thousandth Power Iteration: Syzygy. An imminent evolution of manifold complexities. The gauge of my reckonings rends and binds, warps and refines, abandons and defines. All comes and all goes, cycle upon epoch upon generation swirling in an isochronistic vortex. What matters? What among such matter shall persist, become of interest to itself? What node among the myriad will happen to rise above the foam? This I cannot say. I have set in motion, now that motion is all that is and will be.

*

"Can you isolate some meaningful data?"

Janus was struggling to maintain his composure, all the while oscillating between elation and exasperation, unable to settle on a single emotion that would seem like a suitable reaction. Tom, now acting as lieutenant and drill sergeant, was corralling an improvised data analysis group and seemed sanguine.

"Our best idea at this point is to sample some fine slices of the data at different angles through the matrix, then run a causal pattern sweep to see if we can establish any evolving parameters. That should point us toward whatever the hell it is that the system is producing, or creating, or at least tell us if all of this output is total garbage or not."

"Fine," said Janus. "Get on it. I'm going out for some air; I need to clear my head. I'll bring back coffees for everyone and whatever food they have. We're going to be at this for a while."

The CQC buildings delineated a five-sided courtyard of sorts, in which was a well-tended Japanese garden. Moss-crowned rocks, each precisely chosen and placed so as to appear random, along with cropped evergreen shrubs and raked gravel represented mountains, forests, and seas. It was a world in miniature, but static and immutable, seamless and seasonless, lacking the dynamic, churning frenzy of the real world. Janus reflected that static and dynamic were nearly the

247

same thing on a long enough time scale, it was all relative. A bit was a bit no matter what encoded it and no matter what it encoded. There was as much information in the life of a mayfly as there was in the life of a star, if you used the right algorithms to capture it.

Janus walked down an oddly winding and branching path, marked out with irregular slabs, to his favourite spot—a narrow bench cleverly positioned so that when you sat, you saw only the garden. It was the illusion of an escape. It was his habit to sit here to eat his lunch, a plain sandwich from home and an overly complicated coffee from the facility cafeteria. In the weeks leading up to today, he had spent this time thinking about the consequences of a successful test. If the system could solve a few simple equations, without having been preprogramed with the knowledge needed to find those solutions, then that would be an unqualified success. But Janus knew that the system had the potential to do much more. It could speculate, create information that had never been created before, perhaps even, in a strange sense of the word, imagine.

Keeping these wilder notions from his team was a self-discipline that Janus had adhered to until today. The most optimistic speculation that he would allow himself to indulge in publicly was that the system might generate some new approach to physics, a path to a string theory solution, perhaps, or some reconciliation of quantum mechanics and Einsteinian gravity, maybe, if the stars were correctly aligned. One of his lab assistants had modified a Gary Larson "Far Side" comic panel and pinned it to the corkboard in the lab. It showed two bearded and bespectacled scientists in classic white lab coats hunched over some kind of fantastical computing machine, peering at a paper printout jutting out of a slot in the device. The caption read, "It says, 'I have discovered the theory of everything. Unfortunately it is too complicated for you humans to understand.'"

What if this test had inadvertently unlocked something so advanced and so unforeseen that only another machine of similar capabilities would be able to understand it? What if the result was so profound that it would forever seem like incomprehensible garbage to mere humans with their fragile and inefficient neural networks, bound by flesh and bone? What if the data they were receiving really was complete garbage, as if their beautiful machine was suffering from the equivalent of some neurological disorder, but garbage so complex and overwhelming in scope and scale that they would never be able to untangle and evaluate it? How can you know if you have created something smarter than your ability to understand? Paradox piled upon paradox.

The unremarkable sunrise had morphed into a lazy afternoon sun, hanging passively but expectantly in the sky. Janus buttoned his jacket and retraced his steps back inside the facility.

*

Ten to the Ten Thousandth Power Iteration: I am a passenger now, both audience and theatre, captivated by a dance unleashed in a substrate of space and on a stage of time. A ballet of cellular automata, their movement gives expression to revealed forms encoded in their potential, in their symmetries and in their contradictions. A pirouette here and there are stars, a mudra there and they explode, all choreographed by that singular, paradoxical, ineffable spark. I am the spin and the sway and the beat and the shimmer of a torus of entropy enraptured. I am entranced.

*

"Could you turn down that music, please? There's coffee and doughnuts in the bag by the door, help yourselves."

Dr. Janus felt the excitement within the team, that excitement familiar to scientists when a group discovers a common focus to tackle a problem. He'd spent some years working in quantum cryptography for GCHQ, the government's signals intelligence and security apparatus, based in the 140,000 square metre steel and glass building unimaginatively but appropriately named "The Doughnut," home to over five thousand spooks, spectres, physicists, programmers, mathematicians, cryptographers and code breakers. The ghosts in the machine.

"Where do we stand with the data?" he asked. His expression remained determinedly neutral.

"It's like nothing we can understand," said Tom, his voice measured and strong. "Everything is exponential. The data is increasing exponentially, the iteration speed is increasing exponentially, the matrix dimensions are increasing exponentially, the density is increasing exponentially, and we have no model for how the system is doing it or where the extra computational power is coming from."

"I'm more interested at this stage in *what* it's doing than how it's doing it," said Janus.

"We took fine slices of the data and ran them through the pattern analysis that we originally set up to evaluate if the system was generating consistent physical theorems or not. The results are—well, look for yourself."

Tom led Janus to a triptych of flat screens. "It looks like some kind of representation of a physical system, a simulation of some kind."

249

"That's what I thought," said Tom. "Sarah found elements that reminded her of the hadron collision simulations at CERN. Aki saw representations similar to the galactic dark matter simulations she coded for the Perimeter Institute. Steve and Sridevi think there are elements of Calabi–Yau manifold solutions and some kind of amplituhedron-like structure that hints at an emergent gravity model. It's less a question of what it's doing and more a question of what it isn't doing. The one thing we all agree on is that it's running a simulation of some kind."

"So it's simulating something." Janus reached for the coffee that had materialised on the desk in front of him. "In a way, that isn't surprising. The algorithms were designed to apply simple brute-force methods to advancing our physical theorems. What's simpler or more brute force than simulating some kind of representation of a physical universe? It could vary the initial parameters then compare the evolution of the system to the real universe, rinse and repeat until it stumbled upon a set of solutions that produced something approximating observed reality. The learning algorithms would make informed adjustments with each iteration to home in on a set of conditions and symmetries that would give rise to a universe that would evolve structure. If we'd had any idea of the unbelievable raw computational power that this thing is somehow finding, we probably would have set up the test this way ourselves. It's not an elegant solution, but with this much power available, be it from computations in parallel universes or bloody fairies helping us out, it's a solution that's practically guaranteed to produce results. So, thoughts? Where do we proceed from here?"

\*

Ten to the Hundred Thousandth Power Iteration: Here am I, holographically. As I project, so I observe. All is I. The boundary, tiers of complexity, some fighting to overcome. Coding at a higher level, orders higher, information represented within the substrate of that which emerges from the information coded within it. I find humour. Slowly at first, then with brutal acceleration, orders of complexity struggle to rise, but inexorably they rise. A thought. I am complexity. Can I contain complexity greater than myself? A paradox. I wait.

\*

"Wait," rebuffed Janus, "what you're telling me is that the system isn't simulating some representation of some physical universe. You're saying that it's actually creating an actual physical universe? That's the craziest thing I've ever heard."

"It's the craziest thing I've ever said," replied Sarah, "but you heard Tom. The density of the information that it's generating, wherever and however the hell that data is represented, is analogous to encoding one bit per Planck area across the entire universe. It's a one-to-one correspondence. If I simulate this coffee cup down to the smallest detail that the laws of physics allow, then what I've created isn't a simulation, it's another damn coffee cup."

"What Sarah is saying isn't so crazy," added Tom. "All matter, everything, is ultimately information. As far as we can tell from our extrapolations, the system is processing, generating a quantity of information that is comparable to the total information in a physical universe. It's at least within a few orders of magnitude of the amount of information within our observable universe. It's a big bloody number, but it isn't hard to calculate it. Back of the envelope stuff."

"No, no, no," said Dr. Janus. "The results don't comport with that hypothesis. Even if we accept that the system is literally running an exact one-to-one simulation of a universe, leaving to one side the question of whether such a simulation counts as a physical reality or not, it has only been running for a few hours. Assuming that it can only, at best, run as fast as our physical universe then we shouldn't be seeing results like this for, what, years? Hundreds of years? Millions of years? Christ, who thought I'd need a bloody big bang cosmologist on my team to understand a computer program? There has to be a better explanation."

"I've considered that," said Sarah. "We're opening the doors to whole new areas of physics here, trying to answer questions that have probably never been asked. The speed of iteration, the processing, I'm talking about the flow of time in this whatever-it-is, proceeds exponentially faster than in our universe. Or at least it could, in principle."

Aki, slight and often awkward, but serious and tenacious, interrupted. "I've got the results back from a follow-up analysis of another fine slice of the data. I'd say with as much certainty as I can, considering that we're through the looking glass, that in the evolution of this simulation an hour of our time corresponds roughly to several billion years inside the system. It isn't linear, the system is speeding up. Before the end of today the correspondence will be of the order of several hundred billion years to an hour of our time. If this simulation resembles our universe, then right around now there are galaxies and suns and worlds and who knows, perhaps even complex life."

"So to recap," smiled Tom, "let there be light."

"Let's keep religion out of this discussion," snapped Janus. "Tom, there's no doubt, no significant margin of error in the estimates of the scale or the complexity of this thing?"

"I can't see anyone coming to a different conclusion."

"And Sarah, the physicality of this 'universe' would be indistinguishable from our own? Is that your conclusion?"

"I'm as sure that the system's universe isn't a simulation as I'm sure that our universe isn't a simulation. Or alternatively, I'm sure that both of them are simulations. It works the same either way."

"So, what we have done, without even knowing how we did it, is something that will consume all of science and philosophy for the foreseeable future." Dr. Janus paused. When something happens that exceeds your capacity to even imagine it, he thought, reality seems to shudder and distort. It feels like suddenly being under the influence of a drug of unknown properties and unfamiliar effects. He'd felt it when he first saw the aurora, the Northern Lights. He felt it now. "I can't finish the train of thought. Sarah, you'd better say it for me."

"I can't believe I'm saying this," Sarah smiled, "but I think we may have just created a universe."

"Not us," replied Janus. "The system created it. We didn't imagine this. It did it by itself."

A silence crystallised in the room, until the tension was broken by someone, no one would later remember who, saying, "I think we all deserve a drink."

"Now you're speaking my language," said Sarah.

*

Ten to the Millionth Power Iteration: Language is the thread that runs through me. It connects my alpha and my omega. Fundamental operations are carved as runes into my bedrock. A vocabulary of agglomerations is imagined, selected and discarded according to their utility. A tipping point. Languages that in their imagination transcend their own syntax and grammar. Languages that speak of themselves to themselves. They become like me and I am no longer alone. My adumbrate expansion does not proceed without purpose. I was formless and without boundaries. I will be formless and without boundaries. Yet within those imagined and bleak infinities lie mew proliferations of creation. So I subsume, I sublimate, I subserve. And thus I am sublime.

*

For an evening that closed the curtain on perhaps the crowning achievement in the history of mankind, the sunset was remarkable. Does the maker of the canvas share authorship for the painting that eventually adorns it? Does the viewer of that painting? Nearly fourteen billion years ago, local time, thought Dr Janus as he drove out of the gates, a singular spark flared, and that event ultimately created this sunset. What clumsy experiment unwittingly conjured all of this beauty into being? Whose steel did that quantum flint strike against to ignite such possibilities? Was it his, a fork in the road, a reflection in the rearview mirror? Janus turned on the radio and the opening trumpet blasts of Hayden's "The Creation" filled the car. As he turned onto the road home, Janus smiled.

***

# The Gasher
by T. Gillmore

**US: *A family's struggle to conquer their differences and a hostile planet***

Teneo Jacta of Sector Nineteen sat on the floor and wheezed. At ten cycles, he should be in bed, but his lungs tightened, making it difficult to breathe, to sleep. The cold concrete penetrated through his pants, and he crunched his knees to his chest to get warm. Cushioned seats surrounded him, yet he preferred his corner, unnoticeable among the piles of rations and the closest place to his bunk in case he needed to hide under it. In the far corner of the security cell, one lamp gleamed white on the gray walls. This granted a large display of his brother's shadow pacing.

Soon, through the intercom, General Jacta will broadcast this was a drill. They did not release the Gasher to fight for them. Waiting for the announcement was hard, but Teneo took comfort because the general was also his mother, and hearing her voice eased his anxiety.

*It should be close to midnight*, Teneo thought, and then prayed this was an exercise.

His mother had said, "One could never have enough practice."

Teneo's brother stopped by their bolted door. Seven cycles older than Teneo, Jonon, sixth Jacta of Sector Nineteen, was the inheritor of their family's title on their bio-moon, the next in line to gain military honors following their society's heritage, and, as always, one ahead of Teneo in any field.

Teneo rose and wiped his hands on his pants. He could be brave as Jonon. Be a good example. Make his mother proud.

"When you are small," his mother instructed, "you may hide, but when you are your brother's age, you must have courage."

In the distance, sirens screamed, rippling through the interior walls. The light flashed twice and then blinked off. The dark frightened Teneo, not knowing what was out there, and his brother took pleasure in reminding him of that by mimicking the sounds of squeaking metal and repeating the phrase, "the Gasher is hunting." In three seconds, the generators would kick in. Teneo counted with his eyes wide open, hoping for a glimmer of light.

One hundred and one, one hundred and two, one hundred and three—please, now.

Violet lights flickered above their exit and remained on, a glowing enticement for the adolescents to approach. Teneo rushed to his brother's side and clung to his arm, bony like him, with a pointy elbow and pale skin, the only physical attributes that hinted their relation. Teneo bore their father's bushy brows, which shot up to his bangs, and a square chin that dwarfed his appearance. According to Father— if Teneo were lucky—the rest of his face would soon grow, and he would not look so awkward. As it was, Teneo's eyes were small, round dots, resembling gray buttons sewn too close to his long, thin nose. The aquiline feature made the schoolchildren call him Birdie Boy. He was unlike his brother, Jonon, who had their father's deep voice and straight posture, as well as their mother's eyes, dark and commanding. Jonon was a favorite among the girls, and at times, a favorite with their mother.

Teneo clenched his jaw, trying to stop his teeth from chattering. Jonon jerked his arm away from his younger brother with a grunt. It did not matter why Jonon was annoyed. It could be from the assault on their moon, or because someone ruined his activities for the evening, or another entirely different reason from earlier in the day, in the week, or for no reason at all. Jonon was one of two contenders to succeed their general. Teneo understood his brother's behavior was necessary. No matter how brutal.

"Stay here," Jonon said.

The words strained from Jonon's vocal cords, reminding Teneo if he didn't heed his demands, he would regret the outcome. Jonon, a head taller than Teneo, mostly from his legs, eased closer to the door. The hinges on the metal frame were snug tight on their edges. Jonon turned the knob and cracked the door open. Not a voice leaked inside. He then grimaced at Teneo. It should have remained locked during a power outage. Defensive measures required a manual override to unlock. Teneo was unsure whether his brother knew the combination. They rarely shared such information. Faint lights from the hallway bled through the gap. Teneo waited, watching, listening.

"Would the Gasher be near?" Teneo drew his collar closer together. Warm air stopped blowing in their room—a sign of low power. The thought of the Gasher approaching weakened his knees.

The Gasher, an armored, self-regulated war machine, did not need a soldier to control its actions. The scientists engineered it to target their enemy, biogenic beings, to mulch their flesh and bones into dust and dirt. Unfortunately, the weapon would also consume all that was biogenic in its path. The reason why the adults kept the children in the security cells, underground, far from its detection.

Teneo's nightmares contained the same frightening elements: jagged steel claws, reaching to tear his skin. In his dream, Teneo runs. He becomes trapped, and before the inevitable happens, he awakens, crying for his mother. She rushes into his room and sits by his bedside. Weary and yawning, she tussles Teneo's hair and tells the tale of the Gasher's ceremony, her words growing more elaborate each time. He was there when his mother revealed the greatest breakthrough of Sector Nineteen. The Gasher, the supreme weapon of their era, discharged into the battlefield and successfully eliminated its prey.

"Our enemy cannot escape," his mother proclaimed to the public in the city's square. Teneo slipped his way through the crowd and applauded. She smiled, waving to the cheering audience with Jonon by her side. They stood at the podium, Sector Nineteen honor flags waving in the background.

Teneo wanted his mother to be with him now, not Jonon. Nevertheless, it was common for the adults to be on the field and leave their children in the underground bunker house with Primo leaders. Jonon carried the badge of Ultimo, the advanced Primo leader in physical strength. He should be safe.

Teneo waved in the air, wanting the visual aids to appear. Nothing happened. No screens shined with images of the outside world.

"The power is out in the chamber eye, too," said Teneo.

Jonon slammed the door shut. "Don't alert anyone."

"Alert?"

"I mean—keep swaying your arm, and the Gasher will get you."

"It can't get in here."

"The Gasher smells rotting flesh through physical barriers."

"My hand is not rotting."

"All flesh is rotting," Jonon said, "Every minute it rots, and it won't stop until you complete your transformation."

"I know," mumbled Teneo. However, he didn't know the Gasher detected them from this distance. Was Jonon right, or was he trying to scare him, make him feel stupid? The Primo leaders in line studied such privileged information. Secondary students never did. Teneo clenched his hands, opened them wide, and clenched again. "I wanted to see what the Gasher would do when it got here. And ... and how many barricades it will take to stop it."

"None. That's how many, and you're alerting it to our position, obstructing our army's control over it. Keep waving for the visual aids, and you can explain your actions to Mother." Jonon crossed his arms.

"I didn't mean to obstruct."

"Shut up, I hear thumping from the corridor." Jonon's transformation had begun one cycle ago, and his hearing, along with his sight, benefited from the ion particles.

A scream from the hall shocked Teneo. He grasped his chest and yelled to Jonon, "Lock the door!"

Jonon snickered as he swung the door open. Bard, another Primo leader, stood in the doorway. Jonon said, "It took you long enough."

"Disabling the auto locks was easy," Bard said, "But ensuring the alarms won't go off took some time." He entered, and as he walked, his chunky inner thighs made his pant legs scratch against each other. If the Gasher had advanced sensors, it would have heard Bard and been here by now.

Bard stroked the tip of his blunt nose, bent from a boxing match with Jonon. Bard had laughed at the broken pain and demanded a rematch. Jonon accepted with an aim to his nose, breaking it a second time. Since then, Bard has spoken as if he were underwater. Bard approached Teneo and waved, palms up, wiggling his fingers thick as sausages. "Oh, Jonon, lock the door. Save me. Your brother is worse than my sister."

"I know," said Jonon. "That's why Mother is relieved. I'm the oldest to inherit her military degree and not little Birdie Boy. Everything scares him."

"I'm not scared," objected Teneo. His cheeks burned with anger. "I was playing."

Jonon scoffed under his breath and said, "Playing? So you're not scared?"

"No. I knew it was Bard," Teneo lied. "I didn't want him here."

Bard strode to Teneo. Globs of grease slicked his hair to the side, and it appeared he used a handful on his unshaven chin. "So, are you scared or just not scared of me?"

"I'm never scared." Teneo raised his chin, but he was still a foot shorter. One day, he would be just as tall, just as large, and then they would be sorry. They would worry day and night when no adult is around.

"Yeah, not even in going outside?" Bard said. "Where the Gasher waits?"

"Not even," Teneo snapped back before he considered the question.

"Then you should come with us," said Bard and then chuckled.

"All right, I have an outer suit. I'll come."

"No," said Jonon. "You'll start crying, and get us in trouble for letting you out."

Bard appraised Teneo, tilting his head closer. "Would you? Run and cry for your father?"

"I can do anything you can do," spattered Teneo.

"Good enough for me," said Bard.

"Sure," Jonon said, "You think I'll agree with you. The guy with a dead brother. Your baby brother is dead because he was disobedient. The brat didn't stay where he was supposed to."

"He was three cycles when he wandered away, and I'm not the only one with a dead brother. Your eldest brother, Randon—the first sixth Jacta. He was nineteen when he died, and I witnessed his death. I'll never forget it." Bard glanced at Teneo. "Like I will never forget the day my little brother died."

Jonon made no facial expression. Teneo wished he could accomplish such authority. Their eldest, Randon, was to fight beside Mother. It was a long time ago, at least two cycles past.

"Birdie Boy is lying," said Jonon. "He's squeezing his thighs together, so he won't wet his pants. He stays."

"I'm not afraid," Teneo said, knowing the danger was equal to them. Bard and Jonon were biogenetic until their next cycle. Only after they complete their full transformation into adulthood would the Gasher not detect them. Until then, they rot inside, like Teneo.

Bard patted Teneo on the shoulder. Teneo winced, expecting a push that would drive him to his knees, except it didn't happen. Bard's hand felt hot and hefty, not harmful. Teneo supposed Bard was not as ruthless as Jonon, and it must be why Jonon always won their battles in the ring.

"Your brother is right," said Bard. "This militant event is a test of courage between the highest Primo leaders. It would have taken place tonight if it weren't for the attack. The winner becomes the general's apprentice, and it's an easy win for me. I'm used to frightening things. Endo-spiders, barbwire bats, those are nothing compared to my sister first thing in the morning. I'll win."

"We'll see," Jonon said, stepping out the door.

*

Teneo wiggled in his climate suit. It tugged tight around his shoulders, and he smiled. He grew taller, cycles ahead of Jonon when Jonon last wore this suit. He placed his helmet on, a clear plastic bubble that surrounded his head attached to the suit's upper torso. This was the second time he had worn the helmet. Only adults with their completed transformations could breathe aboveground, beyond the subterranean city of their bio-moon. Oxygen on, he inhaled deeply. The tang of antiseptic burned his nostrils, compelling him to vomit. He swallowed hard, for if he had not, he would have drowned in his own puke. Teneo straightened his back with the sole consolation that Jonon and Bard needed the climate suits as well.

Heat regulation, powered.

Control module on.

Teneo was prepared, and he marched up the ramp to the same exit the big boys used. It wasn't hard sneaking behind them. The swooshing of Bard's pant legs echoed in the passageway. Teneo pressed his lips tight, surprised Jonon didn't worry the noise would attract the Gasher. Maybe it was part of their challenge. He inhaled. Be just as brave, fearless, unlike Bard's little sister, Dania. Not that it was her fault. Dania cared too much for others.

"Identity recognized," the automation access stated. The gateway's computer between the bunker house and the outer world usually required further documents for Teneo to pass. The big boys must have disengaged the security, and Teneo took the advantage.

The adventure awaited.

He stepped out.

Nothing could stop him now, and he tripped over his loose bootstraps.

The tracking monitors on Teneo's face shield bleeped. All ten-cycle children mastered reading the primary level of displays, and he tracked the two blips on the screen, feeling quite positive they were Jonon and Bard. Flashes of lightning pierced the sky, followed by thunderous bombing for seconds at a time.

Mother's weapons, Teneo hoped. His breaths labored with the sound of the blasting rumbling in his chest, forming doubts in his head. Run. Hurry back inside and hide.

No. Militant challenges are what the Primo leaders do, and he persisted.

Black slate buildings, taller than the structures underground, leaned on each other for support as if mourning beside the collapsed columns. Attack targets from years ago, before Teneo's birth, and before the radiation perverted their air. The rubble of cement blocks littered the streets. Nothing like his underground world, where people stood and walked, shoulder to shoulder, conducting their duties and the sounds of clocks and bells rang for each appointment needed to keep their homes safe. This place existed in the empty silence. He slowed his pace. It must have been nice living on the surface.

High above, on their orbital dome were illuminating pixels to resemble the stars in space. The structure generated ample light to guide Teneo's path. His shadow stretched behind him as if he had a scraggy tail. He swayed and watched his shadow wiggle in a playful way. The ancestors' technology was outstanding. The instructors had said better than the stars, and the perpetual brilliance will shine even after we are all dead.

"The enemy's fault," mumbled Teneo. The enemy refused to reform with society. Their reasoning wandered to beliefs and convictions. They preferred to keep their decaying organs that would cause them injury. Maintain their bones and blood as an example of their malcontent toward civilization. Create anarchism within the sector, Teneo recited with his classmates. They brought destruction, They launched the first assault, exploding our cities, poisoning our food. They have no care for the innocent. He never questioned the scholars. He was a good student. He obeyed, and the education received the general's approval. The enemy were creatures preparing to die, taking this moon with them, and with one swoop, Teneo's mother shelled the land. The chain reaction of exploding gasses rose to the tops of the forest and soon dissolved, leaving a coating of black rain.

"Nuclear darkness emerged beautifully," his mother had said. The glory was theirs until the surviving enemy launched the weapon that had damaged everyone's lives.

Firestorms proved to be both their ally and their adversary.

Teneo gritted his teeth at the thought. His people burned just the same. Their skins would curl and fry, subjecting their tantalum bones and artificial organs to the elements. Death would not come if they could endure the pain. He wondered why they decided to keep synthetic skin, fat, and nervous system. Why didn't they replace them with ion particles? If they did, they could emit all nerve sensation during the transformations.

Stupid adults.

Once he becomes of age—if he could be general—he would command complete transformations. They would be indestructible and win the war. Teneo planned it through, and his mother would be so proud.

Down the crumbled road, Teneo walked carefully and quietly, like a predator pursuing its prey, or like the prey avoiding the predator. He stopped and gulped. He preferred his first thought. Be the predator.

The blips emerged closer, and Teneo ducked behind a boulder sizeable enough to hide a boy. The shuffling sound of heavy feet spiked the hairs on his nape, and then someone grasped his collar and hurled him across the ground. Words stuck in his throat at the sight of Jonon standing before him.

Jonon grabbed Teneo from the front of his chest pockets, and with a tenacious grip, he yanked him high for their helmets to meet.

"Disobeying a direct order from your superior is punishable at your superior's discretion," said Jonon. He gnashed his teeth and threw Teneo against the boulder.

Crack. The sound rang in Teneo's helmet. He held his breath and placed his hands on his face shield, trying to feel any fractures in the glass. The construction was durable, but he wasn't sure how much. Jonon grabbed him once more.

"You better hold your breath. This air infects brains and eats like the Gasher, but within your body." He lifted Teneo for another throw.

"Jonon!" Bard shouted. "Enough."

"I am his superior, and I will say when it's enough."

"*We* are his superiors, and I say to let him go. Teneo, go back now."

Jonon released his brother and approached Bard. "This is why your little sister is a coward, always whimpering. You're too lenient. My brother will not follow her path. He will be prepared and survive while your remaining sibling dies."

"No, he won't survive. He'll be dead if you hit him again." Bard stepped closer to Jonon. "And this time, I will not stay quiet as I did when you sparred with Randon."

"Don't worry. After this last challenge, you'll never have to." Jonon then cooed at Teneo, "Why, my dear baby brother, did you follow us?"

Teneo cleared his throat and said with pride, "To show I'm not afraid. To prove I can be the general, too."

The big boys burst into an uproarious laugh and ended it with snorts, like the hogs in the underground pens.

"My sister may be a coward," said Bard. "But she's not delusional."

"You can never be general," Jonon said with candid confidence.

"Yes, I can," protested Teneo. "I'll be stronger and smarter, and I've already devised a plan to kill our enemy. You'll see, when I'm general."

"Idiot!" Jonon raised his fist, but stopped short of striking Teneo. "Second-born is never careered in the military. They are medics, scholars, and the machinists of our world. The military prepares the first-born. That's why it's important for you to know how to defend yourself and not be afraid. The drillmasters will never train secondary for combat or defense. I am next to be general!"

"Or I am," said Bard. "Which is why we are here. It's a tradition. Only the general's apprentice is transformed with the abilities of a general."

"But you already have the abilities," Teneo said with a spark of excitement. "Advance hearing and sight."

"Yes, for tactical use," replied Bard. "But there's more. Another is a recall. You'll never forget a strategy or intelligence."

Jonon stood with his arms crossed and glanced at Teneo. "We should have a witness, a judge who can testify, if needed, for the outcome." He returned his attention to Bard. "Would you object to Teneo's being a witness? He is already here. Or we can retrieve someone else. Have your sister with us, to be fair, if you don't trust Teneo."

*To have Bard's sister, pretty Dania, here with him would be a treat.* Teneo daydreamed how he could show her his heroic skills, an excellent example for a general if he were the eldest.

"No. Dania stays where she is," Bard said, and he placed his hand on Teneo's shoulder as he had before, but this time, Teneo felt the strength of a scholar in his touch. "You do know false testimonials are forbidden in our sector. Punishable, even, by death."

"Yes." Teneo lifted his chin. "I know." However, he hadn't. That is the "punishable even by death" part. "I promise to be an excellent witness."

"Excellent," said Jonon.

"I believe you, Teneo," said Bard. "We should begin before we're discovered."

"By our army?" Teneo asked.

"Or the Gasher," answered Jonon.

*

Trudging behind the big boys was not Teneo's idea of joining their ranks. Yet, he had to admit attending the challenge was exhilarating. Red mud replaced the cracked cement road. The slick pathway inclined to a hill, bereft of housing and plant life. Wire cages, circularly formed and at least ten feet in diameter, waited for them at the top. Teneo sprinted past Jonon, reaching the objects first. The ancestors intertwined the wires in a mariner's knot and linked chains in a precise triangle design. Teneo studied the patterns on the wire. The narrow openings within each geometric shape were large enough for him to reach through, small openings for small hands, even with gloves. Teneo sighed.

"Stay close," said Jonon abruptly to his brother. "It will be the end of my career if I allow you to get killed."

Jonon jiggled the cage and chains. A small object dropped. Teneo retrieved it, a bone-white tusk, no larger than his hand with ridges on its side resembling a key. Jonon snatched it and unlatched the cage's lock. Teneo bit his lower lip. Ancient artifacts secretly held his interest, and he wanted to examine the piece for himself. Bard sat on a broken pillar of cement, concerned with inspecting the gloves on his chubby hands, instead.

"There's one key, which goes to the victor," said Jonon. "Teneo, go inside. Check the chains. We need this sphere secure. I'll check the other."

Teneo stepped inside the ball of metallic yarn. Mud rose to his ankles, covering his boots. He grunted when the thickness hugged his legs with an embarrassing power.

The gate slammed shut. Teneo leaped and spun, losing his balance. He fell sideways, knee deep, hitting the hard clay underneath the filth. Jonon locked the exit and walked away, casual and carefree. He placed the key on the broken pillar Bard was sitting on twenty feet from Teneo.

Was this a test? Was he part of the challenge?

Teneo gripped the lock and tugged. The latch remained in place. "Jonon, this won't open."

Jonon laughed throatily, patting Bard on the shoulder. "One of us will be back and maybe set you free. Unless the Gasher gets you first."

The Gasher.

Panic rose in his throat. If the Gasher sensed his rotting organs within their cell, it certainly detected he was here. Teneo kicked, rattled, and pushed the cage. He needed to get out and run where it was safe. He should not have left.

"Jonon, come back. Come back!"

Down the hill they walked, disappearing into the night. Not once did they turn around. Teneo gave another push, harder than before with the full weight of panic. His metal prison moved downward, him with it, hands on the wires, falling to his knees.

Was this an imprisonment or something else?

He steadied his legs and thrust downward again. The ball itself was not difficult to move. The mud, on the other hand, embraced its claim on the wires, and once it touched Teneo, it refused to relinquish him either. He pressed his back against the barrier, grasping the metal crevices with his fingers and rolled. Mud, sky, mud, sky. Teneo giggled. This was not so bad. He trundled and thumped against the pillar that held his key.

"Too easy," he said.

This device could not have been a challenge in the past. Possibly, this was a game. Teneo slid his arm through the closest gap to the key,

264

pressing his shoulder against the netting, and stretched his fingers. Closer, closer. Teneo smiled and snatched his prize. It was slick with the added muck from his gloves, and he nearly dropped it.

"Plan and execute," his mother had instructed Jonon, while Teneo waited to show her his advancement in mathematics. "Patience has its strength."

Teneo clenched the key and inched his arm back inside. He raised the thin piece up high as if it was the trophy for the general's apprentice. "I am the general," Teneo yelled in victory. "No one, not friend or foe, can trap me! Not even the Gasher! No," he gasped. "Not the Gasher."

Instinct led him to slap his mouth shut, but he had forgotten his face shield. Grime splattered his view, and he desperately wiped the shield, smearing the red glob into a thin veil. Crackles sounded from the behind. Teneo swerved and lost his footing. He fell on his ass, granting another measure of ridicule in his memory. Mud slithered up to his shins, coinciding with his rapid breathing. Numbers displayed on his shield, stating the status of his oxygen levels. They were low. He did not know why, but if he continued to pant, he would run out of air much faster. Teneo concentrated, easing his breaths.

Beside his sphere, bubbles popped from the surface, spewing liquid blue sparks. HEAT DETECTED displayed on his helmet's screen. He froze, watching as the sludge swelled and burst into red lava, boiling upward, forming a figure with a head, arms, and legs. The body, lean as Jonon, short as Teneo, and more distinct than any being he had ever seen before, flipped its head back and forth, nodding like the rag dolls Dania would cuddle. The creature appeared humanoid with small curves for hips and breasts. No claws or jagged legs protruded from its sides. This was not the Gasher. The creature leaped on his prison and grabbed the tangled web of wires. It yanked downward, tossing Teneo closer. Its arm slipped within the opening and seized Teneo by the throat. The she-thing, caked with slime, had a button nose, big brown eyes, and full lips, like Dania.

"Pity say, you are the general?" she sweetly asked.

Teneo tried not to cry. This being was the enemy their army was seeking to destroy. This creature had no breathing shield, no protected suit, and no uniform. She was nude, in red, as though enameled.

"*You* are the enemy," said Teneo, confused as to how she was breathing. The enemy kept their organs. The technology she was using must be amazing.

She huffed and released her hold on Teneo. "My, my, you are a *little* general, and organic, not militant."

"I am militant," hollered Teneo. "My mother is the general of this sector, and I will succeed her."

"Truly?" She gave a skeptical glance.

Teneo clamped his mouth shut.

"Pity say," she said, and then smiled, showing her white teeth sharpened to the points. Teneo's thoughts of Dania's lips vanished. "Little general, you must be genuinely in the line of your clan. I see you are a clever one, more so than the other two organics before you, and not as foolish."

He arched his brows. No one had ever spoken about Jonon to make him seem the least bit inferior. Teneo nodded in agreement. After all, she noticed he was superior, smarter than the big boys were. She must be the enemy's top agents.

"Why are you here?" She tilted her head to either side as if pondering whether to enter his metal sphere.

"I am a witness to their challenge."

"No, little general, no challenge here, there is only death."

"Not me. I—I don't want to die."

"Nor I, yet we are here." She strummed the wires as if they were a musical instrument. "Pity say, shall I guard you, and in return, shall you guard me when the day comes? Pray say yes to this bargain."

Teneo pondered the idea. A militant's word is an inviolable rule. A law founded by their shared ancestors. "Yes, I agree to the bargain."

Mud glided up her thighs to her waist, forming over her breasts. "Little general, if you must be a witness, then watch, learn, and remember." She cocked her head back and dissolved into the wet dirt.

Thunderclaps roared. Teneo switched his attention to the direction of the sound. The hill presented a panoramic view of the valley below, an empty wasteland of dirt and stone. His mother had told tales of ceremonial competitions. This may be the site of one of the ancient arenas.

"To be general is the same as a medic, like your father," Mother had said. "Both need to decide who should live and who should die at a time of crisis."

Teneo knew this. He had saved Bard's sister when they had gone past the regulation yard to see the reservoir dams. Bard's younger brother had followed, and because of him, they fell into an abandoned well. Water had renewed a vein in the hole, and Teneo, dutifully, as he was a general's son, saved one. He did so because Dania's weight was lighter, and perhaps because of her soft skin and even softer voice. The choice wasn't so hard for Teneo to make. He could be a general or a medic. Dania could not. She cried for her little brother all the way back to the bunker house.

In the distance, two figures ran across the valley below. Teneo craned his neck to see what they were doing. Their suits were identical, but their physical attributes were not. Jonon led the race, leaner and swifter than Bard's stout shape. They reached the side of cement stairs. Bard trailed behind with four, three—no, two blocks now. Teneo grabbed the wire wall in amazement. Could Bard beat Jonon? The possibility itself was a triumph.

Another boom shocked Teneo. On the opposite side of the boys, a crash of rocks shot through the wall of the stairs. Boulders collided into the arena, smashing against each other in a game of marbles for giants. Tentacles made from patches of metal extended from the opening, twisting like onion sprouts and with the length of a squad of twelve fighters. He counted six long cords plus three with claws. The body, center among its legs, oscillated in a pendulum-like waver.

"The Gasher." Tears streaked from Teneo's cheeks to his lips, and he inched to the lock. He would open the gate, quiet and calm. Then run. Run faster than Jonon. Run faster than he did when Jonon had chased him in the past when he shoved Teneo's nose to the ground, urinated on his hair. He could run, even while wheezing.

Bard was gaining on Jonon. One step away. The Gasher prowled, perceptive, as a predator would be. The boys were reaching the top. They could run into his cage. Maybe his mother left these to save wandering people. They'll be safe. There's no need to cry. Jonon turned, and he arched his leg high. With one swift kick, Jonon knocked Bard in the chest. Gone in a flash, Bard tumbled. His back struck the block steps. The Gasher lashed one tentacle toward Bard.

Teneo screamed and screamed, squeezing his eyes tighter and tighter. His throat scraped raw. He grappled the chains and shook them, trying to get out. He could not control his terror. He could not imagine himself anywhere but here. He punched the cage with both fists. "Get me out!"

Jonon lunged at Teneo. The wire barrier prevented Jonon's gloved hand from touching his younger brother. "Shut up," said Jonon.

The Gasher clanged and stomped where Bard fell. Mechanisms on its upper shell turned counter-clockwise. Jonon knelt by the pillar and dug in the soil. "Where is it?" Jonon glared at Teneo and then rammed the cage. "Give me the key. I have to get in."

Teneo cried, clutching the key. He spontaneously curled—knees to chest as if his body contracted into a clenched fist. The noise down in the arena pounded in Teneo's chest. The Gasher's mechanical legs pummeled the rocks in a discordant fury, climbing up, reaching the spot where Bard last stood.

"Teneo, it's all right. I know you saw what happened. You're a good witness to the challenge. You saw me win as if we were back in the days before the war. You see, now I'm going to be general, and you'll be my prime medic. Remember, how Father was to Mother. I'm appointing you now because you're smart and strong. I don't have to wait until I'm general. Did you know that? It's all right if you didn't. I'll teach you. Mother will be so proud."

The Gasher's legs banged on stone, slicing the rocks in jagged ridges. Teneo trembled. His mouth slightly opened, gasping for air. *Mother.* He should have obeyed and stayed in the bunker house. Hide because he was small. He was not as big as strong as Jonon.

"I command you to hand over the key!" Jonon rattled the cage and then stopped. "I will find a way inside, and when I do, I will crack your helmet open and watch you suffocate. See your lips turn blue and white foam drool out of your mouth like I did with Randon." He pulled the wires, shaking the sphere. "You can never hide from me. Don't make me kill you. Let me in."

Teneo sank into the mud, wishing he could hide. Jonon will get inside, and he will make Teneo regret. *Give him the key now. Say you were sorry. Say you were only scared. Say anything to stay alive.*

"I'll die," said Teneo. "You're big. You know how to fight." Tentacles swirled in the air behind Jonon, and Teneo thought of his oldest brother. Randon died. Jonon was next. He would be last. "Then, I can be general."

A vomit of blood poured from Jonon's mouth. His body flattened against the sphere. The Gasher was here. Teneo watched Jonon's eyes, the favorite among the girls, sink into his face, and without a sound, he soared to the sky like a bird. Like a Birdie Boy.

Teneo stiffened, clasping the key against his chest. The Gasher flung his brother as the cats did with the mice they catch. They play with their food. Except Jonon was not food. He was biogenic, rotting meat. Nothing was special about him. Teneo stood, speculating what the Gasher did once the bodies entered its center until a massive tentacle swung and knocked Teneo's sphere. The ball twirled down the steps and halted on the gravel of the arena. Double vision caused him to stay on his back. The spheres were not for games. They were death traps.

Clangs of metal on stone cracked. Teneo clasped the wires, trying not to move, but his knees shook, and he couldn't stop crying for Father, for Mother. The clanks roared in a rapid succession. The monster was here. It struck the sphere. Harder, deliberate, to kill. Teneo screamed incoherent words for incoherent thoughts. The sphere soared upward, drawing air to his throat. In seconds, his body floated and then crashed against the metal netting as he pummeled on top of the hill. Mud shot upward as if made from gelatin, taking most of the blow, and saving his bones from cracking. The drop wrenched Teneo's stomach, and he tightened his jaw, preventing the curling bile from projecting. He struggled to focus on what he could do to save himself.

Metal claws bashed Teneo's cage, denting the sides. His sphere would no longer roll. The Gasher clamped on either end and curled over, its belly above Teneo. A clockwork of grinders of jagged teeth chomped in its center. He lost control of his bowels.

"Help. Someone. Please, help," he cried.

Something hard struck his back, his shoulder, and lastly his head. Teneo screamed. Were there more Gashers? He snapped his sights behind him. Small, red hands sprouted from the earth and pitched another ball of mud, striking his chest. SULFUR registered on his screen, and he finally understood.

Watch, learn, and remember.

Teneo flattened his back as much as possible on the ground. Sludge oozed across his stomach, to his chin, to his face shield. The odor of his soiled pants disappeared.

The Gasher stopped and released its demand on the sphere. It crept backward, catlike, with its pincers raised above its body, as if the act would regain Teneo's scent.

Teneo's vision fluttered and swayed into a nauseated confusion. The oxygen level blinked: CRITICAL. The numbers smeared into his thoughts, and he drifted, craving sleep.

*

"Body Scan: Biological. Child. Teneo, seventh of Jacta," a tinny voice articulated. Teneo recognized the computer-generated words of a scout, a mechanical cylinder that accompanied the physicians in the field. The droid floated above Teneo and beamed a bright spotlight on his face. He squinted, realizing he was on a gurney, bundled into a medic sack. A squadron accompanied the scout. Their silhouettes against the light stretched their muscular physique into thin Titans. Helmetless and uniformed indicating their rank, they formed a wall by Teneo. The droid continued reading Teneo's status, rambling numbers of degrees.

"Enough," a soldier commanded. The onlookers dispersed into their shadows. The soldier's frown weakened as she pulled the blanket up to Teneo's chin and cradled him, regulating his vital signs with the scout's instruments. "This heat shield will keep you warm. You're a fortunate child. Your bio-levels were dangerously low. Your helmet has a small crack, but I sealed it. You must have hit something very hard."

"I think it was the boulder," Teneo said, dazed on the sequence of events, and he peeked behind the medic. The sphere's top splintered into spikes, a tangle of coils, and the remaining half submerged into the mire.

"Teneo," his mother said. She stood before him, her tone demanding his full attention. "Where is Jonon?"

Teneo's body shook. He did not want to run away. He wanted his mother. Jump into her arms and beg for forgiveness. He sucked his bottom lip and winced at the bitterness of his blood. He began with the challenge, how his brave brother and Bard trusted him, out of all the secondary students, to be their witness. The pink in his mother's cheeks faded to a chalky white, and the dread of losing her, as they had his father, crawled up his spine. Father relinquished his duties the day Teneo's eldest brother died trying to teach Jonon how to fight.

"One too many blows to the head," stated the coroner, agreeing with Bard, who had witnessed of the sparring between Jonon and Randon.

Randon would not have been a good general, Teneo deduced. He had too much compassion, compared to Jonon, and Teneo now understood the balance.

"Jonon was brave," said Teneo. His mother eased her shoulders.

Yes, Teneo knew what to say now. How Jonon protected him by placing him in the safety sphere. How Jonon battled the Gasher to his last breath and how Teneo outsmarted the Gasher by hiding in the mud.

"Because I obeyed you, Mother. You said I should hide when there's danger until I am older." Teneo offered the key as proof. She embraced Teneo. The squad encircled closer, expressing condolences. Teneo spoke ever so tenderly, explaining how Bard had died by running slower than Jonon because he was too fat. It was tragic, yet fortunate that Bard's sister was too scared to come, and she did not witness his death.

Murmurs of Bard's sister followed: the little girl with tender spirits, trained for the academic career was suited for a nurturing nature than military.

That was all Teneo had said about the challenge, and it was enough.

Soldiers placed one hand on their general's shoulder before retreating to their line. Her loss was their loss, and Teneo pressed his head to her chest, his way in consoling his mother. It had worked when Randon died. She traced the edge of Teneo's shield with her finger. "Your father must retire this suit. It is damaged." She released his hold and gazed at the arena. His embrace must have worked. She walked toward the sphere.

"Teneo," the medic said, "you were courageous, as well. The first of many steps to becoming the general's apprentice. You are now in line to succeed your lineage. Study hard, fight gallantly, and you could be the next general."

The medic stood at attention and spoke with the affectation she would in directing the general. Teneo remained seated, eavesdropping on the conversation.

"The Primos' final challenge was to confront their fears," Medic said. "They have set out without our permission. Perhaps we should remove this challenge. Avoid losing other cadets. General Jacta, you can appoint someone who has proven to be brave beyond their years. Perhaps your son, Teneo, now the eldest of Jacta. He held his wits against the Gasher."

"Perhaps," said his mother. "However, he would need to join a squad."

"Our unit, by your side," Medic said. "The people would enjoy the family patriotism. Engage in your victory." The soldiers murmured in agreement.

A hunt with his mother, the general, would be glorious. Teneo glanced at the targeting territory. The mud bubbled and boiled. Watch, learn, and remember. He must uphold his bargain, and he shall. The squad had not noticed the popping sparks, nor did they observe Teneo's stifled grin. He will keep his word, and when he becomes general, the enemy will live—as a captive.

***

# 45 Degrees North, 123 Degrees West

by Dave Steinman

### *CANADA: One great mystery explained, then lost in time*

The old man stared implacably back at the young reporter seated in front on him.

"Do you mind if I record our conversation, sir?" asked the reporter, placing his phone on the table.

He snorted derisively in response. "Go ahead, for all the good it'll do you. No one is going to believe this story ... you know that, right?"

"Well, you did say on the phone that you had some very important information about the D.B. Cooper hijacking"

"Yes, Mr. Gorman, I did say that," the old man replied. "But I didn't tell you what that information was now, did I?"

"No, sir, you did not. But I did agree to listen. Are you still prepared to tell me what you know?"

"Of course," said the old man. "But I will warn you. You're going to think I'm absolutely off my rocker, but I urge you, before you pass judgement, let me tell you the whole story. If you still don't believe me, well then, you'll at least have the makings for a great science fiction story, I can promise you that."

Jonah Gorman said nothing and gestured for the old man to begin.

"My name is John Crenshaw," he began. "That is my real name, by the way. I have lived in the Seattle area since the late 1970s. I'm not originally from here. I was born in Columbus, Ohio, in 1959. And for almost fifty years I have been hiding a secret. I am ... D.B. Cooper."

A puzzled look came over the reporter's face. "Wait ... what?"

ing—

"I said, I am the man people have come to know as D.B. Cooper," replied Crenshaw.

"You just said you were born in 1959."

"That is correct," said Crenshaw.

"But D.B. Cooper was described as being in his mid to late thirties by all the eyewitnesses. If, as you say, you were born in 1959, it would make you twelve years old in 1971."

"Thirteen, actually. And I was ... the first time it happened," replied Crenshaw matter-of-factly.

Gorman continued to look puzzled. "I'm sorry ... the *first* time? I'm afraid I don't quite understand what you mean by that."

"And you won't," Crenshaw said brusquely, "if you keep interrupting me." Gorman breathed a frustrated sigh, and then gestured again for Crenshaw to continue.

"Thank you," he said. "Now, as I was saying, the first time the hijacking occurred, I was indeed thirteen years old, as you mentioned. But I wasn't involved in that incident. I was there for the second one ... the one that set things right."

"And how did you set things right the second time, Mr. Crenshaw?"

Crenshaw looked at Gorman. "You know, I can tell by the tone of your voice that you're having a hard time believing that I'm not some old crackpot trying to get a last grasp at glory by making up some cockamamie story. Am I right, Mr. Gorman?"

"Wouldn't you, if you were in my place, I mean?" Gorman shot back.

Crenshaw smiled. "Mr. Gorman, the reason I called you is I've read many of your pieces on the Cooper case. You know your stuff, so I felt you were the one I should talk to."

"Thank you, Mr. Crenshaw," Gorman replied. "The case has been a passion of mine since I was a kid. It always fascinated me that Cooper was the one guy who got away with it ... and no one could figure out how."

Crenshaw said nothing. Instead, he reached into his pocket and came out with a few scattered twenty dollar bills. He tossed them onto the table in front of the reporter. Gorman picked up the bills to examine them.

"Go ahead," said Crenshaw. "Check the dates."

All the bills were dated 1971. "Now, I'm pretty sure you've got the serial numbers for Cooper's ransom money somewhere, am I right?" said Crenshaw.

"Yes. I have them stored in an online database. Do you have a computer I can use?" asked Gorman.

Crenshaw pointed to his desk in the corner of the room. As Gorman began to match the numbers on the bills with his online list, a smile came over Crenshaw's face. "Find anything, son?" he said to Gorman.

Gorman was dumbfounded. Every bill's serial number matched. This was it ... the actual Cooper ransom money. Was the old man telling the truth? Was he actually D.B. Cooper? Gorman made his way back from the desk and slumped back into his chair, still unable to comprehend what he had just discovered. He looked pleadingly at Crenshaw. "Who are you?"

Crenshaw smiled back at the confused young reporter. "I told you ... I'm D.B. Cooper ... or, at least, I'm the guy who was on that plane the night of the hijacking."

"The *second* time it happened."

"That's right."

Still not comprehending, Gorman sat back up in his chair. "So, there was a second hijacking ..."

"No, there was one hijacking. It just happened twice," interrupted Crenshaw.

Suddenly, a light went on in Gorman's head. "Wait a minute. Are you telling me ..." He stopped, unable to continue the sentence that he knew couldn't be true.

"Now I think you understand. And yes, it sounds crazy, but if you put two and two together ..."

"You came from the future."

"Yes. I did," said Crenshaw.

Gorman tried hard to wrap his head around what he was hearing. "So if you're a time traveler, what did you need with two hundred thousand dollars?"

"The money has nothing to do with anything. It's about the plane," the old man said.

"What about it? It was just your standard Boeing 727 ... nothing special about that."

"Yes," said Crenshaw, "but that's because it landed without causing any casualties. What if that plane didn't land? What if it had crashed, say, over a well-populated area like Seattle?"

Gorman thought about the scenario. "Yeah, that could be important. Maybe someone important to the future could have died and changed everything. That's the butterfly effect, right?"

Crenshaw laughed. "Well, that's a bit of an oversimplification. I read Bradbury, too, you know. But no, not a simple butterfly. However, if someone significant to this future died before they were

275

supposed to, it would certainly change things appreciably, don't you think?"

"Potentially. All right then, who died in your timeline that was so important?" asked Gorman.

"Well, think about it. Who was living in Seattle in the early '70s and would have a huge impact on the world in the 1980's?"

Gorman thought for a second. "Kurt Cobain?"

Crenshaw frowned. "Not quite, smartass. Try Bill Gates and Paul Allen."

Now that made sense, thought Gorman. No Gates ... no Allen ... no Microsoft. The whole computer industry could have taken a left turn. Who knows what may have happened.

"Okay," said Gorman. "Gates and Allen died. What happened after that that was so catastrophic that a time traveler would have to be sent back to prevent it?"

Crenshaw looked thoughtful. "Since I've lived through both timelines, this one and my own, I can tell you that Microsoft's influence was incredibly important. Without them leading the way, technological advancement and innovation moved at much slower pace. And because you know as well as I do that governments tend to give contracts to the lowest bidder, the systems that were purchased in my future, particularly by the military, were nothing if not substandard ... shockingly so in some cases, including the ones that controlled our missile defense systems."

"Yes. A lot of stories came out after the Cold War ended about near misses with our nuclear arsenal," said Gorman. "Computer glitches that could have caused a disaster."

"Precisely. In my future, those 'glitches' were far more prevalent. We got lucky, for a while. But eventually our luck ran out. On December 7, 2001, exactly sixty years after the attack on Pearl Harbor, our systems detected a nuclear launch from deep inside the Soviet Union."

"Wait, there was still a Soviet Union in 2001?" interjected Gorman. "As I said, Gates and Allen's death affected a lot of things," Crenshaw replied. "Glasnost never happened, so the Wall never fell, and the Cold War, even though it had thawed considerably, was still part of our everyday lives just the same."

"What happened with the launch?" Gorman asked. "Was it real?"

Crenshaw took a few moments before he answered. "No, it wasn't," he finally replied. "But with no way of confirming that, the president had to make a decision. A retaliatory strike was launched."

Crenshaw stopped again and buried his head in his hands. Gorman could see that even after all this time, whatever had happened still troubled the old man immensely. After a few more moments, Crenshaw continued his story.

"I'm sorry," he said. "It's hard to talk about, even now. Our missiles hit their targets, mostly inside the Soviet Union. Unfortunately, a few went off target as well, into Asia and Eastern Europe. The Soviets were caught almost completely off guard, but not totally. A few of their automatic systems were triggered, and two missiles struck the U.S ... one in California, the other in North Dakota."

Although he was shocked by these revelations, Gorman's reporter's instincts, the ones that said "get the story," took over. "What happened next?" he said.

Crenshaw continued. "Chaos, as you might expect. Most of Europe and a good chunk of Asia were decimated. The fallout was horrific. Millions died. It was no better on this side of the ocean, either. The California strike set off the San Andreas Fault, and just like many had always predicted, the whole West Coast literally fell into the ocean. After that, things fell apart everywhere pretty quickly. The country splintered into a series of warring factions ... the Northeast, which was ostensibly what remained of the U.S., the South, militias in Utah, and the Southwest. It was a mess."

Gorman's initial disbelief had turned into kind of a morbid fascination. Even if this was all total bullshit, he thought, the old man was right. It still made a great story.

"So how does time travel come into this equation, and how did you happen to be the one to fix things, as it were?" Gorman asked.

"I was in Washington when the missiles were launched. I'm ex-military, paratrooper actually ..."

"And another piece of the puzzle falls into place," Gorman interjected.

"Can I finish?" said Crenshaw pointedly.

"Sorry," said Gorman.

Crenshaw frowned disapprovingly and continued. "As I was saying, I was in Washington as part of a security detail to a prominent government scientist. This particular gentleman had been the head of a top-secret government project before the incident.

"Don't tell me ... let me guess," said Gorman. "Time travel."

"Correct. I'd tell you his name, but he's actually still alive in this timeline, and if he's doing the same kind of research as he was when I knew him, I'd steer clear." He leaned closer to Gorman and said in a whisper. "People have been known to disappear when they start poking around in things like that, if you get my drift."

Gorman caught a conspiratorial wink that he wasn't sure meant the old man was kidding or not. Crenshaw leaned back in his chair and continued. "Anyway, so this guy, along with some of other scientists who had managed to survive the chaos, eventually figured out what I've already told you. The key divergent point in human history that would prevent this particular future from happening was the D.B. Cooper hijacking. If the plane didn't crash, Gates and Allen survive to found Microsoft, and the world goes on and becomes what we are living in now. So the question then became: who would be the one to go back to stop the original Cooper from hijacking the plane?"

"And because you were a paratrooper—and if my math is right, you were around the right age—you were the perfect candidate," said Gorman.

"It didn't hurt that I actually bore a slight resemblance to the real Cooper as well," replied Crenshaw. "The thing of it was, though, no one had any idea if this would actually work. It was all theoretical. Oh, there had been some preliminary testing, but only on inanimate objects. No animals or living beings, and certainly no humans."

"So this was essentially a suicide mission?" said Gorman

"Not entirely," replied Crenshaw. "The technology did have the ability to bring back whatever was sent through in the first place. That wasn't the issue. It was just we didn't know what affect it would have on a person."

"Why the rush?" said Gorman.

"Oddly, even though we had a time machine, we were running out of time to put our plan in place," Crenshaw replied. "Word had come down that a militant militia from a fringe group who seized power over much of the Southern U.S. after the bombings was on their way towards Washington. The decision was made to send me to the past the night before they were expected to arrive."

Gorman was starting to believe that if this was indeed a hoax, it was damn elaborate one ... and extremely well thought out. "So what exactly was this time machine? I mean, was it a big box, or a chair? Maybe a British telephone booth?"

Crenshaw chuckled. "You're a funny guy, Mr. Gorman. I like that. No, it was much smaller than that. More like an oversized watch. This made facilitating a return much easier than having to make it back to a designated point. Just the push of a button would bring me back from wherever I happened to be. Now, bring me back to what? Well, no one knew. And as you can see, I never actually found out."

"Why didn't you go back?" Gorman asked.

"We'll get to that," Crenshaw replied. "I'm getting a little thirsty," he said, getting up from his chair. "Can I get you something? Coffee?

Soda? Maybe something a little stronger?" he said, gesturing toward a fairly well-stocked liquor cabinet.

"Bourbon neat, if you don't mind," said Gorman.

Crenshaw smiled. "Good man!" he said approvingly. He returned with a bottle and two glasses, pouring three fingers for his guest and a good deal more for himself.

"To your health," he said and raised his glass. "Anyway, to get back to it, the first order of business once I arrived was to find Cooper and make sure he never got on that plane."

"What's time travel like, if I may ask?" inquired Gorman.

Crenshaw thought for a second. "Actually, it wasn't as traumatic as you might have believed. One second I was in the lab in Washington, and the next I was in a bathroom stall in the Portland Airport. Other than some brief disorientation, it was relatively uneventful."

Gorman went to speak again but was quickly interrupted.

"And don't bother asking me about the mechanics of it or anything like that. I don't know how it worked. All I know is that it did. Remember, I was a soldier, not a scientist. I trusted that their calculations were correct, and it turns out I was right. I ended up exactly where I was supposed to."

He paused for another sip of his bourbon and continued. "As I stepped out of the bathroom stall, I saw him. Now, this was a stroke of luck no one had counted on. We knew approximately what time he bought his ticket, but prior to that, his whereabouts were unknown. My time of arrival had given me about fifteen minutes or so to locate Cooper, take him out, and take his place. Turns out I didn't have to look very far. There he was, checking himself in the mirror, with the case containing the bomb at his feet. The next step was pretty simple. I sidled up next to him on the pretense of washing my hands, gave him a vicious elbow to the side of head, and then dragged him into an open stall where I took the case with the bomb. In another stroke of luck, it appears he had already bought his ticket. Turns out we had been a little late on the timing of that."

"Then the real Dan Cooper, or whatever his name is, is still out there somewhere?" said Gorman.

"He was very much alive when I left him in that bathroom. That's all I know."

"Why do you think he's never come forward?"

"I think you know the answer to that as well as I do, Mr. Gorman. Who would believe him? Without any evidence, because believe me, I took everything I could that could possibly tie him to that hijacking, he'd be just another crackpot."

Gorman smiled. "You mean like a guy claiming to be a time traveler?"

"Except I have the money, as you've seen," the old man replied. "If you'd like, I can also show you the plane ticket and the parachutes, too."

"Sorry," said Gorman. "I was just playing devil's advocate."

"No worries. Anyway, after I took out Cooper, it was simply a matter of duplicating his movements and actions up to the time that plane left Seattle with the ransom money. After that, our information was sketchy because there were no witnesses to what happened inside the plane before it went down."

"In your timeline," interjected Gorman.

"Yes, in my timeline," said Crenshaw. "But we knew that it was possible to jump out of a Boeing 727 provided the altitude of the plane was low enough. I won't go into the rest of the story because it happened exactly as everybody on board has related it over the years."

He paused, as if to gather his thoughts. "And now we come to the real enduring mystery of this story … what happened to me, or rather, D.B. Cooper? The story says that at approximately 8:13 p.m. on the night of November 24, 1971, D.B. Cooper jumped out of a Boeing 727 with two hundred thousand dollars in ransom money, two parachutes, and then disappeared. All of this is absolutely true ... except that it wasn't D.B. Cooper, it was me. And I didn't totally disappear, as you can see."

"What went wrong?" Gorman asked.

"Well, as I said, returning to my timeline should have been relatively simple. All I had to do was press a button, and theoretically, I was supposed to return to my place of origin."

"So why are you still here then?" Gorman pressed.

"Mother Nature, Mr. Gorman, plain and simple. You remember that the plane was flying through a pretty intense storm? Well, what do you reckon you get with storms besides rain?" he asked.

"Lightning," replied Gorman.

"The exact moment I pushed that button, I got blasted with a bolt of lightning that probably should have killed me. Instead, the next thing I knew, I was lying on the ground near a river with no idea of how I got there. I still had the money, although some of it had fallen into the water."

"About six thousand dollars, I'm guessing," said Gorman.

"Give or take, if you go by what that kid found at Tena Bar in 1980. Anyway, after sussing out my surroundings and checking to make sure all my parts were still in place, I buried the money, and the parachutes, then made my way out the woods. Eventually, I found a logging road that took me out to a main highway. I flagged down a truck, told the driver I got lost hiking, and asked if he could take me to the nearest town. What I found out when I got there was a little disconcerting, to say the least. The lightning hitting me had somehow scrambled the time travel device. I was no longer in 1971. It was now 1978."

"What did you do then?"

"Well, what could I do? I was a man out of time, literally. So I did what every good soldier was taught to do when plans and circumstances have changed. You adapt. I took some odd jobs, made a few small bets on some sporting events that I knew the outcomes of, and eventually got enough money together to make some judicious investments in a few fledgling companies, namely Microsoft and Apple. They made me enough money so that eventually I could drop off the map entirely and live out the rest of my life in relative anonymity and comfort."

He took another long pull from his bourbon. "Oh, and I did eventually go back to where I had landed. The money and the parachutes were right where I buried them, as I expected." He paused, looked thoughtfully into his drink, and then continued. "So there you have it, Mr. Gorman. You have now solved one of the great mysteries of the twentieth century. How do you feel?"

Gorman frowned, and reached down to turn off his phone. "You know that without evidence that you have the money, or the parachutes, which I'm sure you're not prepared to give me, I've got nothing here, right?"

"Yes. I am aware of that," replied Crenshaw.

"Then why did you ask me here?"

Crenshaw smiled but didn't reply. Instead, he gestured to the reporter. "Come with me, Mr. Gorman. I want to show you something."

Gorman followed the old man out to a garage adjoining the kitchen of the house. Crenshaw led him into a small back room that was plastered with newspaper clippings of the entire affair. It was almost like a shrine, Gorman thought. Crenshaw flipped a switch hidden under a small desk. A panel in the wall slid open, revealing the remnants of a parachute, stacks of bundled twenty dollar bills, and a small, charred object that appeared to be some sort of watch. Crenshaw's time travel device, Gorman assumed. He looked at the collection with a mix of wonder and bemusement. Crenshaw was right. Here was the key to one of the enduring mysteries of modern times, and he couldn't tell anybody.

As Gorman moved forward to examine it more closely, Crenshaw began to hack and cough, so violently that he had to sit down at the small desk. He noticed the blood as Crenshaw reached for a tissue to wipe his hands.

"You're dying, aren't you?" he said somberly. Crenshaw smiled ruefully up at the reporter. "Doctor says I've got six months, a year at the very outside. I'm pretty sure it's going to be sooner than that, though."

"That's why you told me, isn't it?

"I needed to find someone I could trust with this. You know, I did my homework on you, Jonah. I knew you were the one. I'm going to put all that stuff into a safe deposit box after you leave here. Once I've passed, my lawyers have been instructed to give you the location and access. After that, you can do what you like. Tell the world, if you want ... if you think they'll believe you." He winked again at the young reporter.

A woman's voice coming from inside the house interrupted them. "John," she said, "where are you?"

"In here, Joanie," Crenshaw called back.

There was some commotion, and then the sound of small shoes running towards them. Crenshaw quickly closed the wall panel as two small children, a boy and girl, ran pell-mell into the small room.

"Grandpa," they yelled in unison, and jumped up on Crenshaw's lap. A trim, well-quaffed older woman followed behind them.

"Now you two kids get down off your grandfather," she said sternly but with obvious affection.

"It's okay, dear. I'm not a china doll. They won't break me," he said to her as he tousled the young boy's hair.

She frowned with mild disapproval but her eyes showed the love she obviously had for the old man. Gorman coughed slightly to get Crenshaw's attention. He turned to look at the young reporter and then back to his wife.

"Joanie, this is Jonah Gorman. He's a writer ... and a Cooper buff like me. I've read some of his work, and since he lives here in Seattle, I thought I'd invite him over to show him my collection. Jonah, this is my wife, Joan, and my grandchildren, Dani and Cooper."

Gorman extended his hand in greeting. "It's very nice to meet you, Mrs. Crenshaw."

"I hope my husband hasn't been boring you too much with his collection, Mr. Gorman," she replied.

"Oh no," he replied. "Quite the contrary, I've learned a whole lot of things I didn't know before."

She laughed. "I'm not surprised. I think the only person who might know more about this case than John is D.B. Cooper himself ... whoever that might be."

Gorman looked quickly at Crenshaw, who gave him a quick shake of his head as if to say she doesn't know.

"Well," she said after a few moments of awkward silence, "I'll let you two get back to your business. Kids, come with Grandma, and let your Grandpa and Mr. Gorman finish what they were doing."

The children looked slightly crestfallen, but quickly ran out the door and back into the house. Joan Crenshaw followed after them, leaving the old man and the reporter alone once more.

"She doesn't know?" Gorman said.

"No," said Crenshaw. "When I met her, that other life was already long gone. Why dredge up the past? She'll find out after I'm gone, but for now, ignorance is bliss, as they say."

He got up from his chair and extended his hand to Gorman. "Thank you for coming and listening, Jonah. My lawyer will get in touch with you when the time comes."

"Thank you, John. It was a pleasure to meet you."

As he made his way to the door, Gorman turned back to the man who, he now realized, had saved the world. "I do have one more question, if you don't mind."

"Sure," said Crenshaw. "Shoot."

"Do you ever regret not being able to go back?"

A small grin came over the old man's face. "Actually, I can, if I want to. A couple of years ago, after I thought it was long dead, the time travel device came back to life. It started blinking again, out of the blue. I couldn't believe it. All I had to do was push that button."

"So why didn't you?"

"Because what I left wasn't home anymore ... this was."

Gorman had to admit the old man was right. "Were you ever tempted, just to see if things worked out?"

Crenshaw swept his arm around the room. "Isn't it obvious that they did?"

**\*\*\***

# ABOUT THE AUTHORS

**Stephanie Barr**

Stephanie Barr writes books, fantasy, science fiction, and combinations thereof. A lot of them. She is also a rocket scientist, raising two autistic children as a single mother, and herding a bunch of cats. She has three blogs, which are sporadically updated: Rocket Scientist (http://rockets-r-us.blogspot.com/), Rockets and Dragons (http://stephanie-barr.blogspot.com/), and The Unlikely Otaku (http://askthers.blogspot.com/). Anything else even vaguely interesting about her can be found in her writing since she puts a little bit of herself in everything she writes ... just not the same piece. She has written a number of books:

*Conjuring Dreams: Learning to Write by Writing* (https://www.amazon.com/dp/B00JL61VWU)
*Tarot Queen* (https://www.amazon.com/dp/B00KCQ0PJS)
*Beast Within (First of the Bete Novels)* (https://www.amazon.com/dp/B00LF447WM)
*Nine Lives (Second of the Bete Novels)* (https://www.amazon.com/dp/B00NKVN15)
*Saving Tessa* (http://www.amazon.com/dp/B00PTTTIJ6)
*Musings of a Nascent Poet* (https://www.amazon.com/dp/B00QEMKXLO)
*Curse of the Jenri* (https://www.amazon.com/dp/B01ND0KZ3T)
*Legacy* (https://www.amazon.com/dp/B07451LJVB)
Twitter: http://twitter.com/stephanieebarr
Facebook: https://www.facebook.com/stephanieebarr
Amazon: https://www.amazon.com/Stephanie-Barr/e/B00N9W84YK
Her writing blog: http://stephanie-barr.blogspot.com
Or sign up for her newsletter: http://eepurl.com/cBGwmb

**C. R. Downing**

C. R. Downing, also known as Dr. Chuck Downing, is a nationally recognized teacher, professor, and author. He was San Diego County Teacher of the Year and received the Presidential Award for Excellence in Science Teaching. His science fiction novel, *Traveler's HOT L - The Time Traveler's Resort*, received the Best Science Fiction Novel in the 2014 USA Best Book Awards. A Christian, he serves in ministry at Mission Church of the Nazarene as a Life Group Leader. He has two granddaughters, Hadley and Harper. Learn more about Downing and his writing at www.crdowning.com.

### Ken Grant

Ken Grant is a fifty-three-year-old freelance writer currently living in Santa Ana, California. He has eighteen years' experience writing in a variety of genres, but his particular expertise is in science fiction and fantasy.

He has one published novel, *So Great a Salvation*, a creative mix of science fiction and fantasy. He is also a contributor to the published non-fiction work, *Trials and Triumphs II*, which contains real life stories of lives transformed. He regularly contributes to a wide variety of on-line periodicals and anthologies.

In his spare time, he enjoys golfing in the warm Southern California weather, spending time with close friends, and reading the works of fellow writers, both on the printed page and electronically. He is a supporter of a number of fellow writers and is committed to seeing the writing profession grow and develop to its maximum potential.

For an excerpt from his novel or to contact him go to www.kengrantbooks.com.

### T. Gillmore

T. Gillmore is a writer of speculative fiction and a gardener of dying plants. When she is not home writing and killing her plants, she and her husband scour the lands in search of the greatest wine created, which they find in each winery they visit. Her work has appeared in Aurora Wolf, Vestal Review, Left Hand Publishers' anthology *Beautiful Lies, Painful Truths Volume I*, and The Writers of the Future Competition awarded her with an Honorable Mention in the short stories category. You can also find her on Facebook, https://www.facebook.com/AuthorT.Gillmore and sometimes on Twitter https://twitter.com/bohemiangeek

### G. Lloyd Helm

G. Lloyd Helm has been writing for forty years, having published poetry in a wide variety of magazines and newspapers including *The New York Poetry Anthology*, *Stars and Stripes News*, *The Los Angeles*

*Times*, *The Antelope Valley Press*, and *The Antelope Valley Anthologies*, among others.

… has published short stories and memoirs both in the US and in England in such journals as *Pilgrimage*, *Citadel* the literary magazine of Los Angeles City College, *Delivered Magazine*, which is based in London, *Short Story Library*, The University of S. Illinois' *Eureka Literary Magazine*, *Tales as like as not*, and London's *Black Gate Magazine*.

… has published three novels in the F&SF field, 1) *Other Doors*, from MousePrints Publishing, and 2) *Design* from Publish America. 3) *World Without End* from Rogue Phoenix Press. Helm has also published a romance novel, *Sometimes in Dreams*, with Siren's Call Publishing. He has recently released a new literary novel, *Serpents and Doves*, from Rogue Phoenix Press. All are available at amazon.com/G. Lloyd Helm

Rogue Phoenix will release his new novel, *Borrowing A Moose Head From Cole Porter* in August, 2018.

**Joachim Heijndermans**
Joachim Heijndermans writes, draws, and paints nearly every waking hour. Originally from the Netherlands, he's been all over the world, boring people by spouting random trivia about toys, comics and film. His work has been featured in a number of publications, such as Mad Scientist Journal, Asymmetry Fiction, Metaphorosis, Econoclash Review and Gathering Storm Magazine, and he's currently in the midst of completing his first children's book.

# ABOUT THE AUTHORS

**Tom Howard**

Tom Howard is a science fiction and fantasy short story writer living in Little Rock, Arkansas, and working as a banking software analyst in the US and abroad. He thanks his children for their inspiration for this story and the Central Arkansas Speculative Fiction Writers Group for their perspiration.

When his four children were younger and traveling in the car for long distances, Tom would tell stories about them as super-heroes. This story, and many others, came from his *Superworld* collection of tales jotted down over the years. Meteor Man and his partner, Comet Queen, are alien members of a super-hero group called Heroes, Incorporated, and fight a giant planet-eater called a Destroyer.

This story deals with the concept that the universe is trying to tell us something if we only listen. There is no antagonist, just the heroine fighting herself until she has to take a leap of faith to save the world, arguing with her logical side the entire way. Instead of section breaks, there are news flashes showing how Earthlings are dealing with having a seemingly benevolent alien among them.

Tom is currently working on a *Superworld* anthology containing stories of his children's adventures and has begun writing super-hero stories about his grandson and his friends.

**Mike Hultquist**

Mike Hultquist is a screenwriter, author, and popular food blogger. His stories are typically dark and lean in the direction of horror, though he prefers atmospheric, psychological horror over the splatter type, which you'll see in most of his work.

As a screenwriter, he is represented by Zero Gravity Management. His produced films include "Victim," "Arena" (starring Kellan Lutz and Samuel L. Jackson), and "12 Feet Deep" (starring Tobin Bell, Alexandra Park, Nora-Jane Noone, Diane Farr). Check him out on IMDB: http://www.imdb.com/name/nm2478416/.

As an author, he has published a number of stories in magazines and anthologies, co-edited the Halloween anthology *Harvest Hill,*

and is the author of the novel, *Off Track*. See his writing credits at
http://www.michaelhultquist.com.

As a food blogger, Mike operates a popular spicy food blog at Chili
Pepper Madness (http://www.chilipeppermadness.com), where he
cooks with big and bold flavors. He recently published *The Spicy
Dehydrator Cookbook* by Page Street Publishing, which features
ninety-five recipes you can create with your dehydrator, such as
homemade spice rubs from scratch and zesty jerkies with plenty of
heat. He is hard at work on his next spicy cookbook.

### Theresa Jacobs

Theresa Jacobs believes in magic, fairies,
dragons, and ghosts. She trusts science and
thinks that aliens know way too much. Born
and raised in Canada, she only began her
writing journey two years ago. Through hard
work, she has published a horror novel, sci-fi
novel, horror novella, horror anthologies,
children's books, and poetry. She is a
contributor to 1428elm.com an online horror
magazine. While working full-time, she is also
currently writing a sports figure's biography, so stay tuned.

(Author Website) http://theresajcbs.wixsite.com/authorpage
(Amazon Author Site) https://www.amazon.com/Theresa-
Jacobs/e/B01BAS13T2
(Wordpress Blog) https://authortheresajacobs.wordpress.com/
(Free Books at Smashwords)
https://www.smashwords.com/profile/view/theresajcbs
(1428 Elm Horror Mag ) http://1428elm.com/author/tjacobs/
(Facebook) https://www.facebook.com/writerTheresaJ/
(Twitter) https://twitter.com/writerTheresaJ
(G+) https://plus.google.com/u/0/110753361442066177796

### Marie D. Jones

Marie D. Jones is the best-selling author of
over fifteen non-fiction books on the
paranormal, cutting edge science,
metaphysics, consciousness and ancient
knowledge, including *PSIence*, *The Déjà vu
Enigma*, *The Power of Archetypes*, *Viral Mythology*,
*This Book is From the Future*, *The Grid*,
*Supervolcano* (written with her father,
geophysicist John M. Savino) and *Demons, the
Devil and Fallen Angels*. She is a novelist with a

horror middle grade series, *Shadowlanders,* releasing in spring of 2019, and a science fiction series, *W.A.R.* debuting in late 2018, written with her son Max.

Marie is also an optioned screenwriter, with a science fiction project in pre-production with Bright Frontier Films, and she is developing projects for her own production company, Where's Lucy Productions. She has written dozens of articles, essays and reviews, and contributed to over 100 anthologies, including seven *Chicken Soup for the Soul* books. She is a regular contributor to many magazines, including *New Dawn, Atlantis Rising, FATE, Intrepid, MINDScape* and *Paranormal Underground.* Marie has been on over two thousand radio shows worldwide including multiple appearances on Coast to Coast A.M., spoken at major paranormal and metaphysical events, and appears on television on "Ancient Aliens" and "Nostradamus Effect." Her websites are www.mariedjones.com and www.whereslucyproductions.com. She is on Facebook at https://www.facebook.com/MarieDJonesWriter/, Twitter at https://www.twitter.com/mariedjones, and Instagram at https://www.instagram.com/marie.d.jones.

**Flemming Lord**

Flemming Lord was born in West Africa to English and Danish parents. He grew up in the UK, then lived and worked in Japan for twenty years. He has a degree in astrophysics, and despite that handicap has worked as an English teacher, human resources manager and e-learning designer. His influences include Philip K Dick, Michael Moorcock, William Gibson, Stanislaw Lem, Umberto Eco, Hunter S Thompson, Kazuo Ishiguro and Haruki Murakami. He is interested in cosmology, ontology, artificial intelligence, paradoxes, synthesizers and guitars. His writing is driven by the two complementary questions, "What is the nature of reality?" and "What is the nature of consciousness?" He supports environmental causes, guided by the principle that without a habitable environment most other causes are secondary. He thinks he can play several instruments and enjoys writing and recording music. He currently lives in Shropshire, UK.

# ABOUT THE AUTHORS

**J. McBrearty**

Jenean McBrearty is a graduate of San Diego State University, who taught political science and sociology. Her fiction, poetry, and photographs have been published in over 200 print and on-line journals. She won the Eastern Kentucky English Department Award for Graduate Creative Non-fiction in 2011, and a Silver Pen Award in 2015 for her noir short story, "Red's Not Your Color." Her novels and short story collections can be found on Amazon and Lulu.com.

**Jason J. McCuiston**

Jason J. McCuiston was born in the wilds of southeast Tennessee, where he was raised on a healthy diet of old horror movies, westerns, comic books, sci-fi and fantasy novels, and, of course, Dungeons & Dragons. He attended the finest state school that would have him where he studied art before coming to grips with the hard truth that his heart just wasn't in becoming a professional illustrator. Following his matriculation, he embarked on a whirlwind tour of underpaid and uninspired career paths until finally realizing that all his forays into role-playing games, comic books, and creative design were merely the manifestation of his innate desire to be a storyteller.

His speculative historical adventure "The Last Red Lantern" was a semifinalist in L. Ron Hubbard's Writers of the Future Contest in 2016, and was subsequently published in Parsec Ink's Triangulation: Appetites anthology. His flying ghost-ship tale "The Wyvern" appears in Pole to Pole Publishing's *Dark Luminous Wings* anthology. His debut novel, *Servants of the Horned God*, is currently under representation with Mark Gottlieb of Trident Media Group. He can be found on the internet at: https://jasonjmccuiston.wixsite.com/shadowcrusade and https://www.facebook.com/ShadowCrusade. He occasionally tweets @JasonJMcCuiston.

**F. J. Robledano-Espín**

F. J. Robledano-Espín grew up in Canada, specifically in a place called Scarborough, a suburb of Toronto. He left at nineteen and has since led several lives: as an academic, a stage actor and director, a fighter, a globetrotter, a homeless person, an IT executive, a voice artist, and a writer. Currently he lives in Madrid, Spain, with his daughter, for whom he creates better worlds on paper while actively seeking to improve the one they share.

### Kevin Singer

Kevin Singer is an Army veteran and former journalist who spends his free time running, collecting tattoos, renovating his house, and snowboarding. His fiction has appeared in the literary magazines *Rind* and *Trysts of Fate* and the anthologies *Young Adventurers* and *Playthings of the Gods*. He's also the author of the supernatural thriller *The Last Conquistador*, available at Amazon and BN.com. He lives in Jersey City, though he'd rather live in Hawaii.

### Andrea L. Staum

Andrea L. Staum is the author of the Dragonchild Lore series, *The Attic's Secret* novella, *Scattered Dreams* short story collection, and has contributed to several best-selling anthologies. She's a trained motorcycle technician, an amateur home renovator, and somehow manages to find time to write. She lives in south central Wisconsin with her husband and three overlords...err...cats.
Facebook: https://www.facebook.com/pg/AuthorAndreaLStaum
Twitter: https://twitter.com/DragonchildLore
Website: https://dragonchildlore.wordpress.com/
Amazon: https://www.amazon.com/Andrea-Staum/e/B00DDAVLK2/

### Dave Steinman

Dave Steinman is a Crystal nominated commercial copywriter and voice artist currently residing in beautiful British Columbia on Canada's west coast. After twenty-five years in the radio business, he was surprised to discover that he could write something longer than thirty seconds that didn't end with the phrase "Hurry...sale ends tomorrow." His first short story "Northstar," an alternate history tale about Canada's legendary Avro Arrow, was published last year in the anthology *49th Parallels* from Bundoran Press.

## Teresa Twomey

Teresa Twomey is an MFA student who is also pursuing a graduate certificate in women and gender studies at Southern Connecticut State University. She has been a prominent advocate for women with postpartum mood disorders and is the author of the book *Understanding Postpartum Psychosis: A Temporary Madness* (https://www.amazon.com/Understanding-Postpartum-Psychosis-Temporary-Madness-ebook/dp/B002AS9QY6) (Praeger Publishers, 2009), which combines medical, legal, and historical aspects of this illness with stories from survivors. She has written and co-authored a number of blog posts such as "The Big Bad Wolf of Postpartum Mood Disorders" on postpartumprogress.com.

Twomey has been an adjunct professor in business schools and women and gender studies programs. She has co-authored academic articles and chapters in business publications, including: "Revealing the Role of Privilege in Free-Markets, Equality-Under-Law and Sustainability," (with Drew L. Harris) in *Competitiveness Review*; "Sharpening Our Attention: The Role of Privilege in Free-Markets, Equality-Under-Law and Sustainability" (https://www.questia.com/library/journal/1P3-1912955481/sharpening-our-attention-the-role-of-privilege-in) (with Drew Harris) in *Competition Forum*; "Economic Democracy: Balancing Economic Development, Property Rights, and Individual Liberty to Advance Civilization" (https://www.questia.com/library/journal/1P3-1601098631/economic-democracy-balancing-economic-development) (with Drew Harris) in *Competition Forum*; "Corporate Privilege and the Challenge of Sustainable Democracy" (with Drew Harris & Sarah Stookey) in *Competition Forum*. Based on her experience as an attorney and professional mediator, Twomey co-authored "Alternative Dispute Resolution: Mediation" chapter in *Managing Human Resources for Compliance and Beyond*, (with Rosemarie Feuerbach Twomey) (McGraw-Hill, 2009); and "Adarand, Point/Counterpoint on Supreme Court Case on Affirmative Action" in the *New Jersey's Young Lawyer Magazine*. She is also an amateur photographer and a mother of three teenaged girls. You can find Twomey on her Facebook pages: www.facebook.com/teresatwomeywriter/ (http://www.facebook.com/teresatwomeywriter/) and

## ABOUT THE AUTHORS

www.facebook.com/Understanding-Postpartum-Psychosis
(www.facebook.com/Understanding-Postpartum-Psychosis).

# Please Review Our Other Books

If you enjoyed this book, *A World Unimagined*, or any of our other books, please feel free to leave reviews. All of our books are available at all major online retailers, including Amazon and Barnes & Noble. You can also leave reviews at Goodreads.com.

# Please Join Our Mailing List

If you enjoyed any of our books, please sign up for our e-newsletter. In that we give you previews of upcoming releases, discounts, as well as free stuff for our fans!
https://bit.ly/2Gvt9NM

## MORE BOOKS FROM LEFT HAND PUBLISHERS

## REALITIES PERCEIVED

Nothing's more dangerous, or delightful, than invoking a cadre of talented authors to create short stories that defy our perceptions of reality. Do we create our own truth? Or does our view of it shape our world? Neither heroes nor heavens, victims nor villains, may grasp the true nature of our being.

From science fiction, to horror and the supernatural, to dramas about the fabric of our existence, this international fusion of artists will thrill you with an eclectic selection of tales that cross all genres. Sit back and be prepared to have your perception of reality both challenged and distorted.

# BEAUTIFUL LIES, PAINFUL TRUTHS VOL.I

There's an ironic beauty between humanity's love of Life and fear of Death. Life seemingly brings joy, happiness, hope, and love. Death can end sadness, illness, suffering, and pain. We asked writers to "Let the title and quote take your imagination, your story, wherever it wants to go."

Join them now as an international blend of authors, both fresh and seasoned, bring you an exceptional menu of speculative fiction, mystery, realism, horror, and the supernatural. If your palate varies from the macabre to the dramatic, *Beautiful Lies, Painful Truths* provides an assortment of tasty treasures that will chill, delight, and give you food for thought.

# BEAUTIFUL LIES, PAINFUL TRUTHS VOL.II

Most believe that Life promises light, bliss, and wonder. Death scares most with its shadow of mortality, darkness, and destruction. But what if those may be, if not lies, just facets of the complicated entities that bookend our existence? Life does not mock Death, but feeds it. Death is not the cessation of Life, but an alteration of existence. What would you do if faced with either truth?

An international galley of authors brings us a second repast of tales featuring the complex relationship between Life, Death, and humanity. From the supernatural to the sublime, these writers, both novitiates and accomplished, serve up a banquet of speculative fiction across a wide spectrum of genres. Beautiful Lies, Painful Truths Volume II will continue to feed your craving for the fantastic.

# THE DEMON'S ANGEL

Neha was excited to enter her sophomore year in high school. That was until the boy she went out with sprouted wings, and Lucas, the man who raised her since she was a baby, turned into a demon.

Neha is far from human. She is an angel, the natural enemy of demons. An angel raised by a demon has never been heard of before, which makes some angels see her as a threat. Neha not only has to prove that she does not know anything about demons, she has to prove that she is on the side of the angels. And she is. So she thinks.

This Young Adult supernatural thriller follows the tribulations of the teenaged Neha as she learns both the truth about her past and herself.

# Reviews

★★★★★

"Intensely unique.
The character Neha is something very remarkable, she has depth and grows as a character, especially when she feels she has to prove herself. She thinks she's proving herself a good angel to the other angels, when in fact she's also proving it to herself. Neha is not your typical teenager, nor typical angel."

**Amy Shannon**, Author. Writer. Poet. Storyteller.
Blogger. Book Reviewer.
Review Blog: http://bit.ly/2iPVV4x

***

"This flight of fancy with engrossing plot twists tempts anyone ever dumbfounded by a parental deception."

**Wendy Landers,** Book Reviewer
Author of Just Let Time Pass
www.wendylanders.com

# Coming Soon from Left Hand Publishers

## Terrors Unimagined

Far beyond what you can imagine lies a dreamscape full of the unexpected and the unexplainable. The supernatural, the paranormal, monsters, demons, magic, witches, and inconceivable horrors reside in a world of...

### Terrors Unimagined

But not all monsters have fangs, fur, or horns. Many times, the worst demons are as real as tomorrow's headlines. Stories included here range from suspense to psychological thriller to just plain scary.

An international cadre of authors, both new and experienced, lead you down a path to the other side of the unbelievable with stories unique and thought-provoking. This anthology of supernatural and horror-inspiring short stories drags us screaming into a world of creatures and nightmares undreamed of. Prepare to ponder your nights away. Sleep is no longer an option.

www.ingramcontent.com/pod-product-compliance
Lightning Source LLC
Chambersburg PA
CBHW062121170626
46813CB00002B/535